BLESSED
is the
LINK

Titles by Sheri Singerling:

ALFOM SHARED UNIVERSE
NOVELS
Nytho
Neuen
Blessed is the Rot (Bit #1)
Blessed is the Link (Bit #2)

SHORT STORIES
The Seed
The Badge
Rogue
Wireworks
To Keep the Non-Euclidean at Bay (Bit #0.25)
Paper Airplane Poet (Bit #0.5)
Disaffected (Bit #1.5)

Most titles can be standalone reads and read in any order.
Find the author-suggested reading order on her website at
sherisingerling.com.

BLESSED
is the
LINK

SHERI SINGERLING

HypIn

Publishing

Cover design by Geoffrey Bunting
Cover illustration by Jack Hillside

ISBN: 978-1-968638-00-9 (paperback)
First Edition
HypIn Publishing

Visit the author's website at sherisingerling.com

THE DAUGHTER

The Old World greeted Lenore, its cold, its damp, its dark. They were mere paces into it, a line of twelve bodies of varying heights and breadths, no cohesive uniform, not even a sash or armband to indicate their shared purpose and passion. But they didn't need such empty symbolism. They were united in heart and mind. Disaffected through and through.

Deston heaved the stone door, the same they'd come through. His thick arms strained against the weight, veins bulging, muscles taut and likened to cables. Jak moved in to help, and the slab rolled into place with a hollow thud that echoed through the corridor. Lenore tried to peer down its length, but the closing of the entryway had cut off the light. The darkness was total.

"I can't see a damn thing," one of them huffed. The lisp implied it was Jak.

"Firestricker," Deston said. "Who's got it?"

Jingling, rustling, a nervous padding of feet. No one liked to have their sight stolen from them. Not in these catacombs of danger. Not in this moment of peril.

"Here," a husky voice said, Dooreen's most likely.

"Help her over to me," Deston said.

Bodies jostled. Someone tripped and cursed under their breath. A foot stomped Lenore's big toe, but she swallowed the yelp before it could burst forth. A shout was the last thing they needed, and she wasn't going to be the one to give them away. Not after everything she'd done to get them here, to finally be accepted as one of them.

Two clicks, then a spark ignited into flame. The tunnel was illuminated, faintly, but after the pitch black, Lenore had to shield her eyes from Deston's torch. He held it aloft and gazed at their cohort, pointing and counting.

"Good," he said. "We didn't lose anyone. Let's keep it that way, yeah?"

The others chuckled, but Deston frowned and held a finger to his lips.

"Sound travels down here," Lenore explained.

Deston moved to her side. The others loitered, brimming with energy, anxious, excited. Lenore's teeth were prone to chattering all of a sudden, forcing her to clench them into submission.

"Well, luv," Deston said, "you did good getting us this far, but now, I suspect, the hard part begins. Where to?"

Lenore shivered in the low-blood clothing she wore, unaccustomed to the coarse fibers or threadbare nature of it. Still, she ignored the urge to wrap her arms around herself. She belonged here just as much as the others. She wasn't going to have them snicker behind her back and call her a high blood playing at being Disaffected. She was all-in. A true believer in their cause, no matter what blood coursed in her veins or what name followed her given one.

A stray drop of water fell from the rock ceiling and splashed against her forehead. She jumped then wiped the liquid away with the too-long sleeve of her tunic. The movement knocked some of her wavy, strawberry-blonde hairs free from the confines of her low and loose ponytail.

Deston smiled at her and ran his finger under her chin. A fluttering touched her sternum, and a warmth cascaded through. She pulled a parchment from her pants' pocket and unrolled the crude map of the Old World, her furtive handiwork almost illegible even to her. Deston brought the torch in and took hold of one side of the map, freeing up one of Lenore's hands. She inspected her scribblings.

"We're here," she said, tapping a location with a series of haphazard circles. "This is the way we should go." Her finger traced their route from the edge of the map to its center, ending in the heart of the ruins of the subterranean city, at a structure outlined in thick strokes and labeled "Source", the former locus of the Rot of the Link, the point from which all the foulness of distortions and affliction had stemmed. Or so the stories said, but Lenore didn't put much stock in such fairy tales. None of the Disaffected did. If they had, they wouldn't be partaking in this mission.

Deston's eyes followed their path. "When do we hit the road?"

Lenore tapped a spot about halfway along their journey. "Here. We won't have to worry about wardens until then. They don't even know about this other entrance."

"Well, now, that doesn't seem likely. Someone knows about this route, or you wouldn't have found it in the first place."

Lenore frowned and folded the map before stowing it for safekeeping. The official road from the surface into the Old World was direct, and if they were following that one, their journey would be brief, totaling no more than a half hour's time. But they weren't following the route carved out by the wardens, at least not at first. Theirs was a lost path.

"It's forgotten knowledge," Lenore said. "I found it in the archives. Buried and dust-covered, molding even. If anyone knew, it was from the time of the Church."

"You make it sound like the distant past when we've got former clergyfolk still walking the streets of Simetria all chipper and spry. Your folks among them."

Lenore's blood raced at the mention of her parents. They were a sore spot for her, and now, in the belly of the beast, they were the last thing she wanted to think of. She could almost hear their gasps, see the disapproval written on their faces, feel their disappointment. Her mother most especially.

"Should we continue to argue about the secrecy of the route," Lenore asked, "or get on with following it?"

Deston's broad grin ripped across his face, but this one time, he held his powerful laugh in check. Silence was their friend on this treacherous mission. Instead, he held the torch off to the side and planted a kiss on Lenore's lips. She simply looked back at him with wide eyes. He never displayed his affection so openly among the Disaffected. Lenore glanced at the others. A few were watching them, their eyes fleeing on spying hers. She didn't have time to think about what it meant, whether a good sign or ill omens, because Deston was already gathering the others into a marching order. As the torchbearer, he took the lead with Lenore as the navigator just behind.

The way was narrow and winding. They could never see more than a few dozen paces ahead before the path curved sharply left or right. At some point, the slope dived. They moved deeper and deeper into the Old World, into this land of unknowns, all the horrors of the past gone now, but the memory of that asymmetry seemingly etched into the stone, soaked in the puddles, saturating the earthy vapors.

This was the realm of their twisted past, twice over. The world of the Bygones, the people who had come centuries before and nigh worshipped synthetics only to be undone by their own hand, the Rot of the Link shackling them by creating the distortions, the Church of Impermanence stepping in and spouting lies, claiming the Rot of the Link was blessed and the distortions stemmed from other causes. Except eventually, the Church's lies were made known, the truth shattering the old system and paving the way for the Order of the New Day.

The Order. It was the only motivation Lenore needed. When her courage wavered, when doubt consumed her, when she wanted nothing more than to flee back to the surface, all she had to do was to think of the Order. The corruption. The injustice. The inequalities. Memories of her visits to the lower city, the children wearing rags, bare feet covered in filth, faces all grime, too-large eyes staring back at her blankly. Or the elderly hunched over, backs bowed, knees wider than their thighs, then learning they weren't even six decades old and already so battered and broken. It had to change. All of it. This was why she was here.

How often did she tell herself this on the journey? The Old World warped time, but bodily needs managed to track the minutes as well as any clock. It couldn't have been more than an hour or two into their trek when their tight corridor of poorly hewn stone hit a wall. Deston turned to Lenore. She inspected her map. They ought to be nearing the intersection with the road, that straight, clean shot from the surface to the Source. Lenore glanced at their surroundings and spotted it, a small gap nestled near the top of the tunnel. She pointed. The others followed her finger then groaned.

"Anyone got a rope?" Hanna said in her breathy tenor.

"Hold on," Jak added, rummaging in his bag. He tossed a bundle, and a thick cable smacked the stone ground.

"Someone's still got to be the first to make it up there," Hanna said, crossing her arms and tapping her foot. As the leanest amongst them, she was the obvious choice. And she knew it.

Deston and Jak, the two broadest of the cohort, interlaced

their fingers and each lifted one of Hanna's feet. They were almost too successful, Hanna only narrowly avoiding knocking her skull against the stone ceiling. She whispered curses back to them then caught the rope tossed up to her, waited for it to be secured by several strong bodies, then dropped through the opening to the other side. She pulled twice on the rope then each member of the group went up, over, and down, lightest to heaviest. Fran, Arnuld, Olevea, Lenore, Timofee, Jordun, Dooreen, Georg, Randel, and Jak, each new arrival helping to secure the rope to counteract the heavier and heavier loads. Deston was last. The torch was a complication and caused some bickering whispers on both sides of the wall, but in the end, Deston stomped the flame out, tossed the torch through, made his way up and over, then relit it on the other side.

"First obstacle down," Deston said. "On to the Old World proper?" he asked Lenore.

She inspected the map then angled her head to her left. "That way."

After the previous passage, the road was almost too spacious and level and free of jagged edges. Lenore couldn't be sure if it was just her nerves, but she swore there was a faint clinking of chain. She stopped and turned. Dooreen rammed into her.

"What are you doing?" Dooreen hissed. "You forget how to walk or what?"

"I thought I heard something," Lenore said.

"It's probably that." Jak pointed forward.

Lenore glanced ahead. Mere steps away, the tunnel opened into an impossible expanse. The cohort shuffled forward in silence and found themselves on a cliff's edge. Their mouths were agape at the city-sized cavern. The crumbling ruins of a dead metropolis hovered just out of sight, holding strange shapes and forms, filled with foreign materials. It was an endless stretch that put Simetria to shame in its scale, the miniscule portion they could even glimpse, because in the face of that vastness, Deston's meager torchlight was useless.

He moved to Lenore's side and tapped the map sticking out of her pocket. "Let me take a look at that."

She pulled it free and unfolded it then took Deston's torch so he could handle the map. He gripped the parchment in both hands and inspected its contents. It gave her time to take him in—the bulge of his arms threatening to burst from his beige shirt, the sway of his hips as he shifted from one leg to the other, that enormous smile that broke out when he found what he sought.

"We're nearly there," he said, tapping the map.

Their cohort of ten lingered nearby, waiting for instructions, eager to dive into the heart of the ruins.

"Onward?" she asked, offering the torch and reaching for the map.

Deston's grin faded. He folded the parchment and stowed it in the pocket of his dun linen pants.

Lenore's brow twitched. "Are you the navigator now?"

"Something like that," Deston said, refusing to look at her directly. Instead, he raised his eyebrows to the Disaffected and offered a nod.

Lenore followed his gaze. Their comrades' eyes ran from hers. Something was amiss.

"Let's me and you chat a bit," Deston said.

He grabbed her by the elbow and steered her several paces back into the wide tunnel they'd come from, but that way was the surface and Simetria, not onward at all. Lenore compressed her lips, the movement only making their asymmetry more prevalent. Larger on the bottom and smaller on top, they gave the impression she was perpetually pouting. But this time she really was because, without Deston saying a word, she knew what came next.

"You aren't letting me come," she said, setting her torch-free hand to her hips and widening her stance. He was not doing this to her. She angled her head down and glared. "You wouldn't even have gotten this far if it wasn't for me."

Deston was tall, but Lenore was too, though with her, this mostly stemmed from a life of good fare. The same couldn't be said of Deston or the cohort pacing in the distance.

"Is it because of who I am?" she asked.

Deston sighed and slumped. He rubbed his hand against his head, the short hairs springing back into position instantly. "It's not safe down there."

Lenore dug her fingernails into her pelvis and gritted her teeth. "Don't give me that. If it's dangerous for me, then it's deadly for you all."

"*Warden's* training doesn't prepare *you* for the Old World."

There it was, the first crack in Deston's façade. The word choice alone wasn't telling, but the tone in which he'd said it gave him away. "Warden's" with a look of contempt and disgust and, worse, that same inflection repeated when he'd gotten to the "you."

"I'm no warden," Lenore said. "You know that."

Deston shrugged and smirked. Another crack that threatened to widen and splinter the whole of him. He wasn't even trying to hide it anymore, his loathing of her. Lenore's veins were frozen in an instant, and she abandoned all hostility in the face of losing Deston. She rushed in, dropping the torch in the process, and grabbed and held him, but he was inert in her embrace. After a few seconds, he pushed her away then picked up the torch.

"Why are you doing this?" she asked.

"You mean, treating a high blood like you deserve?"

How could he aim that wide smile at her after those horrid words? And his infectious laugh came next, but oh how he'd turned it to such a foul purpose. Lenore was spinning. The walls of the tunnel and the ceiling and floor, all of those were just as fixed as before, but the world was upended somehow.

She reached for the stone nearby and used a hand to support her. Deston turned and walked to the others while Lenore looked on helpless. What was she meant to do? How could she convince him she belonged?

"My father is a low blood," she said.

Deston stopped and turned to face her. The others shuffled with impatience.

"Oh, don't we all know about Fenrir Roshem," he said. "Blessed toller turned renegade. Destroyer of the Rot of the Link. Mey was his name before, wasn't it? When he was an actual low blood. Before he married into wealth and privilege and never looked back. Sorry, luv, but just because your pa was born in the filth doesn't mean you know two things about it."

"But—"

Deston held up a hand and tsked. Five long strides and he was back at her side.

"Tell me, Lady Roshem, what sheets line your bed? Silk, maybe? And your shoes, how many pairs clutter your wardrobes?"

Lenore looked away.

Deston leaned in. "Too embarrassed to answer? Or have you lost count?"

"I'm on your side. I want the Order to fall too. And you need me. You need high bloods."

"Needed. We needed high bloods, but we got what we were after." He tapped the map peeking from his pocket. "Thanks for leading the way, but we'll take it from here."

Deston turned and hurried to the others. They huddled in a group. Lenore slumped against the cold stone wall and stared down at her hands. There was no convincing her former companions; she saw that. She'd only ever been a tool to use, and now she'd served her purpose, they were discarding her. Six months of comradeship, of meeting and plotting and risking everything, and none of it had meant anything.

And Deston. How many times had her lips graced his? What a fool she'd been. Lies. All of it. Nineteen years should have made her an adult, but she was still a child. She knew that now. Too late.

Chain links clinked. She heard them clear as day, together with footsteps, faint and diffuse, echoing down the length of the tunnel, back toward Simetria. Deston and the others were too fixated on their chattering, trying to glimpse a route down to the ancient city. Only Lenore could hear what was approaching, that characteristic jingle of a warden's chain sash.

If she had only ever been a warden in Deston's eyes, she ought to keep her peace. Let come what may. She gritted her teeth and slipped into the shadows. Then, she was running down the tunnel, away from those who had abandoned her. She kept her stride light and silent, graceful like a deer, just as wardens were taught. And suddenly, there they were. A veritable lance of them rushing the tunnel. A solid mass of black and forest green, the uniform of their guild—tight leather pants, high-laced boots, frocks buttoned all down their length, short in the front, long in the back. Only the tricorn hats helped Lenore distinguish the parts from the whole, discrete peaks, though bobbing in unison.

Lenore threw herself against the stone of the tunnel wall, hoping they wouldn't trample her in their onslaught. As they rushed by, a familiar form peeled away. A shout from Deston meant the Disaffected had finally spotted the ambush. Lenore knew how it would play out. The few against the many. The poorly trained and equipped against the expert warriors. It didn't please her. Despite the betrayal, she couldn't discard half a year's worth of connections at a moment's notice. More still, she believed in their cause.

But even if she had a change of heart potent enough to force her to run headlong into the fray and aid her erstwhile companions, she couldn't. A familiar form stood between her and them. Emerald eyes so similar to her own held her in stasis. A much-loved face peered back, framed by hair the color of hay, illuminated faintly by a synthetic attached to his lapel.

"Lenore," Fenrir said.

"Papa, they lied to me. They tricked me."

"We need to right this wrong, you understand?"

"Deston Kerk," she said, "he's their leader."

Fenrir shook his head. "Not that. I mean *your* wrong. You leading them here."

Wrong? No, wrong was what Deston had done to her, not the bigger picture of what they were doing, dismantling a corrupt system so they could build a better world. But Fenrir wouldn't see it that way. He was as much a part of that system as Sophie. They'd built it, after all—the Order of the New Day—their other labor of love, maybe even the favored child.

"I—" Lenore said.

"We'll talk about this later. For now, you go back to the surface. Your Mama is waiting."

Lenore bit her lip but refused to budge.

"Lenore," Fenrir said. "Do as I ask. You can't be here. You can't be implicated."

"But."

Fenrir waited. He wore a look somewhere between pain and pride and understanding. Lenore sighed, turned, and trudged down the tunnel. She moved slowly, partly from the ache that embedded itself in her chest and partly because she had to grope her way along. She had no light source. She was lost, adrift, but not quite aimless. She knew the direction she had to travel, but how she feared what awaited her. The surface, Simetria, and a mother who would give her no leniency, would wear that perpetual look of disappointment. Never enough. Lenore, what she achieved, who she was.

A faint glow marked the tunnel's exit. As Lenore neared it, her gait slowed then stalled. She wasn't ready. Deston's betrayal had wounded her, and she needed every ounce of strength to face her mother. But waiting would do her no good. She just had to get on with it, take her chastisement and accept her failure, in her own eyes, in Sophie's.

Lenore slipped through the gap between the massive stone doors and blinked her eyes, letting them adjust to the glare. Sophie waited in the circular room of stone bricks, with arms crossed and boot tapping. Lenore dragged her feet onward until she stood just in front of her mother. So alike but different, in appearance and temperament. Both tall and lean, but Sophie had a softness to her form that was boxier in Lenore. The eyes were striking in their similarity of hue and shape, but the rest of Lenore's face must have come from her father—strong jaw and nose, the tendency to furrow her brow. Still, any passerby couldn't fail to see the link between the two women. Although, despite her forty-nine years, Sophie's youthful appearance made Lenore look more the part of younger sister than daughter.

"May you bask in a light which casts no shadow." The Order's motto. Of course Sophie would level that at Lenore, given the circumstances. "Although, it seems, lately, you prefer slinking in the shadows, my silly little corvid."

Sophie shook her head, orange-red curls near her face bouncing, the rest secured in a long braid. She wore her warden's attire, just like the others who had run by and joined the fray, which meant she'd come in more than her guildmaster capacity. She'd been prepared to fight too or, more likely, look the part. That's all she was, as far as Lenore could tell. A role, a figurehead. If there were any depth to her, it was buried deep and long dormant.

"Papa said to come here. To you."

"And you always listen to your Papa, don't you?"

Lenore glared. Sophie stared back. They sat like that for several seconds until Lenore looked away. She couldn't battle her mother, not in that moment of fragility. Everything she'd believed in was suspect. The ground beneath her might give at a moment's notice. How then could she even try to stand against her mother, a woman who knew exactly who she was and what she stood for?

"What will happen to me?" Lenore asked.

"For treason?"

Lenore's eyes snapped back to her mother's. Had her crime been so extreme?

"That's what it is," Sophie said. "What you and your little friends were getting up to down there. The Source, no? That's what they were after?"

Lenore nodded.

"I need you to tell me everything," Sophie said. She took a step forward and placed her hands on Lenore's shoulders. Her glare softened, and that perpetual smile danced on her lips. Was it even real? Or was she playing a part even then?

"You mean their plans?" Lenore asked.

"I have my suspicions of what they were trying to do, but it would be best for everyone involved if you were to tell me outright."

"Because then my punishment wouldn't be so harsh?"

Sophie brought her head closer to Lenore's and dropped her voice to a whisper. "Why, my corvid, there's no punishment to be had, so long as you play this right. You were only pretending to be one of them, weren't you? At the request of your father and myself, at that. Our lovely mole feeding us oh-so-valuable information on those who would seek to undermine all the Order stands for. You were never not on our side. You were simply a very good player, such that you fooled the lot of the Disaffected. They never saw the ambush coming until it was too late, and now, we have them on bona fide charges of treason. All that's left is for you to say what their aims were."

Lenore's mouth hung open. Treachery built on treachery. Used by both sides.

"You knew?" she said. "All along, you knew what I was up to?"

"Of course. How could we not? We gave you this task, didn't we?"

There would be no denying it, even if she wanted to help Deston and the others, it would only mean damning herself. Why would she ever do such a thing to those so ungrateful? She'd played right into Sophie's hands. And Fenrir's. He'd known too. That realization crushed her even more than Deston's betrayal had.

Lenore's shoulders sagged, but Sophie's grip on them held firm.

"Go on then," Sophie said. "Tell me what they were after. Say the words, and let's be done with it."

"The Disaffected were seeking the Source. They wanted to destroy the Link."

Sophie nodded and released Lenore then turned on her heel and strode to the arched doorway. At the threshold, she stopped and turned. Back straight, head held high, regal, perfection. It was misery being the daughter of such a goddess. To be held to that impossible standard. To fall short on all fronts.

"Well?" Sophie said. "Are you coming or not?"

"Do I have a choice? Ever? About anything in my life?"

Sophie sighed and shook her head. There it was, that look of disappointment that routinely graced her mother's face. Just another knife jab to accompany the series of them Lenore had suffered this day.

"We let you choose to make a mistake, didn't we?" Sophie asked. "You have plenty of choices day in and out, but it's easier to pretend you're trapped and blame circumstance on your failures."

Lenore glared but forced her feet forward. Step by step, she plodded along, always three paces behind her mother. Even after they emerged from the ruins of the Church, now the Wardens Guildhall, in the heart of Simetria's upper city and were out under the autumn sun, Lenore lingered back, trapped in her mother's shadow. As always.

THE FATHER

Lenore's retreating form sent a pang through Fenrir's chest. She was reeling, and her meeting with Sophie would only make the vertigo all the worse. But he couldn't focus on his daughter's pain. He had work to do, and securing the Link came before anything else. Even Lenore.

Fenrir turned away from the tunnel and headed toward the sound of battle. Chains clattering. Clubs smacking. Fists planting. By the time he jogged up to his fellow wardens, the Disaffected were in complete disarray. It wasn't a surprise considering how few they were and how ill-equipped. Just disgruntled low bloods with next to no martial training and too much passion and anger to sit idle with.

Maybe Fenrir could have viewed them with compassion and sympathy if they hadn't used his poor Lenore, but his father's blood boiled when he caught sight of their ringleader, Deston Kerk. Two wardens were wrestling with him, and he still hadn't fallen. He flung his long, thick arms, oblivious to the blows from the wardens' chains. Even when they managed to catch Deston's arms with the roped metal, he simply pulled the wardens to and fro like dolls on strings, their own weapons turned against them.

Fenrir would use this opportunity to exact revenge. He strode over to the scuffle, pushed the two wardens aside, and shot his fist straight into Deston's throat. The movement was lightning-fast, and the Disaffected's leader doubled over, gasping for breath that wouldn't come. Fenrir planted a kick in the man's gut, and Deston sank to his knees, grasping his throat with one hand and cradling his stomach with the other.

Fenrir glanced at the two wardens, and they rushed in to secure the prisoner. A third warden hurried to the side, holding a light source high, synthetic, casting white-blue rays. The illumination was potent and put the Disaffected's pathetic torchlight to shame. It also revealed their surroundings. Fenrir's eyes strayed to the murky shapes beyond the cliff's edge. In an instant, he was twenty years into the past, in this same spot, accompanied by a motley crew—a cartographer, an archaeologist, a cultist, and a fellow surveyor. He hadn't been this deep into the Old World since that fateful journey, and until that moment, he hadn't consciously realized he'd been avoiding it. But he had been. Fenrir saw that now.

All the feelings from that time came flooding back. His self-loathing, his pain, his death wish. But they were distant now and couldn't grip him like they had back then. Time had healed him. That and Sophie and Lenore. He'd lost one family but gained another. Two decades ago, when he'd opened his shack's door, taken Sophie into his arms, and chosen to be the father Lenore needed, he had buried the past once and for all.

Fenrir lived in the present now. Such idle reminiscing did him no good, as evidenced by the present situation. Instead of focusing on the task, on the threat Deston still posed, whether subdued or not, Fenrir was absentminded. It was all the distraction Deston needed. Even with the wardens slapping shackles on him, he managed to burst free and bolted down the ramp that led into the decaying city. The wardens shouted and moved to give chase, but Fenrir stopped them with a raised hand. Deston Kerk was his to hunt. His to punish.

Fenrir tore down the smooth stone incline. Despite his bulk, Deston was fast. Having his very life on the line likely played a part in his speed, but Fenrir had something driving him too, maybe equally potent—hatred.

Within a minute, Fenrir caught up to Deston and threw all of his weight onto the man. They both tumbled and rolled on the stone ramp. Deston recovered first then crushed Fenrir under his bulk. Fenrir tried to wrestle free, but Deston had him pinned. All of Fenrir's finesse was useless in the face of the raw mass of the man. Deston raised a fist and slammed it into Fenrir's jaw. The world went black. There was a high-pitched whine.

But Fenrir wasn't done. Deston had the upper hand, true, but that meant he would be careless. Fenrir pretended to reel long after he'd regained his faculties. He flailed his arms and groaned then sent a knee into a pressure point on Deston's thigh. The man gasped and fell over. Fenrir rolled away and rose to his feet, but Deston's blow had done more damage than Fenrir had realized. His balance was off. He wavered and caught himself with a hand to the ground.

Deston was on him before he managed to right himself. One push. Two hands to his chest. Fenrir was walking back, back, toward the precipice. Then his feet touched air, and he was crashing down, slamming and bumping and scraping against rock. Suddenly, everything was black. The sound was wholly gone, not even that whine to accompany him anymore.

***

Fenrir woke to agony gripping the whole of his body. He hissed and cracked his eyes open. There was a ceiling of light blue and geometric molding that ran the length of the room. He knew these. He shifted his gaze downward and spied white, airy curtains set against floor-to-ceiling windows. His fingers brushed against navy blue silk sheets. This was his bed. And there, sitting on its edge, was his wife. And daughter.

"Papa?" Lenore said. She grabbed his hand, and it burned with the contact.

"Ah," he said.

Lenore released him but leaned in. Her eyes were wide and red-lined. Her hair had broken free of its perpetual bondage, the ribbon that normally secured her wavy locks dangling pathetically. She wore such a look of worry.

"Get the doctor," Sophie said to someone Fenrir couldn't see. She was at his other side, pushing his hair away from his forehead. "Well, my love, you look a frightful mess, if I'm being honest."

Lenore glared at her mother then looked back at Fenrir. "She's so rude and a liar. You look divine, Papa, all things considered."

Fenrir furrowed his brow. What did they mean? "What happened?"

Even talking was taxing. Despite just waking up, he was already exhausted, but he forced his eyes to stay open. He didn't want to go back to the darkness and silence. He wanted to be here with his family.

"You took a nasty tumble," Sophie said. She brushed his hair with her fingers. It was the only part of his body that wasn't screaming at him. A focal point of healing that stemmed from her and her alone.

"Deston pushed you off the cliff in the Old World," Lenore said, "and for that, I'll never forgive him."

It all came back. The Disaffected. The Old World. His wrestling with Deston Kerk. He'd been bested and by someone with no training. It was a bad look with the potential to embolden their opponents.

"The wardens captured them?" Fenrir asked.

"Yes, and carted them away to the penitentiary," Sophie

said, "but don't you worry your silly head about that. You need to focus on healing."

"How long have I been out?" Fenrir asked.

"Only a few hours," Sophie said.

Footsteps sounded down the hall, and Sophie and Lenore turned to the doorway.

"The patient is awake?" A doctor approached, everything about the man harkening to a square. A solid, squat body, and a jaw of hard angles. Lenore moved to make room for him, and he sat on the side of the bed.

"He only just came to," Sophie said, standing now, hands clasped.

The doctor inspected Fenrir. For the next few minutes, it was poking and prodding, and Fenrir hissing or groaning with nearly every touch and movement, but by the end of it, the doctor had his diagnosis.

"He's very fortunate. Mostly just bruising and cuts. One broken rib. There might be a slight head injury, so we'll want to keep an eye on him for the next few days. Watch for slurred speech, confusion, issues with his vision, nausea, that kind of thing."

"How long will he need to stay in bed?" Sophie asked.

"A few weeks to be safe. I'll be able to say more within the next couple of days. For now, don't let him leave the bed, even if he demands it. Understood?"

"Oh, if Mama tells him to stay put, he'll follow her instructions to the letter."

Sophie's eyes snapped to Lenore. She forced a laugh at her daughter's words, shook the doctor's hand, then sent everyone away. It was just Sophie and Lenore now, both looking less concerned, gazing down at Fenrir lovingly as his eyelids grew heavier and heavier until he couldn't fight sleep any longer.

***

"Silly man," Sophie said.

Her fingers stroked Fenrir's cheek, and the touch brought him back. It was hard though, returning. Sleep was numbness and oblivion, whereas the alternative was an incessant pain. Yet if anyone could force Fenrir to weather such pangs, it was Sophie.

"You mean stupid man," Fenrir said.

"I rather think if I did mean those words, I would've used them."

"You wouldn't dare hit a man laid so low already."

Fenrir peeled his eyes open, and there was Sophie, grinning. She wore her warden's attire. The look of her filled him with pride. Twenty years they'd been married, and still, he was smitten. But Sophie had that way, with him, with everyone. It was why she was their guildmaster and not he. It was why Simetria bowed down to her and no other.

"What is this self-loathing?" she asked. "Last I checked, we did what we set out to do. Deston Kerk and his cohort are locked away, nicely and neatly."

That name. Before, Fenrir's hatred for it stemmed purely from a father's protectiveness, but now, the antipathy was much more personal.

"He bested me," Fenrir said. "Him. A man with no training. It's a bad look. For all of us."

Sophie sighed and pulled her hand away from his cheek. She pursed her lips and shook her head. "Please don't be the oh-so-exhausting stereotype of your sex. That's a bad look, Fenrir."

"What do you mean?"

"Oh, you know, the man must be the protector, the most competent, unassailable. That was never you, my love. Don't start with such nonsense. I need your level head, now most of all."

"Why?" Fenrir asked. "What's happened?" He made the mistake of trying to sit up in bed. He froze then sank back into his pillows, his very nerves forcing him into submission. He groaned.

"You have to stay put. Dr. Kerk's orders."

"I've no desire to try that again for a good long while. Wait, Dr. Kerk? Is that a coincidence?"

"My, aren't you sharp?" Sophie said. "No, there's a relation between him and Deston. He's his uncle, apparently. When he heard what happened, he insisted on treating you, despite the fact that he's busy running one of the upper city clinics."

"Insisted?"

"Penitence or something. He says he doesn't have anything to do with that part of the family, but he shares the name. I suspect he wants to keep on good terms with us. In any case, I was happy to have expertise. Try not to hold it against him?"

"Why would I do that? It's not like he pushed me off the cliff."

"Well, good," Sophie said. "It seems you're indeed still quite levelheaded."

Sophie rose from the bed and walked to the nearest window. She pushed the curtain aside with a finger and peered out. The light was soft and faint with no rays trickling in through the sheer curtains. It was overcast. Winter was making its slow and steady approach, geared to grip Simetria and hold her hostage for the long and dismal months ahead.

"Trouble's brewing," she said. "Yes, we have the ringleader and his closest associates in hand, but keeping them under lock and key will only make others sympathetic to their cause. We can't sit idle on this Disaffected threat. The time for passivity is over."

"What did you have in mind?" Fenrir asked.

"We talk to Nytho. He reached out, asking to speak with the two of us. I suspect he has suggestions on how we can convince the people to see the error of their ways."

Sophie released the curtain and walked back to the bed. She reached behind her ear with one hand and dug in her pocket with the other. Two small metal disks sat in each of her palms. She placed the one on her forehead, just above her brow. She sat on the bed, leaned over, and held the metal just over the same spot on Fenrir's head.

"Are you fit enough for this?" she asked.

"My mind is the only thing that doesn't hurt, so yes, I would say so."

Sophie brought the disk in contact with his skin. Then, they ceased to see the physical world anymore. Bed, curtains, windows, walls, all gone. They existed in a non-space now, a place that had no need for anything as mundane as the human form. Fenrir and Sophie didn't see so much as feel one another's presence.

It had been a long time since they'd visited the world within their Third Eyes. Or rather, the world their Third Eyes allowed them to spy. Something akin to the Digisphere of the Old World or maybe a sad and sorry substitute for that vast and limitless realm. The Church had destroyed the Digisphere in its earliest days. Fenrir and Sophie existed in just an echo of it now.

You called? Sophie said.

I did. Thank you for answering.

It was always Nytho who they spoke with. There were other alfom, but neither Fenrir nor Sophie had ever conversed with another. Where did the alfom exist? How did they always answer in an instant? Fenrir and Sophie had been protecting the Link for them, as they'd pledged to do, for years, and despite that, they still knew next to nothing about the alfom despite innumerable attempts to learn more. It wasn't so much that Nytho was tight-lipped. On discussions of synthetics and the Old World, he could be quite garrulous. But for the deeper truths—what the alfom were, why the

Lady was their greatest enemy despite being akin to them, why she was so intent on bringing the Rot of the Link back—Nytho was evasive.

Still, the alfom had lived up to their promises and didn't interfere with Simetria's doings. After a time, Fenrir and Sophie simply accepted the situation for what it was. The alfom were powerful, wise, and mysterious, likekly with aims as incomprehensible as their own would be to an ant crawling toward their cake at afternoon tea.

I take it this is about the Disaffected and their latest stunt? she asked.

Yes, I'm afraid so. You did a good job protecting the Link. However...

It will happen again, Sophie said. *The Disaffected have made severing the Link their call to arms, and unfortunately, it's resonating with the people.*

You have to reroute their angst to something else.

Or appease their angst altogether, Sophie said.

Which is what you've been trying to do without success. What you're missing here is that human nature veers toward an us-versus-them mentality, so your best option is to give the people another "them" to despise. Perhaps something more tangible. Something they see and interact with day in and out. An especially corrupt guild, maybe?

We're not going to create a fictitious enemy, Fenrir said, *or get innocent people hurt.*

Something to dwell on then, but that alone isn't sufficient. Not anymore. This situation with the Disaffected has exposed our vulnerability, which brings me to the real reason I reached out. I had hoped to mention this later, ideally to the next generation of wardens, but circumstances have accelerated the timeline. We need to ensure if even one Link node is lost, it won't completely sever the connection.

Link node was a new term for Fenrir, and he didn't like the foreboding in Nytho's words. Still, Sophie held the reins here. He would follow her lead.

What did you have in mind? she asked.

Try not to feel betrayed by what I say next.

That sounds awfully ominous, Sophie said.

The Source in Simetria isn't the only of its kind. There were twenty before the Old World fell, but all were corrupted like the one in Simetria. Yours was the first and, so far, only to have been restored. I had hoped to have your descendants spread out and restore the others, but we don't have the luxury of time.

You mean, there are other Rots of the Link? she asked.

Yes, each Link node was corrupted by the Linkrot virus but by different people. Scores of other Marcos Frenwiths who Yir had do her bidding.

Which means the distortions still exist, Fenrir said, *and afflicted still suffer.*

Why didn't you tell us? Sophie asked.

I didn't want your achievements to be diminished, and asking you to restore the other nodes would have been too demanding.

All those lives still forced to exist alongside the non-Euclidean, in constant fear of coming in contact with those foul motes. And yet, why did Fenrir suddenly feel so energized, so full of hope and wonder and promise? Had he missed them so dearly? Or was it just the old life of rituals and wards and being a surveyor?

A warden was a fine role to play, but it was no surveyor. It was a custodian. There was no art to it. No Axioms to study or wards to perfect or mercy killings to give. He really did miss it, all of it, and the idea that everything he'd thought was lost to time was out there somewhere, waiting for him, filled him with an eagerness he hadn't felt in ages.

Why wouldn't we want to cleanse those Sources too? Fenrir asked. *Why would you think we wouldn't leap at the chance to free others as we freed ourselves?*

You don't know what it's like out there. How big the world is. How different. Even restoring one other node will be a feat. I didn't think it would be appropriate for me to ask, given everything you two had already done.

Would it be the same process? Sophie asked. *Use the diskette again in those consoles to remove the Rot of the Link?*

Yes. The malware removal program will work on all instances of the Linkrot virus.

Where's the closest Link node? Fenrir asked.

Across the water to the east.

You said it wasn't safe to venture there, Sophie said.

It isn't, but the danger mostly lies in our ignorance of the place and its people. My eyes are as blinded to that far shore as they were for Simetria until you cleansed your Link node.

Well, then, Sophie said, *I suppose it's high time we set about restoring your sight.*

LOVER'S LETTER

To Lenore,

Last night, I was walking in the lower city. My eyes went up to the rooftops, and there was one of those attuners stuck in a cobble of chimneys. I guess that's why no one ever bothered to take it down. Maybe you can't even see it during the day, but I saw it. In the background kind of lighting it up for me was your window.

It was like a sign. You, the attuner, our cause. I know I've kept you at arm's length. Truth be told, I figured you just wanted to play at being a revolutionary, but I've been watching you. You probably didn't notice because I'm real careful with that kind of thing. I've had too many angry mothers chase after me with roller pins and fire pokers and walking sticks when I eyed their daughters too openly.

Anyway, I learned how to look without looking, if that makes sense, and in my not looking at you, I've been impressed. The lot of us don't treat you real well, but you just let it slide right off you. You work as hard as any of us maybe harder just to prove you belong.

That's what I'm here to say. You do belong, Lenore. You

deserve to be more involved and to know where we want to take this whole thing. It's not safe to write more. Let's meet and talk about it face-to-face. Just you and me. There's a nice little spot near our regular place. I think you can even see that attuner from there. It all comes back round, see? You, me, the things we aim for. I'd be glad to have you at my side for the part that comes next. Who knows? Maybe for the times that come after too.

Deston

THE MOTHER

Nytho needed them to restore another Link node, and Sophie would see it was done. But diving into the unknown without Fenrir at her side was paralyzing. It wasn't her skill she doubted. Her anxiety stemmed from something more nebulous. She didn't always trust her instincts, and worse, she found herself becoming the kind of leader she didn't like all that much. Who better to accompany her than her loudest critic?

Sophie rapped on Lenore's door. After a few seconds with no response, she tried again. The silence persisted, and Sophie grabbed the knob and turned. The door was unlocked. It opened to reveal Lenore hunched over her desk, her head turned on its side, resting on a stack of pages, eyes closed. Sophie tiptoed over, making it to her daughter's side without waking her.

Lenore's lips were parted, and a stray lock of her fair hair swayed with her breath. She wore her nightclothes still, and in that oversized frock, Lenore almost looked like the child she wasn't anymore. Nineteen, her heart newly broken, the innocence lost. Had it been so long already since she'd left Sophie's womb and been placed in her arms, screaming and howling, a fighter from the outset?

Sophie gazed at her and spotted the contents of the papers under her head. Love letters. Scores of them signed "Deston." Sophie sighed. All that passion and drive turned to pleasing a man. Such wasted potential.

Lenore's breathing stopped, and her eyes shot open. She jolted on catching Sophie so near at hand.

"Goodness," Sophie said. "I didn't mean to startle you."

"Then perhaps you ought to avoid hovering over me while I sleep."

Lenore glared then pulled her arms away from the desk and took note of what had served as her pillow. She scrambled to collect the leaves of paper, but Sophie grabbed one and held it out of reach.

"Dwelling on the past is rarely a worthwhile exercise," Sophie said, "and lamenting over a man who betrayed you is the height of foolishness."

Lenore jumped from her chair and snatched the letter from Sophie's hand. "I'm not lamenting over Deston. I was trying to see through his lies and make sense of how I got duped so badly."

"Well, in that case, good work, my little corvid."

"I hardly deserve that moniker anymore. I'm the opposite of clever."

"That's not entirely true. In fact, it seems like you've already learned the first lesson from your mishaps—grow from one's mistakes."

Lenore crushed the paper into a ball and glowered. "Is that why you came, to shove my failures in my face?"

Lenore's venom was like a knife to Sophie's sternum. Consolation was supposed to be Fenrir's task. He knew how to handle Lenore, to appease her, to comfort her. Sophie was a poor substitute, maybe the very worst one, because no matter what she said or did, Lenore seemed resolved to despise her.

"I would never do a thing so cruel," Sophie said. "Besides,

you seem well aware of your failures without me pointing them out to you. Now, make yourself presentable, preferably with trousers and sturdy boots. We're going on a little outing."

Lenore slumped but didn't bother to argue. Instead, she moved to her wardrobe, rummaged in its contents, and retrieved a tunic and trousers. She stopped and looked back at Sophie. "Do you mind?"

Sophie turned away to give her daughter privacy.

Within minutes, Lenore was ready, boots laced, coat and hat on, a hand on her hip, and her foot tapping. "Where are we going?"

Sophie moved into the hallway. "You'll see soon enough, won't you?"

Lenore sighed but followed Sophie through the corridors of their estate. The house was old, as old as the Roshem family itself, and all those lives seemed to haunt the halls. Or maybe that's just how Sophie felt moving past the portraits of her ancestors all the way back to the founding of the Church of Impermanence.

Her history was fraught. Her present was everything she'd tried to avoid, but Vergil's betrayal and Lenore's inadvertent conception had forced her into this life. She was a reluctant leader, an unwilling saint, and maybe a bad mother. She didn't know how to be one. Trisht, her old housekeeper, had been the closest thing Sophie had had to a mother, but Trisht was many years gone. All Sophie had were her memories, and those were hardly good for more than idle reminiscing.

As Sophie and Lenore strode down the halls, the dark, wood-paneled walls and thick, burgundy carpets absorbed their footsteps. A humming was left in wake of the deadened thuds. The air was close. This was Sophie's home, but she didn't like it all that much. Despite the fact she could change it with the wave of a hand, something stymied her. Maybe it was the need to keep up appearances, being the high blood others expected her to be, maintaining tradition. Or maybe she was terrified of change.

Once outside, Sophie buttoned her coat and flipped up its collar. She rested her warden's tricorn on her head and angled it down. The day was young. The dew still clung to the rosebush thorns in her garden. The sun hid behind the clouds. The wrought-iron gates wheezed on their hinges as a guard let them out. Sophie strode with perfect posture, took long strides, and moved her arms with a graceful sway. Those she passed in the streets stopped and stared. They knew who she was. Everyone in Simetria did. Their saint of the Order of the New Day and the Warden Guildmaster. The woman who had wrestled Simetria free from the iron hold of the Lady and her followers, the Church of Impermanence.

Sophie glanced at the mostly shuttered windows of the high-blood homes. They looked much as they had during the time of the Church. Well-kept, clean, sporting opulent touches. In the molding above one door, a griffin screeched without sound. On the knocker of another, a lion clamped down on a brass ring. Window boxes overflowed with marigolds drying and fading.

But this hadn't always been the case. These same homes had been pillaged and looted between the fall of the Church and the establishment of the Order. The law and decorum only returned with Sophie's own homecoming, from the villa Vergil had locked her away in back to her estate in the upper city. In those early days, she hadn't had to do much to cement her following. The low bloods and high alike welcomed her, not too surprising considering she had destroyed the Rot of the Link and freed them from centuries of living in fear of the distortions. That and she had supposedly returned from the dead.

The human mind was a fickle thing, however, and it wasn't long before unrest started to rear its ugly head. And so, Sophie had slipped into the role Vergil had created for her without even meaning to. She had led the effort to create a new-world order which had yielded the guild system, her Order of the New Day.

It was only a few blocks from her estate to what had once been the Church of Impermanence and was now the Wardens Guildhall. Two sentries stood guard at the gate. Sophie smiled at the man and woman, wrapped the first two fingers of each hand around one another, and formed an "x" with her arms. The sentries returned the Wardens Guild gesture and let her and Lenore pass.

Every warden was critical. Sophie couldn't afford to take their loyalty for granted. Fenrir knew this too. Together, they'd managed to amass a following they could rely on, but every edifice held flaws. Two such defects, as Sophie saw them, were standing nearby on the paved stones, chatting. Nicolus Yevin and Laurenz Frenwith. They glanced at her then quieted, straightened, and strolled over.

"Guildmaster Roshem," Nicolus said.

He gave the warden's gesture, and Laurenz followed suit. Sophie returned it to each.

"Masters Yevin and Frenwith," she said, nodding at them.

"How fares Master Roshem?" Nicolus asked.

"Well enough, all things considered. A broken rib, bruising both in terms of body and ego but on the mend."

"That's a relief to hear," Laurenz said with a broad but empty smile, blue eyes dead.

Was his characteristic ennui simply a defense mechanism he'd built in his earliest days? To bear the weight of the name Frenwith had always been a burden. A happy one in the days of the Church. A blighted one in Simetria now. But if the change in his circumstances had rattled Laurenz, she hadn't been able to tell. The man could play at being a statue. Stolid, stern, cold. All the rancor directed at him and his family in the aftermath of the Church's fall, and he let it glide right off him. A stalwartness? More likely, a disbelief in his own vulnerability. A high blood through and through. And in a sense, he'd been right. Here he was, two decades later, strolling the grounds of that erstwhile Church, wearing the garb of a warden, swearing to protect the same Link Saint Marcos Frenwith, his ancestor, had tainted and, in doing so, secretly cursed their city. Yet power and prestige were not so easily lost, at least not to a Frenwith.

"And here is the savior of the day," Nicolus said, angling his head at Lenore, throwing his arm out to the side, and offering a deep bow.

"Me?" Lenore asked.

Nicolus glanced up from his still inclined position and grinned. "Well, you are the same Lenore Roshem who infiltrated the ranks of the Disaffected, discovered their treachery, and turned them in to us wardens, are you not?"

Lenore blushed. Nicolus was striking, with his black hair slicked back and reaching to his neckline, and still sporting the body of a dancer. He'd aged like a fine wine and, as such, tended to have a way with nearly all the high-blood women. But Lenore didn't swoon over him in that way. Nicolus was more like family to her. He'd taken to Sophie's daughter from the outset, acting the part of a surrogate uncle, and to Sophie's unending annoyance, a bond had taken between the two.

"Lenore and I are taking a little trip into the Old World," Sophie said.

Lenore started.

"It's a bit of journey," Sophie said, "so if you don't mind, I'd like to be off so I can check on Master Roshem before too long."

"Don't let us delay you a minute more, please, and a pleasant journey to you both," Nicolus said, stepping aside and waving them through.

"May you bask in a light which casts no shadow," Laurenz said, reciting the Order's maxim.

"Come along, Lenore," Sophie said over her shoulder.

They followed the manicured paths, grass cut short, bushes trimmed into sharp boxes, vestiges of the time before the Order, when the specifications for harmonious spaces dictated their physical environs. Despite the Church being long gone and no worries of distortions taking root anymore, such tendencies persisted. Tradition could be a tenacious beast. Best to let it be and fade when society had no need for it anymore.

Once they entered the guildhall, Sophie slowed and moved to Lenore's side. Her daughter looked at her with a furrowed brow, so serious and grim more often than not.

"Just so you know," Sophie said, "only your Papa and I are aware of the true role you played in the Disaffected's stunt. Not even Nicolus knows the truth."

Lenore's lips parted then closed again.

"All to say, be careful what you tell him."

Lenore shook her head.

"Do you have something to add?" Sophie asked.

"I don't know why you dislike him so."

"I like Nicolus as much as he deserves. Now, come along. We've a long way to go."

They continued on. At the end of the grand hall, they plunged down a series of stairs, darkness becoming the norm, broken only by the occasional flame, until they arrived at a door bearing a bronze plaque with the word "Vault" etched into it. Sophie pulled a key from her pocket, inserted it into the keyhole, and granted them access.

They entered the Vault, but how changed since the days of the Church. No longer filled with dust, barely lit by rotting torches affixed to rusting sconces. Now, it boasted smooth gray walls and floors, cold crisp lighting, pure air, all the better for the synthetics to flourish here. Because that's what this place was made for, fashioned in this way, not to simply hold old relics with unknown purposes but to study those relics and, maybe one day, bring them back to relevance.

A head appeared from behind a row of shelving. Flaxen hair worn short in a bob. Dark black eyes. Olive skin. If Sophie didn't already know her, she'd mistake Feowna Moldgrove for an overeager teen, but her appearance was exceptionally misleading. Feowna was well into adulthood, nearing four decades. Her movements were quick, and she was at Sophie's side in seconds.

"Guildmaster Roshem," she said, "I have the devices you asked for."

Smudges of gray peppered her round cheeks. The source of the grime rested in her hands, some synthetic pried open, spewing wires. Feowna hurried away, around the corner to the rear of the room. Sophie followed, and Lenore trailed and peered with a mix of wonder and fear at the synthetics crowding the space. Few were permitted into the Vault. Lenore had never seen its interior.

"This is my daughter, Lenore Roshem," Sophie said to Feowna then to her daughter added, "This is Journeyman Feowna Moldgrove, the wardens' resident syntheticsmith. She maintains the Vault for us."

Feowna glanced at Lenore and offered a curt nod then trained her eyes back on Sophie. No time for social pleasantries. Or rather, no use for them in Feowna's mind.

"I activated the Third Eye as you requested," Feowna said. "It's ready for its bearer." She held a small gray box in her hands and offered it to her guildmaster.

Sophie took it, opened it by pressing a depression set into its top, and gazed at the contents. Nearly a dozen metal disks, indistinguishable from her own Third Eye, arranged edge on, held in place by a soft, synthetic material that gave when she plucked one free.

"One moment," Feowna said, moving too close to Sophie, sticking a lens into one eye, and inspecting the disk. "No, not that one." Feowna snatched the box from Sophie, mumbled to herself, and proceeded to move through the disks until she found what she sought. "This is it. Registered to a Lenore Roshem. Serial number XGY79521BU." Feowna glanced at Lenore. "She's not a warden though, is she?"

Sophie tried not to react, aimed to keep her voice level and calm, but she was ill-used to defiance, what with being the de facto leader of the Wardens Guild and, by extension, Simetria. Still, Feowna was an invaluable asset to the guild, and Sophie had to remind herself of the woman's oddities. This wasn't impertinence, just a lack of social grace.

"Not yet, no," Sophie said.

"Not ever," Lenore muttered.

Sophie glared at her then looked back at Feowna, smiled, and shrugged. "Willful, like her mother. In any case, where in our guild charter does it specify only wardens can bear a synthetic?"

Feowna thought for a moment then shook her head.

"A hint?" Sophie said. "Nowhere. I wrote the document. I didn't put anything about synthetics in it. This Vault and all its contents are overseen by the guildmaster, which means, I say who can and cannot use the devices within it."

"That makes perfect sense," Feowna said then handed the disk and the box of others to Sophie.

"We won't take up any more of your valuable time. Thank you, Journeyman Moldgrove."

Feowna nodded and immediately returned to the shelving she'd issued from, rummaging through synthetics, in search of something strange and mysterious, no doubt. Even with the Vault at Sophie's disposal, with the knowledge granted by Nytho, the synthetics were still nigh magic to her. While she'd delighted in learning the esotericism of mathematics when she'd been a surveyor, she couldn't warm to studies of these devices. There was something cold and almost hostile about these relics of the Old World. They held secrets but ones seemingly laced with poison. After all, hadn't they, in part, been the cause of the downfall of the Bygones?

Sophie and Lenore took their leave of Feowna and the Vault and dove further still into the bowels of the old Church, parts no longer used by the Wardens Guild, ones left to rot and crumble, but the path itself was well-maintained. Maybe too much so. The upkeep of this particular route had likely allowed Lenore to find that other access point to the Old World in the first place. The one she'd led the Disaffected to.

It boggled Sophie's mind how anyone could be foolish enough to want to destroy the Link and bring the distortions back, but she was resolved to understand the reasoning behind the Disaffected's act. She hoped to gain insight courtesy of her wayward daughter. In the meantime, she had ordered the wardens to seal off that other route.

As she and Lenore entered the large circular room that led into the Old World, the two guards stationed there straightened. She smiled and nodded to them and gave the guild gesture. They returned it, cradling their glaives in the bends of their arms.

"Truth, protection, connection," Sophie said.

"Truth, protection, connection," they replied.

"I sent word ahead I was coming."

"Yes, Guildmaster Roshem."

The one moved aside as the other used the bulk of his mass to push the doors in. Once there was enough room to permit Sophie and Lenore to pass through, he stopped, retrieved his polearm, and stood to the side, tall and alert.

"You'll close it behind us and open once you hear my knocks," Sophie said.

"Yes, Guildmaster," both guards said in tandem.

"Come," Sophie said to Lenore.

They passed through the gap and entered the Old World. Sophie tapped a synthetic attached to her coat's lapel, and a steely blue glow illuminated the way. She knew the path. She'd overseen the project to clear it years ago. After all, direct access to the Source was essential to protecting the Link. Instead of the two or three days it had taken their fateful expedition of the past to reach the Source, the journey in would total less than a half hour now.

But how time dragged. Lenore plodded along, stamping her feet, frowning and scowling. Then they exited the same tunnel Lenore had run back down a mere three days prior, and suddenly, they were in an enormous cavern. Lenore couldn't have seen its extent before. Her torchlight would have been too dim, and the synthetic illumination had only come after Fenrir had sent her back to Sophie. This was her first time really seeing the Old World. Sophie stood back and let her take it in.

Buildings were falling into ruin but still impressive in their height and girth. Synthetics abounded. Roadways were made of a single stone worn smooth somehow. Carriages of metal cluttered the streets. And then, there was the sheer scale of it. Structure on structure on structure, all equally vast and dizzying, stretching up into the heights, looped off by the sarcophagus that entombed it all, Simetria sitting above. Their whole world but a mote in comparison to this one.

Sophie stood abreast with Lenore. "This was my first view of it too."

"You came this way during your expedition?" Lenore asked.

"Yes, and back then, we had no idea what was waiting for us down there. Distortions. Afflicted. We knew they'd be there, but not how many or how prevalent."

Lenore leaned forward and looked down the cliff they stood on. She kicked a rock off the edge. It clattered down, down, down. Then, the silence returned.

"No more distortions or afflicted now," Sophie said. "Just a still and quiet tomb for the past. Until you and your companions decided to break your way in."

Lenore's scowl returned. She crossed her arms and looked away from Sophie.

"This is also the spot where your Papa almost died, thanks to your friend. Can you imagine falling down these heights? That was your doing as much as Deston Kerk's."

Lenore's hostility evaporated, and she looked nauseous.

"But we're not here for the view," Sophie said. "Come."

The rest of the journey saw Lenore more subdued. Her feet dragged, her sour look replaced by a forlorn one. This outing was doing just what it needed to. Lenore gazed at the wonders of a bygone era with vacant eyes. Her mind had to be leagues away, back on the surface, in Simetria, sitting in a room with airy curtains, stroking the hand of a man she adored, his body a ruined wreck.

In short order, they left the streets and entered a building that was remarkably preserved. The synthetics of its cladding reflected Sophie's light source. Inside, the halls were empty and pristine, so far removed from her first passage. Back then, this space had been saturated with distortions. Straight lines, hard angles, depth perception, all of that had been upended. It had been walking through a world of undulations, like water forever swirling in a vortex. Now, it was calm and predictable. Beautiful in its Euclidean nature.

Sophie led them to a door of silver metal. She pulled her Third Eye from behind her ear and placed in on her forehead.

She thought of what she sought, the sequence of letters and numbers that would grant them entry, then there they were, overlain on her vision as a ghostly glow. Sophie pressed her fingers lightly to a smooth surface and entered the code. A lock released, and the door slid to the side.

Sophie looked over her shoulder at Lenore, who simply gaped. The door and lock were unlike any synthetics. These were more newly foundered under Nytho's direct guidance. It had been the first major project for securing the Link, and the wardens had kept the secret well.

"You and your friends would've had a lovely time trying to get past that door," Sophie said. "But come, set your eyes on the thing you so hungered to destroy." She entered the room.

It was modest and bare, eight large paces in length and width, gray walls and ceiling and floor. It was warm, and a hum permeated the space, originating from the sole contents of the room—a console and the object that infused it with power. Lenore crept in, and the door slid shut behind her.

Sophie waved a hand at the console. "The Link's Source. Or more accurately, a Link node."

It was just a gray rectangle with a smooth reflective surface set into it, and beside it, another gray box with little lights that blinked on and off in rapid succession. The whole of it rested on a table no more than two arms' span in width. Cables snaked off the backs of the synthetics and plunged into the housing that imparted the console with power.

"Is it the vile, horrid thing you imagined it to be?" Sophie asked.

Lenore was waking from her daze at last. She settled her eyes on Sophie and shook her head. "You just don't understand."

"Then enlighten me."

"It's the Order I despise. The guilds. This"—Lenore pointed to the console—"is just the smallest part of that."

"I see. And you thought, the last world order was usurped by affecting the Source, so why not perform a repeat to achieve the same results? Was that the brilliant idea?"

Lenore grimaced and crossed her arms. "The guilds don't work or only work for the very few. The masters and journeymen, maybe, but certainly not the apprentices or novices. Definitely not those who don't belong to a guild."

The idealism, the naivety, the beautiful obliviousness of youth. Sophie had to suppress the laugh that threatened to erupt from her throat.

"Every form of governance is flawed because we are," Sophie said. "Selfishness, greed, ambition, that's what the system has to contend with. You'll never stamp them out wholly. The best you can do is minimize the corruption."

Lenore shook her head and stiffened. "The guilds aren't the way."

"Perhaps. There may very well be a superior system, but if there is, I haven't stumbled across it in all my research. I created the Order because it was the best option. Better than another religion, which was what some of the others wanted. Blessed is the Link, they said, but it felt all too similar to the Church. I wanted to distance ourselves from it as much as possible, opting for a series of hierarchies rather than a single one. Each guild responsible for protecting its members' interests. Every member an active part of the whole. Skill and expertise determining relative influence. Countless guilds to check one another, no single one dominating, necessitating compromises and alliances."

"Ignoring the fact it doesn't play out in that manner," Lenore said, "where does such a system leave the people who choose not to be in a guild? They have no voice. They're as good as nonexistent."

"They make that choice."

Lenore threw up her hands and scoffed. "Yes, either join the twisted system or be satisfied not having a say."

Sophie walked to the console's table and rested against it. "It's not perfect, I'm well aware, but what I'd like to know is just how destroying our connection to the Link would create a wonderful new utopia? What exactly did you all have planned? If you'd made it here into this room against all odds, what then?"

Lenore's eyes shifted from side to side. The self-righteousness persisted, but the confidence faded. Her arms loosened and fell slack to her sides.

Sophie tilted her head and tapped her finger to her chin. "Did you have the Rot of the Link? Would you use that and bring back all the horrors it entails? Distortions. Afflicted."

"I don't even know what the Rot of the Link is or was."

"Of course not. It's beyond your understanding, any of you. So, tell me, how you would have done it?"

Lenore tightened her hands into fists. "We'd destroy it, the Source."

Sophie continued to tap her chin, her head still askew. "And how would you manage that?"

"Smash the synthetics to pieces," Lenore said, tossing her hand at the console and smirking.

Sophie nodded then pushed herself off the table and stepped to the side. The console was in full view again, and she waved at it. "Look closely. Tell me what you see."

"Synthetics. Lights. A black mirror. Worms and snakes coming off of it."

"And around it? Hovering in the space just beyond those obvious physical objects?"

Lenore squinted then her lips parted. She hadn't noticed until then, no doubt too preoccupied with their conversation to see what the Source really was, where it really was.

"The air around it is strange," Lenore said. "It's undulating or wavering."

Sophie moved close to the console and reached into those irregularities, rotated her hand, wiggled her fingers.

"Some strange side effect of the synthetics?" Lenore asked.

"No, this is the Link's Source. The console is simply a means to interact with it. If you had destroyed the console, it wouldn't have done a thing."

Lenore gaped and shifted her eyes. Sophie let her take in the truth, understand its ramifications and the futility of what her and the Disaffected had wanted to do.

"Why do you think the Church used the Rot of the Link in the first place?" Sophie asked. "If the Link could have been destroyed, why wouldn't they have done that? They lived with distortions because the Rot of the Link was the only way to sever the connection."

Lenore narrowed her eyes. "You kept that fact hidden on purpose."

"At long last my little corvid sees the full picture."

"Don't call me that silly name. I'm an adult, and I'd appreciate you speaking to me like one."

So, even Lenore was aware of the paradigm shift that had occurred owing to her actions. From child to woman in the blink of an eye. All it had taken was a monumental betrayal. The poor thing, but she would weather this difficult time and come out all the stronger so long as she had the proper guide.

"As you like," Sophie said.

Install the update on the Third Eyes, Nytho's voice sounded in Sophie's head.

This was the other task she'd come into the Old World to do, essential to their mission. Sophie dug in her coat's pocket and retrieved Lenore's Third Eye and the gray box containing the others. She placed the latter on the table and held the former between them.

"Yours first," Sophie said.

Put the Third Eye in the slot set into the tower.

Sophie laid the disk on a depression in the large rectangle with the blinking lights.

Wake up the console up selecting the Enter key on the keyboard.

She brought the reflective surface to life with the tap of a button. A black window flashed into view holding a small amount of text and a white rectangle that appeared and disappeared over and over again.

Key in this text.

A string of letters and numbers and symbols appeared in Sophie's vision: "cd E:" [Enter key] then "start 3rdEyev4.2.0.exe" [Enter key]

Sophie entered the text, and the console performed a flurry of actions.

Wait for the installation to complete then repeat the process with each Third Eye.

"What are you doing?" Lenore asked.

"A necessary first step in correcting your mistakes."

"I always thought that metal disk you and Papa wore was symbolic, but it's not, is it?"

Sophie switched out Lenore's Third Eye for another and ran the installation again.

"No, it most certainly is not," Sophie said, moving to Lenore. "Give me your hand."

Lenore reluctantly did as instructed, and Sophie placed the metal disk in her daughter's palm.

"Your very own Third Eye," Sophie said. "Seeing as you're such an adult now."

"I thought you were going to punish me for helping the Disaffected."

"Who says this isn't punishment? You'll travel with me to the far shore to right the wrong you set into motion."

Lenore started and frowned. Her fingers closed over the

metal disk in her palm. "The far shore? I thought there was nothing out there."

"So we believed, but we were wrong," Sophie said. "Your little stunt exposed just how vulnerable the Link is at present. The best solution is to bolster it, to ensure if the Source, our Link node, is compromised, there will be other Link nodes that will safeguard our connection to the alfom."

"There are other Sources?"

"So it would seem. Other Link nodes, other Rots of the Link, distortions, afflicted, all of that is likely lying in wait for us."

Lenore blanched. This would be an apt lesson for her in multiple ways. Let her see with her own eyes just what the world was like before the Order of the New Day. Have her understand why the duty of the wardens was so fundamentally important.

"And if I refuse to go with you?" Lenore asked.

Sophie stepped in and placed her hands around Lenore's. She smiled. "Let me put it this way, either you recognize the importance of the Link and assist your mother in a quest to bolster it, or you admit to aiding the Disaffected and join them in a cell."

"You're bluffing. You'd never do that to me."

Sophie squeezed Lenore's hands. "I wouldn't be doing a thing. This is your choice to make, just like the one where you let yourself fall for a con man. Let's hope you make the wiser call this time around."

She released Lenore and returned to the console, switching out the Third Eyes and initiating the installations.

Lenore stood by fuming. "Papa wouldn't let you do it."

"Your Papa was the one to suggest this ultimatum. He can't come with me because of the injuries he incurred wrestling with your beau. He wouldn't hear of me going alone, so here we are. If you don't like it, take it up with him."

Lenore slumped, the fire in her extinguished. Sophie had won. A few more minutes and all the Third Eyes carried the updated software.

Retrieve the M-disc.

Sophie pulled a worn synthetic case from a pouch on her belt and pressed a button on the console. The device expelled a tray holding the diskette that had changed her life and world. Sophie lifted it with care and placed it in its case then closed it with a snap.

"Is that the relic you used?" Lenore asked. "To destroy the Rot of the Link?"

"Yes, and we'll put it to good use again. We have multiple copies of the code writ on it, so we can take this one without worry."

"What did you do with these then?" Lenore asked, lifting her palm and the Third Eye sitting on it.

Sophie moved to her side and took the metal disk between thumb and forefinger. "These are our most important tool. They're how we stay connected and, with the update I just ran, will allow us to see the distortions. A rather important skill to have. But your Third Eye must be used with care. Know that when you don it, a voice may speak to you. Heed the one who calls itself Nytho, but be wary of another. If a woman's voice speaks, be on your guard. She may go by Yir or the Lady. Either way, she can't be trusted. She represents everything we're fighting against."

"Everything you're fighting against, you mean," Lenore said. "Don't lump me in with you and your wardens."

"This is your second chance, Lenore. Stay on the right side of history this time, won't you?"

ADDRESS

Good people of Simetria, I am here today to have an honest conversation with you. As the founder of the Order of the New Day and Warden Guildmaster, this task falls to me. I do not come bearing happy tidings. It is quite the opposite. I come with a grave message. Perhaps you have heard some rumors of what recently transpired, but I would like to set the record straight and remove any room for doubt. We are under attack.

Four days ago, a small group of Simetrians calling themselves the Disaffected set out to do the unthinkable. They snuck into the Old World with the horrid aim of harming the Source. Their goal was to sever the Link and, with it, our connection to the alfom. Fortunately, the wardens stayed true to their oath and protected the Link nobly. The Disaffected were captured and are under lock and key.

I am aware these Disaffected are not alone in their qualms with the Order of the New Day, but we have procedures in place precisely for this. If you are unhappy with any aspect of our system, whether it be your guildmasters or other seniors in your guild or actions by other guilds, I urge you to file a complaint. The wardens investigate every matter brought to our attention. We pledge to protect the Link, which includes the guild system that is meant to support the people.

What I urge you not to do is sympathize with these Disaffected or, worse, support their twisted aims. I cannot believe I must say this, but we cannot and will not return to a life with the Link befouled. We will not live again with distortions and the constant fear of affliction. The Disaffected will tell you they only aim to destroy the Link, that they will not make use of the Rot of the Link and so will avoid the return of the non-Euclidean. I tell you they lie. There is no way to destroy the Link. It can only be severed and that with the Rot of the Link. This is why the Church hid the truth from us.

Do you see now how foolish the cause of the Disaffected is? How misplaced? They want to tear down the Order, but doing so would only bring about our ruin. Some of you are too young to remember the world before I destroyed the Rot of the Link. Some of you were not yet born. So, take heed of your elders. Listen as they describe what our lives were like. Picture yourself in their shoes. Your mother or father or sister or lover or child succumbing to affliction. Their body warped into horrid forms. Their mind lost to that siren's song. It is a fate infinitely worse than death because even with a mercy killing, they do not die, tormented for eternity so long as the Rot of the Link persists.

I repeat, we cannot and will not return to that life. If you are unhappy, there are ways to protest, ways to demand your voice be heard. I am telling you, I am here. I am listening. I am open to change. I am not the Church. I am you. You are me. We are one. We escaped the shadows and bask in the light. Do not be tempted by flawed ideology. Do not willingly plunge back into the dark depths. The Link is not our enemy. In fact, our only enemy is ourselves if we are foolish enough to turn against one another.

A CONFRONTATION

The crowd erupted into a roar. The guildmasters hovering behind Sophie whispered to one another. Sophie waved and waved and gave the Wardens Guild gesture. She soaked in the love of the masses, got drunk on it, so that by the time she stepped away from the balcony and back into the guildhall, she looked giddy.

Lenore grimaced. Her mother was her worst in moments like this. So far removed from the serious and composed woman who had taken her into the Old World and shown her the Source. That woman must have been the surveyor in her. This one was the hollow head of a gluttonous beast. What was worse was how sweet her words did sound. She had such a way with them. And even if Lenore turned her nose up at her mother's high-pitched laugh and flippant ways, everyone else was mesmerized.

Lenore was alone in her disdain. Before, the Disaffected had seen things her way, but they were gone now, their bodies trapped in cells, their minds turned against her or, better yet, never having been with her. She was forsaken, but sulking served no purpose. Besides, she was here for a specific reason; she had a request. The best she could do was linger in a corner of the hall, bite her tongue, and wait for her mother to notice her.

Lenore took up her station in an alcove sporting thick forest green curtains and molding with geometric forms. The door to the balcony was shut now. The roar of the crowd had faded. The guildmasters were swarming Sophie.

"A moving speech, Guildmaster Roshem," a man said.

"You've such a way with words," another added.

The groveling continued until Lenore's feet began to ache. She unfocused her eyes, and the cloaks of the guildmasters blended into a kaleidoscope of colors. There was the stone gray and white of the Masons Guild complementing the spring green and brown of the Farmers. These more natural hues and tones contrasted with the bold blue and yellow of the Teachers Guild and the silver and gold sheen of the Merchants. There were scores more. All the guildmasters were present, roughly fifty at the moment. Sophie must have demanded it. A show of unity.

But they were far from unified. There was constant in-fighting. Guilds combined and splintered from month to month, in attempts to gain more power and influence by sheer number but ultimately flung apart by disparate interests and loyalties. Lenore couldn't understand it. How could such a volatile and ever-shifting system even hope to function for the people it was meant to serve?

The answer was it didn't. Not from what the common folk said, the same who would laugh away her mother's suggestion that the disgruntled simply file a complaint. They had already lost all trust in the Order. Why would they willingly label themselves as potential enemies by airing their grievances?

Lenore preferred to think her parents were too far removed to understand how the world actually worked. That they meant well but were ill-informed. The alternative was too painful to consider. Her stunt with the Disaffected had, at least, grabbed their attention. Maybe they would finally start to see her as an equal, listen to what she had to say, take her feedback seriously. It was her only bit of hope left after the Disaffected's failure and Deston's betrayal.

That betrayal weighed on her mind. Lenore needed some kind of solace, and she had an inkling of what might do the trick, but it required a favor only her mother could grant hence the endless standing and waiting and suppressing sighs that kept forming in her throat.

Bored and restless, Lenore eventually wandered out of her alcove and skirted the edge of the room. She wasn't supposed to be there, but the wardens hesitated at turning her away from their guildhall. They all seemed to think she wielded some kind of power. That or they suspected she would stand in her mother's place one day. But they were wrong; Lenore would never be a warden.

"And how, oh how, did the little vixen make her way into our hallowed guildhall?"

Lenore turned and caught sight of Nicolus lingering nearby, leaning against the wall, legs crossed at the ankle, smirking.

"Your wardens aren't vigilant enough, I suppose. It was child's play making it in, even to your innermost circle."

Nicolus pushed himself off the wall and came to Lenore's side. They stood abreast, watching the crowd, Sophie still meandering through it, the throngs trailing her eagerly.

"Discovering our weaknesses?" he asked. "A clever tactic and much needed in these days of traitorous intent. Tell me, little vixen, was this something your mother tasked you with?"

"More like something she necessitated. I need to speak with her, and I'd rather not wait until evening."

Nicolus nodded and stroked his chin. "Well, you'll be waiting a long while yet. That is, unless you'd rather me fetch her?"

Lenore brightened. "Would you?"

"For you, anything."

Nicolus strode forward and slipped through the crowd. His movements were adept, measured, more akin to a dance than the navigation of a loitering mass of overindulgent guildmasters. Within minutes, he was at Sophie's side, whispering in her ear.

Sophie kept her smile, forced it to remain intact, as she nodded and shook hands and slowly, agonizingly so, moved out of a crowd that persisted in coagulating around her, like pond scum to a waterlily. Nicolus took her place, fielding questions, applying his charm, and in doing so, Sophie was able to make it to Lenore without the bulk of the perpetual entourage. Still, some held on fast and watched the interaction between mother and daughter.

"Lenore," Sophie said, "when did you arrive?"

She really meant "how did you arrive," but Lenore only smiled and looked down at the tiled floor, hands clasped behind her back. Sweet and innocent. These onlookers would never have suspected the part she'd played in the crisis averted, the same they were congratulating themselves over.

"Can I have a word?" Lenore asked.

"Why, of course, child," the Weavers Guildmaster said. "A mother's duty comes before all else."

Sophie nodded at her peers as they broke away. She slipped her arm through Lenore's and guided her into the corridor.

"Somewhere more private," Lenore said.

Sophie steered them toward a vacant room with a vast assortment of chairs and small tables. Once inside, she released her hold on Lenore and closed the door behind them. Then they were alone, and their masks vanished. Sophie's smile faded, leaving only lines near the edges of her eyes and around her mouth. Lenore's bashfulness was replaced by pursed lips and a hard stare.

"Did you hear my address?" Sophie asked.

"I did."

"And did you take what I said to heart?"

"I already understood the gravity of what I'd done. You made that perfectly clear in the Old World."

Sophie moved to a set of chairs, upholstered in patterns of triangles, remnants of the Church, repurposed for the guild. She sat in one and waved to the other. Lenore breathed in deeply then took the seat. Sophie crossed her legs, clasped her hands, and rested them on a knee, leaning forward.

"Thank you for rescuing me from the other guildmasters," Sophie said.

The words were a shock. They were something her mother never would have said before. No crack in her façade. No hint of doubt or disdain. Why was she suddenly showing this side of herself? Had Lenore's stunt changed so much in their dynamic?

"You don't like their company?" Lenore asked. "Even with all their false love and adoration and flattery?"

"Heavens, no. Some of them are tolerable when there's actual work to be done, but occasions like this are nigh torture for me to wade through."

Lenore side-eyed Sophie. Her mother had a tell when she lied, a crinkle of her nose, but Lenore didn't spy it. "You're acting differently toward me. Honest for once. Why?"

"You requested I treat you like an adult. This is that. Have you had enough time to think over our offer, your Papa's and mine?"

"I have, and I agree to go with you on your journey but only on one condition."

"Let's hear it then."

"I want to go to the penitentiary and speak with Deston."

"I don't think that's advisable."

"It's not what you think. I don't pine for him, Mama. I

want to tell him what my role was. How *I* was the one to use *him*. How I was never on his side. How I told the wardens what he was up to so they could stop him before he did any damage."

Lenore was a contradiction, and she knew it. She hated the Order as much as ever. She wanted the system to change, and yet she knew things now that complicated the picture. About the Link, the alfom, the wider world. But more than anything else, she was a woman spurned, and she was not going to let that betrayal define her. She needed him to know she felt nothing for him because if she made that clear, if he believed it to be true, maybe she would too.

"But this is what everyone's already has been gossiping about," Sophie said. "Even in a cell, the rumors will make their way to him. You visiting isn't necessary. In fact, it only gives him a kind of power over you. You're still raw and wounded. You might say things you'll regret."

"I won't. I have more control over myself than that."

Sophie shook her head. "It's not something I'm willing to risk. Besides, it would look strange, you visiting him."

Lenore rose from her chair. "These are my conditions."

"And I refuse to agree to them, but that doesn't mean you suddenly get out of accompanying me on the journey. This is your punishment, Lenore. You don't get to choose terms. And before you have a tantrum, take some time to think, actually think, over what I've said. I suspect, with a cool head, you'll see the wisdom of my words."

Lenore glared, but Sophie only met her gaze with equal intensity. A wall stood between them, tall and broad and treacherous to any who aimed to scale it. It had always been there, looming, but even if it was the norm, Lenore knew it wasn't right. There ought to be a bond between mother and daughter. She saw it in others, and when she'd been young and hopeful, she'd craved it for her and Sophie too. Yet, no matter what she did, that wall persisted, taking on dangerous new implements over the years, as Sophie's callousness wounded Lenore bit by bit. Small, innocuous acts adding a moat here and some machicolations there. When taken in total, though, the fortifications were nigh insurmountable.

~~~

The bow's hairs lifted lightly off the violin's strings. Lenore beamed, stood, curtsied, blushed, a lass of just twelve summers, with this having been her first real performance. So many adults clapped with gusto. For her. Fenrir nodded and smiled, but when Lenore's eyes strayed to her mother, they met a familiar sight—Sophie preoccupied, already chattering with other high bloods. The applause gave way to conversation, and Lenore stowed her violin and bow in their case.

Fenrir came to her side, laying a hand on her shoulder. "It was beautiful."

"Thank you, Papa. I was so nervous, I worried my bow rattled the strings."

"It did a touch," Sophie said, slipping into the conversation.

Fenrir turned to her and frowned. Lenore's mouth just hung open. She couldn't find the words to respond, and even if she did, the crack in her voice would have betrayed her roiling emotions. And how Sophie despised public outbursts.

"Well, I didn't notice," Fenrir said. "As I said, it was beautiful."

"If you lie to her, she'll never improve," Sophie said to Fenrir.

He glared at Sophie while Lenore focused all her efforts on keeping the tears at bay.

"It wasn't a lie," Fenrir said.

"I'm tired," Lenore said. "I'll excuse myself now."

She didn't wait for a response and instead simply snatched her violin case and dove into the crowd still loitering in
~~~

the parlor. As she did, smiles met her, pats, congratulatory comments. The dark clouds lifted so that Lenore slowed her exit and lingered. Fenrir and Sophie's voices drifted to her through a cluster of adults who shielded Lenore from her parents' sight.

"It wasn't kind," Fenrir said. "And it was the first thing you said to her after the performance."

"She's not such a delicate flower that my handful of words would cut her so."

"Do you really not know the power you wield? All she wants is your approval, Sophie. Why can't you just give it to her?"

"My approval? What a silly thing to crave. No, I refuse to believe our child is so simple."

A jab that Lenore never forgot. Just another brick added to that infernal wall.

~~~

After her failed proposition concerning a visit to Deston, Lenore wandered the guildhall corridors then migrated to the grounds. Her boots crunched the loose stone paths as she looped around and around the massive domed structure. After her third such circuit, she stopped and glanced at the top of the guildhall, where a flag flapped in the wind. It was attached to a spire with a globe on its tip, now dark, although once, it had shone a bright blue, a sign that the Rot of the Link persisted. Somewhere, out there in the wider world, it still did. Or so Sophie claimed.

Stones crunched, but not from Lenore's motionless boots. She glanced to her left, and there was Nicolus, strolling toward her, the wind tossing his wavy black locks and the tails of his warden's frock, his tricorn in one hand.

"Still loitering about?" he asked.

Lenore sighed, and her shoulders slumped. "I don't know what else to do with myself."
~~~

Nicolus raised an eyebrow. "I take it your talk with the guildmaster didn't go well?"

"What gave me away?"

Nicolus pointed to her face. "You wear your heart on your sleeve, though you actually looked five times worse when you came out of that room."

"She's heartless. I asked for one little favor, but she refuses to give me even a mote of mercy."

"She's being cautious," Nicolus said.

Lenore's brow furrowed. "What do you mean?"

"There's always a chance some guard at the penitentiary talks, rumors spread, your visit to Deston gets around, people let their imaginations run wild, someone happens to land on the truth."

Lenore's stomach dropped. Nicolus knew then, but how? Sophie wouldn't have even hinted at Lenore's true role to him.

"Don't fret," he added. "Your secret is safe with me."

"How did you know?"

"Well, I know you, and I know you'd never play along with a scheme like that, not for the wardens. I also may have spotted you venturing into the lower city a handful of times and caught sight of you with one Deston Kerk."

Lenore sucked in a breath and narrowed her eyes. "You told them about me and him."

Nicolus held up his hands. "Never. I would never betray you like that. I didn't breathe a word."

No, he wouldn't have. How many secrets had she shared with Nicolus over the years? All secrets well kept. Besides, if she'd been lax enough for Nicolus to take note of her nighttime escapades, surely her parents had also stumbled on her outings. She'd thought she'd been clever, but she'd been a fool, many times over.

"Your request is a reasonable one," he said, "and there

are plenty of ways we could frame it to be consistent with the 'truth.'"

"How do you even know what I requested? Were you eavesdropping?"

Nicolus grinned and placed his tricorn on his head. "I'll take you. I'll make sure it's all kosher, and if your mother even hears of it, I'll take the brunt of her wrath."

"Why would you do that?" Lenore asked.

"Because I know what it's like to be a pawn in her games. You deserve this much agency, don't you think?"

Lenore offered a quivering smile and nodded. She'd always felt a kindredness to Nicolus despite the lack of blood ties. After all, he lived in her parents' shadow too, and he'd endured the shade far longer than she. To be a beautiful thing with a sharp mind but to be denied the light that would let him flourish. Her mother claimed Nicolus was vapid, but he wasn't that at all. He only pretended to be, to fit the mold Sophie and society had set for him.

"When can we go?" Lenore asked.

"Now, if you're free."

He offered an arm, and Lenore took it gladly. She was suddenly all smiles, her heart light as air. Her feet too barely seemed to touch the cobblestones as she and Nicolus ventured toward the lower city. They first passed stately homes with fresh paint and vibrant splashes of colors on their shutters or molding then moved by simpler abodes with plain wooden doors. As they neared the penitentiary, the solemn tower loomed, dwarfing any other structures in its vicinity.

Lenore stared at the black façade as they approached its gate. "Why did you all keep it?"

"As opposed to dismantling it? No matter what we built after the fall of the Church, we'd always have need of a place to lock away those who didn't play by the rules."

Lenore tilted her head back and took in the whole of the dark tower. The windows were thin strips, sunken into the stone walls. Which one of those held Deston?

"My parents were kept here after destroying the Rot of the Link, weren't they?"

"Yes. Shall we?"

Nicolus stepped forward, and Lenore followed. Their path was direct. This prison had been built according to the specifications for harmonious spaces, which meant hard edges, straight lines, crisp angles. There were no flourishes or excesses here, a color palette limited to black and gray and brown, materials restricted to stone, iron, wood. A frigid atmosphere. Lenore couldn't imagine spending more than mere minutes in such a place. How long had her parents been held here? They didn't talk much about that time. Few Simetrians did.

"What was it like just after the Rot of the Link was destroyed?" she asked, now walking abreast with Nicolus.

"That's a difficult question to answer. If I asked you, what was Simetria like two years past, how would you convey that?"

"Please don't dodge my question. My parents always do. It's always the same bland statements, like they're just reciting lines to a play. Why?"

"A trauma response, perhaps? They both went through a lot. I don't even know what hell their journey into the Old World was. They were a party of five, you know, but only your mother and father returned to the surface."

Lenore sighed and shook her head. The same vague details, no emotion, no weight. "And then they were in captivity. Mama was executed. Papa was released or escaped, another detail he's vague about."

They reached a set of stairs that wound up and up. Lenore followed behind Nicolus, letting him set the pace. She had a spring in her step, but it wasn't just the vigor of youth;

she was keen to reach their destination, eager to exact her revenge.

"But how was it for you?" Lenore asked. "You were a clergyfolk?"

"A priest."

"It must have been strange serving the Church after learning of their lies. You became some kind of maverick though, didn't you? Working against them from the inside and out."

"I did. Along with Vergil."

"Who was he to Mama? She always gets a hollowed-out look when his name's mentioned."

"She never told you?"

"Told me what?"

Nicolus broke into a grin and wagged a finger at Lenore. "I won't fall for your tricks, little vixen. I know you too well, or did you forget? It's not my place to say such things. Ask your mother. Now, let's get on with this so you can have your grand showdown with that bastard."

Lenore pulled back. Nicolus had a way with words and rarely stooped to base insults. But in that one slip-up, she saw this for what it was. Deston had hurt Lenore, and Nicolus despised the man for it.

The next landing led to the cell blocks, and Lenore and Nicolus quit their hike. A guard met them near the entrance to the wing and brought them to a hall. He unlocked the barred door then allowed them to continue on alone. As they passed the barred enclosures, Lenore glanced in. Most cells were empty. The ones that weren't held indistinct forms bathed in shadow, hunched over, leaning against the wet stone walls, lying on thin mats, coughing, groaning.

"It used to be much worse," Nicolus said, "when the Church put its prisoners here."

"I can't imagine either of my parents in one of these cells. How long were they locked away?"

"Your father, for five days. Your mother, for nine, officially." He dropped his voice to a whisper and leaned toward Lenore. "In reality, only four."

"What does that mean?"

Nicolus pulled away, stopped, and pointed to a cell several paces distant. "There's your destination. Talk to him through the bars, and don't get too close. I'll be waiting back with the guard."

Lenore barely registered that Nicolus's footfalls had become distant thuds. She was frozen. Terrified. But that realization filled her with rage. She shouldn't be the one immobilized by fear. That should be Deston. She clenched her teeth, straightened her back, and marched to his cell.

Deston had been stuck in this place for five days, and it showed. He wore rags in place of his low-blood attire. Bruising and dirt covered his face. The wardens and the guards here had left their mark on him. Some of those blows would be payback for what he'd done to Fenrir. The wardens loved Lenore's father.

Deston sat with his back to the wall, the barred door to his left. His forearms rested on his knees, and he stared at the wall opposite even after Lenore came into view. But then, his swollen lips flickered into their poor attempt at a smile.

"I was wondering when you'd come," he said. He grunted and rose. His movements were labored, and spasms shot across his face.

These were his just desserts, so why was pity gripping her heart? No. Absolutely not. She wouldn't give him a sliver of compassion, not after what he'd done.

"How did you know I wasn't in a cell too?" Lenore asked.

Deston lumbered over until he stood at the bars. Lenore took a step back so that his long arms would fail to reach her. He grabbed a rod of iron and used it to support himself. He leaned his head against the metal and smiled at her. That look, it sent a pang through her, a thousand thoughts, the hopes and dreams, the yearning, she choked it all off and glared at him.

"Word travels, even in this place," he said. "Besides, we both know how your folks operate. There was no way in hell they'd let their darling daughter be thrown in a cell. The high-blood special treatment in action."

Lenore clasped her hands behind her back to hide their trembling.

"But not for me," he said. "Nope, no such cushy treatment for poor Deston Kerk. Thrown back in a cell just when I'd almost managed to forget the stench of this place. Last round, it was four years. What do you think it'll be this time? Most probably no time at all. Easier to stamp me out altogether and be done with it, don't you think?"

"My parents won't have you executed," Lenore said. "It would make them look desperate. Take that how you will, but I didn't come here to offer comfort."

"What did you come for then, luv?"

"Answers. It was all a lie, was it? Your letters, your fine words, your promises."

"I never made a promise. I said lots of 'maybes' and hinted at possibilities, but I never swore you anything."

"So, a lie then?"

Deston sighed and tapped his forehead against the iron. "Maybe not every last little slice of it. My loins did happen to burn from us sharing spit."

Lenore scowled and took a step forward, hands clenched at her sides. Deston's eyes gleamed. She let the rage cool and came in close. She reached a hand out and touched his wrecked and ruined face. She stroked his cheek and ran her fingers through his short hair. Then, she grabbed his ear and pulled hard, slamming his face against the bars. He howled and swiped at her, but Lenore sprang back just in time.

"You high-blood whore," he shouted then groaned and fell to the floor.

"See, I can play a role too, Deston, and that's exactly what I did. It was all a lie to me. I'm on this side of the bars not because of my blood or name, but because I worked you and yours. Who do you think clued the wardens in on what you were up to? How do you think they knew exactly where and when to find you?"

Deston went quiet and still. He glared at Lenore then used the bars to pull himself up. "You're lying."

Lenore grinned and shook her head. "I believed in the cause but not in you or how you were going about things. Destroying the Link? No, enacting the change Simetria needs requires a more delicate touch. What you aimed to do was reckless."

"You hide in your little castle, pretending to have a stake in the lower city, but you're clueless. The Link is just as much a part of the problem as the guilds. It's the Church all over again. Secrets and lies and half-truths designed to keep us common folk in line. But what do we really know about the Link, Lenore? Why do the alfom need it so much?"

This wasn't how the conversation was meant to go. She didn't want to mull Deston's words. She was done being manipulated by him.

"Enough," she said. "There's no way to destroy the Link. I came here to tell you your cause is dead. Nothing you could say would sway me. In fact, nothing you said ever did." She turned on her heel and marched down the hall.

"Whatever you have to tell yourself, Lenore," Deston called after. "Whatever lies help you cope."

***

Lenore was lost. She didn't know what she felt anymore, what she stood for. She had hated the guild system, but she'd never dived deeply into the why. On the surface, yes, it was corrupt and hurt the low bloods, but she wasn't them. Did she only pretend to care about their injustices because it gave her an excuse to rebel? She was never good enough for her mother's standards, so why then bother to follow them at all? Was it all just an elaborate ploy to be something other than what was expected of her?

If Lenore had dwelled on such musings, they might have nettled her, but her time was quickly not her own. The day after her ill-fated visit to Deston, her training commenced. From sunrise to sunset, she drilled with the wardens. By day, there were techniques for fighting afflicted to master and simple but effective wards to refine. By night, a hoard of mathematical texts begged to be devoured. Two weeks passed in this way. Lenore picked up the polearm maneuvers with ease. Straight, clean swipes of the scythe she'd settled on as her weapon of choice. Solid and firm footwork.

"Fast and elegant," said Journeyman Zacharay Frye, her trainer.

She couldn't help but smile. It wasn't hard to find joy in her abilities, to bask in her martial prowess. Young and strong with boundless energy, or so it was until Sophie took to haunting the training sessions. She moved in slow strides along the edges of the indoor arena. It distracted Lenore to no end. After dropping her scythe for the third time, she nearly howled with rage.

"No need for that," Zacharay said, picking up her polearm and tossing it to her. "Anger is just wasted energy. Channel it into something useful."

Lenore tried to block out Sophie. She focused on Zacharay, took in every minute detail of his face—the crooked nose, the wide mouth, the narrow eyes. She widened her grip and leaned more heavily on her back leg. When Zacharay charged, she was ready. The butt of her scythe arched toward his foot, him distracted by the gleam of her unsharpened dummy blade all the while. The pole made contact with his boot. His grunt of pain meant Lenore had gotten the better of him this pass.

"That was good," he said. "Unexpected."

"For a human," Sophie said, striding into the combat area. "But you have to remember what it is we'll be up against, the both of you."

Zacharay nodded. He wasn't as young as Lenore. He most certainly had lived a life with distortions and affliction, but even so, he would have been a child then. By the time he'd taken up a polearm, the Rot of the Link had been long gone.

Sophie held out her hand, and Zacharay offered his halberd before moving several paces away. Lenore readied herself, her heart racing at the prospect of facing her mother. Sophie crouched in a strange pose, doubled over, back to Lenore, head turned peering over her shoulder. Lenore waited, but Sophie refused to make the first move. Impatient and overeager, Lenore stepped in to strike. A spray of dirt flew at her. She spat, dropped her scythe, and frantically wiped at her eyes. A polearm's butt smacked her in the gut, and the air fled from her lungs and refused to return. She gasped and gasped, and after what felt like an eternity, the wind came flooding back in. Through dirt and tears, she looked at her mother, standing over her.

"The afflicted have scores of surprises," Sophie said. "They don't play fair. Expect the unexpected. With them, it won't be dirt. It'll be death or a fate worse than it."

By the time Lenore recovered, Sophie was gone but so too was Lenore's drive. For the remaining days, she swiped her scythe, drew her wards, read her tomes, but it was all a hollow act now, laced with doubt. She made a point of spending that last night with the only person who could infuse her with hope, convince her she was prepared for what lay ahead.

She sat with Fenrir in a chair beside his bed. He was healing quickly and had even taken a short walk outdoors that day. Lenore read from one of the tomes Sophie had assigned her. Fenrir lay on his pillow with eyes closed, hands on his chest, fingers intertwined. He looked so peaceful. When she stopped, his eyes shot open. He hadn't been asleep after all.

"I won't be able to finish it before we set out," Lenore said.

"Take it with you," Fenrir suggested.

"We have to travel light. Besides, I don't know that I'll have much time for reading." She closed the text and drummed her fingers on its leather cover.

Fenrir frowned. "I should be the one going, not you, not your mother."

"Then try not falling off a cliff next time, Papa."

Fenrir grabbed a pillow and threw it at her. Lenore caught it and laughed.

"If you weren't so feeble, I'd hurl this right back at you."

"Is this a taste of what you'll treat me like in my old age?" Fenrir asked, shaking his head.

"Oh, don't you know? I'll be sending you away to some sad little hovel. I can't be bothered to attend to your every need. I'll be far too busy with my grand life." Lenore's grin cracked.

What kind of life awaited her? If she managed to make it back to Simetria, what did fate have in store for her? To follow in her parents' footsteps? To be a warden and protect the Link? She fidgeted, tucking the hair behind her ears. Her finger brushed against a metal disk, and she pulled the Third Eye free from its hiding place. She gazed down at it.

"Have you used it yet?" Fenrir asked.

Lenore angled her hand, and the metal disk reflected the room's candlelight in strange patterns, swirls and fractures and bursts, forever changing.

"No," Lenore said.

"Why not? You aren't curious to see what it can do?"

"I'm afraid of it, of the voices in it."

Fenrir pulled himself up on his pillows then patted the bed. Lenore closed her hand and migrated to his side, nuzzling her head against his arm. He brushed her hair from her forehead and planted a kiss there.

"You've no reason to fear Nytho," he said. "He helped your Mama and me and even you. He's been true to his word all along the way."

Lenore looked straight ahead at the windows on the far wall. The night was deep, moonless, starless. She ought to be sleeping. It would be a busy day tomorrow, but she couldn't stand to pull herself away from Fenrir's side.

"And the other alfom?" she asked.

"They don't speak with us. It's always Nytho."

"What of the Lady? Mama warned me about her."

"The Lady knows the wardens won't fall for her lies. She may reach out to you, but if you ignore her, she'll eventually go silent."

Lenore sat up and looked at Fenrir. "What are they? Gods? Beings from another realm?"

"I don't know."

"And the Link, what do they need it for?"

Fenrir shook his head.

"That doesn't bother you?" Lenore asked. "That you protect this thing at all costs without even knowing what it does?"

"It used to concern me more, but it's been here for a long time now and hasn't had any negative effect on Simetria."

Lenore watched Fenrir intently. "Have you asked them? Who they are, and why they need the Link?"

Fenrir sighed and smiled, and when he did that, Lenore marveled at him. Over five decades in age but still so handsome. She could imagine how a high-blood woman had fallen in love with him against all better judgement. Had that been part of why she'd fallen for Deston? A sad attempt at repeating her parents' epic romance?

"I've tried prying information from Nytho," Fenrir said, "but he always manages to steer the conversation away without you realizing he's done it. In any case, if he was willing to tell us more, he would have."

"And the fact that he isn't willing to tell you doesn't worry you? He's obviously hiding something."

"No doubt, but not all truths are worth learning. Some of them break you."

Lenore huffed and scrambled off the bed. She paced the room a few times then stopped and stood with her hands on her hips. "I'll never be a warden. I refuse to pledge myself to something I don't understand."

Fenrir was silent. His face gave nothing away. Lenore met his stare until her eyes ached then she threw up her arms, grabbed the tome from her chair, and headed to the door.

"Before you go," Fenrir said, "I have something for you."

Lenore turned and moved back to Fenrir. He pointed to the bedside table where an envelope sat, unmarked and yellowed with age.

"For you," he said.

Lenore took it then went to tear it open.

"Not now. Later, when you're doubting us the most, your Mama and me, and wondering why we did what we did."

Lenore nodded and placed the letter on top of the tome she carried. "She's going to drive me insane on this journey. You know that, don't you?"

"Try not to be so hard on her."

Lenore narrowed her eyes and pursed her lips. "Me hard on her? I rather think it's the other way around. Did you hear about her throwing dirt in my eyes?"

Fenrir sighed. "Yes, I did. You have to understand, she's

trying to prepare you for what lies ahead. She thinks pushing you to your limits is that."

"She doesn't understand me at all."

"She's doing the best she can."

"Yes, yes, I know, she didn't have a mother of her own and so on."

"She's dealt with a lot," Fenrir said, furrowing his brow. "Things neither of us ever told you. What happened with you and Deston Kerk, your mother suffered a similar betrayal, only hers was at least tenfold as painful. Be kind to her. Please? For me?"

Lenore smiled, leaned in, and kissed her father on his forehead. "That's all you had to say. I'd do anything for you, Papa."

ARTICLES OF THE ORDER

ACT OF THE ORDER OF THE NEW DAY OF THE CITY OF SIMETRIA

WHEREAS the Stewards of the city of Simetria have agreed to certain articles for the establishment of a new form of governance for the city of Simetria.

~~~

ARTICLE I. The title of this establishment shall be "The Order of the New Day."

ARTICLE II. The function of this establishment shall be to provide protection for the citizens of Simetria and oversight for the governing of the city.

ARTICLE III. The structure of this establishment shall be composed of any number of Guilds, representing the interests of their members.
~~~

ARTICLE IV. The said Guilds shall not deny membership to any citizen of Simetria without due cause.

ARTICLE V. The said Guilds shall act as checks and balances on one another, with final arbitration of any disputes provided by the Wardens Guild.

ARTICLE VI. No Guild or member of a Guild may interfere with the functioning of the Link or any support system associated with it. To do so is to threaten the Order and all it stands for.

~~~

IN WITNESS, WHEREOF we have hereunto set our hands in unity. DONE in Simetria the first day of the ninth month in the year of the current era five hundred and thirty.

The Stewards of Simetria

We bask in a light which casts no shadow
~~~

THE JOURNEY

Sophie tried to ignore the annoyance radiating from Lenore, tried not to notice her fidgeting with her forest green frock. Instead, Sophie reframed it. Lenore looked the part of a warden. She wore their uniform and stood in their ranks. She was indistinguishable from the four men and two women assembled in front of the guildhall, save for the lack of a chain intertwined in her black sash. That was the true sign of a warden, one who had taken the Oath, and Lenore had refused to do so.

"I'm only agreeing to go on this journey with you, not become a warden," she'd said.

Sophie had hoped that two weeks of associating with wardens from dawn to dusk would change Lenore's perspective. But despite excelling at her training, Lenore remained obstinate. Even Fenrir hadn't been able to convince her.

Sophie angled her tricorn, flipped the collar of her coat, and marched to the collection of wardens. They stood in clusters, two here, three there, one tending to the horses. Sophie had selected only the best and most loyal, but even so, she didn't know how they would fare when faced with the horrors of affliction. The two journeymen wardens, Zacharay Frye and Gewyn Reys, had seen three decades, but the others hadn't lived much more than two, having been young children or unborn before Sophie had destroyed the Rot of the Link.

On seeing their guildmaster approach, the wardens went silent and straightened then arranged themselves in a line. The journeymen understood the inherent dangers of their mission, both in the ways of the non-Euclidean and the ways of humankind. The people of this new land were an additional threat and not to be taken lightly. The other four wardens all sported the rank of apprentice, but despite their lower placement in the guild's hierarchy, they were skilled. Sophie had handpicked them—Harry Heathford, Terrance Grosefield, Eugene Weathers, and Jasmine Potts.

Sophie glanced at Lenore, standing off to the side, leaning against the courtyard wall, hands in her pockets, tricorn almost eclipsing her eyes. So dour and aloof despite the initial promise she'd shown, excelling in her martial training. Whatever had spurred Lenore on, pushed her to strive so hard, had, at some point, petered out. A flame snuffed by a gust of wind. This extended to Lenore's relations with the other wardens. Sophie had expected her daughter to find comradery amongst the ones joining them on their mission, but as if to spite Sophie, Lenore withdrew the closer they came to their departure date. Lenore kept to herself, never initiated conversation, and answered any question posed by the others curtly. She didn't want to belong. That much was blindingly clear. Still, Sophie couldn't help but hope the journey itself might do wonders in thawing Lenore. After all, bonds take strongest and fastest through danger and hardship.

The wardens gave Sophie their guild gesture almost in unison.

"Are we all set then?" she asked.

The wardens nodded and murmured. Their nervous

excitement seeped out and infected Sophie. What they were about to do was novel, to say the least. In the days of the Church, leaving Simetria's immediate environs had been a rarity reserved for traders or high bloods with villas in the hills. With the paradigm shift brought about by the Order, venturing beyond the city was commonplace. After all, there were no distortions or afflicted to worry about anymore. But journeying as far as they would and attempting to cross the waters to the far shore? They would be the first.

"We have a long way to travel today," Sophie said. "Let's be off. Journeyman Frye has the route so he takes the lead. Any questions?"

The wardens shook their heads, smiled, chattered.

"Mount up."

Sophie secured her saddlebags, took the reins of her horse, and hopped on. She shifted into a comfortable position and waited for the others. Some were less than elegant in their attempts at mounting. Few of them had made use of these creatures previously. The past two weeks had seen them ride every day, but an hour here and there was nothing compared to what their travel entailed. It would take over five days to reach the coastal village where their boat was waiting.

They'd sent word ahead via carrier pigeon, and the good folk of the fishing village had offered a suitable vessel as well as a few capable sailors to get them to their destination. But after that? When they landed on that far shore, Sophie would be operating in the dark. Nytho could only see so far into the murkiness bred by the Rot of the Link gnawing at the node there. He had told Sophie where to go, but beyond that, he couldn't offer much.

The Linkrot there clouds the view like it did with Simetria before you restored the Link node. That means I don't know much about that society except what it was like during the Old World. The language will be different, but you can use your Third Eye to analyze it, translate it, and even speak it back to them. However, the process won't be instantaneous. The program requires data to function, which means you'll need to interact with the locals before it can work.

The wardens were mounted and ready. Sophie pulled on her reins and guided her horse out of the courtyard of the Wardens Guildhall. A cluster of their peers waited in the street just beyond, familiar faces from the highest of their ranks. Nicolus and Laurenz were foremost, hands clasped, smiling serenely, exuding the calm and authority Sophie had instructed them to project. The particulars of their mission were being kept secret. The less the people knew, the better. Let them be safe and happy in their predictable lives. Don't let them know that those horrors she'd effaced from their city were out there, lurking. Still, her leaving would breed rumors and uncertainty, and in these increasingly volatile times, the people had to feel secure. This started with the wardens. They set the tone for the city. Everyone looked to them for guidance.

"Masters Yevin and Frenwith," Sophie said with a nod and a tap to her tricorn, slowing her horse.

The two master wardens stepped forward.

"I expect you to assist Guildmaster Fenrir Roshem in my absence," she said. "Anything he asks, take it as though it came directly from my lips."

"Of course, Guildmaster," Nicolus said, giving the warden's gesture. "Truth, protection, connection."

"Truth, protection, connection," Sophie replied before urging her horse onward.

They navigated the mostly empty streets of the upper city before advancing into the more bustling thoroughfares of the lower one. Markets were filling their stalls with the day's goods. Blacksmiths and masons and woodworkers carried their tools, heading to their work. Everyone they passed stopped and stared.

She smiled and nodded at the low bloods, and most returned the good graces. But not all. Some simply frowned and glared. Not many, but enough. Trouble was brewing still, despite her address and the fact that Deston was locked up. Fenrir would have his work cut out for him.

As they ventured deeper into the lower city, the decay increasingly reared its head. Buildings were falling into ruin— roofs patched haphazardly, cloth covering the broken panes of windows, whole walls slumped and sagging. The people too reflected their environs. Bare feet, tattered skirts and trouser hems, dirt-encrusted faces, gaunt cheeks. Had it really gotten so bad? And when exactly?

Sophie glanced back to the rear of her company. Lenore bobbed in her saddle, looking down at the faces. Maybe the corruption of the guilds was worse than she'd realized. Sophie moved her Third Eye from behind her ear to her forehead. She thought of Fenrir, imagined her mind reaching for his, then there he was.

You call, I answer, he said.

Aren't you the model of reliability? But don't let me get distracted singing your praises. I'm in the lower city coming up on the southern gate, and the state of the place is atrocious. The streets, the homes, and the people, it's almost as bad as when the Church controlled things.

She imagined sharing her sight with Fenrir. Then his eyes and hers were one. He gazed on the same scenes she did.

That really is bad, he said, *and it explains the people's support for the Disaffected. We shouldn't have gone so long without visiting.*

We shouldn't have trusted the word of the guildmasters. Deal with this while I'm away, will you?

Leave it to me and be safe.

Sophie let her love of Fenrir fill her heart. He did the same. Their dedication and passion grew and grew until it threatened to erupt. Then Sophie sighed and cut the connection. It would be torture being away from that man, but at least they had their Third Eyes. With those, they would never be truly sundered.

After the wardens exited Simetria's gates, they urged their horses into a trot. Zacharay took the lead, and the others could let their minds wander or their tongues wag as they pleased. Even the weather was on their side. Large fluffy white clouds peppered the blue expanse. The wind rustled the manes and tails of their mounts. The long grasses in the fields swayed. Sophie sometimes forgot how beautiful their slice of the world could be. She needed to get out more, away from the guildhall. When she returned, things would be different. For her. For Simetria.

The good weather held for another day, then on the third, it reverted to the usual thick cloud cover and perpetual drizzle. The temperature dropped and, with it, morale. Still, they slogged on. Their hands grew accustomed to gripping the leather of their reins, the skin of their thighs thickened in opposition to the perpetual rubbing of the saddle, their chattering died down. It was too much effort to talk all day. Better to save what few words they had to share until nightfall, sitting around their campfire.

Sophie tried to treat the wardens equally and avoid showing any favoritism, but she overcompensated, avoiding Lenore entirely. Her daughter did likewise and opted to keep to herself, even as the others reveled in their card games by the fire. Sophie knew her daughter's nature too well. Even hinting at the possibility of Lenore joining them would only result in her daughter resisting and receding further. Instead, Sophie let her be.

On their fourth day, the strange, cragged nature of the horizon resolved into the ruins of a vast city. Sophie knew of its presence. The Church archives held maps she'd studied long ago. In a world where travel was once again a possibility, she'd made the effort to send scouts. People had even resettled much further afield, the village that was their destination being a fine example. But this city, they'd avoided. Too filled with bad omens, with relics, a kind of tainted aura. Her people had told her of the crater here, but she'd never laid eyes on it herself.

The fastest route was forward, skirting the crater, and time was of the essence. Besides, the city itself didn't pose a threat. It was haunted, to be sure, but she had little fear of ghosts, not with more tangible threats still lurking out in the world—distortions, afflicted, the Rot of the Link.

Zacharay had his map out and was inspecting it, biting his lower lip as he tended to do when in thought. His eyes were narrow slits, almost like he wore a perpetual glare from combating a too-bright light or eyeing an enemy.

"Lead us onward, Journeyman Frye," Sophie said.

He glanced up and set his auburn eyes on her, now quizzical and alert.

"The route we discussed," she added.

Zacharay nodded, the movement swaying the low ponytail he kept his jet-black hair in. He folded the map and stowed it then donned his gloves. Each hand slipped into a brown leather nearly the same shade as his own skin. He was dark in the way that Nicolus was, but poor Zacharay didn't have the same advantages as his colleague. He was far from beautiful with a brow that protruded, lips that were too big for his face, and a nose that mimicked a sinuous river.

"Is it Rotatia?" Lenore asked, nodding at the crumbled ruins in the distance.

"No, Rotatia is far north of Simetria," Zacharay said. "We move southeast."

"This is a ruin from the Old World," Sophie replied.

But what is it besides that? Sophie asked Nytho. He was there. She could sense when he was present somehow, like a slight pressure on the skull or a breath on the neck bristling the delicate hairs there.

London, Nytho said, *one of the greatest of the Old World's cities.*

They advanced at a steady pace, but as the detritus of this ruined city became more frequent, their progress slowed. They didn't rush their horses; the last thing they needed was for one of them to slip and sprain an ankle. As they crawled along, they looked at the wreckage of the past. The sights that greeted them weren't wholly foreign to Sophie, but to the others, those who hadn't plunged into the depths of the Old World or rummaged through the stores of the Vault, what they laid eyes on must have appeared bizarre and incomprehensible. Rotting synthetics. Wires hanging and strewn from crumbling building to building. The windows hollowed out like empty eye sockets in a skull.

"This was a city?" Jasmine asked, her mouth hanging open, dark eyes fixed on her surroundings.

"It's so different from Simetria," Eugene said, the next youngest of their cohort after Lenore and Jasmine.

Children born after the cleansing of the Link node, oblivious to the horrors that had been existence in the time of the Rot of the Link. She'd saved them from a dark and grim future, freed them from the grip of the distortions, and yet, in some ways, she so longed to shatter their naïve illusions, to expose them to that which she'd liberated them from in the first place.

"Don't stray too close," she said to Eugene.

His horse's hooves crunched piles of blasted stone near the edge of their path.

"We know too little of the Old World," Sophie added. "That lack of knowledge is danger."

"Then maybe we ought to learn instead of languish in ignorance," Lenore said.

Sophie held her head high and trained her eyes forward. "We are, but the process takes time. Rushing to regain the past would be the height of folly. Slow and steady, that's the safest and truest path forward."

Her advice applied to their progress through the ruins as well. They moved deeper into them, struggling to find a route through until the rubble was wholly gone, replaced by grasslands. Flora had made its relentless inroads, as it was wont to do. The unending, plodding, persistent march of life, intent on spreading itself far and wide, blanketing the world.

As they neared a cliff's edge, the crater's grandeur showed itself. It was vast, impossibly so. In breadth. In depth. Sophie inhaled sharply, gazing at the gouge that dove leagues down. A puncture into the earth with trees and bushes sprouting in abundance. All the travelers' eyes were fixed on the topological irregularity. In awe. In wonder. In fear. What could have done this? What horrid synthetics had the Bygones leveled at themselves, and why?

What happened to this place? Sophie asked Nytho.

I don't know the specifics. We were shut out from your world by the Linkrot virus when this occurred.

What could have happened then?

The Bygones had plenty of weapons capable of doing this. As for why, this is how it goes. Their world was overly complex, and highly specialized systems go first. The fall would have been long and hard. Maybe the Bygones warring amongst themselves for limited resources? Or a preemptive strike by Marcos and his cohort? It doesn't matter what exactly caused the damage. The point is, something like this was bound to happen.

Let's just hope it doesn't happen again, Sophie said. *Yet another reason to be conservative in bringing the synthetics back.*

They followed the crater rim and so, eventually, came out the other side of the forgotten city and continued on into the green hills. The wind shifted, no longer at their backs but instead rushing at them headlong. They were nearing their destination.

On the fifth day, the coast showed itself, sheer cliffs of a startling white dropping from the fields above to the smallest strip of sand over one-hundred meters below. A scent of salt floated in the air. Sophie had never seen the ocean, and she got lost in its vastness, its rhythmic motion, its soft hiss, droning but peaceful. The wardens stared into the horizon, mouths hanging open. Even Lenore seemed mesmerized.

"The village ought to be nearby," Sophie said, looking at Zacharay.

He pulled himself out of his reverie and fiddled with the map. "We follow the coast south."

The fishing village was purported to be composed of only a dozen or so huts. A little cluster of civilization such as this would have been impossible in the days of the Church. As the bishops had warned, distortions infected the world and, without surveyors to contain them, ran wild. But how true had those stories been? If the Rot of the Link created the distortions, wouldn't they, in fact, be less abundant with distance from their source? More likely than not, these untamed lands of supposed danger had been the safest place to be.

Even with real or supposed danger long gone now, little villages such as this were still rarities, life in them being isolated and difficult, but there was something inherent to humanity that forced a subset of people to train their eyes outward. The possibilities of what lay beyond the horizon goading them to tempt fate.

Once arrived at their destination, the wardens' morale improved thanks in no small part to the feast the villagers presented them. Hot food, good drink, song, and dance. This place technically had no affiliation with either of the former Church-controlled cities of Simetria or Scalium, being an independent entity, but practically speaking, it relied on Simetria, in particular, for goods it couldn't otherwise craft. Relations were healthy, and as such, Sophie hadn't felt odd requesting assistance from the villagers for the journey across the water. She was pleased that the goodwill between their people was real, that the villagers were eager to meet with their cousins from the north, to share victuals, stories, laughter. Sophie let the wardens enjoy themselves. It would be their last chance. Tomorrow morning, they would cross the ocean, and when their feet touched that foreign soil, a perpetual guard would be required.

But that last night was all laughter and revelry. The fire and merriment even thawed Lenore. She sat with the villagers and sang their songs. One young man even convinced her to dance. Sophie watched and shared the sight with Fenrir, so near yet far. She spent an hour or so of her night synced with him. Their two minds became one, thoughts, desires, hopes, dreams. When Sophie woke the next morning to a thick fog, she was ready to face the unknown.

"The shore's hidden behind this soup," the boat captain said. He pointed a gnarled finger across the restless waters.

"Should we wait for it to lift?" Sophie asked.

"Aye. I know this side of the waters, but landing over yonder in this would be folly. The fog will lift with the heat of day. I'm sure your wardens wouldn't mind the extra sleep besides. We all had a bit too much fun, didn't we?"

Sophie would let her wardens dream, let them be as babes once more, blinded to the trials lying in wait.

"How long for the crossing?" she asked.

"It depends on the currents but likely a bit over a handful of hours."

While she waited, Sophie brushed her horse and said her goodbyes. They had become friends on their journey, but the far shore was no place for such a creature. The wardens would travel by foot in that foreign land.

Sophie's wardens woke, munched on bread, slurped tea. Lenore sat with them, yawning and rubbing her eyes. This life suited her. She looked more at home in the attire of a traveler than that of a high blood. She'd always spurned the fine silk and lace and lamented over the discomfort of her dresses. Any opportunity she got, Lenore donned trousers and a tunic and wore her hair loose and low, pulled back by a simple black band.

"The fog is lifted," the captain said.

"Time to cast off then." Sophie rose from the log she sat on and dusted off her trousers.

The wardens hurried to finish their breakfast then gathered their things. The boat was ready. All it needed was its passengers. They embarked. Seven wardens, one high blood who looked the part but hadn't taken the Oath, and three of the villagers. The latter were busy untying knots and stowing and pulling ropes. Once all the travelers were on board, the captain gave a sharp whistle. A sail unfurled, and they were pulled away from the only land they'd ever known toward one filled with mystery.

The wardens leaned against the bulwark and gazed ahead. As the minutes turned to hours, they rested on the deck, tending to their polearms, staring up at the clouded sky. Only Lenore stayed fixed, scanning the horizon for the far shore still invisible through a haze. Sophie migrated to her daughter's side and rested her arms against the boat's worn and weathered wood.

"She deigns to speak to me at long last," Lenore said.

"I assumed you wanted your space. Either that or you were still angry with me for dragging you along."

Lenore shifted and leaned away from the boat's edge. She looked down at the deck and kicked the wooden railing. "I am angry, but not about that." Lenore continued to ram her boot into the wood and avoid eye contact.

"And what are you angry about then?" Sophie asked.

Lenore dug in the pocket of her coat and retrieved an envelope, yellowed and wrinkled. She offered it to Sophie.

"A letter from Papa, or rather, Papa of the past. He says many interesting things in it, but the part I honed in on was him talking about my future."

Sophie took the envelope and removed the letter. Fenrir had never told her about writing it. She skimmed its contents.

"He says the choice to become a warden is mine," Lenore said, "but it's not, is it? It's like me choosing not to come on this journey, an option but not one I could take."

Sophie folded the letter and tucked it into its covering then offered them to Lenore. "You do have the choice, but you're right, it's only a choice in name. We need you to become a warden. We pledged ourselves to the alfom, us and all our descendants."

Lenore scowled and snatched the letter. "And when were you planning on telling me how you sold my soul to the alfom?"

"Don't be so dramatic."

"Fine then, sold my future to them."

Sophie removed her tricorn and sat down on the deck, her back to the bulwark. She tussled the hair not held by her long braid, and the orange-red curls sprang back to life. Lenore knelt beside her.

"You wouldn't have a future at all if it wasn't for them," Sophie said. "They saved you and me and your Papa. In exchange, we swore to protect the Link for them."

"Saved us from what?"

"Whom. The short answer is Vergil Holdsworth. The long one will have to wait for a more appropriate time and location. In any case, your Papa was wise to share that letter with you when he did. It's high time you learn who you are and what you need to become."

Lenore turned the envelope in her hands, corner to corner to corner to corner, round in circles. "Papa said he had a wife and child before you and me, but he never talks about his past. Who was he?"

"Have you ever heard of Ashtin Broodfell?" Sophie asked.

Lenore shook her head.

"I suppose you wouldn't have. He was a high-blood surveyor of exceptional skill, tier 1, the best of the best. He even helmed a Holy purge."

Sophie paused and looked to gauge how close the other wardens were. The slap of the waves against the hull and the shouts of the sailors hid her voice. Nevertheless, she dropped it further, forcing Lenore to crane her neck to hear.

"Ashtin's son became afflicted, but instead of reporting it to the Church, he tried to save the poor boy. If anyone could have, it would've been Ashtin. But no one could cure affliction, and in his desperation, Ashtin used forbidden relics. He was found out, imprisoned for crimes against the Church, and supposedly executed, only he wasn't. Five years he spent in the penitentiary, then he was released." Sophie's voice turned to a whisper, and she beckoned Lenore closer. "The man who left those gates was Fenrir Mey, a low blood who became a blessed toller. I made his acquaintance when he reported a distortion in his bell tower. Things moved on from there."

"Papa is a high blood?" Lenore asked.

Sophie held her finger to her lips. "Ashtin Broodfell is dead. Even with the Church gone, it's best it stays that way."

"Why?"

"It keeps the story simple. Besides, your Papa is Fenrir. Ashtin really did die in that penitentiary."

Lenore went silent and stared into nothingness. Sophie let her digest the revelations.

"And you?" Lenore said. "You have secrets too, no doubt. Who were you really?"

Sophie smiled, stood, and offered a hand to Lenore. Her daughter took it, and she pulled her to a stand.

"Someone's been chattering in your ear about me, haven't they? A Nicolus Yevin, perhaps?"

"You think you're quite the clever one, but sometimes you can be utterly blind. Nicolus wouldn't tell me anything about you."

"I'm honestly shocked to hear that. It's out of character for him. He so savors gossip, especially the kind that involves my name."

Lenore crossed her arms and glared at Sophie. She shook her head and scoffed, boot tapping. "He's a master of your guild, a fellow architect of your precious Order, a friend to Papa, and like a second father to me. Despite everything he does for us and Simetria, all you can do is turn your nose up at him."

"I'm only ever civil toward Master Yevin."

"Civil but not kind."

"There's a reason for my feelings toward Nicolus. Believe you me."

"I'm sure, but vague statements like that are hardly going to convince me your disdain is warranted." Lenore stuck her hands in her pockets and walked to the opposite side of the boat.

Sophie sighed. All the innumerable things there were to tell her daughter. All the unpleasant truths. She'd put it off for so long, telling herself it wasn't time yet, but she couldn't use that tired excuse anymore. Lenore deserved to know. If Sophie was ever going to convince her to take up the mantle of a warden, she would need to dig deep into the past and dreg up those horrid memories, rotting and stinking.

But it wasn't just an avoidance of reliving those dark times. Sophie knew the reason she hesitated. She was terrified of how Lenore would look back at her once she knew the truth. That Sophie was no saint or martyr. That she'd been duped and used by Vergil, emotionally, physically. That she'd done what needed to be done to save the three of them—herself, Fenrir, and Lenore—which had necessitated killing that man in cold blood. Would Lenore pity her? Or despise her? Which would be worse?

And then, there was the darkest secret, kept buried so deep even Sophie forgot its existence. The question of parentage. Whose seed had given her Lenore? It was a momentary weakness in even straying to such a toxic, unanswerable question. Sophie pushed it down, crushing it with vehemence. There was no time for such musings. Too much uncertainty lay ahead. She needed all her mental faculties devoted to her task. Cleansing the Link node was all that mattered.

WARDEN'S OATH

Truth, protection, connection.
These are a warden's ideals.

Truth—to arbitrate the guilds.
Protection—to safeguard the Order of the New Day.
Connection—to maintain the Link.

The wardens are a guiding hand.
I am a finger of that hand.
The wardens are a soft heart.
I am a vein of that heart.
The wardens are the Order's foundation.
I am a brick of that foundation.

I pledge this oath to be a warden for all of my days.
Truth, protection, connection.
These are my ideals.

ANOTHER GUILDMASTER ROSHEM

It was hell watching Sophie walk away and letting Lenore go with her. And there Fenrir was stuck like a fool in Simetria all because he'd let his guard down and been bested by a nobody. But Deston was hardly a nobody anymore. His name was everywhere. Whispered by confederate lips, spat out by antagonistic ones. It had even been found scrawled in chalk on a high-blood home. The storm was looming, and it was Fenrir's job to contain it.

"Master Roshem."

Fenrir turned and threw a weak smile at Willum. The man was well past his prime but persisted in sporting the latest fads in hairstyle, clothing, and ornamentation. Almost every day brought something new—today, a wig dyed a deep purple with the hair cropped short. It matched the trim on his frock and the paint on his nails.

"What is it?" Fenrir asked.

"Master Yevin is in the drawing room, sir. He asks to speak with you at your earliest convenience."

Fenrir's smile faded, and furrows formed on his brow, seeming to originate from the Third Eye still fixed to his forehead. He moved it to that safe spot behind his ear. Out of sight but still accessible for when Sophie called next.

"I'll be there soon," Fenrir said.

Nicolus wasn't even going to give him one day of peace. Then again, they didn't have the luxury of time. That storm wasn't going to wait for the ache of Sophie's and Lenore's absence to abate. Besides, at least dealing with the threat of the Disaffected gave him something to set his mind on, something besides his worry over and envy for the journey his wife and daugther were undertaking.

Willum straightened and folded his hands behind his back. Fenrir frowned. The formalities still irked him even after all these years of living like a high blood again.

"I'll be there soon," Fenrir repeated.

"Sir, perhaps you require assistance getting dressed?"

Fenrir glanced down at his silk robe and loose pants. He could walk on his own now, but Willum was right. Dressing was an exercise filled with pain and one he couldn't hope to complete alone. His face burned, but he didn't let his shame manifest in an outburst. This wasn't Willum's fault; it was his.

"Yes," Fenrir said, "I do, in fact."

Willum nodded then flew into action. He pulled clothes from Fenrir's wardrobe and laid them on the bed. Standard high-blood garb—a frock and trousers with too many buttons and unnecessary stitching. It wouldn't do, not for what Fenrir had in mind. He walked to the wardrobe, and Willum arrested his rummaging.

"Sir?" he asked.

"Not this," Fenrir said, tossing his hand at the clothing on the bed.

He dove into the hoard of garb. So many items he'd never worn or even seen. That would be Sophie's doing. When they'd married, she'd insisted he act the part of a high blood. She was convinced few would accept him as her life partner if he didn't do the song and dance. But Fenrir's aversion to this clothing wasn't just because it wasn't to his personal taste. It was also a practical consideration.

Fenrir's time in the penitentiary had changed his person, making him leaner, more angular. Still, behind all the alterations borne of time and pain, Ashtin Broodfell lurked. He worried that if he looked too much like his former self, someone might see the resemblance and put two and two together. If one could see the link, so could others, then it would only be a matter of time until word got around. Soon enough, the whole of Simetria would know Fenrir Mey hadn't always borne that name. Him being Ashtin would complicate matters, and matters had always been sufficiently complicated.

Fenrir retrieved a black tunic and leather pants. "This." He held them out to Willum.

"Sir?"

"Along with sturdy but simple boots and a well-worn coat and hat. I'm venturing into the lower city today."

Willum stumbled over his words. Then the man got ahold of himself, smoothed his frock, and cleared his throat. "Are you sure you're up for that kind of excitement, sir?"

Fenrir smiled, untied his robe, and tossed it onto the bed. His torso was a bandaged bulk still, but his wounds had closed, at least the external ones. In truth, he was still seething, and sitting idle in his home wouldn't do him or Simetria any favors. The time for convalescence was over. Action. That's what was required in the face of the maelstrom heading their way.

"Help me put these things on," Fenrir said.

Willum sighed and shook his head but didn't object. Within five minutes, Fenrir was entering the drawing room. Nicolus stood by a window, hands clasped behind his back, gazing out on the estate's grounds. He turned on hearing Fenrir.

"Master Roshem," Nicolus said, executing that overstated bow he always did.

Fenrir gave a brief inclination of the head mostly owing to his limited movement. In truth, Fenrir rather liked Nicolus. The man had been one of the first to truly accept Fenrir into their cohort in the early days of the Order's founding. He was loyal to their cause. And, most significantly, Nicolus got on well with Lenore. Fenrir doted on his daughter and couldn't help but warm toward another who did the same.

"You're doing better, I hope?" Nicolus asked.

"Almost back to normal. Just in time to stand in for the guildmaster."

Nicolus eyed a set of high-backed upholstered chairs tucked into a nook. The room was darker than usual with all its curtains drawn. Between Fenrir being confined to his bed from injuries and Sophie being preoccupied with the fallout from the Disaffected's actions, they hadn't frequented this place in recent days.

Fenrir gestured at the chairs then made his way to a curtain and tried to pull it aside. The movement elicited pain. Abrupt. Sharp. Loud. He held the groan in. He debated attempting the maneuver again but couldn't risk failing twice in a row. Even if Nicolus was on their side, a warden through and through, he was still covetous. Fenrir couldn't afford to show weakness, not without Sophie around and everything falling into chaos.

Fenrir released the curtain and migrated to the chair beside Nicolus's. He lowered himself into it, slowly but without a grimace. Nicolus intertwined his fingers and rested his hands on his knee, one leg crossed over the other.

"If you don't mind, let's skip the pleasantries," Fenrir said. "There's a lot I need to do today."

"Of course, Guildmaster Roshem."

Switching the honorifics over so smoothly and effortlessly,

but then these kinds of things were Nicolus's forte. Attention to detail. Flattery. Winning others to his side.

"I'm assuming your visit has a purpose?" Fenrir asked.

"I thought we might discuss how you plan to deal with the unrest caused by the Disaffected. Namely, who we want to turn the people's anger on?"

Fenrir blinked. Had he missed something? Was his memory failing him? Then, his and Sophie's conversation with Nytho came to mind.

"Sophie suggested this?" Fenrir asked.

"She said it was one avenue to explore."

It was a possibility but not one Fenrir wanted to entertain, and it didn't sound like Sophie. Then again, these were troubling times. Perhaps she was overwhelmed by all the tasks set out before them. This was what Fenrir was here for, exactly this. Sophie called him her guiding voice. She counted on him to challenge her; even she had admitted her growing influence had come in tandem with other less desirable qualities. Power had that kind of effect. A tendency to erode empathy and make one cold and callous. Sophie wasn't those things, yet. Her reaching out to Fenrir as she'd passed through the lower city and sharing those horrid sights was proof she did still care.

"We won't be pursuing that," Fenrir said. "I don't approve, and I don't think the guildmaster really does either. It's a short-term solution, diverting anger and hate. The trick is to regain the people's love and respect."

Nicolus burst into laughter, but when Fenrir stayed stony-faced, Nicolus turned grim.

"Idealism and innocence have no place in a leader's head," Nicolus said. "Guildmaster Sophie Roshem knows this."

"She also happened to leave me in charge, did she not?" Fenrir asked.

Nicolus inclined his head.

"Then we do things my way."

"But of course, Guildmaster Roshem." Nicolus rose from his chair and gave off another of those exaggerated bows. "May you bask in a light which casts no shadow."

Nicolus made his exit. He was loyal, but that didn't mean Fenrir trusted him unerringly. After all, he had once been the staunchest ally of their greatest enemy. Nicolus had been at Vergil's beck and call. Perhaps a part of it was practical; Nicolus seeing Vergil's star rising had hoped to throw his hat in and advance by proxy. Nicolus was always so pragmatic, but Fenrir couldn't forget what he'd heard all those years ago. How Nicolus and Vergil had spent an inordinate amount of time together for a bishop and a priest and how Nicolus had reacted to the news of Vergil's death. Inconsolable. Lost. Adrift. Had Vergil been a kind of idol to him?

In truth, these misgivings were faint and minor, vague whispers in the back of Fenrir's mind, mostly given weight by Sophie's dislike for the man. But in the present moment, Fenrir didn't have time to fret about such things. He had work to do. He needed to look into the state of the lower city himself. He headed there directly by foot in his low-blood disguise. He flipped his collar and angled his cap and hoped it would be enough. Few knew him. Sophie was the figurehead of the Order; he worked in the background.

Within the quarter hour, Fenrir walked the cobblestoned streets of the lower city. Even if the change in the thoroughfares' slopes hadn't clued him in, the increase in refuse would have. It was different here, just like Sophie had said. He'd walked these same streets, bought food at these same stalls, frequented that well, and yet it had been so long ago since his feet had tread here. It was the Old World all over again, an unconscious avoidance of a place that only served to remind him of a past he didn't have any fondness for. His time as a low blood had been fraught. What good did revisiting such memories serve?

Even so, he saw the other side of his evasion now. The place was changed. Part of it was time and another circumstance, but that wasn't the whole story. No, the lower city had decayed while he'd been away, living his plush high-blood life. To convince himself his eyes weren't misleading him, that he wasn't just too accustomed to fine sights, Fenrir made a point of visiting a place he knew well—his old shack near the Most-Holy Southeast Bell Tower. The latter was in ruins. The former wasn't much better off.

Fenrir peered into the sole window of his onetime abode, but a thick layer of grime protected the interior from his prying eyes. Still, the exterior told him all he needed to know. A roof half caved in. Mortar crumbling between sagging stones. A door liberated from one of its hinges. And it wasn't just his former home. The whole of the neighborhood was in an advanced state of deterioration. When had it gotten so bad? He navigated deeper into this part of the city, but it was the same sad story. Rot. Rot everywhere, even when it was no longer framed to be blessed.

Fenrir wandered into a bustling market and perused the options, but even there the state of things was abysmal. Malformed vegetables and fruits. Baskets half-emptied even before midday. The coup de grace? A long line snaking through the tight streets with the queuers waiting for access to a well.

Fenrir gaped for many minutes. But then, a familiar mane of black curls entered his line of sight, and his stomach leapt. Twenty years had passed since he'd last spied her in these streets, but Amilia was still Amilia. At her side stood a grown woman with features reminiscent of that toddler Fenrir had seen playing in the dirt so long ago, Amilia's daughter by another man. The woman locked eyes with Fenrir then the mother too looked his way. There was a moment, a fraction of a second, where Amilia inspected him more closely, but

Fenrir dove into the nearest pub before the recognition could truly dawn on her.

If anyone could spy the Ashtin in him, it would be Amilia, his former wife. But Ashtin Broodfell was dead, and he had to stay that way. The last thing the Order needed was a scandal, and that's what the discovery would be. A secret. A truth hidden. A lie. The Church all over again, but the Order was not the Church and couldn't afford to be perceived that way. Not with all the current unrest.

Fenrir moved into the thick of the pub and scouted the place. It was cramped and smoky. He headed to an empty table in a corner, removed his hat, and ruffled his hair. Then he quickly slipped his Third Eye into place. It would aid him in cutting through the noise and honing in on individual exchanges of interest. How better to test the temperature of the lower city than eavesdrop on chatter in a local pub?

"What you having?" the barkeep asked, cleaning a glass with a dirty rag.

"Just an ale."

The man nodded and waddled back to the bar. Fenrir took the time to listen to the conversations floating in the air around him.

"—wardens came through not two hours past—Sophie Roshem was with 'em—"

"—impossible—no mention of her leaving the city— wouldn't do that at a time like this—"

"—been how many days—still no word on when the Disaffected'll be tried—"

"—course not—still too hot and testy for that—want us low bloods to simmer down a bit first—"

And on it went. Fenrir continued to listen as he nursed his ale, but all his snooping only confirmed what he already suspected—the low bloods were unhappy. Sophie's speech had done little to placate them. He had his work cut out for him.

Fenrir downed the last bit of ale in his glass, warm and bitter. He waved the barkeep over, paid his dues, and headed out. It had been at least a half hour since he'd taken refuge, but even so, he took his exit slowly, peeked his head one way then the other. No Amilia. He breathed out in relief then steeled himself and moved on to his next destination.

But it wasn't easy returning to the place where he'd spent the worst five years of his life. As the black iron gates of the penitentiary loomed, Fenrir's legs lost their rigidity. He'd avoided it ever since he'd been tossed out a second time, that fateful night when Sophie had sacrificed her freedom to save him. But right now, he didn't have a choice. There was a prisoner he very much needed to talk with.

Fenrir crushed his discomfort and strode into the prison with a straight back. He ignored the torrent of thoughts as those familiar sights and sounds and smells accosted him. He pinched his leg between his fingers to quell the rising panic. Pain brought him back to his body and out of his head. His injuries, at least, worked in his favor in that respect.

He followed a guard through the corridors and arrived at Deston's cell.

"Watch his reach, sir," the guard said. "He's got the longest arms I ever did see."

Fenrir nodded, and the guard retreated.

"Well, well, if it isn't my Old World sparring partner," Deston said.

He was a dark, huddled form in the corner of the cell farthest from the bars. There was grunting then the light brought Deston's face into view. Bruised and battered but healing, which meant the guards had gotten all they could out of him. Not much from what Sophie had told Fenrir. Not even an ally's name passed those busted lips. His or the other Disaffected's.

"Did wifey send you to strong-arm me?" Deston asked.

He leaned against the bars, but Fenrir didn't back away. Long reach or not, he wasn't going to let this man think he felt threatened, and in truth, Fenrir wanted Deston to try grabbing him. It would give him an excuse to strike.

"Strong-arming you isn't doing any good," Fenrir said, "so no, that's not the purpose of my visit."

Deston tapped his head against the metal bars, a hollow dong sounding with each thud. Once, twice, thrice.

"I'm here to talk," Fenrir said. "You seem to have a head on those broad shoulders, so I thought it worth an attempt at appealing to your reason."

"I'm listening, Pa."

Fenrir's blood quickened, but he kept his calm. "I understand why you did what you did. I saw the state the lower city is in just before coming here. It's an embarrassment. Things have to change, that much is clear."

"I wonder, if I hadn't turned on Lenore, if I'd opted to sell out like you did, is that what I'd call you? Pa?"

Fenrir pressed on through clenched teeth. "I want to fix things, but I can't do that without help from the lower city. The people listen to you. How about you put that power to good use? I'm willing to advocate for your release if you give a public apology and work with me to calm the rising tensions."

"I mean, you and wifey couldn't turn your noses up at me just because I'm a low blood. You'd be hypocrites if you did. If Lenore had wanted it, would you have rolled over and let her tie her pretty little self to an oaf like me?"

The blood was rushing now, reckless, threatening to overspill its banks, but still Fenrir pushed. "I'm willing to forgive your misdeeds if you work with me to restore Simetria.

Convince those who follow you the Link isn't the issue. The guilds simply need to be reformed."

"You're a pushy bastard, aren't you? Hold fast and firm until you get your way, huh? That the tactic you used to snag wifey? I mean, Lenore definitely takes after you in that way. When that girl wants something, she goes after it, hard. I barely had to do a thing to draw her in. She was fixated on me before I even held her in my arms and told her I'd give her the world."

It was too much, the searing rage that came in tandem with Deston's twisted words. To use Lenore was one thing. To speak of her like this? Fenrir's arm shot through the bars and squeezed Deston's windpipe. He grabbed at Fenrir's fingers and clawed, but Fenrir held firm. This was his punishment for hurting Lenore. Yes. This man deserved to be in pain and fear for his very life. A smile spread across Fenrir's lips as the life faded from Deston's eyes.

Once big and strong, a force to be reckoned with, one that had sent Fenrir tumbling down a sheer cliff, now reduced to this shadow of his former self. But the victory wouldn't be sweet; this wasn't a fair fight. Fenrir's opponent was weak from sickness and malnourishment, much as Fenrir had been when he'd been confined to a similar cell. More than that though, Fenrir saw through the lies he told himself. This wasn't for Lenore. It was for him, revenge for Deston having bested him.

Fenrir's fingers relaxed, and he retracted his hand. Deston crumpled to the floor, grabbing at his neck, gasping for air. Fenrir turned and walked away, too ashamed of his actions to look on their results. This wasn't him. What would Sophie think?

***

It was time for action. Time to step out of the shadows and make that much-needed change. Sophie had left Fenrir in charge of Simetria for a reason. He wasn't meant to be a simple placeholder. Something had to be done, and Fenrir was resolved to make it so. Appealing to Deston hadn't worked. Instead, he aimed to repair the system itself, starting with the guilds and those who controlled them.

"Are they all here?" Fenrir asked Nicolus.

They waited in a small sitting room adjacent to the guildhall. Fenrir's tea was long cold. Nicolus sipped his own, pinky out, left hand supporting the base of the cup, the model high blood.

"Patience," Nicolus said. "I tasked one of the journeymen with informing us once everyone's assembled, but you know how these things go, even with the other Guildmaster Roshem at the helm." Nicolus sipped his tea.

"I don't," Fenrir said. "I usually leave these kinds of affairs up to her."

"Oh, yes, that's right. My apologies."

It was strategic, Nicolus pretending he hadn't noticed Fenrir's perpetual absence from these guildmaster meetings. He wasn't happy about the route Fenrir had settled on and had subtly hinted at his stance for the past two days, ever since Fenrir had floated the idea of this meeting following his failed attempt to enlist Deston.

"I know you don't approve," Fenrir said.

"Not at all, Guildmaster. I defer to your sagacious judgement."

This barely detectable sarcasm was new too. They couldn't afford to fight within their own ranks. It was time to spell the situation out clearly. Unlike Sophie, Fenrir had no patience for subtext and subterfuge.

"This is only helping the Disaffected," Fenrir said, "you working against me."

"I would never deign—"

Fenrir held up a hand and rose from his seat. He walked

the few paces to Nicolus's side. The man placed his tea down and stood. Fenrir held his gaze until Nicolus's discomfort was apparent.

"The false flattery and false words too," Fenrir said. "They only harm the guild. Stop using this moment to play politics, Master Yevin. Simetria's survival is at stake."

Nicolus's shoulders slumped. He had no fine words to offer, not in the face of Fenrir's bluntness.

"If we don't move quickly to repair the system, it will fall," Fenrir said. "We get the guildmasters to see their role in this, however uncomfortable it may be. We hold the mirror up so they see just how warped their images have become."

"They won't listen," Nicolus said, shaking his head. "You should hear how they talk with one another in private. I've been privy to those conversations. They don't care a mote for the low bloods or fairness or even the Link."

Fenrir knew this. He had hoped it might not be true, hoped his cynicism was clouding his judgement, but he'd been part of a corrupt institution before. The filth rose to the top and choked off everything below. The most effective cleansing was a purge of the system, but that was what the Disaffected wanted. Fenrir had to offer something else, a solution with more precision.

"Well then," Fenrir said, "we'll just have to find people who do care for those things."

Nicolus's eyes bulged. "You can't remove them as guildmasters. You're playing with fire. You'll get an awful scalding, you and your family."

"Because these guildmasters have influence? So did the Church, but look at what happened to it. There comes a tipping point when the people decide they've had enough. We're nearly there. I'm trying to avoid such a fate."

The door opened, and a warden entered, offering a stiff bow. He bore the journeyman's insignia: three larger chain links in his sash. "Nearly all of the guildmasters are present, Masters Roshem and Yevin."

"He's Guildmaster Roshem," Nicolus said, pointing to Fenrir.

"Yes, that's right," the warden replied. "My apologies, Guildmaster."

Fenrir waved the mistake away then marched to the door. The journeyman turned and led them to the guildhall just adjacent. He threw the doors open then stood to the side to allow Fenrir and Nicolus to enter. The room was swarming with guildmasters. Old and fat and overwhelmingly male. Even with Sophie at their helm, women were still the minority when it came to guildmasters. It made a kind of sense. After all, the Church's upper echelons had been dominated by men to such an extent that, discounting the founding members, there had only ever been one female bishop, an Eleiza Horens who had gone to Rotatia and met her end when that city had fallen to affliction. That was before Fenrir's time even, and in all the intervening years between her death and his time as a surveyor, no other female had risen to the level of bishop.

Though Sophie's position seemed to buck the trend of male dominance, in most ways, it was an anomaly rather than a meaningful change. It was that age-old desire for a mother and caretaker simply manifesting in governance. They were all willing to stomach this one-off exception, but how their world would have been shaken to the core for it to be the norm. Such a strange tendency.

As Fenrir made his way to a raised platform on the far end of the hall, he forced a smile and nodded at those he passed. The room went still and quiet save whispering. Fenrir didn't know what these people thought of him, but the fact he didn't grovel at their feet, like Nicolus, or feign respect, like Sophie, meant he was starting off on a bad footing. Fortunately, he wasn't trying to win them over. Fear could be an effective tool, as he'd learned from the Church, and the storm bearing down on them was pure terror in the minds of vacuous high bloods.

Fenrir strode to the platform, took the step up, and turned to face his audience. His wounds weren't completely healed, but he made every effort to hide any trace of weakness. He looped his thumbs in his warden's sash, the five large links on its chain indicating his new rank as guildmaster. He took his time looking from one end of the room to the other, catching as many eyes as he could in the process.

"I'm Fenrir Roshem, Sophie Roshem's husband and acting Guildmaster of the Wardens Guild in her absence."

He stopped and let the smirks flitter about the room. Of course they knew who he was. In their minds, he was the fool who didn't know them, who didn't play politics, who let his wife take the reins. And that had been true. Fenrir had existed in the shadows. A warden, a master of his guild, but one who had preferred to remain out of the spotlight and all the scrutiny that came with it, always fearful someone might look too hard at him and be reminded of a former tier 1 surveyor and high blood who had been executed for his grave crimes against the Church.

And it wasn't just the worry of recognition. When Fenrir had been Ashtin and lauded for his talents, he'd tasted the sweet sweet nectar of adoration by the masses and got drunk on it. It had fed his hubris. True, he was much changed since those days, but he also didn't quite trust himself not to fall prey to the beast yet again. Better to reject it altogether. Starve it into submission. Only, he had no choice now but to rise to the occasion. Sophie had left him with this task, and for her, he was willing to do whatsoever was required.

"Thank you all for coming today," he said. "I suspect you'll find your decision to attend this assembly was well-founded because, as of this moment, any guildmaster not present is no longer a guildmaster." Fenrir's blood raced at the collective gasp, the mouths hanging open, the eyes wide and restless. "I requested all guildmasters attend and made it abundantly clear this assembly was of vital importance to Simetria's security as well as that of the Link. Those who couldn't be bothered to come obviously don't cherish our fair city or Order enough to deserve the title of guildmaster. All affected guilds will hold elections at their earliest convenience to find suitable replacements."

Fenrir spotted Nicolus near at hand. His eyes were blinking rapidly.

"Now, on to the business I called you all here for."

Fenrir took two steps to the edge of the platform, thumbs still looped in his sash, stance strong and stalwart. Shock was giving way to disbelief. Outrage would follow shortly.

"The Disaffected, they're on all our minds. High and low blood alike. Plans thwarted. Imprisoned. Damaged contained? No to the last in that list. Not in the least. A storm is brewing, and this act by the Disaffected has set the maelstrom in motion. I suspect many of you are considering using brute force to crush any resistance. But to that, I say, absolutely not. We got to this point not because of twisted ideas by a fringe group but because of our own ineptitude as leaders. Ours. We've been asleep too long, shying our eyes away from unpleasant truths. Our guild system is corrupt, and we know where the rot stems from. On high, as ever. The guildmasters."

The outrage was coming to the forefront now. Lips snarled. Teeth gritted. Jaws clenched. Hands balled into fists.

"But not all of you," Fenrir added. "That's why I asked you here instead of ordering some grotesque purge. We heal that which is sick, not amputate it without thought. I need your help. To save Simetria, to calm this storm, those of you who care about your guild, about our city, about the Link, speak to me, work with me. We must do better for all. The people turn to the Disaffected because the Disaffected offer change. They hunger for change because the current world they inhabit crushes them. No more."

Fenrir threw his hands to his sides, fingers splayed, arms tense. He jumped down from the platform and walked amongst his enemies. As he did so, he watched for soft eyes, knowing looks, furtive smiles.

"Did the Warden Guildmaster, the real Guildmaster Roshem, agree to this drastic tack?" a voice shouted.

"Fenrir Roshem is the Warden Guildmaster," Nicolus said, pushing his way through the crowd.

"Acting," another voice said.

"Fenrir Roshem is the only Warden Guildmaster Simetria has in this moment," Nicolus said, "and that should be all that matters to you."

"Everything I say, I do, all of it, she knows," Fenrir said, touching a finger to the Third Eye affixed to his forehead.

"You're one guildmaster," a voice said. "We are many."

Fenrir whipped his head in the direction it emanated from and narrowed his eyes. He pushed through the crowd until others backed away to reveal the latest opponent, wearing the orange and brown of the Tanners Guild. A man with a flat nose and a jaw lost in his neck.

"I'm giving us all a path out of this mess," Fenrir said. "Those who defy me only tell us one thing: they're the corrupt ones."

The Tanners Guildmaster grimaced but went silent. Fenrir turned and moved through the horde, saving every expression to the memory of his Third Eye. It would tell him which of these were the cause of their sickened city. The ones who came to him and outed their fellows would become his most trusted cohort. It would be a purge but a surgical one, cutting out the tumors, saving the good tissue just adjacent.

"Henceforth, I'll hold private audiences every day," Fenrir said. "From dawn to dusk. Come to me. Tell me all the sordid secrets you know of one another. Rot isn't blessed, we know that now, so why would we let it return to sit and fester in our city?" He was done. The Third Eye had seen all it needed to. "Come to me, and help me save Simetria."

With that, Fenrir moved to the door. Nicolus hurried behind. A cacophony of voices followed but was cut off once Fenrir and Nicolus entered the hall then the sitting room they'd come from, the journeyman from earlier stationed outside. Fenrir eased himself into a high-backed chair, his wounds making themselves known. That jump he'd taken from the platform had almost done him in. He needed to be more careful. Sitting for these meetings was the safest bet because there would be many, and they would be long.

Nicolus took the seat adjacent to Fenrir's, leaving a small sofa across from theirs open, the witness stand in this unofficial trial against the guildmasters. Nicolus leaned an elbow on his armrest and cupped his chin in his hand. He shook his head at Fenrir and laughed. "You're mad. Here I thought you were going to give them a scolding, tell them to behave, and then brush your hands off and claim job well done."

"This is the only way. We're out of time."

"You'll make many enemies."

"We'll make many enemies. You backed me up in there."

"You didn't leave me much choice," Nicolus said, frowning. "You're my guildmaster."

This was no good. Fenrir needed Nicolus to truly be on his side, not forced into doing his bidding by rank. They had to work together. Nicolus knew these people, the ins and outs of their lives, the drama, the intrigue, how best to ply or press them.

"How would you have approached it?" Fenrir asked. "How to undo the Disaffected's rising influence?"

"Cut off the head of the beast and watch the limbs

wither. Execute the Disaffected we have in custody. Send a very clear and very loud message, one even the low bloods would understand." Nicolus was usually more careful. He started, catching his error too late. "Some low bloods. Not all are the same, mind you."

To Nicolus, Fenrir was Fenrir, a former low blood. Nicolus had no way of knowing the man he spoke to was as much a high blood as him.

"You would show the people a fist," Fenrir said. "I offer them a helping hand. I'm telling them we see the sickness too and are intent on curing it."

"I suppose we'll see how it all plays out soon enough. Too late to turn back now."

Fenrir's concern was creeping up. Shouldn't the uncorrupt guildmasters be flocking to him by now, asking for admittance from the journeyman on the other side of the door? How many minutes had it been? How long did they need to do the right thing?

"You know, I rarely bring up the past or ruminate on what-could-have-beens," Nicolus added, "but I had us on a path that could've avoided all of this nonsense with the Disaffected. This was before you joined the cause, back when it was still Lady rather than Guildmaster Roshem. I wanted to take a religious route. When it came to how to reshape Simetria, how to protect the Link, I rather liked 'blessed is the Link.' A sacred thing. A holy one. People would've been far more reluctant to attack it outright."

Fenrir shook his head and tapped his finger on his knee. "I know all about that. Sophie told me. She didn't want it that way."

The door opened. The journeyman stepped in and gave the guild gesture.

"Guildmaster Roshem, Master Yevin, there are a number of guildmasters who have asked to share a word with you."

Fenrir grinned, and his finger stilled. "By all means, send them in. One by one."

HORROR REVISITED

A lonesome cry sounded from above, accompanied by the flap of wings. Lenore glanced up. A gray and white bird glided on the wind, the same she'd seen in abundance at the fishing village, a creature of these sea-touched lands, so different from the pigeons or sparrows that frequented Simetria. It alighted on the sand several paces away and gazed at her with the intensity of a lidless yellow eye. A strange land awaited them with creatures far more baffling than this bird.

Lenore gripped her scythe to steady her hands. She shifted, and her feet sank into the soft sand. The sailors shouted in the distance, running with the dinghies back into the surf, fighting the constant onslaught of waves, bobbing with the crest and dipping with the trough of each. She set her back to them. Her attention needed to be forward, fixed on the next task. Back was a pang and ache. Back was Deston and his betrayal.

She couldn't afford to wallow. They were on the far shore now where uncertainty and danger loomed. If she wanted to stay alive, she had to focus. So she did. She scanned the dunes, tufts of grass swaying in the wind. This place didn't look all that different from the one they'd come from, but looks could be deceiving. Like a smile and soft eyes that had seemed to tell her they loved her, when in reality, they'd only ever been mocking her. Enough. She pushed the thoughts of Deston away and strode to her mother's side. The other wardens were gathering their things and readying their polearms. Only Sophie was still, calm, stoic. Everything Lenore longed to be.

"What's our next step?" Sophie asked.

Lenore trained her eyes on the dunes and thought for a few moments. "To find people."

"How do we do that?"

What did people gravitate toward? The basics— company, shelter, food, water. One of these came before all the others.

"We look for water, fresh water," Lenore said. "People tend to live near it."

"How do we find it?"

"We walk along the beach and follow any stream we come across. It should lead us to a river or larger body of water, eventually."

"Very good," Sophie said. She whistled, and the wardens looked in her direction. "Gather your things. Make it as if we were never here."

Lenore glanced out to sea. The sailors and their dinghies were nearing their ship. Once aboard, they would cast off, back home. They couldn't put a deadline on their mission, not without knowing more. Better to have the sailors return to that other shore and wait for word. Communication was tricky. Pigeons could only carry messages to familiar territory, but Sophie and Fenrir had their Third Eyes, an ethereal bridge across the waters.

Lenore, Sophie, and the wardens set off. They kept to where the sand was more compact and easier to traverse. It wasn't ideal. Being distant from the dunes meant they would be more visible from afar. Still, they didn't have much of a choice. There was no knowing how long their trek would be until they came across a tributary.

In fact, the day was nearly gone by the time they found a stream. Lenore's boots were heavy from the sand that had wheedled its way in over the hours, and her calves ached from walking on the uneven surface. But their find gave her a burst of energy, and she was all but ready to climb over the dunes and into the adjacent fields.

"We camp here for the night," Sophie said, dropping her bags.

The wardens did likewise then crashed into the sand, unlaced their boots, knocked the minuscule pebbles out. Lenore found a piece of driftwood and used it as a seat.

"I'm afraid we can't risk a fire," Sophie said. "We want to see the locals before they see us."

The wardens nodded and dug dried goods from their things. Lenore stared out over the water to the sun sinking behind it and the spray of colors set against the sky—soft pinks and pale oranges and violent reds. The water reflected the scene. It was stunning, but it couldn't reach her. She was far away, buried beneath her surficial flesh.

Lenore's mood plummeted with the setting sun. Even after its last rays had flashed against the lapping water, still she sat there, letting the chill of an autumn evening seep into her. Then boots padded sand, and the log she sat on shifted. Her mother was beside her but was hazed out by some liquid veil that floated between them.

"He doesn't deserve your tears," Sophie said.

"How could I forget? A Roshem can't afford to show her true feelings. Just bottle it up and wait for it to explode later."

"We have work to do. I need you to be focused."

Lenore grimaced and crossed her arms. "I didn't ask to come on this little quest of yours. You forced me into it. I would have much rather stayed with Papa and helped him with Simetria. But no, you couldn't stand to feel left out."

It felt good to lash out. Lenore needed an outlet, and Sophie was the only option in her immediate vicinity. But her mother was accustomed to such outbursts. She weathered Lenore's harsh words with a pinched mouth and raised eyebrows.

"That's enough of that," Sophie said. "This isn't our estate. We're with wardens, and I won't have you making a scene."

"Then let me be," Lenore said, turning on the log and setting her back to Sophie.

"Oh, I'll be glad to, but we need to discuss our tactics for tomorrow. You and I are the only ones with a Third Eye, so that means we're the ones scouting ahead."

Lenore faced her mother again with her mouth hanging open. "I'm not even a warden, and you're sending me into who knows what? Are your actual wardens not up to the task?"

"Have you worn it yet?" Sophie asked. "The Third Eye?"

"Why do I have to be the one to wear it? Why not give it to Journeyman Frye?"

Sophie shook her head. "We're very careful about who we let use a Third Eye or any synthetics. You'll be taking my place one day, so it makes sense to have you use it now. I'll ask again: Have you worn it?"

"No," Lenore said.

"It's nothing to fear."

"I'm not afraid of it." Lenore huffed and stood from the log.

Sophie rose too, as though they were tethered. Lenore stomped toward the water.

"Don't wander off," Sophie said.

"Then stop following me. I'm only trying to put some distance between us."

"Fine, I'll let you be. But you really ought to wear your Third Eye tonight, otherwise you risk being disoriented by it tomorrow. Get it out of the way now."

Sophie turned on her heel and headed back to the wardens. She sat down among them, so at ease, so at home. Lenore wished she could belong to something like that but something she'd chosen and hadn't been forced on her.

The alfom. This was their fault. Her parents had pledged themselves and her to their cause. She shouldn't be afraid to speak with them. She should be eager to give them a piece of her mind, to tell them she wasn't interested in being their pawn, no matter what her parents had promised.

Lenore reached behind her ear to the metal disk and pulled it free. She inspected it in the deepening night. It was smooth and silver and bore no markings obvious to the naked eye. How did it work? How could such a small thing do all it seemed capable of doing—enabling her parents to speak from afar, letting them share their minds, guiding them in the use of synthetics, reaching out to beings beyond their reality? This small, unassuming disk of metal.

Lenore placed it on her forehead, and when she removed her fingers, it stayed fixed in place. She sucked in a breath and waited, waited for that voice, the one who bore a strange name, but it never came. There was only silence. By degrees, Lenore noticed other sensations, a pressure and tugging originating from her mother's direction, another much further afield across the waters. Beyond that? Nothing. She couldn't help but think she had somehow failed a test.

***

The next morning was dismal. Thick fog had rolled in overnight and lingered. A chill too. Lenore rubbed her gloves together and longed for a fire. The wardens were subdued, eyeing their surroundings, straining their ears. Only the crashing of the waves and the call of seabirds greeted them.

Lenore took a deep breath, salt-tinged air rejuvenating her, soaking into her skin and covering the trails of salty waters that had streamed down her cheeks the night before.

"Let's move," Sophie said.

"In this fog?" Zacharay asked. He held a notepad and graphite stick. Even here, where they had no maps, he still acted as their guide. They would need to know the way home, after all.

"The fog is our friend," Sophie said. "It hides us as well as any we may run across."

The wardens accepted her ultimatum. They were much less rebellious than Lenore, but this once Lenore had no desire to oppose her mother. She was out of her element, whereas Sophie seemed perfectly at home. Focused. Certain.

The group of eight set out. The only signs of their camp now were depressions in the sand. Otherwise, it was as though they'd never even been here. They walked in a line with Sophie in the lead and Zacharay in the rear. Lenore was somewhere in the middle trying her utmost to hide her mounting unease. There was one positive to her fear; it pushed all other thoughts from her mind.

They followed the stream. When it splintered, they opted for the largest branch. It was hard going as the dunes transformed into hills and those to forests. The undergrowth was thinning with the changing season, but the brush held on tenaciously. Lenore couldn't count the number of spiderwebs that crossed her path. She had to hold in the gasp that came with each unwelcome encounter. How was she running into them when the others in front of her somehow avoided the sticky silk threads? Bad luck. Ill omens.

The fog persisted into the afternoon, and the wardens' pace slowed. They trudged for hours through bramble and mud and the loose, slippery stones of the stream's bed. With the venture into foliage, it became difficult to tell what was a harmless shrub and what could be a malformed threat. Afflicted—that's what they had to contend with. Creatures infected with distortions, corrupted motes of non-Euclidean space that, in turn, warped the minds of those they were embedded in. Lenore had heard the stories. How the afflicted were literal horrors to behold. How even the mere act of looking at them could drive one insane. How the same fate lurked for any who brushed up against a distortion on the creatures. So she'd been told. So had all the younger Simetrians, but without seeing the afflicted for herself, with only the word of her elders to go on, Lenore had rolled her eyes at the stories.

But when the story became reality, her eyes behaved quite differently. A strange form came into view, and she honed in on the movement, trying in vain to decipher the form. There was a lumbering and lurching. A hollow wheeze shifted into a scream. The wardens all snapped their heads in the direction of the noise. Lenore dropped her polearm.

The clatter of wood and metal drew the afflicted's attention. In too little time, its bulk barreled through the fog straight toward her. A mass of flesh and cloth. A mixture of colors, brown and beige and black and a dark green. A conglomerate of sheens, matte and lustrous and metallic. She tried to make sense of it, but it changed and morphed from one second to the next. There was a hand that became a mouth then an eye.

And all of that was horrifying, but the part that undid her, truly caused her body to freeze and her mind to turn inward, were the distortions. She knew them as soon as she saw them, or rather, their effects. Spheres of impossibility, pulsing, contracting, rising and falling, in and out, endlessly. The sounds too were shattering her being. Frequencies accosted her beyond comprehension, hitting some resonance that began to erode the matrix of her. She couldn't handle it. It was all too much.

The creature was close, almost on top of her, when a ranser's pointed tip sliced the air and embedded itself into the mass. The polearm's wielder though lost her balance. Jasmine's eyes were impossibly wide as she toppled over and collided with the horrid beast. But before it could concern itself with the young warden, Sophie's form leapt into view. Her orange-red braid whipped like a wild creature. Her eyes were fixed on her target, her mouth pursed and set. Sophie's voulge arced across her body. That moment of infinite time collapsed into a thousand actions and reactions. Sophie moved in equal parts dancer and butcher.

Twists and twirls, ducking, dodging. Viscera splattered. Sophie was a thing of beauty set against the horror born of some other reality's disease. She was their balm. She brought them back, Lenore and the other wardens. She struck and lopped off limbs that appeared unending. Other wardens dove in. Within seconds, the creature had been reduced to palm-sized chunks that quivered but did little else.

Jasmine staggered away from the pile of gore, holding her right shoulder, the same that had touched the afflicted. Sophie turned on hearing the movement.

"Stop," she said, leveling her voulge at Jasmine.

The young warden froze and snapped her eyes to her guildmaster.

"You touched the afflicted," Sophie said. "You know what that means."

"No," Jasmine said. "I'm fine, really. Just bruised is all. No distortions or anything like that."

Through Jasmine's fingers, there was the complex movement of the non-Euclidean. Sophie narrowed her eyes and pursed her mouth. Lenore knew that look too well. A mind set.

Jasmine went to speak, but before the words could even escape her throat, Sophie's voulge sliced it clean through. Jasmine's head slipped from her neck and tumbled to the forest floor. Sophie repeated her dance of death, cleaving Jasmine every which way until she too was an inert mass, indistinguishable from the afflicted.

Both deaths had been mercy killings, only they knew there was no such thing. As long as the Rot of the Link persisted, the distortions birthed from it would too, along with the lives stuck in eternity. This is what they'd come here to do. To erase this evil. To free the poor souls caught up in it. Lenore saw that now. How could she have ever doubted the stories, scoffed at the strain in the old voices who talked of the dark times of the past? So naïve. So blind. But not anymore. She gazed at that twistedness bred of corrupted space-time, and it infused her with resolve.

"Is everyone else untouched?" Sophie asked.

"Aye," the wardens who could find their words said.

"Take a moment to clean your polearms," Sophie added. She opened a flask of water, doused her blade with it, then rubbed it dry with a ward-embroidered cloth.

Lenore came to her side.

"One moment," Sophie said. "This has to be done with the utmost care."

Lenore simply looked on in a daze. This woman was her mother? Dashing toward certain death, flying through the air, twirling her polearm like a vortex, dispatching the afflicted then her former ally. She hadn't hesitated. Maybe this side of Sophie was why she led Simetria. Not a woman spouting empty words but one who didn't flinch from the hard deeds.

"We should construct a ward around it all," Sophie said, waving at the carnage.

"I couldn't move," Lenore said. She let her eyes defocus

as she looked through the pile that had been the afflicted and Jasmine both.

"The initial encounter is always particularly difficult. We surveyors were shown our first afflicted in a controlled setting precisely for that reason."

"She did that because of me. She was trying to save me, and I got her killed."

Sophie stared at Lenore for several seconds. "I highly doubt you'll freeze up again." She dug into a pouch on her belt and pulled a piece of chalk free then looked at the other wardens. "Gather stones, the flatter the better."

SPIRALE

Sophie was making her final touches to the makeshift ward when the foreign man wandered into sight. His eyes were trained on the ground, searching for something, maybe a type of nut or berry. The basket he carried implied he was foraging, that and the state of his attire. A low blood, if he had been in Simetria. Here? Doubtless some similar name in whatever strange tongue they spoke.

Sophie reached for Nytho with her Third Eye. *I've found one of the foreigners.*

Nytho's answer was faint, so diffuse she could barely hear it. *Too close to the Link node...Blocking the signal...Speak through Fenrir.*

Of course. The connection would be affected. This was different from her speaking with Fenrir. This was the alfom and some other reality they resided in. The Rot of the Link had been used precisely for this reason. Nytho's voice would be silenced the closer Sophie got to the Link node.

She reached for Fenrir. *I can't speak to Nytho. I'm too close to the Rot of the Link.*

He's here and able to speak through me, Fenrir said.

We found someone, Sophie said to them both.

The man glanced up then down then up again on realizing he'd seen something besides foliage. His eyes flitted over the seven people sporting light armor and long weapons. The wardens stayed motionless. They waited for Sophie to make the next move.

Good, Nytho said.

Sophie held her hands out, palms down, chalk intertwined with the fingers of her right one. The look in the man's eyes screamed of fear and confusion. They presented a strange sight to him, no doubt. Even if his clothing looked similar to a low blood's, theirs had to be unique from whatever the high bloods here wore. Two civilizations isolated for centuries with only the well-to-do having the time and energy to spend on appearances.

Sophie took a step forward, and the man crouched, ready to sprint.

"We mean you no harm," she said.

Another step. The man cocked his head, curiosity holding him in place.

"We would like to talk. Do you understand?"

The man's eyes jumped to Sophie's companions before settling on the remnants of the afflicted. On seeing that sight, his mouth popped open, and he let out a gasp.

"It's all right," Sophie said. "This creature is no threat to anyone anymore."

The man pointed to the afflicted's remains and gave off a flurry of words, too fast to catch any one sound. He jabbed his finger at the viscera, and his voice grew louder. Without knowing exactly what he said, Sophie was certain of the tone—outrage.

"What's he going on about?" Zacharay asked.

"I haven't the faintest idea," Sophie said.

"He doesn't look happy about the afflicted," Lenore added.

"Let him ramble on a bit," Sophie said. "I'll be able to understand his words at some point."

But the man wasn't going to give them the opportunity. Without warning, he bolted in the direction he'd come from, dropping his basket in the process. Lenore cried out.

"Let him go," Sophie said. "He'll lead us to our destination."

She stowed her chalk in the pouch on her belt then rummaged in her bag, pulled the diskette free, and held it out to Zacharay.

"For safekeeping. Lenore and I go alone to scout. The rest of you stay put. In the meantime, Journeyman Frye, you take the lead."

He grabbed the diskette with care.

"Watch our polearms too," she added. "We can't bring them unless we want to frighten the locals."

"Of course, Guildmaster Roshem," Zacharay said. "And if something happens to you and your daughter?"

"Fenrir is watching. He'll find a means to instruct you."

Sophie slung her bag over her shoulder. "Come, Lenore."

Lenore scrambled to gather her things. Then they both trotted after the man who was, fortunately, slower than they were. They caught sight of him just as he fled from the forest into open fields. That's when the city revealed itself to them. It was still a fair distance away, but even so, its grandeur was apparent.

Towers soared with one that appeared to reflect the sky. Its height was impossible, nearly triple that of any Simetrian structure, but Sophie didn't have time to gaze in wonder at this foreign city. They had work to do, and the task ahead required the utmost delicacy. They were outsiders entering the unknown. Information would be their friend, but for that, they needed to understand the words of these people.

Sophie slowed to a walk.

Lenore jogged ahead a few paces before realizing, stopping, and turning. "What are you doing? He'll reach the city if we don't sprint."

"Let him. He did what we needed him to. We have our destination in sight. Now, we go and try to get our Third Eyes to make sense of this strange tongue."

Lenore planted her legs wide and frowned. Her chest heaved as she tried to catch her breath. Her tricorn was askew. One of her coat's flaps was caught in the loop of her bag. She looked a mess but at the same time perfectly at home.

"That's what you meant by scouting?" Lenore asked. "Literally going into the city and amongst these people?"

Sophie adjusted her own tricorn, coat, and bag then walked forward, taking long, leisurely strides. Lenore stayed abreast.

"What did you think I meant?" Sophie asked.

"Watching from afar. Assessing the threat. Learning what we're dealing with. It's not just the foreign language. Their whole culture could be completely different from ours."

"And we'll learn that from spying on them? No, my dear, we need to jump into the thick of it and make meaningful contact. But yes, we must use care, which is why we stick to conversing with the low bloods." Sophie pointed to a cluster of fabric stalls. "The market, outside the walls, which likely means no guards. We can move in and out unseen. To top it all off, there's no better place for low-blood idle chatter, just what our Third Eyes require."

"I don't think this is wise. At all."

"This is the plan. Now, put your Third Eye in place then cover it with your hat."

Lenore sighed and grumbled but did as instructed. Her actually heeding Sophie's words was a new development and likely a result of their encounter with the afflicted. Maybe it even indicated a newfound respect.

They set off. The man wasn't visible anymore, but he wasn't their concern. Exposure to this foreign tongue, that's what they needed. The more, the better. They approached without anyone taking notice of them until they neared the outermost stall. That's when the people stopped and stared. Vendors craned out of their stalls to catch a glimpse. The collective hum of voices near at hand thinned. It didn't bode well. It meant travelers were a rare sight in this city.

"Everyone's looking at us," Lenore said.

"I'm aware. Here, let's head to this first stall."

The structure Sophie bore down on was a flimsy thing. Just a few wooden posts with cloth draped over. Vegetables and fruits sat on display. Sophie walked straight to the stall, smiled at the vendor, and gazed at the produce on offer. She clasped her hands behind her back.

"These look familiar at least," she said to Lenore.

Lenore's lips were even more pursed than usual, and her shoulders were high and stiff.

"Relax," Sophie said. "Your nervousness will only put them on guard."

Lenore forced a smile and mimicked Sophie's stance, hands behind her back.

"These look delicious," Sophie said to the vendor.

The woman stared. She was probably a bit older than Lenore, but it was hard to tell with all the grime clouding her features and the shawl wrapped around her hair.

"Is that an apple?" Sophie asked, pointing to the fruit. She needed this woman to talk.

"J'comprends pas," the woman said.

This was good. A start, at the very least.

Sophie pointed to the apple again. "Apple."

"C'est quoi ces mots?"

Sophie pointed to the apple with one hand and gave a shrug with the other.

"Tu veux acheter une pomme? C'est ça?"

Sophie dug in a pouch on her belt and pulled out a Simetrian coin. It was worth at least ten apples. She held it out and dropped it into the vendor's palm. The woman brought the coin close and inspected it.

"C'est quoi ça? Non, non, c'est pas bon. Qu'est ce que tu veux que je fasse de cette pièce bizarre?"

The woman pushed the coin back on Sophie and shooed her away from her stall with her hands. Sophie and Lenore retreated.

"Well, that could have gone worse," Sophie said. "At least we got some words from her."

"Such a strange sounding language," Lenore said.

"Let's try again with another vendor."

They moved from stall to stall to stall—ones selling cloth, shoes, cheeses, spreads, all manner of goods. At each, Sophie ran through the same tactic, coaxing the vendors to speak, exposing their Third Eyes to the sonorous hum of this new language. All the while, the people in the market watched her and Lenore, like prey wary of a new potential predator.

When they were at the fifth stall, a disturbance broke out close to the gate set in the city walls. As the people peeled away, a trio of guards came into view and headed straight for Sophie and Lenore.

"Mama," Lenore said.

"I see them."

Their Third Eyes only needed a little longer to make sense of what they heard then allow them to speak, but if the guards were hostile, weren't open to dialogue, their synthetics would be useless.

"Be ready to run if things go south," Sophie said.

The guards strode up to them and stopped, hands on sword hilts, heavily armored, so unlike their counterparts in Simetria who prized agility above all else.

"Who es-tu? Why es-tu ici?" one of them said.

Some of the words were comprehensible, but even without knowing the ones that weren't, the gruff tone of his voice imparted the meaning. These guards weren't pleased with their presence.

Sophie held her hands out, palms down. "Well met. I don't speak your tongue yet, but if you would give us but a little while longer, I could properly converse."

"Des mots wicked pour des gens malfaisants," another guard said then spat on the ground.

"That's not a good sign," Lenore said.

The third guard barked something then shoved someone into the space between them. It was the man from the forest, wringing his hands and blubbering in an endless stream. The third guard growled and grabbed the man by the shoulder.

"C'est ceux-là?" he asked.

The man nodded and pointed to Sophie and Lenore. "Wicked ones qui ont mal agi."

"Did you hear that?" Lenore asked. "Wicked ones. Us?"

The guards and man all snapped their heads to Lenore. Her words were becoming clear to them, as theirs were to Sophie and Lenore.

"Vous avez tué les poor unworthy?" a guard said.

The man from the forest gestured wildly, jumping in place, jabbing his finger at Sophie and Lenore.

"Wicked, wicked, wicked," he said.

"Mama, I think it's time we flee."

"Flee?" a guard said. "Je n'pense pas, wicked ones."

Lenore's face went pale. Sophie's stomach dropped. She twirled around ready to sprint, but a wall of people stood in her way. A crowd of low bloods blocked their escape, their dark eyes boring holes into the foreigners in their midst, foreigners who were somehow wicked in their minds. Fleeing back to the forest wasn't an option anymore.

Sophie reached for Fenrir. *Are you seeing this?*

You have to get out of there, he said.

Sophie grabbed Lenore's wrist with her left hand then slammed her right arm into the helmet of the nearest guard. A crunch and a howling from him told her he, at least, wouldn't be a threat. No such luck for the other two, but Sophie wouldn't give them the chance to process what had just happened. She slipped through the gap made in the wall of bodies by the fallen guard and rammed her way forward. The low bloods peeled away with yelps and screams. To see one of their bulky guards dispatched with such ease had to be a shock. Sophie used their confusion and fear to her advantage, blending in with them as they rushed the gate set in the thick stone wall that girdled the city, the handful of guards posted to it suddenly overwhelmed by the massive influx.

Sophie and Lenore passed the gate and tore down a thoroughfare. Sophie pushed Lenore in front and let her lead the way while Sophie watched their rear. Their actions had birthed bedlam, but the chaos wasn't quite total enough to aid in their escape. A few guards were already bearing down on them, and despite the Simetrians' superior speed, they were at a massive disadvantage in being utterly out of their element.

It wasn't just a new place with unknown streets. The city they found themselves in was incomprehensible in its twisted geometries. Curves everywhere, sinuous and irregular, so at odds with everything they as Simetrians had ever known. Vertigo gripped Sophie and sent her crashing against one of the walls of a tight alley. Lenore too was unsteady, legs wobbling, arms reaching for the bowed wooden walls of the nearest structure in hopes of finding safe harbor.

"This place," Sophie said. "It's foul."

And it wasn't just the geometries and their tendency for cursed forms so reminiscent of the non-Euclidean. Beyond her disorientation, she sensed something, something long forgotten, like a scratch that couldn't be itched or a lash irritating an eye, the same sensation she'd felt with the afflicted in the forest. She'd doubted it then, thinking it some kind of placebo effect. Her body being so accustomed to that feeling on seeing an afflicted had only mimicked that long-gone ability. But it wasn't so long-gone after all because it was unmistakable now. Even without one in her own navel, Sophie sensed the distortions. And they were everywhere.

There was no time to mull the horrors surrounding them because more tangible foes had found them, backed into a narrow alley. Feet clattered. Voices called out. Then, Lenore shouted, a wild, savage scream filled with a rage Sophie didn't even realize her daughter possessed, or rather, pretended she didn't possess. The truth was, Sophie saw the darkness lurking. She always had, even from those early days.

~~~

"Such perfect weather," Sophie said, tossing her braid off her shoulder, leaning back, and gazing up at the azure sky dotted with fluffy white clouds.

Melodi Yevin sighed and fanned herself feverishly. "It could be less warm. Just a skosh."

She sat next to Sophie on a blanket laid on the rolling green hills surrounding Simetria. Sweat hung in beads on her brow and upper lip. She was like a wilting flower, although even in fairer circumstances, Melodi didn't quite fit the metaphor. She was more a weed than anything else. Not particularly beautiful, what with those Frenwith features—the thin lips, the aquiline nose, the weak chin. Try as the Church might, they never could make Marcos Frenwith's silhouette look noble. If Marcos had been anything like his descendant, the Church had taken great liberties in rendering him. No wonder they'd always opted to depict him face on with eyes closed, head lifted skyward, barely recognizable.
~~~

"I'll take a touch of heat if it comes with that sun we see too little of," Sophie said. "Besides, the breeze helps."

"Not enough," Melodi said, fanning herself more frantically.

"Try to see the bright side, will you, darling?" Nicolus asked, standing nearby, swirling his wine. "At least, now, we get to enjoy these hills. No worries of afflicted. Our children frolicking about."

Lenore and Gilbur were two motes of white linen following the crests and troughs of the topography. As much as the children were enjoying themselves, Sophie found these forced outings with the Yevins so very tiresome, but Fenrir insisted they keep on good terms, telling Sophie it was for the good of the guild. And it was, but she wasn't a fool. Fenrir liked Nicolus, despite everything that had happened. Then again, maybe the only way he'd been able to cope with their past was by pushing such unpleasant memories completely out of his mind.

"The wind would be perfect for kiting," Sophie said.

"I could go fetch one," Fenrir replied. He was stationed next to Nicolus, a nearly empty wineglass in hand.

"It'd be a good excuse to grab another bottle," Nicolus said, angling his head at his glass.

"Oh, and I could find some relief in the shade of the city," Melodi added. "Even grab my parasol from the house."

"Well, don't be too long," Sophie said. "If those two decide to run off, I'll wear myself out sprinting after them. Their energy is boundless."

The others headed toward the city gates, and Sophie trained her eyes on two little meandering forms in the distance. Lenore and Gilbur playing, although the nearly four years' gap in age made for a strained dynamic, especially since Lenore was starting to view time with Gilbur as an embarrassment. To associate with a child of six when she was already ten? She'd put up a fight until Fenrir had calmed and coaxed her into submission. After all the drama of the morning, there they were running about, tumbling down the hills, getting their clean white clothes grass-stained.

Sophie laid on the blanket and closed her eyes, letting the sun soak into her skin. She couldn't have been that way for more than a few minutes when a howling sounded, a child's scream of terror. She shot upright, stood, and scanned the fields. The two little white dots were farther away, and she couldn't make out the particulars. She hiked up her skirt and bolted down the hill in their direction, bare feet flying. Within minutes, she topped the last crest, panting, sweat rolling down her face. Gilbur was still howling, folded over into a kneel. Lenore stood by and looked on with only a crinkle of her brow, either from confusion or annoyance.

Sophie hurried to Gilbur and laid a hand on his arm. He had his knees brought into his chest and his arms wrapped around those, crying, shivering, then Sophie saw why. A thick black cord was draped over his back and shoulders, moving on its own, slithering. Its head turned to Sophie, a pink, forked tongue darting out. She let off a yelp of her own, and Lenore burst into laughter.

"You're both so silly," she said. "It's just a little snake."

Sophie turned to Lenore and glared then grabbed the snake by its tail and launched it into the grass far over the hill. She was enraged because without any explanation being required, she knew exactly what had happened. She could almost see it play out in her mind's eye. Lenore hearing a slithering, seeing the snake moving through the grass, grabbing it, and tossing it on Gilbur.

"Gilbur, it's all right now," Sophie said, taking hold of the boy and stroking his dark hair. "The creature is gone."

His cries softened then turned to sniffles.

"Why was he so afraid?" Lenore asked, hands behind her back, rocking on her heels.

"Snakes can be deadly, Lenore," Sophie said. "We never put our friends in harm's way, do you understand?"

"That one wasn't deadly. I read a book that showed pictures of the ones to look out for."

"And if you were wrong?" Sophie asked, releasing Gilbur and standing.

"I wasn't. I'm not stupid."

"Well, I beg to differ. Today, I think you've been incredibly stupid. Even if the snake wasn't dangerous, you hurt Gilbur. Don't you see that?" Sophie pointed to the boy, who was wiping the snot and tears from his face, his chest still heaving from the aftershocks of terror.

Lenore crossed her arms. "If he wants to be a warden one day, he needs to be braver."

"And if you want to be one, you need to be kinder. Ruthlessness is not a trait the wardens welcome in our ranks."

~~~

Except in that moment, ruthlessness from a pseudo-warden was exactly what was required to escape captivity in the foreign city. Lenore rushed past Sophie, heading straight at the cluster of guards hurrying down the alley. As she did so, she let off another scream, the sheer force of it, the bloodlust nestled within, unsettled them, and that hesitation was all Lenore needed. Sophie had taught her well. Too well. Because even after dodging the foremost guard's blow and liberating his sword from his grasp, Lenore didn't falter or blink before turning the sword back on him and driving it into the gap between his armored torso and arm.

And Lenore wouldn't have stopped there. She would have lopped off his head. Sophie recognized the grip and positioning she used, but Lenore had no time to execute the death blow. The other guards were too quick, knocking the
~~~

sword away and tackling her. The smack of her flesh against the hard stone put a sickening pit in Sophie's gut and forced her to her feet. She rushed to the pile of guards and pulled at them, clawing, ripping, rending with her hands until she'd reached Lenore, battered and bruised but alive and awake.

"Enough," Sophie shouted, dropping to her knees and lifting her hands, wrists touching in what she hoped was a universal sign of surrender.

Sophie, Fenrir said.

I don't see that we have a choice but to submit for now. You send word to the wardens. I'll do everything I can to get us out.

The guards murmured with one another. The injured one removed his plate armor, and another helped him wrap the wound. Exposed, it didn't look as grievous as Sophie feared it might be. The last thing they needed was to kill one of the locals and ruin any hope of peaceful relations. Sophie glanced at Lenore, still slumped on the stones, breathing heavily.

"Don't fight them," Sophie said to her. "When they know why we've come, they'll treat us like their saviors."

Lenore glanced up. She was pale. Whatever fire had propelled her forward with such vehemence was quenched. She simply nodded to Sophie. The guards reached a kind of consensus. One grabbed Lenore and another Sophie and dragged them to their feet. Having lost their tricorns in the scuffle, Sophie and Lenore's Third Eyes were now exposed. One of the guards took note of the shiny metallic disk on Sophie's head.

"Elles portent d'étranges accessoires synthétiques," he said.

Lenore's guard twirled her around and inspected her Third Eye.

"No," Sophie whispered.

The guards grabbed the Third Eyes and pried them free from the women's foreheads. The connection to Fenrir and

Nytho was severed. The language these people spoke was again a mystery. The two guards handed the Third Eyes to one of their companions then bound Sophie and Lenore's hands behind their backs and pushed them out of the alley. The low bloods loitered in the square near the gate. With the threat neutralized, they were safe to jeer at the captives.

"Des gens malfaisants, des gens malfaisants, des gens malfaisants," they chanted.

"They're mad," Lenore said.

The guard steering her gave an especially savage push, and Lenore took the hint from it. Both mother and daughter stayed quiet as they moved from the square into the adjacent thoroughfares. The buildings here were low and shabby, and the streets were more mud than cobblestone. It was similar to Simetria in that sense, but that's where the similarities ended. As they ventured deeper into the city, Sophie's initial impression was reinforced. There was no holy symmetry underlying the layout. No straight streets. Buildings were dominated by curvilinear forms, undulations, irregularities, everything the bygone Church had preached against.

Sophie's eyes strayed upward. That shard that reflected the sky loomed, and as they approached it, she was able to make out more details. The tower wasn't clad in synthetics salvaged from the Old World. It wasn't even simply the ancient ruins from that time. This structure that stretched toward the clouds looked as new as the day it had been built. Timeless. And Sophie knew why. She felt the amalgamation of distortions within it. That shard was where their Link node laid. Not buried deep below the city, as had been the case with Simetria. Here, the Link node was elevated, a perpetual reminder of the distortions, the people cowering at its feet. Or so she thought.

But as they passed through a square, a statue drew her eye and told a different story. It was a smooth black marble carved in the shape of a woman. She stood at least four meters tall, back straight, head held high, arms open at her sides with the palms facing up. Her dress reached to her feet and covered her arms, but it was form-fitting with the deepest neckline that Sophie had ever seen.

Still, the risqué cut wasn't what caught Sophie's attention. It was the strange patterns etched into the skin on the woman's bosom. Twists and turns and swirls and spirals. So many spirals. The left eye of the woman too bore the same pattern but made from a white vein set in the stone. And it was the woman's eye that told Sophie what the spirals were meant to represent.

Distortions.

Her mind raced even as her feet dragged. She tried to make sense of all the pieces, to put them together and glimpse the coherent whole, but in too little time, they were brought into a building made of pitch-black stone, severe yet opulent, sporting the spiral motif. The guards ushered Sophie and Lenore through a few corridors before forcing them to their knees in an expansive hall. To Sophie's dismay, non-Euclidean geometries abounded. Hyperbolas, parabolas, a disdain for hard angles and edges. The opposite of Simetria and in blatant defiance of the Axioms.

Footsteps thudded. A man advanced from the far end of the room where a line of chairs sat. Five with backs twice the height of the people sitting in them. They were far away, and the light was dim, but the woman in the center emanated something, an aura, that drew Sophie's eye to her. Straight black hair, the bangs cut above the brow in a hard line, the rest of it tumbling down to the floor. She wore black, tight at the arms and chest and thighs but long. She sat with her elbow on her armrest and her chin in her hand. A veil hid the upper half of the face, only the bright red lips visible, a smile spreading on them.

Sophie had to tear her eyes away to view the man approaching. His garb was similar to the woman's—black robes reaching to his feet and covering his arms but elsewhere fitted to his form. A plunging neckline revealed a roiling embedded in his chest. Sophie held her breath on spying it, his distortion. And despite his condition, the guards bowed down to this afflicted.

He spoke. "Les gardes m'ont rapportés que vous aviez tué un pauvre indigne. Est-ce vrai?"

Without her Third Eye, Sophie couldn't comprehend even one of the words. She hoped that amongst the powerful, there would be the educated and maybe even one who understood her tongue.

"There's been a mistake," Sophie said. "If I could just explain who we are and why we're here."

The afflicted smiled and shook his head. Black eyes and black hair with pale skin, a long, straight nose. He didn't look all that different from a Simetrian, except for the foul mote sitting in his chest.

"Do any of your people speak my language?" Sophie asked. "I could learn yours if only your men would return those metal disks they took from us."

"Que dit-elle?" the afflicted asked.

"Des mots malfaisantes," one of the guards said.

The afflicted sighed and waved his hand. "Emmenez-les et mettez-les au cachot. Je n'ai pas le temps de m'occuper de cela pour le moment."

The guards grabbed Sophie and Lenore and forced them to their feet.

"Wait," Sophie said. "Please, we're here to help. Do you understand?"

A guard shoved her toward the door. The afflicted turned, his robes lofting with the movement. To bear a distortion was to be afflicted, and yet the man hardly fit that label. No, he was much more akin to another, one who'd borne a distortion that was different, one that didn't spread or grow and was satisfied with endlessly turning in Sophie's navel until it had disappeared along with the Rot of the Link.

"Be strong," Sophie said to Lenore.

The comment got her an especially forceful push. It was the last thing she said to her daughter before they threw her in a cell in the bowels of that opulent building. Twenty years later and here she was, put in confinement for again trying to rid the world of the Rot of the Link.

MISSIVE

Voyant Supreme,

I do not wish to disturb you, busy as you are with preparations for the gala. As such, I have opted to send a message in lieu of my person. I wish to provide you with more information on those strange persons apprehended near the southern market, the same ones brought to the grand hall earlier this day.

Your ears did not deceive you. They do indeed speak in a foreign tongue, as has now been confirmed. Of course, the guards did not merely apprehend them owing to their foreignness. Rather, one of the sightless claims he stumbled on them in the woods where he observed them murder a poor unworthy. We have not been able to make sense of their odd words, but I already have my people asking the Sect scribes for aid in untangling their speech. Rest assured, as soon as I know more, I will pass word on to you.

I would rather not speculate, but I cannot help but wonder if these might be the people we have spied out on the water, from the other landmass. Why they have decided to come to our fair city after all these years, I cannot say. I suspect it

does not bode well, but I will let off with my idle musings
until I have more concrete information to share. Of course,
as soon as we procure the services of a suitable scribe, I will
personally see to their interrogation.

Your most humble servant,
Hubert Pomeau
Voyant Superior of Spirale

THE GAMBLE

Fenrir stood at his bedroom window, appearing to gaze out on Simetria, but in actuality, scenes leagues away unfolded before him. He smelled salt-tinged air and caught the laughs and whoops of sea-side villagers. Then there was Lenore, smiling, dancing. It was his wife and daughter's last night in the land they called home. The next day, they sailed to the far shore. It weighed heavily on Fenrir and crowded his thoughts.

A knock sounded on his door, and Fenrir returned to the place his body inhabited.

"That'll be all for tonight, Willum," Fenrir said.

The door cracked open, but it wasn't the wigged head of his helper that appeared through the gap. It was the suave smile of Nicolus. Fenrir squinted his eyes, almost doubting them, but there was the warden still wearing their guild's garb despite the late hour.

"Nicolus?" Fenrir asked.

"Apologies for the intrusion, but this couldn't wait until morning."

Fenrir's smile faded. Grimness took its place. Fenrir waved him in and tied his robe around his nightclothes. He gestured at a set of chairs with their backs to the windows.

Nicolus entered the room and sat, while Fenrir closed the curtains before taking the seat next to Nicolus's.

"Three days," Nicolus said, "and they're already digging up dirt on you."

"The guildmasters?"

"Former ones, yes."

Fenrir planted his elbow on his armrest, hand up. "They're even less efficient than I thought they'd be. Three days is an eternity."

Nicolus's sternness wavered, and a smile flitted across his lips.

"And?" Fenrir asked. "Tell me about this dirt they uncovered."

"Fenrir Mey didn't exist prior to his assignment to the Most-Holy Southeast Bell Tower on the second of January, year 529. No family. No close acquaintances. No past to speak of. Who are you really?" Nicolus asked, staring hard at Fenrir.

His secret was always going to come out, but that knowledge didn't appease the fear of everyone knowing his old name, his past deeds, his failures and shame. Fenrir sighed.

"I need the truth," Nicolus said, "in order to engineer a solution."

Ever the pragmatist, the weaver. Nicolus was right. They had to beat their enemies to the punch and tell Fenrir's secret themselves. Take the offensive to avoid being forced into the defensive.

"Before I was Fenrir, I was locked in the penitentiary for five long, hard years. The Church put me there for defying them. I laid hands to blasphemous objects and didn't initially give a mercy killing to my afflicted son. I was a surveyor."

That moment of recognition, the parting of the lips, the O-shape of the mouth, the whisper of sound that came with the gasp.

"By the Order," Nicolus said, "I see it now. Ashtin Broodfell, is it?"

Fenrir nodded and leaned back in his chair, elbows flush with his body, hands on his thighs, palms down.

"That's a secret that would turn the low bloods against us," Nicolus said. "You were never one of them. You only pretended to be in order to earn their trust then went back to the upper city the first chance you got. That's what your enemies will say anyway."

Fenrir shook his head slowly then quickly like a failing clock's second hand rushing to make up for the lost time. The path forward wasn't shallow words to feed the masses. It was the truth.

"Or I'm both a high blood and low. As Ashtin, I was the former, and as Fenrir, the latter. It's not that I was trying to hide my past. I'm simply not a high blood anymore. I'm Fenrir. I lived the life of a low blood. I have a foot in both worlds, and only I can see this archaic distinction serves no one. A guildmaster isn't a high or low blood. They're a guildmaster. Same for a master, journeyman, apprentice, novice. It's time we unify the city. Fenrir who was Ashtin, wronged by the Church, forced to live a lie, a broken man made whole again."

"That's one way to frame it."

They told Simetria the next day via pamphlets in the upper city and heralds in the lower one. Fenrir's truth. Who he really was. Why he'd hidden it. Why he was resolved to be honest and open with Simetrians moving forward. Then, the coup de grace—his plan for the future, a restructuring of the guilds. The reaction could go either way. Condemned or applauded. The early hours were uncertain. Fenrir paced his room, while Nicolus stood near at hand. They waited for word from the handful of wardens they'd sent out to do reconnaissance.

By midday, a collection of low bloods appeared outside

the Roshem Estate's gates. Another was said to be amassed at the Wardens Guildhall.

"What do they want?" Nicolus asked.

"Why don't we ask them?" Fenrir said.

He hadn't told Sophie about this. She had too much on her plate as it was. Besides, he was resolved to find a solution to their dilemma on his own. They waited hours more until the autumn sun hung just over the rooftops. Fenrir threw on his warden coat and tricorn then strode the lengths of his home's halls. When he burst through the double doors that led to the grounds, the crowd murmured. It had only grown since those first reports. Fenrir met them, only a line of iron posts standing between him and the people.

"Open the gate," Fenrir said to the guards.

Nicolus reached out and grabbed Fenrir's wrist. "Are you sure?"

Fenrir smiled. Of course he wasn't. He had no idea what the low bloods thought of him. He could be walking into their murderous arms, but what was the alternative? Hide in his plush home, ruling from afar, cold and distant?

He marched through the gates and up to the low bloods. "I'm listening."

They looked back at him, mute, dumb, but their reaction didn't actually stem from a lack of intelligence, just surprise, shock that he would actually be open to their words.

"I'm listening, truly," he said.

Those nearby, who could hear his words directly, came out of their daze. A few even smiled, but of course, the most brazen and coarsest spoke first.

"Are you now? Well, that's a start, but how 'bout you try your hand at using those pretty eyeballs of yours?" a weathered man with windburn and pockmarks on his cheeks said.

"How so?" Fenrir asked.

The man stuttered, having clearly expected a fight or to be ignored entirely.

Before he could recover and reply, another cut in. "He means to set your peepers on the lower city, Guildmaster." It was an old woman with a bowed back, wearing a tattered wrap to hide a head with too few hairs. "You say you're listening, but he wants you to also look."

"I will," Fenrir said. "I intend to visit it myself."

"Visiting it is one thing. Living it another." This came from a younger man with a shock of short blond hair. His face was covered in a fine layer of dust, and the leather apron he wore told Fenrir he was a craftsman just come from his work.

The silence had been breached. The floodwaters released. The comments poured forth from low blood after low blood, so fast Fenrir couldn't keep track of who said what.

"Don't he already know that?"

"He lived in the lower city."

"That was ages ago. It's worse now."

"Did he actually live there though, or was that another lie too?"

"No, he did. I remember seeing him head to the bell tower. I lived nearby."

"You're full of shite. You'd have been a lad of what, three back then?"

Fenrir waited for the torrent of words to fade to a hushed surf. They looked at him, expectant, pleading almost. Did they want a reason to trust him? Were they finally so exhausted by the plethora of hate?

"I lived in the lower city," Fenrir said. "But only for just shy of two years. And it was long ago. Things have certainly changed."

"Why did the Church let you live?" This was shouted by the same antagonist of the windburnt and pockmarked cheeks.

Fenrir sighed, shrugged, and shook his head. "They never told me why, and I was too stunned to ask. Five years I'd been a prisoner. I was in a daze for a long while after being released. By the time I was able to even think about such things, I was already living my life as a toller. Discarded and forgotten by the Church. I wanted to keep it that way."

There were murmurs, nods of heads, smiles, frowns, coughs. He couldn't gauge how they really felt, but in truth, he didn't want to. He wasn't there to manipulate them into feeling what suited his purposes. He was there to have an open dialogue, plain and simple.

And it was the right tactic to take. The low bloods must have sensed the sincerity and savored this rarity from a high blood. By the time the sun sank behind the horizon and the street lamps were being lit, the crowd had largely dispersed. They'd learned his truth and hadn't turned against him. The low bloods had decided to see things Fenrir's way. They were appeased for the moment.

But Fenrir didn't have time to watch his efforts take root and flower. The next day, Sophie reached out and showed him the strange foreign city. He observed through her eyes as mother and daughter wandered the market and tried to make contact with the people. Unease gripped him when three guards came lumbering toward them. Raw terror enslaved him as his wife and daughter attempted to flee into the city then fought the guards before giving themselves up. Their Third Eyes were ripped from their foreheads, and the link between them was lost. Fenrir was blind to their fate.

He jumped from his seat in the sitting room that had become the receiving chambers for guests of the Wardens Guildhall. Nicolus was seated next to him and started. A journeyman was just bringing in a woman who bore the colors of the Publishers Guild. Fenrir shook his head at the journeyman, and the warden ushered the woman out of the room.

"What is it?" Nicolus asked.

The words were too difficult to form. How to say it? In what order? With what context?

"They took Sophie and Lenore," Fenrir said.

"Who? The far-shore dwellers?"

Fenrir nodded then tore out of the room. Nicolus called after him, but he couldn't be bothered to turn the sounds into coherence. Fenrir's mind was all aflutter. He took refuge in an alcove in a side corridor.

They took their Third Eyes, Fenrir said. *We're completely blind now.*

It's a bad turn of events, Nytho said.

Fenrir flew through the halls and up a central staircase, around and around until he was on a rooftop platform. He huffed with the exertion of his climb but couldn't stand to stop. He strode over to the woman tending to the pigeons in their coop.

"I need to send a message to the fishing village on the coast," he said. "The one Guildmaster Roshem visited."

"Of course, Master, err Guildmaster Roshem." She crammed the seed she'd been clutching into a pouch on her belt then fumbled with a set of drawers just adjacent to the coop. Out came a graphite stick and small scrap of parchment.

She looked at Fenrir. "Message?"

"Fenrir comes riding hard and fast. Pick up the wardens from the far shore and have them wait in the village. Be ready to carry Fenrir and the others back to the far shore as soon as he arrives."

"Should it be Guildmaster Roshem rather than Fenrir?" she asked.

"No, leave it and send it immediately. Two copies on two different birds, just in case."

Then, he tore back down the steps and through the halls,

deep into the bowels of the old parts of the structure not used since the days of the Church. Narrow corridors. Dark. Winding. Crumbling. Fenrir stopped at the door to the Vault, using a key to open it. The light flooded out and bathed the corridor in a cold illumination.

Fenrir couldn't understand how the syntheticsmith stood it, working in such a tomb day after day, alone, surrounded by relics from a past long gone. Then, there she was. Before he'd taken even three steps into the room, Feowna was bearing down on him, stomping and frowning until recognition took hold.

"Oh, Master Roshem," she said, slowing her stride and growing meek.

"I'm only here to retrieve something," he said, pushing past her and heading to the rear of the room, making for a table set against the wall.

Feowna shuffled after him with short steps that hugged the floor. She liked to chatter, especially when she had a rare visitor to the Vault, but Fenrir didn't have time for her endless lectures on synthetics, on what she'd learned, on what she was making. His mind was fixated on one thing. He spotted it on the table, a gray box no larger than his hand. He opened it and was greeted by a host of small metal disks. He plucked one, pinching it between thumb and forefinger, then closed the box. When he turned, Feowna was blocking the way. She gazed at the Third Eye in his grip.

"Guildmaster Roshem didn't give you permission to take that," she said.

Fenrir glared at her. Sophie had been the one to give Feowna the job as a syntheticsmith and rightly so; Feowna was skilled. Despite that, Fenrir didn't particularly like the woman. It wasn't owing to her cultist roots. In the time of the Rot of the Link, Feowna had been like Theopold, worshipping synthetics and the Others, but none of that mattered now. All the biases Fenrir had had back then were shattered when he'd learned the truth—about Theopold's role, or lack thereof, in Fenrir's imprisonment, about the Others, and the Rot of the Link. Fenrir's disdain for Feowna was ill-defined. More akin to a knee-jerk reaction than a conscience opinion. In that moment of distress, he couldn't be bothered to force civility.

"I'm Guildmaster Roshem, in case you hadn't heard, holed up as you always are down here. And this," he said, holding the Third Eye up between them, "will help Sophie. Now, move."

Feowna narrowed her eyes and compressed her lips. "I need the serial number to note which one was taken and for whom." She held out her hand.

Fenrir gritted his teeth and shoved it into her palm. Feowna turned the disk over, squinted at it, angled it to catch the light just so, and used a lens to inspect it. She muttered to herself and hurried to a console nearby. She brought the tool to life with a tap of a key then let her fingers fly over others.

"Whose?" she asked.

"Nicolus. Master Nicolus Yevin. Of our guild, obviously." Fenrir held his palm out and shook it at her.

As soon as the disk touched his skin, he rushed from the Vault. Then, it was back the way he'd come, navigating the labyrinth. Fenrir took the steps two at a time and pumped his arms. At least this way, he could try to pretend his racing heart was only a product of his exertion and not the terror that gripped him over the fate of his wife and daughter.

You'll keep an eye on Nicolus while I'm gone? Fenrir asked Nytho.

Are you sure it's wise for both you and Sophie to be absent from the city?

I don't know about wisdom, but I don't see what choice I have.

Fenrir mounted his last step then flew through the halls until he arrived back at the sitting room. The journeyman stood alert at the door. A line of people waited, some moving toward Fenrir on seeing him. He waved them away and stole inside. Nicolus looked up as he entered, as did the Publishers Guildmaster. Fenrir uttered his apologies and took his seat, his mind preoccupied by his wordless conversation with Nytho while Nicolus dealt with guild business.

What do you intend to do when you get there?

Free my wife and daughter, Fenrir said.

By force?

Ideally not, but if it comes to it, then yes.

Nicolus said something and looked at Fenrir. Fenrir gave a weak smile but stayed silent.

I won't be able to help you once you're there. You'll be on your own.

I know, but you need us to do this, don't you? Fenrir asked.

Yes, unless you'd like to go back to the old ways.

I can't trust anyone else with this task, with either part, the saving of my family or the destruction of the Rot of the Link. I do, however, trust Nicolus with Simetria.

And if you don't return?

The Publishers Guildmaster was walking toward the door, her back to them.

Fenrir grinned savagely. *Then you'll have a whole horde of wardens to choose from to be your new favorites.*

"Where did you go?" Nicolus asked.

The journeyman moved to let another guest in, but Fenrir held up his hand and shook his head. "We need a minute."

The journeyman nodded and retreated. Fenrir and Nicolus had the room to themselves, sitting in their pseudo-thrones with no one in attendance.

"I have to go," Fenrir said. "Sophie is in trouble, and I don't trust the wardens there to know what to do."

"You? To the far shore? You're not even fully healed, and what about Simetria and everything you started?"

Fenrir smiled, leaned over, and patted Nicolus's shoulder. "I'm healed enough, and this is the best option, Guildmaster Yevin."

Fenrir lifted his hand and held the Third Eye out to Nicolus. He pointed to the metal disk attached to his own forehead. "This will allow us to stay in touch. Instantaneous communication."

"Synthetics," Nicolus said. He brought his hands in, cupped, open, waiting for the treasure on offer.

Fenrir tilted his hand, and the Third Eye tumbled into Nicolus's palms.

"You place it here when not in use," Fenrir said, showing the spot behind his ear, "and here when you need access to it." He tapped the spot where his own sat.

Nicolus brought the disk to his eye and inspected it. "So this will be all that links us?"

"Yes, but it's reliable. If something does happen to it, Feowna Moldgrove will be able to help."

"The cultist in the Vault?"

"Former cultist. She's the guild's syntheticsmith. She's knowledgeable."

"And how do I speak with you?" Nicolus asked.

"Simply think of me and the words you would say. The Third Eye does the rest. Even if I'm not wearing it on my forehead, I'll feel you reaching for me and vice versa."

"You trust me with a great treasure," Nicolus said, stern, his usual smile effaced by the severity of his charge.

"You're our most stalwart ally," Fenrir said. "You've been with us since the beginning, been a warden since the first days. If anyone deserves to bear that relic, it's you, but be wary of its powers." Fenrir dropped off as Nicolus's eyes shot to his.

The man would know what Fenrir alluded to. Vergil and his untimely demise, attributed to playing with synthetics he didn't understand. His Third Eye had still been attached to his head when they'd finally gotten to his body, so Sophie had said. What Fenrir implied wasn't a complete lie. The relic had killed him, in a way.

"Just use it for communication," Fenrir said, "and you'll be fine."

"And the alfom? Will they hold audience with me through it?"

"If they choose to. The one called Nytho is our ally. The one called Yir is not. That's the Lady. Push her words aside."

Fenrir didn't need to elaborate because, in Nicolus's mind, the Lady was just as deadly as the Third Eye could be. Vergil's death was also tied up with her. Those were the rumors Sophie had spread in those days, and they had stuck. The Lady was not to be trusted. The alfom were.

Fenrir rose from his chair, and Nicolus jumped up. He vibrated with a nervous energy. How could he not? Fenrir was leaving him with great power and even more responsibility.

"We'll be back as soon as possible," Fenrir said, "but I can't say when that will be. Just don't do anything with the Disaffected while I'm gone, understood? Focus on cleaning up the guilds."

"I've only ever had the best interests of the Order at heart," Nicolus said, straightening and giving the warden's gesture. "May you bask in a light which casts no shadow."

A fine sentiment but misapplied in this particular case because, in fact, Fenrir was doing the opposite. He was leaving the light and plunging into a land of shadows, a place where Nytho's voice was silenced, where distortions still pulsed, where the non-Euclidean reigned supreme. If he was smart and careful and most especially lucky, maybe he could manage to bask in light even in that land of darkness. It was a fine thought, a noble one, but what really gave him the courage and resolve to set out was a simple image in his mind's eye. Two women with green eyes, one bearing orange-red curls and another strawberry-blond waves. His pride and joy, both. His whole reason for existing. He had to protect them, come what may.

COMMUNIQUES

Falcon,

The loveliest of sights and sounds graced my eyes and ears just this afternoon. A gift was delivered to the Fleur-de-lis in the form of two women. They arrived in Spirale speaking a strange tongue, wearing odd clothing, and picking and nearly winning a fight with several heavily-armored guards. I saw and heard it all. I followed as far as I could, but they brought the women into the Sanctum. I need your contacts within to find out more. The sooner, the better.

Your Starling

***

Starling,

Thomas handed me your message, covered in sweat and breathing hard and fast. Ticktock, I take it? I reached out to my people in the Sanctum. What they say is the two foreign women were brought in, shown to Pomeau who could not understand a word they said, then tossed in separate cells. This is all so far. Pomeau asked after Sect scribes who know the tongue the women speak. I suspect the questioning of the women will start tomorrow with the aid of the scribe. It is all exciting, to be sure, but why, little Starling, are you so intrigued? What does any of this mean for the Fleur-de-lis?

Your Falcon

***

Falcon,

We are just shy of three weeks out from a significant event. I find it odd these women would appear so close to said event. Coincidence? Perhaps, but in our line of work, it would be foolish to ignore other possibilities. Who are these women, and what exactly are they here for? Are they working with another faction? Was getting captured a part of their plan? If so, for what purpose? These are a sampling of the questions I have. It would behoove us to learn more, given everything at stake in the very near future.

To that end, I propose a more active role in retrieving such information. Your contacts are to be applauded for their efforts, but we need to hear what we seek directly from the source. I have an idea, but I do not know that you will like it. The Sect requires the services of a scribe who speaks the strange tongue. I happen to be both a scribe and one versed in said tongue. All that remains is to find a way for me to be approached for the work. If there are Sect scribes who fit these requirements, we have no choice but to remove them from the pool. You understand?

Your Starling

***

Starling,

You show a side of yourself I do not often see. Am I

rubbing off on you? Why would you think I would not like this route? Perhaps you forget who your Falcon has become. I have no qualms with using violence in pursuit of our cause. Against voyants. Against those who aid them, sightless or no. However, I do find fault with your plan in one way, and maybe this is what you referred to. I do not like you being the one to go into the lion's den and for something so vague. In short, is the reward worth the risk? Only you can answer this, Starling. I will trust your judgment, as always.

Your Falcon

***

Falcon,

I am pleased we are in agreement regarding what must be done. Move forward with the plan. Remove the obstacles but preferably with minimal violence. Remember, Sect scribe or not, these sightless do not know what we do about their masters. They could be innocents. That being said, we cannot risk exposure. Only you can evaluate what is best. As for your question of risks and rewards, you will sigh and scoff at my answer, but you asked for it, so here it is. This cannot be a mere chance encounter. It is all happening for a reason. Now, perhaps this is the work of another faction, in which case, we need to be informed. Or, and more meaningful in my opinion, these women are here unrelated to any of us and our schemes.

Do you see what that would mean? Foreigners arriving on the eve of a revolution. Coming from a land not under the thumb of the Sect. Potential allies? Guides? Fate, Falcon, that is what I view this as. Chuckle all you like, but then set about your task. Ensure Pomeau reaches out to me to be his translator. Again, the sooner, the better.

Your Starling

***

Starling,

I am a skeptic, this we know, but where you lead, I follow. You have the vision. You have the mind. I am merely a handy tool. Use me as you will. I am happy to do whatsoever you ask if it means we get our justice. Rest assured, you will soon walk through the Sanctum's gates at the direct request of the Voyant Superior himself.

Your Falcon

THE SCRIBE

Sophie had said to be strong, and Lenore took her mother's words to heart. But it was hard. Being thrown in a cold, wet cell. Barely given food or drink. Yelled at by guards. She curled into a ball, hugging her knees, resting her head on them. In all of her nineteen years, she'd never known discomfort; this imprisonment was a shock to her. Whenever despair crept in, she would silence the beast with one thought—how many low bloods spend their nights like this?

Lenore hardened herself and refused to let tears grace her lashes. Sophie had said to be strong, and so she would. Lenore forced herself to see the good. It could have been worse, much worse. After tossing her in her cell, no one had bothered with her. She'd heard horror stories of what women could be put through in situations like this, but she escaped that nightmare at least.

Yet another kind of terror visited her in the dead of night. A woman clad in black, stalking the halls, passing back and forth and back and forth then staring in at Lenore. She spoke no words and instead bored holes into Lenore with her eyes. A black lace veil pushed aside, one eye of bright green, another roiling with an impossible foulness. Lenore shrank and retreated into the corner of her cell. She told herself it was a bad dream, the stress of her capture getting to her and making her mind play tricks.

They came for her on the second day. Two guards. Unlocking the barred door, shouting at her and waving their hands, grabbing her by the arm much tighter than they needed to. But Lenore held her tongue and let her eyes tell them all the things words could not. They laughed at her harsh looks then pushed her into a small room with only a table and two seats. One guard pulled a chair out while the other forced her into it. They attached heavy metal cuffs to her wrists and ankles then left.

Not long after, footsteps bounced off the stone walls of the corridor. A face appeared in the small barred window set into the door. It was that same man from the grand hall, the one with a distortion in his chest. She didn't know how she could spy it without the aid of her Third Eye, but so it was. Lenore gritted her teeth to keep them from chattering. She wasn't cold, but she couldn't get them to stay still. There was something about the man, some foulness other than the distortion, a manic light in his eyes.

He entered the room with a middle-aged man wrapped in gray robes and carrying a stack of tomes. Ink covered his fingers. His back was stooped. His eyes squinted. A scholar, if Lenore had ever seen one. So pale from all the hours spent in darkened rooms smelling of dust and parchment. The scholar glanced at Lenore then looked away, at the table, the walls, the floor, anywhere but her eyes.

The afflicted closed the door. The scholar grunted and deposited his books on the table then took the chair. The afflicted stayed standing and watched Lenore, inspecting her, evaluating her. He was clearly the one in charge, the other just a lackey.

"Comprenez-vous les paroles de ce scribe?" the afflicted asked.

"Do you understand the words this scribe speaks?" the scholar said.

There was an odd inflection to the sounds, but Lenore understood him.

"Yes," Lenore said.

"Oui," the scholar said to the afflicted.

That manic light in the afflicted's eyes only became more pronounced. "Why are you here?" he asked through the scholar.

What was she supposed to say? Surely she couldn't tell the truth. They were in this very position because they'd killed an afflicted, and that was seemingly a wicked thing to do. It was as Lenore had warned—their culture was completely different. What had been blessed in Simetria was most certainly not in this place.

"My city sent us to make contact with your people."

The afflicted eyed Lenore then clicked his tongue and wagged a finger at her. "Do not tell me lies, little traveler. It does you no favors."

"They're not lies. Our ruler sent us to explore the waters beyond our lands. He's newly come to power and has an adventurous spirit."

"Over five hundred years, and suddenly, you all decide to see what else is out there?"

Lenore despised lying. There were too many loose ends to keep in mind, too many ways to trip up, but she had no choice at the moment.

"There was a brutal regime change," she said. "We're trying something new."

"Why come with weapons if you simply wanted to make contact? Yes, the sightless saw your little cohort's arms and reported that along with your murder of a poor unworthy."

She was digging herself deeper, but there was nothing for it.

"That was a misunderstanding," she said. "The creature attacked us first."

The afflicted planted his hands on the table, leaning in to peer at Lenore. Her eyes strayed to the distortion pulsing and swirling on his chest. An afflicted and yet there he stood. His mind his own.

He noticed where her gaze went and smiled. "I do not know what it is like where you hail from, wicked one, but in Spirale, we do not lay hand to the poor unworthy. If they decide to gift you with insight, you willingly take on the vitre they so graciously offer."

"I don't understand what that means," she said to the scholar.

"Which part?" he asked.

"Any of it."

"Que dit-elle?" the afflicted asked.

"Elle ne comprend pas ma traduction. Est-il possible que j'utilise des mots qui n'existent pas dans leur langue?"

The afflicted grimaced and threw a hand. "You want to play this game? Fine. That cell will be your home until you stop with the lies and give us the truth. Remember, we have two of you. What you say does not match what the other woman says, so either one or the both of you are lying."

With that, he pushed himself away from the table and headed to the door. The scholar hurried to gather his things then scurried after his superior. The guards came and returned Lenore to her cell. She spent the whole of the night wracking her brain for a solution. How could she speak with her mother and get their stories to line up? Was there any way out of this that didn't involve her father coming and storming this city? Because that's what he'd do. She knew Fenrir would burn the world down to save them.

***

The next day, the guards retrieved Lenore late, the sun's light already starting to fade. They brought her to the same small room and locked her in shackles yet again. A few minutes later, a face looked through the window set in the door, but this time, it wasn't the afflicted man or the stooped scholar but rather a young woman with thick braids and dark skin. The door opened, and she entered, wearing loose beige robes tightened at the forearms. A guard closed the door behind, and the woman's auburn eyes settled on Lenore then refused to budge. Like the scholar who had preceded her, this scribe too held a stack of tomes and loose sheets of parchment she offloaded on the table before sitting.

"Yours is a new face," Lenore said. "Where are the two men from yesterday?"

The scribe smiled, sorted her parchments, pulled a graphite stick from her robes, and set her hand at the ready. "Today, it will just be me. Monsieur Pomeau is much too busy for such parleys."

"Monsieur Pomeau was the younger man, the one who seemed to be in charge?"

"Younger? No, though he would seem it. The one in charge? Yes."

Lenore furrowed her brow. It was hard enough following the words with all the strange flavors peppering them, but to also read between the lines at the subtleties? She couldn't hope to do so in that moment, nerves on edge, hungry and thirsty and haggard.

"And the other man, your colleague, the translator?" Lenore asked. "He's also too busy to bother with me, I take it?"

The scribe's smile morphed, the lips curling further, puckering, but still hiding her teeth. Something about the grin implied a hint of mockery. "Not colleague. He works for the Sect. I do not."

After two days in the dark, of wondering what she was up against, here was a fragment of something. A name at least.

Lenore straightened in her chair, the chains clanking with the movement. "The Sect?"

"The ones who rule the city. You really are a foreigner to not know the name. To answer your question, the other scribe will not be joining us. He never showed up. I am his replacement. Now, I have questions, and I hope you will offer answers."

The scribe wrote a few words on the parchment then shot her eyes back to Lenore. She offered that sphinx smile again, only this time, Lenore realized it wasn't mockery nestled in the expression but rather something more akin to a jest, or a player in a game.

"Why are you here?" the scribe asked.

"Where is here? This city, what's it called?"

The scribe shook her head. "I ask the questions. You answer. Again, why are you here?"

Lenore had no choice but to repeat the story she had told yesterday.

"My city sent us to make contact with your people. Our ruler has newly come to power and has an adventurous spirit."

The scribe's hand moved frantically as she set Lenore's words to parchment. "What message does your ruler send then?"

Lenore thought quickly, making sure to keep her response simple, all the better to recall it at a moment's notice.

"He sends you greetings. He wishes to know your people."

"And the poor unworthy in the forest?" the scribe asked. "Was killing it a part of the greeting too?"

"That's what you call the afflicted here?"

The scribe's grin faded. "I am asking the questions. You are answering."

"No, killing the afflicted, poor unworthy, whatever you

want to call the creature, was not part of the greeting. It attacked us. We had to defend ourselves."

The scribe's mouth popped open, and she seemed to struggle with whether to wear her grin or dispense with it altogether. "So, you have no qualms with laying hand to poor unworthy then? And voyants? Would you lay hand to them too?"

"Voyants?"

The scribe tossed her head at the door and lowered her voice. "Monsieur Pomeau and his kind, the ones who bear the vitres."

"The distortions, you mean? The people who are afflicted but with their minds intact?"

The scribe simply stared back at Lenore, immobile, as if balancing on a knife's fine-honed edge. Then, without warning, she stowed her graphite stick and gathered her papers and books.

"Did I do something wrong? Say something untoward?" Lenore asked.

"Far from it, but I need to think." The scribe heaved her things and staggered to the door then kicked it a few times to summon the guard.

"Will you be back tomorrow?" Lenore asked.

"Would you like me to be?"

"If you offer answers, then yes."

The scribe shook her head and tsked. "That is not how this works. Remember, I ask the questions, and you answer."

***

The woman scribe was already waiting when the guards delivered Lenore to the small room the following day. Without preamble or greeting, the scribe ran through the same set of questions. Lenore answered with the same set of words. Faithfully. But therein was the problem.

"Do you know how I know you are both lying?" the scribe asked.

Lenore sat up straighter in her shackles, the metal rubbing her wrists. "Because we tell different stories?"

"No, that hints one of you lies, but I said both of you do." She went silent and stared at Lenore with those probing eyes, lined by long, dark lashes and tapered at the ends. "Since you offer no guesses, shall I tell you?"

"I don't know why you would. It would only aid me in outsmarting you."

The scribe laughed, the sound sending a bright pulse that shot through Lenore. "Both times we have met, you said the exact same thing. The same words in the same order. If you spoke the truth, you would not have to do such a thing."

Sticking to the script. Lenore had thought it was the right tack to take, but now she saw how flawed it had been.

"Maybe I'm keeping my words simple so you can understand them," Lenore said.

The scribe's grin fell. "You are the ones who come to our city without knowing our language. You are lucky I know it at all."

"How do you?" Lenore asked.

The scribe waved her hand at the tomes set on the table. "I read. Many things, things from the Old Times, some of which have your language. It seems it was a widespread one, spoken across many lands."

"But I'm the first you've met who speaks it?"

"No, there are others in Spirale who know it. Not many, but some."

"That's this city?" Lenore asked. "Spirale?"

"Why did you come here when you knew so little of this place? You had to know it would not end well."

"How are we supposed to learn anything about a place without visiting it?"

The scribe raised her eyebrows. "A valid point."

Lenore couldn't be sure if it was just wishful thinking,

but she sensed something from the scribe, something hiding behind her words and false smiles. Curiosity maybe? No, it was more potent than that, an eagerness to the eyes, their refusal to budge from Lenore, the hanging on to every word.

"That Pomeau who was here the first day," Lenore said, "who is he exactly?"

"Hubert Pomeau, a very powerful member of the Sect, the Voyant Superior of Spirale. He rules the city."

"The Sect is like your church?" Lenore asked.

"We do not worship a god, but in other ways, yes, the Sect of Sight is a bit like a religion of the Old Times. It controls Spirale. It shapes our society. It gives the sightless hope."

"Sightless?"

"The poor and powerless."

Low bloods then.

"And this Hubert," Lenore said, "he's special, a voyant you called him, because he bears a distortion?"

The scribe's brow wrinkled.

"The motes of non-Euclidean space, the thing on his chest," Lenore said, "you called them something else."

"Vitres," the scribe said. "We call them vitres. 'For the voyants are gifted the eyes within and are open to another sight.' Or so the Sect claims."

An unease crept up on Lenore. These sayings were nothing like those the Church would have leveled at the distortions. Coupled with the fact these people didn't give afflicted a mercy killing, seemingly made it illegal to do so, it all painted a terrifying picture.

"You worship them," Lenore said. "That's why Hubert rules the city, and why the statue of that woman bore so many of these vitres. You see them as blessed things."

The scribe's face hardened into an almost grimace.

"Or they see them as blessed," Lenore added. "The others, but not you?"

The accusation jolted the scribe, and she was back to her former self, the disdain pinched off and buried away. But Lenore had seen it clear as day, and it offered so much potential. She had to push now. She might not get a chance again. It was a risk, to be sure, but she was out of options.

"We call them distortions," Lenore said. "They're foul motes that warp and twist everything. We call the poor souls who come in contact with them afflicted. We give them a mercy killing, or we did until we learned our Church had been lying to us. There's no death for an afflicted. At least, there wasn't until we destroyed the Rot of the Link. It caused the distortions. Another lie of the Church's that was their true undoing."

The scribe's mouth was agape by the time Lenore closed her own. After a few seconds of silence, she hurried to hide the shock and become that inscrutable scribe again.

"Is that what you came for?" she asked. "To destroy the source of our vitres?"

Lenore stared down at the table, her eyes defocused, tightlipped and stern. It was done. Come what may, she'd taken the leap. Now, she could only wait and see if the seed she'd planted took.

***

"Helice," the scribe said. It was the first word from her mouth since their last session. "My name, Helice Valin."

Lenore tried to temper her expectations, but she couldn't help but see all the grand possibilities this confidence represented.

"Lenore Roshem."

"You said some very interesting things yesterday, Lenore. You will be relieved to hear I chose to keep them to myself."

Lenore leaned in, trying and failing to rest her hands on the table, the chains arresting her movement. "That surprises me. It's what Hubert longs to know, isn't it? The real reason we're here."

"Is it the reason? You never answered me."

Lenore looked away from those intense eyes and down at her shackled hands. Sores were forming. Grime was sticking. Her hair was becoming a matted mess. She was desperate to escape, but she needed to use care in how she went about it. Besides, they still had to do what they'd come to this place for. The Rot of the Link was here, and whether the populace wanted it or not, it had to go.

"Did you speak with my companion, the other woman, about it?" Lenore asked.

Helice shook her head. "I spoke with her before you yesterday, and I decided to start with you today. You are more forthcoming."

Of course her mother would be a rock. Sophie had gone through trying times before, but just how trying, even Lenore didn't know.

"What if I told you that you and I have like minds?" Helice said.

"About the distortions?"

"About many things. I may be here talking to you on behalf of the Sect, but that does not mean I believe in what they do."

It could be a trap. Maybe Helice hadn't told Hubert yet because she wanted to pry yet more information from Lenore. What was their city like? How many were they? What kind of threat did they represent? How had they destroyed the Rot of the Link? She had to be careful. She had a bad habit of confiding in people who didn't deserve her trust. Hadn't she been sucked in by another set of brown eyes already?

"It just so happens I stumble on the one Spiralean who isn't a true believer in the Sect," Lenore said. "How fortuitous."

"One? You think our city is such a restful place that we are all happy little sheep eager to be marched off to the slaughter?"

Lenore's eyes widened. This was the first true break in Helice's performance, previously so calm and composed, now struggling to suppress rage.

"Spirale is not of one mind," Helice said. "Or even two or three, for that matter."

Helice rose from her chair, lifted it by its back, and moved it to Lenore's side of the table. She sat then leaned in close. Those tapered eyes were fixed on Lenore's emerald ones.

"Not all sightless are alike," Helice said. "Not all are devout."

"And where do you fall?"

Helice leaned in further until her lips were just adjacent to Lenore's ear, her words barely audible.

"I did not just happen to be asked to this prison. The other translator did not come for a reason. A beating, a gag, bonds. These stood in his way. When the Sect frantically looked for another to step in, my allies ensured they would have none but myself to turn to. Just a simple scribe to them, but I am the definition of a wolf draped in sheep's wool." Helice pulled away.

Lenore gaped. "What are you saying? You pried your way in to speak with me?"

"Or the other woman, it did not matter which. I saw the chase and heard the strange tongue. I thought you might be working with another faction, maybe Blindfold. Porte did not seem likely; turning a guard's sword on himself is too violent for them."

"Factions?"

"Those not devout. Those who want nothing more than for the Sect to be turned to ash. Obviously, you are not in league with one of these, or else you do a better job lying now than when I questioned you before."

Lenore's face burned at the jab, and she instinctively tried to cross her arms. Her chains prevented the movement and stubbornly dug into her wrists.

"But what luck for the Fleur-de-lis," Helice said. "We supposed you might be useful. A source of chaos to distract the voyants at the very least, but yesterday, you spoke words that offered so much more. To destroy the source of the vitres? Is this truly possible?"

"We did it in our city nearly twenty years past."

Helice grabbed Lenore's forearm and stared into her eyes. "How?"

"Why would you want this when so many of your people worship the distortions?"

"They do not know better. If we can remove the voyants from power, everything else will fall into place. And if you aim to destroy the vitres, this will undo the voyants in more ways than one."

Lenore had a flash of that roiling in Hubert's chest. How could he survive if the distortion embedded in there was suddenly gone? If the same was true of all the other voyants, cleansing the Link node would mean death for them. Instantaneous and total.

"How do we do this?" Helice pressed.

"I'm not a fool. If I tell you, you'll just leave me and my companion behind to rot in our cells while you go on your merry way to start your revolution. Only it would be a flawed endeavor. Without us, you have no hope of cleansing your Link node. Get us out of this prison, help us get to your Link node, and we'll do the rest."

Helice grinned, not her sphinx smile but a real and genuine expression of joy, creases on the edges of the eyes, lips pulled back to reveal equant teeth. "We will ensure you are put in the other woman's cell so you can explain things to her."

"One request," Lenore said, reaching for Helice's arm,

the chains arresting the movement. "We wore two small metal disks on our foreheads when the guards took us in. We need them. They're essential to our mission."

"Then we will retrieve them. Tomorrow. Be ready. I won't be back to question you."

SECT TENETS

I. Forgo the synthetics—they cloud the eyes.

II. Seek out the vitres—they open the eyes.

III. Any person is free to take on a vitre.

IV. Those unable to bear the truth of the vitres are poor unworthy.

V. Poor unworthy must come to no harm.

VI. Those able to bear the truth of the vitres are voyants.

VII. The voyants are gifted the eyes within and open to another sight.

VIII. The voyants lead the Sect of Sight.

IX. The Sect of Sight will guide us to ascendance.

NEW ALLIES

Without warning, a guard brought Lenore to Sophie's cell. Sophie didn't dare move, afraid this was only some kind of error, that they had mistaken her cell for Lenore's. She stayed huddled in the shadows, nestled in the corner of the stone-walled enclosure, even after Lenore had stepped in and the door had been shut behind her. Sophie held her breath as she waited for the guard's steps to retreat down the corridor, only stirring when they were lost to distance.

"Mama?" Lenore said.

"Don't use that. I'm Sophie to you in this place."

Her words came out in a croak. Her throat was dry and achy. She didn't want to think what picture she painted for her daughter. Somehow, the sun's coming and going implied it had only been four full days, but that couldn't be right. She couldn't have gotten so filthy in so little time. She couldn't have lost so much of her sense already. Time was blurred. The past was so far away, the future uncertain.

"It's safer to just be two women rather than mother and daughter," Lenore said. "Something like that?"

Sophie stood slowly, her head spinning with the

movement. She'd taken food and water only sparingly. She didn't trust her captors. She knew too little about them.

"You were right," Sophie said. "We should've been more careful in approaching this place and these people. I ought to have listened to you."

Lenore didn't offer a smug smile or cross her arms. That's what she would have done before this place. Had it changed her so much already? Sophie was most certainly a bad mother. She knew that without a doubt now. To have brought her daughter into this situation.

"I don't know if any amount of careful scouting would've ever prepared us for Spirale," Lenore said, walking the few paces to Sophie's side and leaning her back against the cold stone.

"That's the name of this city?" Sophie asked.

"Yes, or so the scribe said."

"How are you here?" Even as Sophie said it, she knew. Lenore's averted gaze confirmed her suspicions. "You told them why we came."

Lenore's eyes snapped to Sophie's and narrowed. "Not *them*, and not like you think."

Sophie slumped to the ground and held her head in her hands. "They'll be executing us. That's why it doesn't matter if they put us in the same cell or not."

Lenore lowered herself to the floor and came in close to Sophie. "I only told Helice, the scribe, and she didn't tell another. She's on our side."

"They don't hate the distortions," Sophie said with a forlorn smile. "They worship them. And for us to come with talk of destroying them for good? We're their truest enemy."

If she'd only realized it sooner. The reaction of the man in the forest should have been enough to clue her in, but she'd been distracted and overconfident. If only she'd seen that statue of the woman before the guards had got ahold of them. But it didn't matter now. That's not how things had played out.

"Not all of them worship the distortions," Lenore said. "Helice, for one. She hates them. She wants them gone. There are others too, multiple factions, and when we destroy the Rot of the Link, they'll thank us."

"And how will we do that while locked away in this cell?"

Lenore scooted closer to Sophie and lowered her voice. "Helice will come tomorrow night. She's going to get us out."

Those eager eyes, so like Fenrir's. That surety, so like herself. Sophie reached out and tucked a lock of Lenore's hair behind her ear. "My poor child, I would've thought you learned your lesson with Deston about the dangers of trust."

Lenore pulled back and frowned. "You think she lied? She knew yesterday why we came to Spirale, and she didn't turn us in. Why go through all this song and dance? Why pretend she's on our side if she's not?"

Sophie shrugged and tossed her hands before holding her head in them again. She was delirious from hunger and thirst and couldn't think straight to see why these people would play them as they had.

"It was a risk," Lenore said, "but I had to do something. We can only hope you're wrong, and I'm right." She looked down at her hands. "I wish Papa was here."

"I don't because then we'd all be stuck in this dreadful place, and Simetria would be vulnerable."

Lenore laughed, the sound so at odds with their environment.

"I don't know why you find that humorous," Sophie said.

"The irony. You and Papa think you're so essential. You think Simetria would crumble at a moment's notice without you. You claim to love the city but have so little faith in it."

"You don't know what it's like, having such a weight on your shoulders, year after year."

Sophie tried not to think about it. She'd spent the past two decades running from the truth. After everything she'd done to break free, first from her distortion then from Vergil, she'd ended up building a prison around herself.

"I could never play pretend all the time like you do," Lenore said.

"Oh, it's dreadful," Sophie said. "I so despise being the figurehead."

"I've a hard time believing that," Lenore said. "You seem to enjoy it well enough from where I stand."

"Seem, my dear. Seeming is not being. I do a good job of pretending. That's all."

Lenore peered at Sophie. What did she see in that faint light trickling in from a moon mostly eclipsed by clouds? A woman strong and proud and so sure of herself. Or did her daughter glimpse the truth? The incessant uncertainty and doubt.

Sophie was tired, worn down by her long and unending watch, of being everything Simetria needed her to be, of always having the answers, of exuding charm, of appeasing male egos, of having given up her own daughter to save her. Had it been worth it?

"I'm sorry we never told you about our pledge to the alfom," Sophie said. "The truth is, it pains me to know I've backed you into this corner. I despise cages with all my being, and to know I placed you in one, it's a difficult pill to swallow."

Lenore moved in and laid her head in Sophie's lap. She'd taken this position so often in her childhood, but it had been years since she'd let Sophie hold her so. She played with Lenore's hair, at least the parts that weren't a tangled mess. To have brought her daughter into this. What a fool she'd been.

"Why did you do it?" Lenore asked. "You said it was to save us from Vergil Holdsworth, but wasn't he the man who freed us from the Church's grip?"

"That's the lie we tell. It's easier that way, but no, he was nothing like any of the stories you've heard. He sent me into the Old World with your Papa and others to destroy the Rot of the Link, only he didn't tell us that's what we were doing. We took the blame when we returned to the surface while Vergil schemed away in the shadows, undoing the Church from the inside and out. He wanted their power. He wanted Simetria to be his. And he wanted me."

It was easier saying these things to the back of Lenore's head. She stroked her daughter's hair and pressed on, letting her tongue say names it had avoided, imagining scenes she'd pushed away all these long years.

"He was obsessed with me. We'd been betrothed since we were children, but I'd glimpsed his darkness. I didn't want any part of it. I just couldn't find a way to free myself from him. He knew things about me, secrets. I suppose I have something in common with these strange people in that way. I too bore a distortion, but one that didn't cause affliction."

Lenore lifted her head and turned to Sophie. "A distortion?"

"I was born with it, but it was different. It could be seen with the naked eye. It didn't grow or change, but that didn't matter. If anyone had found out, it would've meant a mercy killing. Vergil knew my secret, and it hung over my head my whole life until we destroyed the Rot of the Link. Then, Vergil used my role in that act to imprison me anew."

Sophie stopped and hesitated. To tell Lenore of Nicolus's role or not? To shatter her image of that man? Would she only be doing it out of pettiness, jealous of the bond between that man and her daughter, or would it be to warn her of his true nature? The latter, most assuredly. Lenore wasn't a child anymore; she deserved the truth.

"He kept me locked in the cellar of one Nicolus Yevin for nearly a month."

Lenore sucked in a breath.

"And yes, Nicolus knew. It was all part of Vergil's plan, and Nicolus was his most trusted ally. They needed to keep me out of sight so a woman who shared my face could die on my behalf. Sophie Roshem would rise from the ashes and become a saint. Nicolus knew this and assisted Vergil. He also knew what Vergil got up to when he visited me nightly in that cellar."

Lenore locked eyes with Sophie. Such pain, empathy, to feel so strongly on her behalf. Had Sophie only imagined that darkness in her daughter during their chase? When she'd plunged the sword into the Spiralean guard, had a trace of a smile graced Lenore's lips or had she been stony and inert, undertaking an unpleasant but necessary action?

"What are you saying, Mama?"

Sophie smiled sadly, brushing the locks from Lenore's eyes. She didn't bother scolding her for using "Mama." Besides speaking in a foreign tongue, their words were barely even whispers now.

"I think you know what I'm saying. What Vergil did and how Nicolus helped him do it or, at the very least, didn't lift a finger to stop it. Of course, Nicolus would claim he'd believed I was in love with Vergil and wanted that. But the truth is, Nicolus didn't spare a thought for me. He only ever considered Vergil's desires."

"I find this very hard to understand," Lenore said. "It's so at odds with the Nicolus I know."

"I'm not excusing Nicolus, far from it, and the choices he made tells you the kind of man he is underneath it all, but part of the explanation for his behavior lies in Vergil. He had this way with people. You would fall under his spell so effortlessly. Even me. I'd let myself get trapped by him and only realized it too late. No matter what I did, I couldn't shake free of the man."

"Until he died."

"That wasn't an act of fate. We killed him, your Papa and me. The alfom told us how to do it, forcing Vergil to overtax himself while he bore his Third Eye. It was the only way. I was pregnant with you, and once he found out, he would've killed you and Fenrir."

Lenore pulled her knees into her chest and wrapped her arms around them. Even with their wardens' garb, the cell was cold in the late autumn evening.

"A word of warning," Sophie said. "If we ever manage to escape and return to Simetria, you must keep the truth of Vergil's death to yourself. As should be obvious now, Nicolus was close to him, and I don't know how he would react to finding out his idol's death wasn't, in fact, a tragic accident."

"I wouldn't dream of telling him," Lenore said before going silent. How was she taking this new, unflattering vision of the man she viewed as a second father?

"And your Papa, he's aware of my trials, but it's best not to dreg up such horrid memories."

It wasn't actually a lie, but it wasn't the unvarnished truth either. Sophie had never told Fenrir in so many words about her time in Nicolus's cellar. Even after she'd reunited with him in his shack on that fateful day, her belly swollen with Lenore. Even after they'd synced, sitting on his bedding of hay. She had opened her mind completely, exposing the ugly truth, the not knowing who Lenore's father truly was. But Fenrir hadn't commented on it, then or in all the intervening years. Sophie had taken it as a sign that he didn't care and was claiming Lenore as his own, but it was entirely possible that, in all the chaos of their minds, all the overwhelming emotions, he hadn't actually glimpsed the possibility.

"I see now why you both dislike discussing that time," Lenore said. "Thank you for sharing the truth with me. I understand why you made the choices you did, but I can't give my life away to something I don't comprehend. The alfom. The Link. I won't serve masters or protect an object that are complete enigmas. I'll help destroy the Rot of the Link here, but beyond that, I make no promises."

"Of course you won't, my clever child," Sophie whispered.

"Your little corvid, you mean?"

"You said not to call you that anymore."

Lenore smiled bashfully. "In all honesty, I rather miss the moniker."

"Well, if that scribe does happen to spring us, you'll most certainly deserve the name."

***

Helice came deep in the night, the second since Lenore had come to Sophie's cell. The woman was soundless, standing at the barred door without warning, no light to guide her, a key slipping silently into the lock, even the hinges mute in her presence. Two steps into the cell, an arm waving indistinctly in the dimness. Sophie roused Lenore, slumbering on her lap. Lenore's eyes fluttered open, and Sophie nodded in Helice's direction.

"Wear these over your clothes," Helice whispered, handing each of them a cloak. "Come, we do not have much time. As soon as we step out of the cell, your lips must stay shut."

Sophie and Lenore nodded. They wrapped themselves in the cloaks, smelling of smoke and damp. Helice went to the door, stuck her head out, and waved them along. She closed and relocked the cell without a sound, then they were gliding through halls, empty, dark, still. There was the occasional cough of a prisoner in other cells or the snoring of guards. Helice led them through the labyrinth, and in short order, they were out, under the open sky, breathing fresh air, wind tossing their cloaks.

Within ten paces, Helice had them diving through a

nondescript wooden door set in a stone building that led almost immediately to a set of steps. They navigated by groping in the dark.

Once they reached a landing, Helice threw her arms wide and blocked the path. "Careful, there is a hole that leads down." She knelt and patted the ground then beckoned them.

"Where are we going?" Sophie asked.

Helice hissed and held her finger to her lips, the details visible only as slight gradations in shadow. "Your lips stay shut. Now, down."

Sophie reached for where Helice's hands were and found the edges of a ladder plunging into a hole. She moved slowly, and eventually, her feet found the rungs. Down she went, Lenore just above, and Helice at the top. Step by step. Sophie set the pace. She was weak and tired and hated being robbed of sight for so long, but she couldn't afford to slip. She had no way of knowing how long the fall would be.

After a space, the echoes of their foot- and hand-falls were shortened, then Sophie's feet touched solid ground. She stepped aside. Lenore came down followed by Helice.

"Come," Helice said, taking the lead.

The tunnels they traversed grew waterlogged. As they trudged through, Sophie tried not to dwell on what the stench of the liquid implied about its contents. Soon, a faint light showed itself at the far end of a tunnel. They pulled themselves onto a narrow stone walkway set above the muck. They followed the path to the light, a single torch flickering in this lonely place, just next to a simple wooden door.

"We are here," Helice said.

She pulled a set of keys from her pocket, fit one into the lock's slot, and turned. The door gave way to a darkened opening. Helice waved for Sophie and Lenore to enter. They found themselves in a small room filled with boxes and crates, a heap of hay in one corner, a small wooden table with a few chairs in another. Helice lit a candle then shut and locked the door.

"The sewer?" Sophie asked.

"What did you expect?" Helice said.

"You think they won't look here to find two fugitives?"

Helice smiled, the movement slow and deliberate. She had a wisdom to her that was beyond her years and gave off the kind of aura that only comes from great suffering. Sophie could see why Lenore had trusted her, and so far, her daughter's intuition had been spot-on.

"They will not look here," Helice said. "Or rather, cannot. This is not their domain."

"The realm of your faction?" Lenore asked.

"Partly, although the Sect thinks it mostly thieves who frequent this place," Helice said. "They know to leave it be if they hope for Spirale to continue functioning."

"An uneasy alliance of convenience," Sophie said, "but will that survive two highly sought prisoners potentially hiding here?"

Helice moved to the table and took up residence in one of the chairs. She removed her cloak and unlaced her boots. "They do not know what I do about you. The Sect does not understand just how valuable you are. Or dangerous."

"So they won't be so desperate to find us?" Lenore asked.

"They will want to find you, but they will not be reckless in their pursuit."

Lenore took the chair next to Helice's, removed her cloak, and undid her boots. Sophie caught sight of a bucket under the table, complete with a bar of soap and a rag. She could use a good cleaning even before their trek through sewage.

She sat in the third chair and followed suit, removing her own cloak and boots. The three women scrubbed grime from their feet and legs then moved to cleaning the clothing that had been soiled by their journey. They sat in their undergarments, waiting for their things to dry in the close and still air of the storage room.

Helice pointed to the hay pile. "You can get rest there. We will bring you to a better place soon." She retrieved a pouch from the pocket of her robes and laid it on the table. "Your little trinkets."

"You got them?" Lenore asked, untying the leather band holding the fabric in place and unrolling it.

Two metal disks gleamed in the flickering candlelight.

"Oh," Sophie said.

She stared at the Third Eyes for a full five seconds before snatching one then putting it in place. She reached for Fenrir, her numbness fading and an urgency rushing in. To speak with him. To hear his voice. To feel his presence after far too many days without it.

Fenrir.

Sophie? Is it really you?

It's me, and I have Lenore with me. We're safe. For now.

Where are you? What happened? I lost contact. Those guards. It's been six days. I thought you were…

His pain and fear infected her. After the elation of that initial connection, it was like a gut punch. Sophie was nauseous and dizzy from the ache of him. She could barely stand it.

We escaped, Sophie said.

Thanks to me, Lenore added.

Sophie focused on the physical space around her and looked for Lenore. Her daughter sat beside her, a Third Eye in place, smirking. She'd connected to them so effortlessly, finding the way to them all on her own and inserting herself into their conversation without being let in.

Lenore, Fenrir said.

Another wave of raw emotion smacked them, but this time, it was pure relief. The balm was soothing. Fenrir was safety again, Sophie's harbor, her anchor.

Lenore has done well, Sophie said. *Better than I would've ever hoped for, under the circumstances.*

Managing to make a compliment a jab? Lenore said. *Back to your old self already, I see.*

Her daughter's words cut Sophie deeply, but Lenore wouldn't feel that, only Fenrir could. Although Lenore was connected to them, communicating wordlessly, she wasn't synced. Not like Sophie and Fenrir.

Sophie could feel him. Close. So very close. Closer than he should be.

Fenrir, Sophie said, *where are you?*

Guilt. Panic. Pride. His masquerading as hers.

You left Simetria, Sophie said.

To save you, you and Lenore. I'm at the fishing village. I sail to the far shore tomorrow at first light.

Annoyance. Disgust. Disappointment. Hers.

Save us? Sophie said. *Come to rescue the two silly maidens locked away in the evil tower? Oh, my love, this look doesn't suit you. Not at all.*

Hurt. Anger. Defiance. His.

What was I supposed to do, Sophie? You and Lenore were captured, and I had no further information to work from. Of course I would come. I had to do everything in my power.

The model protector because we can't be expected to protect ourselves.

Sophie's bitterness surprised even her, but at the same time, she knew it had always been there. This savior routine wasn't unique to Fenrir. It was an annoying trait of his sex, and one she increasingly had no patience for. She didn't need protecting or coddling because those were just lovely words hiding an ugly truth—protection was just another kind of cage. Well, she'd had quite enough of cages.

I needed you in Simetria, Sophie said. *Not here.*

Simetria is fine. I left Nicolus in charge.

Panic. Irritation. Shame. Hers then his. He felt then saw the source of her fears.

He's on our side, Fenrir said. *He's been loyal all these years. A friend and ally in all ways.*

Only because we were there to keep his worst tendencies suppressed. He can't be trusted on his own. He's power hungry.

I'm watching him.

Not a sync? Sophie said.

Irritation. Impatience. His.

I'm not a fool, Fenrir said. *No, just the Third Eye.*

That's bad enough. You know who lurks in here. She could reach out to him and tell him everything.

Why would he believe her? He knows the Lady lies.

But they're not lies.

A hot, swirling vortex of anger. They were both caught in it, getting pulled under by the current that only grew more potent with each exchange.

Fine, Fenrir said. *I'll just turn around. I'll go back to Simetria and keep your throne warm.*

Oh, stop it, you two. Lenore's voice cut in and stilled their troubled waters. *Enough. Papa, come. Help us finish this thing. Simetria will survive a few days without the two of you.*

Lenore was right. Sophie's little corvid. They had escaped the confines of their cell, but they were by no means free. They would be hunted in a foreign city with customs they knew so little of. They had to navigate this strange place with care if they had any hope of doing what they'd come for. They needed Fenrir.

It could be that I'm being overly reactionary, Sophie said. *Let's blame it on the imprisonment. You'll come to Spirale, Fenrir, but only you. The wardens ought to stay in the village. Numbers work against us just now.*

Warmth. Wholeness. Belonging.

Where will I find you? he asked.

Sophie looked back into the physical world, where Helice sat.

"We have an ally coming tomorrow," Sophie said. "How can he get safe passage into the city and to us?"

"I will bring him," Helice said. "Tell him to meet me on the forest's tree line. Nearest to Spirale's gate, the same you entered through."

"A bit before sunset," Sophie said. "He should be there by then. His name is Fenrir."

I'll see you both soon, Fenrir said. *You don't know how hard it's been.*

Sophie did know. She felt his ache, still palpable, a gaping hole in him poorly concealed. But it would heal, and in a short while, they would be reunited. Whatever came next, whether they restored the Link node or not, at least they would be together.

BOUNTY

****ANNOUNCING AN ESCAPE OF PRISONERS****

In the night past, two prisoners held in Spirale for the atrocious MURDER of a poor unworthy in the Southern Forest escaped from their confinement in the Sanctum of the Sect of Sight. Said criminals are foreigners from another land who speak a strange tongue.

The appearances of the prisoners are as follows: One woman, red of hair and green of eye, young of age, tall and lean. One woman, blond of hair and green of eye, young of age, tall and lean though shorter than the other. Both are garbed in black trousers and dark green frocks.

Whosoever provides information vital to the apprehension of said criminals shall receive a handsome and gracious award of TWENTY coins-of-plenty upon their safe procurement. If any person concerned in the above escape will make a confession of their offense and aid in the apprehension of said criminals, a pardon for their crimes shall be on offer.

***Contact Voyant Superior Hubert Pomeau—
Sanctum of the Sect of Sight***

THE THIEF

"Keep going," Sophie said.

"How much longer?" Helice asked.

Sophie scowled and shook her head. Dirt had settled into the fine lines on her brow and made her look older. The flickering candlelight didn't help. Or the cold and smell of their haven in the sewer.

"Say it in your language," Sophie said. "Just a little more."

Helice sighed then gave off a string of gibberish interspersed with meaning. Each sentence brought more coherence. It was working. Lenore wore her Third Eye too. Helice's words benefited them both.

"I don't know ce que you voulez que je dise, but here I am chattering away. Should I speak of my city or the Sect? Or my work? Avant votre arrivée you and your sister—."

"Sister?" Sophie said.

Helice looked from Sophie to Lenore and back. "Sisters," she said, pointing at the two of them. "No? Between your looks and how you act toward one another, it seemed likely."

"We're blood relations, yes," Lenore said, "but she's got nearly three decades on me."

"Your mother?"

"Graced with fine looks still," Lenore said.

Sophie tossed her hand then used it to support her chin, elbow to the table, back hunched over. They were all exhausted. Despite the hay sitting in the corner, offering itself as a bed, none of them had slept.

"Mother and daughter, yes," Sophie said. "Now, shall we continue? The synthetics are nearly there."

"Understanding my words is one thing," Helice said, "but what about your speech?"

"This synthetic works both ways," Sophie said, pointing to her Third Eye with her words coming out in the foreign tongue.

Helice gaped. "You sound like us, not even a trace of an accent."

"Keep going," Sophie said. "If we're to converse with your friend when he arrives—"

"Not my friend," Helice said. "Better than that. He is blood and co-founder of the Fleur-de-lis."

"Is that the name you call yourselves?" Lenore asked. "The ones who stand against the Sect?"

"Yes, but our faction is only one of four dominant ones in Spirale. All with a shared hatred of the Sect but very different ideas on how we might defy them and what a world without them might look like."

Sophie slapped the table, and Helice and Lenore drew back.

"How many times must I say it? Use your foreign tongue. Everything you're saying right now should be in your language, not ours."

It was a strange sensation. Even though the words came to Lenore's mind in a form she could decipher, whether her own tongue or Helice's was used, there was a kind of flavor that distinguished them. Her mother was right though; they needed to practice and not just to get the vocabulary down.

They had to be able to intuitively switch between languages. One slip-up could be their undoing.

The door rattled, and the women went silent.

Someone's fist hammered on it then a gravelly voice called out. "Oh étourneau, étourneau, let me into your nest, won't you?"

"It's him," Helice said, jumping from her seat.

Sophie and Lenore stood in still damp but mildly cleaner clothing. Helice hurried to the door, unlatched the bolt, and cracked it a sliver.

"Good morning, Starling," a man said, still invisible through the door's narrow gap.

"Good morning, Falcon," Helice replied.

She swung the door aside and made way for their guest. In he strode, chest out, shoulders back, grin wide. He was striking—dark skin and eyes and hair, the latter kept in small braids and those held up in a high knot. His smile danced, sending constant currents through his light dusting of facial hair. He stepped into the cramped room and threw an arm to the side, the metal trinkets on his fingers, wrists, and neck jangling with the movement. He bowed then moved to Sophie, placed his hands on her shoulders, and planted a kiss to each cheek.

"What in the world?" Sophie said.

"You don't greet one another in this way?" Helice asked, in her own tongue this time.

"Not at all," Sophie said.

The man moved to Lenore and dropped two brief kisses on her cheeks. He gave off a scent of wood shavings.

"This is Guy," Helice said. "My cousin."

"Guy Zanon," he said.

Guy wore leather armor interspersed with common clothing, fitted trousers that left little to the imagination, a cloth sash striped in black and yellow, a vest with nothing underneath, his curled and wiry chest hairs peeking out. He was older than Lenore but younger than her mother, probably having seen just over three decades. A warmth stole over Lenore's cheeks owing to Guy's proximity, but his eyes were fixed on Sophie.

"They match the bounty's description," Guy said.

"They already have a bounty up?" Helice asked.

Guy dug in his pocket and pulled out a folded parchment. He handed it to Helice then picked up his former burden and offered the cloth sack to Sophie. "Ma chère, for you and the little lady."

Lenore clenched her jaw.

Sophie took the sack, opened, and peered inside. "What is it?"

"Clothing," Helice said. "We can't have you walking the streets in your strange garb."

"Walking the streets?" Lenore said.

Guy snapped his head to Helice and tsked her. "You didn't tell them?"

"Not yet," Helice said. She looked at Lenore and Sophie. "We need to move fast. The Sect still doesn't know why you came to Spirale, and that's to our advantage."

Sophie searched through the clothing, laying out each item on the table. Lenore moved to her side. The options were dismal, but then what else would they be? They needed to blend in with the locals, become invisible, which meant looking poor and unremarkable. Lenore never imagined she'd be so reluctant to remove her warden's garb.

"I'm taking you out into the city," Guy said. "I've things to show you, and we've plans to hatch."

Helice's and Guy's speech was clear now with only the occasional strange word. Lenore marveled at what the synthetics could do. No wonder her parents guarded the objects so jealously. Synthetics were knowledge. And power.

"I must go," Helice said. "Guy will take care of you. I'll be back with your ally come sunset."

"Where are you off to now?" Lenore asked.

"The Sect's Sanctum," Helice said. "This simple little sightless has no way of knowing the prisoners escaped. It would be odd for me not to go."

"But won't they suspect you of helping us?" Lenore asked.

Helice grinned. "The quiet and shy and obedient scribe freeing the two prisoners? It would never cross their minds."

"You had them put us in the same cell," Sophie said. "You can't know no one saw you come to us so late. There are too many loose threads they'll unravel once they dig deeply enough."

"Fret not," Guy said. "It's all been taken care of. An outside job, that's how we framed it. A couple of our people dressed strangely, moving through the streets near the Sanctum in the dead of night. A door's lock busted in. A guard knocked out cold but not before we slipped in some of your strange words for him to hear. Helice is safe. Don't you worry your lovely head. This isn't our first time toying with them."

"My, you've been busy," Sophie said with a grin.

Lenore rummaged through the clothing then shoved a particularly drab dress at her mother. "That's perfect for you."

Sophie took it, grimaced, and sighed.

"Don't forget the bonnets," Helice said, "to cover those synthetics and your hair." She moved to the door, slid the bar out of the way, and squeezed the latch. "Don't take unnecessary risks, Falcon," Helice said to Guy.

He laughed then grew grim, the contrast abrupt and unsettling. "Be safe, Starling."

Then Helice was gone, leaving the two women with this stranger in a foreign city hostile to them in all ways. Lenore spotted the parchment Guy had handed Helice. She picked it up and stared at the letters. They started as a jumbled mess that resolved into coherence within several seconds. The Third Eye even translated the written word.

"Is twenty coins-of-plenty a fair amount of money?" she asked.

Guy was at Sophie's side, holding up bonnets. "These are all too ugly to be set against such a face," he said.

What was this rage that filled Lenore? A roiling queasiness that wasn't nausea. She'd felt it before in her mother's presence but never so potently. When Guy twirled a lock of Sophie's hair and her mother just looked back with a knowing smile, the sensation made itself known. Jealousy. That's what she'd always felt and never put a name to. It was a part of that wall that existed between her and her mother, growing taller and more robust with the passing years. As Lenore had moved into womanhood, her own beauty flowered, but her mother's stubbornly persisted, managing to somehow bypass those unfailing laws of time. If Sophie hadn't already been labeled a saint, some might have taken to calling her a witch.

Lenore leaned over and snatched the bonnet from Guy's hand. "I think it's a perfect fit. Now, if you don't mind, we need some privacy." Lenore pointed to the door.

Guy shrugged and sauntered over and out. When the women were alone again, Lenore disrobed and donned a simple beige dress and white bonnet with a fringed hem. She pushed her hair in it and pulled it down to cover her Third Eye.

"You could stand to be a little more pleasant," Sophie said.

"You could stand to be a little less flirtatious."

Sophie slipped out of her warden's garb and into the dress and bonnet Lenore had suggested, both a pale blue. Sophie fluffed the dress and shook her head. "He's an ally, and I'm only responding in turn. It doesn't hurt anything to play his little game."

"You're leading him on."

"He doesn't mean anything by it. Trust me, I know his type."

Lenore stuffed the remaining clothing back into the sack, jamming it in harder than needed. "You don't know these people. This isn't Simetria."

Sophie reached a hand out and placed it on Lenore's. "I know men, and this is the game you have to play with them. We don't have many options, and if me idly flirting with this Guy earns us his trust faster than we could otherwise, I'll do it in an instant. There's no place for a moral high ground in these situations, little corvid."

"But Papa—"

"Will be here soon. In the meantime, we ensure Guy thinks kindly of us. Blood or not, it's best not to assume trust. Now, are we all set?"

Lenore looked her mother over, suddenly transformed into a low blood. "Let's see this Spirale."

***

Out on the city streets, Guy was a different person. He tucked his hands in his pockets, hunched his shoulders, and hurried through the sinuous thoroughfares. Lenore and Sophie followed just behind, terrified to lose their guide in the non-Euclidean chaos of the city. There was a kind of beauty to the randomness, a flavor of the organic, but it was incomprehensible. For all Lenore knew, they could be walking in circles.

The fog didn't help. It was nearly midday, so the chiming clocktower told them, and still the thick soup of vapors hadn't dispersed.

"This haze is so thick," Lenore said.

"It's the time of year for it," Guy said. "Let's just hope it clears soon. Visibility is key for where we go."

He led them through the city, a smell of salt on the air

pierced by the occasional high-pitched cries of those gray and white seabirds. The curves and bends of the buildings and streets bled together. The people too became a blurred mass, but their words at least were no longer a mystery. Lenore caught bits of conversation, idle chatter, gossip, phrasings not unlike those in Simetria's lower city. They weren't so different after all, at least when it came to the fundamentals of life— food, work, shelter, people. That's what dominated their talk. Nothing of sightless or vitres or voyants, but their distorted views did make themselves known in the place itself.

Spiral motifs abounded. Black appeared to be a favored shade. And then, there were the distortions themselves. Lenore hadn't known what life had been like in Simetria in the time of the Rot of the Link, but she'd heard stories. Of how distortions had been warded off and balustraded. Of the attuners that had crowded the roofscape. Of the surveyors who had frequented the streets in their trench coats and leather and glyph-inscribed garb.

Spirale was nothing like those stories. Distortions sat in the open pulsing, throbbing, wavering in the fog. Or so it was for Lenore whose Third Eye let her spot them. For the others, makeshift barriers of simple wood were painted a bright yellow in warning, the people of the city skirting them, tripping over one another as they were forced into bottlenecks. Some streets were completely lost to the things. Houses too. The distortions were an inconvenience for them. Just another obstacle in their daily comings and goings. Nothing like the horrors they had been framed as in Simetria.

That was strange for Lenore, but she didn't have the context her mother did. She glanced at Sophie as they passed a distortion and caught a pursing of her lips and a widening of her eyes. This had to be hard for her mother, to be so near these foul motes, to pretend it was the definition of normalcy when it had to be a sacrilegious perversion to her. Still, the distortions themselves did little besides their tireless dance of in and out. It was those they had come in contact with that disturbed Lenore most.

They passed a poor unworthy, one likely newly afflicted, lingering in an alley. Sophie grabbed Lenore's arm and stopped. Guy turned back.

"It's just out here?" Sophie said. "In the street? Free to brush up against any of us?"

"Shhh," Guy said. "Come."

Sophie shook herself out of her daze then walked abreast with Guy. Lenore followed just behind, craning in to catch their whispers.

"Why do they let them wander in your city?" Sophie asked. "It's just begging for more affliction."

"Affliction?" Guy asked.

"It's what happens to those who come in contact with vitres," Lenore said.

Guy stroked his chin, his other hand still tucked away in a pocket. "The fifth tenet of the Sect—poor unworthy must come to no harm."

Sophie's lip curled. "How are you all not afflicted?"

"The Sect corrals the poor unworthy every so often and tucks them away in the depths of the Fortress."

They passed a market filled with people, all surfaces covered in flyers. Their bounty was amongst them, but their disguises made them nigh unrecognizable. Lenore glanced at the other postings. Advertisements for goods and services. Appeals for lost items and pets. Announcements about the city and the Sect. One of the latter caught Lenore's attention mostly owing to its prevalence. It was the same sign over and over again bearing the words "Ascension Day" along with a man's face with two spirals for eyes.

They trudged on. More winding streets that grew ever thicker with bodies coupled with a droning murmur of a collection of voices. They pushed their way into an open square and found themselves in a kind of mass gathering with the prison they had only just escaped as the backdrop.

Lenore's stomach clenched. "Why do you bring us here?"

Guy furrowed his brow and shook his head. "Not the time to say such things." Then louder, "We come to hear the wisdom of the Voyant Supreme." He smirked and rolled his eyes then dropped his voice. "You should see our enemy in the flesh. To know what it is you're up against. She gives a speech soon."

Lenore recalled the statue they had walked past with the guards, that eerie presence sitting on a throne and staring at them from across a long and dimly lit hall, and that stalker who had walked by her cell that first night in the Sanctum. They were all one and the same, a woman who emanated a darkness. But as the woman marched out of the Sanctum's wrought-iron gates, flanked by a set of three guards on each side, swaying with every stride, arms arcing across her body, Lenore realized she'd misjudged. The woman didn't give but rather took, not emanating darkness but absorbing the light, warmth, wholeness. She was an absence, a void.

"Celeste Wilmot," Guy said. "Leader of the Sect of Sight. Voyant Supreme since its founding over five centuries ago."

"She's lived for centuries?" Sophie said.

"So the stories say," Guy added. "Another mystery surrounding the voyants—their timelessness."

Celeste ascended the wooden stage set before the crowd. The construction was only large enough for one person, elevating her above the masses. She rested her hands on the railing, and the crowd went silent. It was unnatural, the speed and totality of the loss of sound. The crowd waited in expectation. Lenore squinted, but the finer details of their nemesis were lost to distance. A slender woman dressed in a fitted black gown with a plunging neckline, long black hair, but that was all she could make out.

"Today marks two weeks until our much-anticipated Ascension Day," Celeste said, her voice carrying effortlessly, seeming to defy physics and sounding just next to the ear. "Preparations will begin in earnest for the festivities, the carnival for the sightless and the gala for the voyants. This is my gift to you as it has been for all these long years. It is a chance for us to come together, not just as Spiraleans, but as loyal servants of the Sect of Sight, in the hope that, one day, we too may follow my father's path of enlightenment and ascend to another plane of existence. Remember, we are all gifted the eyes within and so capable of becoming voyants, but only the worthiest will join our ranks. Stay true, and you may find you too are open to another sight."

The crowd burst into cheers so loud and potent Lenore feared a frenzy would overtake them all. A hand grabbed hers and tugged. Guy pulled her and Sophie along until they found refuge in an alley. They looked at one another with frantic eyes.

"What was that?" Sophie asked. "To command the crowd in such a way."

"You see now," Guy said. "The voyants are no mere ruling class. Empty words she speaks at every such occasion, and yet the response shows more is at play."

"What is this Ascension Day?" Lenore asked.

"A celebration, but more on this later. Come, we have one last stop."

They navigated the alleys, avoiding the main thoroughfares. They could hear the crowd dispersing. After several blocks, they stopped at the foot of a tower holding the face of a clock. A set of stairs led to a wooden door. Guy rummaged in his trouser pocket and fished a skeleton key from it. He glanced down the street and over his shoulder then unlocked the door and ushered them in. The air was close and musty, the only light filtering in through the rafters overhead.

"Follow me and stay close," Guy said, his hands patting the stone of the walls and guiding them. He stopped. "We climb."

A ladder creaked as he ascended. Pigeons cooed overhead. Lenore followed Sophie who followed Guy. They climbed, rung by rung, at least five stories. Their ascent brought more light along with the ticking of a clock's second hand. Near the top, the mechanics of the timepiece came into view. Scores of cogs in a complex arrangement. Pulleys here and there. They dismounted the ladder and stepped onto a landing. A waist-high rope separated their walkway from all the temporal mechanisms. Guy led them to a door then they were stepping into fresh, salt-laden air with Spirale sitting below, the fog largely gone now.

Lenore placed her hands on the stone rail and leaned over before Guy grabbed her shoulder and pulled her back.

He wagged a finger and tsked. "Best not to be seen here. Just because I have a key doesn't mean I'm welcome. You two even less so."

Lenore nodded and kept her back pressed against the wall of the tower.

"Come this way," Guy said.

He rounded a corner, and Sophie and Lenore followed. Their eyes met a striking skyline. Even at these heights, Spirale's uniqueness was apparent. To their left, an expanse of silver stretched to the horizon. So close to the water, and they hadn't even known it, holed up as they'd been. Their long trek along the beach then through the forest, a waste bred from ignorance of this land. If the fishing village sailors had brought them directly to Spirale's port, decorated by scores of masts, maybe Jasmine would still be alive. Maybe they never would have killed an afflicted, been branded as wicked ones, and stuck in this awful mess. Then again, Spirale was what it was. They had come to cleanse the Link node, and the voyants never would have taken kindly to their aims. No, better that things had worked out as they had, despite their suffering. They had found Helice and now Guy, potential allies to help them navigate this odd city and its customs.

Guy pointed, and his outstretched arm forced Lenore's gaze to her right where clusters of chimneys and windows were set into sharply sloped roofs. But Guy gestured to another construction set in the background, a shard of glass reflecting its surrounds, climbing into the very sky. A relic of the Old World in their midst looking timeless, not buried under the city.

"The Sect's Fortress," Guy said. His arm swung farther to the right to the domed structure of black stone Celeste had given her speech in front of. The same Lenore and Sophie been imprisoned in. "And their Sanctum, which you know only too well."

Lenore took a step forward then remembered she had to stay unseen. She squinted to try to make out the finer details, but even with the fog lifted, distance blurred the scene. Guy grabbed a cylindrical pouch attached to his sash, popped the lid off, and pulled a metallic tube from it.

He extended the spyglass then offered it to Sophie. "Take a peek."

Sophie peered down the tube. "What am I looking for?"

Guy came in close, wrapped an arm around her shoulder, and pointed with his other hand at the Fortress. "Study it. Commit its structure to memory. Learn every little thing you can about it. This is where the object of your aims is housed."

"You mean the console?" Sophie asked.

"If that is what you call it, then yes. Sect doctrine says it is the Hole, the source of all the vitres. It's why the Fortress is there."

Sophie moved the spyglass and inspected the structure. Lenore looked on with impatience.

"How does one get in?" Sophie asked. "I don't see any gates in the walls around it."

Guy grinned and shrugged. "A very good question. Only the voyants are allowed in. Only they know how to enter."

The framing was so unlike Simetria, where the Source had been buried and hidden, but the Fortress was similar in its dominant purpose—to keep the people away from the Link node.

Lenore's mind strayed to the Old World. "Tunnels?" she asked.

"Most probably," Guy said, "but there's a way for us to gain access without needing to answer such questions ahead of time."

Sophie handed the spyglass back to Guy. "And that is?"

"The gala Celeste spoke of. We make sure to get ourselves invited to it, and it'll be our ticket into the Fortress."

REUNION

Fenrir fought the urge to activate his Third Eye. He would see Sophie soon. There was no need to pester her. Still, he longed to hear her voice after the extended silence. His hand twitched, and he gripped his fauchard tighter. He was all nerves. The dark of the forest to his back, the openness of the field before him. He was alone, having followed Sophie's advice. The wardens who had accompanied her waited at the ready in the fishing village across the water. This was a covert operation now. If that changed, if they needed strength in numbers, Nicolus was one thought away with his Third Eye, and he would have pigeons sent to the wardens to instruct them as Fenrir wished. But that was the plan in reserve. The present situation called for delicacy and patience.

Just as his excess energy forced Fenrir to pace, a figure approached from the fields, but the movement was hurried and chaotic. As they neared, the details resolved. Arms were pumping, legs were scurrying, the chest was heaving, yet it was no ordinary jog. This person was frantic in their fleeing from the creature pursuing them. Fenrir didn't need sight to tell him what it was because as both prey and predator neared the tree line, that characteristic tug of distortions accosted him.

Fenrir sprinted forward, out of the forest, fauchard at the ready, boots padding the dying grass. The pursued passed him, her dark eyes wide as he bore down on her pursuer. It was low to the ground, partly covered by the field's growth, but this worked to Fenrir's advantage. Having gone so many years without seeing an afflicted, Fenrir didn't know just how he would react to his first encounter with one—to freeze at the mere sight of it or power through the terror and let muscle memory take over even while the mind flattered?

Without a clear view of the horror itself, any hold the afflicted might otherwise have had on him was diminished. A mass of hair and claws, limbs uselessly sticking from its back, a nausea-inducing stench, that was all Fenrir took note of before he was enacting his mercy killing. Clean swipes, a cleaving of the thing in two then four then onward until he lost count of the bisections, of the chunks of twisted flesh this onetime fauna had become. It wailed and screeched, the sonic onslaught tearing at the fabric of Fenrir. There was no other surveyor here to sweep in and save him were he to drop his fauchard and shield his ears. There would be no role reversal this time, Sophie saving him as he had done so long ago in the Old World with her.

All he could do was resist, and he did. So close now to his wife and daughter, after braving the long journey alone to this shore, to lose himself now? It was unthinkable. A cruel jest of fate he would have no part it. His fauchard sliced and sliced until whatever mouth or mouths the beast's howls erupted from were hacked into nothingness, only stopping when the afflicted had been reduced to a quivering mass of flesh, viscera, and offal.

Fenrir's chest heaved. His ears rang. The entirety of him buzzed. Was it any surprise a smile spread across his lips, him having performed the very act he'd been so lauded for, decades past? A sliver of his faded youth returned. A long-lost hunger satiated. A physical release of all his worry and angst during his travels, of a wife and daughter captured, beaten, maybe even defiled.

But they were safe now, this he knew. Yet the aftereffects of his anxieties lingered. The bile that had built up as he'd fretted on horseback, sat in a waterlogged tent cursing the darkness of night that stymied his efforts, bobbed in a boat as he crossed the waters. Here, at last, he'd found a kind of release so that his mind sang even while his body screamed. He wasn't fully healed from his fall off that cliff in the Old World. He only hoped the new aches stemmed from unhappy muscles, tendons, and ligaments and didn't correlate to wounds reopened.

"Thank you," the woman said in Fenrir's tongue, though with an accent. She was young, dark of skin and hair, wearing beige robes, carrying a sack. "I am Helice, and based on what you just did, I assume you must be Fenrir?"

"I am," he said then gestured with his fauchard at the remains of the afflicted. "Was this the only afflicted?"

"Yes, it took me by surprise hiding in the grass. And, just so you know, we call them poor unworthy in Spirale. Make sure to use our words from here on."

Fenrir nodded then returned to the forest for his pack. From it, he retrieved a cloth with delicate triangular patterns stitched into it and wiped the gore from his blade with care.

Helice pointed to his Third Eye. "Sophie said you would have such a synthetic. We need to train it to understand our language. Let us sit a while and do that."

Fenrir finished tending to his polearm then stood. "First, I need to construct a ward around the afflict—or rather, poor unworthy."

"A ward?"

"A kind of buffer or shield that will keep its distortions from affecting our Euclidean space. Just chalk to stone." He pulled a stick of chalk from a pouch on his belt and held it up between them.

"I would caution against that," Helice said. "If one of my people were to find a poor unworthy maimed so with strange symbols arranged around it, they would know it had something to do with foreigners."

Fenrir tucked the chalk back in its pouch and nodded. "A sound point. Well then, shall we?" He tossed his hand at the log.

They both took up residence on it.

"Are you ready?" Helice asked.

Fenrir nodded. They spent the next half hour talking in only the loosest of terms. In actuality, Helice spouted strings of nonsense at him. He waited for comprehension to sink in, and it did, slowly. Stray words were coherent then phrases then sentences until the odd words became the exception rather than the norm. This continued until he was able to truly converse, to hear and understand and be understood in turn.

"This is good," Helice said. "We're nearly ready to go into the city."

Fenrir rose from the log.

Helice nudged a cloth sack with her boot. "Find something you like and change into it then stow your garb."

She stood and walked to the tree line, her back to Fenrir. He looked through the options and settled on a simple set of pants and a tunic, not all that dissimilar from the attire he'd worn as a toller. He switched his clothing out then stuffed his warden's garb into the sack. He brought it and his polearm along with him until he stood at Helice's side.

Her eyes strayed to his polearm. "You can't bring that into Spirale. You'll have to hide it."

Fenrir was loath to part with his fauchard, to be defenseless in a hostile city, but it would be pointless to argue. Moving forward, he would just have to do without.

"Very well," he said.

Helice took the sack from him while he found a place to stow his beloved weapon, constructing a makeshift marker with stones and sticks so he might find it later. Then, they set off into the open field, passing the afflicted's quivering and steaming remains, then onward to the city, closer to Sophie and Lenore, nearer to their goal. Fenrir felt it. Even at such a distance, the distortions made themselves known. That old familiar unease and discomfort tugged at him. They were everywhere, and they were many.

He grimaced then smiled. The surveyor in him was waking like an old friend almost forgotten but well received. It made the march into danger less harrowing. A film buffered Fenrir. Everything felt so far away. He glided along, tracing Helice's footsteps, moving among these foreigners, their city become his, a staunch desire to cleanse it taking hold of him. They had erred. Made a mistake. Captured his wife and daughter and treated them horridly. No matter. It was done, the past, and he resolved to hold no grudges. They were lost, like all of Simetria had been.

Or, so Fenrir imagined until he heard the truth, sitting with Helice in a shack somewhere deep in the winding chaos of the city with Sophie and Lenore set to arrive in short order.

"The Sect rules Spirale," Helice said. "They worship the vitres, what you call distortions. They bear them, those who lead the Sect, the voyants. The rest of us are sightless. We obey with the hope that, one day, we too can become voyants. Gifted the eyes within and open to another sight."

It didn't make sense. Any of it. How could anyone frame the distortions as holy? The afflicted as blessed?

"But they lie," Helice said. "I don't know how they take on the vitres, but it isn't what they claim. They know something the rest of us don't. Something that lets them take on vitres and survive with their mind intact, their bodies timeless."

"When you say timeless, do you mean they don't age?" Fenrir asked.

"Or age unequally. After taking on a vitre for the first time, they might mature for a little while longer, but at some point, yes, they cease to age as we do. None look older than middle age."

Fenrir glanced at the sole window, coated with dust or grime or both. The light out there was failing. He felt Sophie drawing near. He stood then a series of knocks sounded at the door, complex, a code. Helice hurried to the threshold and tapped a response. She waited a few seconds then unlatched and opened the door. Three figures slipped in, the door shut and barred behind them without delay. A man and two women. Even with their disguises, Fenrir knew them both as soon as he laid eyes on them. He rushed in.

Lenore met him first. "Papa, you don't know how glad I am to see you."

"Lenore," he said, holding her, her face pressed into his chest.

He looked over her head at Sophie, smiling, lingering. No dramatic outward display of affection from her. Composed, assured, professional. But Fenrir didn't require such blatant signs of his wife's love for him. He knew how pleased she was to see him too.

"He's your father?" Helice asked.

"Couldn't you tell?" Sophie said. "She takes after him more than me, I'd say."

"Your husband?" the man asked, inspecting Fenrir from head to toe, his eyes lingering longer than they needed to on certain parts, a rival inspecting the competition, no doubt.

He was lean and lithe, like Fenrir, but more roguish with a dangerous grin.

"This is Guy," Sophie said to Fenrir then added to Guy,

"Did you think a woman like me wouldn't already be spoken for?"

She moved closer to Fenrir and placed a hand on his cheek. She was playing a game, and Sophie didn't do such things without reason. Fenrir took her hand in his and kissed the palm. He watched Guy from the corner of his eye. Guy's grin only widened; he liked the game, it seemed.

"I would give much to stay a while longer," Guy said, "but I've delivered my charges. Too much still to do, and far too little time. I'll return soon."

"Take care, Falcon," Helice said.

"Starling," he replied, before slipping out the door.

Lenore released Fenrir. Sophie migrated to the table Fenrir and Helice had been sitting at the past few hours, a bowl of cold gruel half eaten. Fenrir and Lenore followed Sophie. The three sat down, beaming, in disbelief at their luck in making it back to one another.

"Did you have any trouble getting here?" Sophie asked.

"The trip to the fishing village went smoothly. The same with crossing the water, but I had a run-in with an afflicted in the forest."

"And?" Sophie asked.

"I brought rot to the undying, although I might have overexerted myself in the process."

Sophie shook her head and clicked her tongue. "Silly man."

Fenrir leaned over and rummaged in his bag then pulled a diskette free and set it on the table. "As instructed, I retrieved the relic from Journeyman Frye."

Sophie ran her fingers along the diskette's case then pulled it toward her. "Very good, my love."

"And you?" Fenrir asked. "How have you been?"

He already knew. Even when they weren't synced, Fenrir could feel emotions in Sophie. They were faded and indistinct, like a cousin to déjà vu or the remnants of a potent dream that's fled from one's memory on waking. Sophie was better, especially since seeing him, but her spirit was wounded from her ordeal. And what of Lenore? He'd had no sync with her, not yet, and so didn't have a window into her mind.

"We're ready to do what needs to be done," Lenore said.

"Good," Fenrir said. "The sooner we restore the Link node, the better."

The three of them glanced at Helice, lingering in the shadows. Lenore pulled the only remaining chair out and waved for Helice to sit. She came over and stood behind it, her hands resting on its back, gripping the wood.

"I'd like to thank you for bringing Fenrir," Sophie said to her. "He'll be invaluable in achieving our goal, and I know you put yourself at risk getting him to us."

"You could have mentioned he was your husband," she said.

"Why does that matter?" Lenore asked.

"Strong bonds can make people do foolish things," Helice said.

"Fenrir will be invaluable in achieving our goal," Sophie repeated.

Helice moved into her seat and sat with her hands folded in her lap. "Guy showed you what we're up against?"

Sophie and Lenore nodded, their smiles shifting to frowns.

"The woman and her Fortress," Sophie said to Helice then looked at Fenrir and added, "Their Link node is in that enormous tower. I'm sure you saw it on your way in."

A glass shard that made all other structures cower in its presence. How could he not?

"Only voyants can enter their Fortress freely," Sophie said. "The ones who bear distortions like badges of pride. Do you know they worship them?"

"I told him," Helice said. "We were in the middle of discussing the ways of Spirale when you arrived."

"So, what is it we're up against?" Fenrir asked.

Helice moved her hands to the table, balled into one fist with the fingers intertwined. The candlelight was faint and unsteady, but even so, traces of ink were visible under her fingernails.

"Nine cities," she said. "This is what the Sect of Sight lays claim to, and you would be aiming to destroy all it holds dear. The vitres are everything to the Sect. The head of the beast is Celeste Wilmot. Timeless, like the rest of the voyants, but alive for far, far longer. Centuries."

With an immortal at the helm, it was no wonder Spirale put Simetria to shame. No petty conflicts over a transfer of power when an Archbishop died or resigned. No changes in policy with the passing years. Just a solid, unerring presence guiding them.

"We saw her today," Lenore said. "She gave a speech. The words were generic, but she had such an aura. It was unsettling."

"Where did she come from?" Fenrir asked.

"Here," Helice said, "or the city Spirale was before. Her father, Henri, founded the Sect. He was the first to learn how to take on vitres."

A woman from the time just after the Old World. The daughter of Spirale's version of Marcos Frenwith.

"And the people, they support her?" Fenrir asked.

"They seemed in awe of her," Sophie said.

"The Sect lies," Helice cut in. "When we expose that lie, our people will turn against her."

"What lie exactly?" Sophie asked.

Helice let a few seconds pass then rose from her chair. "They dangle paradise in front of us. The promise of another sight, of timelessness, but they know we'll never have it. They decide who becomes a voyant, not fate or destiny. They use it to control us, silence us, keep us inactive and obedient. If the people knew, they would tear the whole twisted system apart in an instant."

"And you have proof?" Sophie asked. "Not just theories or heresy but bona fide proof?"

Helice grinned. "We will, soon, very soon, but that's not your concern. You're not here to ignite our revolution. You're here to destroy the source of the vitres, no? This is what we need. It's the missing piece in our coup. Without it, we'd never be able to entirely remove the voyants from power, at least not without much time and effort."

"But with the vitres gone, disappearing from our world in seconds," Lenore said, "the voyants would die." She looked to Fenrir and Sophie. They nodded grimly to confirm her words. They'd seen it happen firsthand in the Old World when they'd destroyed the Rot of the Link.

"Exactly," Helice said. "Your goal aligns with ours. The trouble is where it lies. In the Sect Fortress with no known entry or exit. And where within the Fortress itself, I can't say."

"Tracking down the exact location of the Link node won't be an issue," Sophie said, nodding at Fenrir then speaking to him within their minds. *I can feel them, even with my distortion gone. And Lenore can spy them too with the update installed on our Third Eyes.*

Fenrir gave the slightest of nods to her then looked at Helice. "So then, how do we gain access to the Fortress?"

"There's a celebration taking place in two weeks' time," Helice said, "one that occurs every year. Ascension Day. Scores of voyants from other Sect cities come for a gala held in the Fortress. The visiting voyants and their servants are housed there. It's our best chance for gaining access."

"Two weeks isn't a lot of time," Fenrir said, strumming his fingers on the wood of the table, made irregular by the numerous nooks and crannies etched into it. "If you aim to infiltrate their gala, it will likely take impeccable planning."

"And so it has," Helice said. "We've been working on this for months. We've had the idea for far longer. You all just happen to fall into our laps at this critical moment. Fate perhaps?"

"Fate on both ends," Lenore added. "I don't see how we would ever make our way into the Fortress without this gala."

Fenrir was pleased. His daughter and wife had done remarkably well, taking such a disastrous miscalculation—the assumption that these people would despise the distortions as Simetria had—and turning it on its head.

"So how exactly do we get into the gala?" Sophie asked.

Helice pursed her lips and narrowed her eyes, back to that inscrutable scribe. "Not yet. Such things are closely guarded secrets. Only the Fleur-de-lis are privy to them."

"How can we be expected to help if you won't tell us what we're doing?" Sophie asked.

"We'll tell you everything, but only once you've proven yourselves to us."

"How do we do that?" Lenore asked, leaning forward, eyes locked on Helice.

"Guy will explain this to you when he returns. It's his idea."

***

"We're after a very specific document," Guy said.

They were in the cellar of the house now, flanking a large pine table covered in books and parchment, more materials piled on crates nearby. This place was well-used and frequented. Guy unrolled a document, laid it flat on the table, and used cups to hold the edges down. Fenrir, Sophie, and Lenore craned in to see what was set to the worn and wrinkled paper. Black ink mimicked an overhead view of Spiral, sketches of little houses and thoroughfares.

Guy tapped a spot on the map. "Us." He dragged his finger to a portion of the map where the buildings were spaced farther apart and took up larger swathes of land. "Our target—the Bain Manor, home of voyants Jean and Julie Bain." Guy wore a grin, but his eyes screamed of poorly concealed rage. "They have the document we seek in a lockbox in Monsieur Bain's study."

Guy retrieved another rolled parchment and overlaid it on the map of Spirale. This one depicted a home's interior, bare bones, sans furnishings.

"The Bain Manor." He tapped a finger on the kitchen and the servants' entrance. "Our means in." His finger slid to the second story and a room there. "The study."

"We have someone on the inside," Helice added. "They know the combination to the lockbox and will guide you there."

"*You*, as in *us*?" Sophie asked.

"One of you and me," Guy said. "Whichever you like. We let you choose, although stealth is invaluable. Quicker and quieter are preferred."

"I'll go," Lenore said, hands on the table, eyes hard.

She'd changed from her trials in this foreign land. Confident and eager yet stern. Being locked in a cell after a lifetime of comfort and freedom tended to instigate a transformation. It had for Ashtin, at any rate.

"Brave and pretty," Guy said.

A burst of red showed on Lenore's cheeks. Like mother, like daughter. Guy didn't seem to care whether Fenrir was present or not. He flirted openly with Sophie and Lenore alike.

"Brave she may be," Sophie said, "but I won't hear of it."

"Mama, I can do this."

Sophie held up a hand. "I'm sure you could, my little corvid, but I already made the mistake of putting you in harm's way unnecessarily. This is my mess. I'll be the one to clean it up."

Lenore's lower lip stuck out, and she gripped the table with both hands. "But I'm the reason we're here in the first place, aren't I?"

"No, you're actually not," Sophie said. "You may have helped the Disaffected, but you didn't create them. They were always going to threaten the Link. Their little stunt simply pushed us into action. Now, I'm going, and my decision is final."

Sophie stared Lenore down until she'd won. She glanced at Fenrir, but he only shook his head and smiled with no objections to voice. Sophie knew her own limitations. Her taking on this task meant she could handle it.

"Now that's settled," Sophie said, "tell us more about this document we're pilfering."

"The proof of the lie," Helice said.

"A Permission," Guy added.

The Spiraleans both went silent.

"Which is what exactly?" Sophie asked.

Guy glanced at Helice then back to Sophie. "That's not for you to know just now. Prove yourself to us first, then we share such details."

"I don't like this," Fenrir said. "You're asking an awful lot of us but not being very forthcoming yourselves. Trust goes both ways."

Sophie shook her head. "No, no, it's understandable. And they've already shown us immense trust, freeing Lenore and me, retrieving you. So, we do things their way. We help to snatch this Permission from the voyant home, and then we get our answers, yes?"

"Yes," Helice said.

"Tomorrow night," Guy said. "We've waited for this long enough already." He looked at Helice who met his eyes, frowned, and nodded. No grin for either of them, just determination and an ache.

INVITATION

Occasion: Ascension Day Gala
Location: Sect of Sight Fortress, Spirale
Date: 19th November

To my fellow voyants,

I welcome you to celebrate the day marking the ascension of my father, Henri Wilmot, to another plane. Each delegation is encouraged to send six delegates, to be chosen by your city's Voyant Superior, to represent your fine city at the festivities.

Upon arriving in Spirale, report to the north entrance of the Sect of Sight's Sanctum between midday and nightfall. Accommodations and service will be provided on the grounds of the Sect of Sight's Fortress. Let us celebrate all that makes our Sect flourish and give the sightless hope to which they can aspire.

Celeste Wilmot
Voyant Supreme

For we are gifted the eyes within and open to another sight

A THEFT

A vagabond scurrying through the night, that's what Sophie felt like, decked in all black, a mask covering the lower half of her face, hair concealed by a hood. When Guy moved, she followed. When he halted, she froze. Far too many starts and stops for her liking. Then again, caution was warranted. Even in the thick of the night, Spiraleans were afoot and, worse, the afflicted. Their cries of agony echoed through the narrow corridors.

Guy and Sophie were hurrying down a street when the clatter of plate armor sounded from around a bend. Guy stiffened. Sophie backtracked to an alley they had only just passed. Guy followed, and they took cover behind a stack of crates. The ground was waterlogged and stinking. If that wasn't enough, a veritable tangle of vermin writhed in the shadows, chattering, squeaking. Sophie's skin crawled at their sheer number and the violence of their whirlwind movements.

The duo of guards walked by, eyes trained forward, hands on sword hilts. Once the armored footfalls were only distant clanks, Sophie and Guy ventured out of their refuge. A gate sat in the distance. A city within the city, the walled enclave of the voyants, the estates separated from the rabble by stone and mortar and armored guards. Guy sprinted forward, and Sophie had no choice but to follow, her heart beating violently, her lungs heaving. Give her an afflicted to face down, and she would be almost serene. Not so with such human antagonists. She'd only ever caused the death of two unafflicted persons directly, Leida and Vergil, and she hoped to never again repeat such a heinous act. De facto leader of Simetria or not, Sophie refused to let herself become callous to death.

Guy and Sophie migrated from alcove to alcove, nearing the inner wall by degrees. Once they were adjacent to the barrier, Guy led them along its periphery to a cart sitting idle. A man leaned against it, chewing on a bit of hay, arms and ankles crossed, a hood shielding his face.

"Did you know," he said, "flowers flourish when watered by tears?"

"Only lilies," Guy replied.

The man removed his cloak's hood, the pale moonlight exposing him as a youth, not much older than Lenore, with long and wavy black hair worn in a loose ponytail. His blue eyes, seemingly stuck in a perpetual squint, ran over Sophie then strayed back to Guy.

"Is everything set?" Guy asked.

The young man nodded and spat out his bit of straw. He rubbed the back of his gloveless hand across his nose vigorously. A nervous tick? A release of pent-up energy? Sophie hoped Guy's people weren't as green as this one looked.

"I'll go in first to help Esme with the servants," the young man said. "You'll wait in the cart under the burlap." He glanced at Sophie. "So she's one of them then?"

"Sophie," Guy said, pointing to her then to the man, "Bastien. Other pleasantries will have to wait. Ticktock."

Bastien looked up and down the street then flung aside the burlap in the cart's rear. "In you go."

Guy hopped onto the cart, and Sophie did likewise. Bastien tossed the burlap over them and secured it with rope.

"Don't make a sound," he said, just a voice to Sophie now, her world reduced to fibrous-laden air, ever warming from her and Guy's breath.

The cart jostled then lunged forward. The wheels creaked. Bastien huffed and groaned, pulling the collective weight of the cart and its load of two concealed riders. A murmuring sounded then resolved into banter between two guards standing watch at the inner wall's gate.

"I'm telling you, she was falling all over herself at the look of me," a nasally voice whined. "Hips swaying, tits almost falling out of her bodice."

"A whore," a deeper, cracked voice said.

"No, I know the whores."

"I bet you do."

"Not like that. They're always peddling their goods in the street near where I live. She wasn't one of them."

Bastien stopped and cleared his throat. "I've a delivery for the Bain Manor."

There was a rustling of cloth and a crinkling of parchment, Bastien retrieving a document, then a clattering of metal against stone from a guard stepping forward.

"Bit late for deliveries," the deep voice said.

"Running behind," Bastien replied. "Too little hands what with Ascension Day bearing down on us."

"A fine time for everyone except us guards and you delivery folk. Well, your papers are good. Go on in."

The cart rocked and clattered along, the guards' voices resuming their conversation then fading altogether. The journey seemed to take ages without Sophie's dominant sense to guide her. Even once the cart stopped, Sophie and Guy stayed motionless. She had a thousand questions to ask but knew better than to utter a sound. This wasn't her mission.

She was only here to prove she would help these Fleur-de-lis with their cause. Her curiosity would have to be unappeased for the time being.

Just when the heat and lack of fresh air were becoming unbearable, a door creaked open, shoes stomped against cobblestone, and a labored breath huffed. Then the burlap was pulled aside. A young woman peered down, the spitting image of Bastien complete with the same pinched features.

"We're ready," she said to Guy.

He jumped from the cart and offered a hand to Sophie. She laid hers in his and smiled as he helped her down. They stood in a courtyard, stone on all sides, the walls, the ground. The only exception was one lonely tree, a small thing, but its gnarled branches and the deep crevasses in its bark hinted at the deception. Not a sapling but rather simply stunted by malnourishment. The wind rustled the few leaves stubbornly hanging on its branches, the ones already shed caught in cyclones. It was a clear night with a moon far too luminous, exposing them and their furtive deeds.

Guy tossed his hand at the young woman. "Esme," he said to Sophie then to Esme, "Sophie."

The two women nodded at one another before Esme turned on her heel and strode stiffly into the manor. Even with the courtyard's stone walls shielding them from curious eyes, it was best not to linger. Guy and Sophie entered, masks still covering their faces. Esme guided them into the kitchen. It was chaos in the aftermath of dinner, plates and glasses cluttering the countertops and in need of a cleaning, half eaten dishes in their pots and pans. Sophie glanced around, but there was no one to see or hear.

"The servants?" she asked.

"In the cellar, locked away," Esme replied then to Guy added, "The voyants are in the parlor. Bastien is ready when you are."

"The lockbox first," Guy said.

Esme trotted up a staircase, and they followed. Given Spirale's penchant for twisted geometries, Sophie suspected the interior of the voyants' homes would err toward those unholy perversions, but to her surprise, the halls were linear, lacking bowing or irregularities. In fact, the only signs of homage to the non-Euclidean were slight flourishes present on doorways and in picture frames. Then again, at some point, practicality had to win out. How much easier was it to construct a straight passage than one with infinite complexities? Sophie was thankful for the familiarity. She needed all her mental energies focused on the task ahead, not grappling with vertigo or unease.

After ascending the steps, Esme led Sophie and Guy down a hall to a shut door. She pulled a ring of keys from her pocket. Taken with her appearance, Sophie was beginning to piece the situation together. Esme wasn't just a Fleur who'd stolen her way into this manor. She was a servant who'd called this place home for some time, dressed in maid's attire, trusted with the housekeys, able to fool and imprison her fellows.

Esme unlocked the door, opened it, and crept in. The room was cluttered and mostly occupied by shelving crammed with books. The sole article of furniture—a massive oak desk. The study was dark with the only illumination coming from a single beam of moonlight filtering in through a partly cracked curtain and cleaving the room in half.

"Here," Esme said, waving to a metal safe no taller than her knee. It sat on the floor, tucked behind the desk.

Guy hurried to her side. They knelt, Esme turning the lock's dial, one number after another, Guy grimacing more with each movement. Finally, the lock gave, and Guy greedily grabbed at the handle. Esme backed away and stood, hands clasped in front, patient and somber. Guy retrieved the contents and tossed aside anything not made of parchment—jeweled necklaces, coins, a bar of gold. After rifling through the entirety of the safe, he deposited a stack of documents on the desktop and ran through each, one by one. His eyes were hungry for the bounty he sought, the moment he found it marked by the smile lines that formed at his eyes' corners, a large grin gracing his face under his mask, no doubt.

Guy scanned the contents then tapped a finger to the parchment and looked at his two companions. "This is it." Before Sophie could step closer to inspect the find, he folded it and stowed it in his vest's pocket. "Now," he said, "let's visit the Bains."

Sophie frowned. They had come for the document, the same they had in hand. What else was there to be done? Guy rounded the desk. Esme took the lead again, bringing them back down the way they'd come, through the kitchen then into a hall. Guy moved differently now, more relaxed, no longer in a partial crouch with light steps. As they passed open doorways, he didn't bother to check for any inhabitants. He took long and powerful strides until they found Bastien, standing silent a few paces from an open doorway, light streaming out, soft voices murmuring from within. Esme pointed at the threshold. Guy nodded, and the Fleurs flew into action.

Guy was the first into the room followed by Bastien then Esme. Sophie rounded the corner and hovered near the doorway. Guy and Bastien rushed the voyants, Jean and Julie Bain. Esme was in and out of the room in seconds, running past Sophie, carrying a small bundle whose terrified cries exposed it as a child. Sophie was frozen, watching as Guy wrestled with Jean and Bastien subdued Julie. Guy kneed Jean in the groin, and down he went. Julie wailed, helpless in Bastien's iron grip, one hand on her throat, the other securing both her wrists. Jean was slumped over attempting to recover from the blow when Guy grabbed a handful of his fair hair. He pulled Jean's head back, slipped a dagger from his boot, and spoke into the voyant's ear.

"This is for Antonette, you swine."

Guy ran the knife across Jean's throat. Blood sprayed. Guy released Jean who grabbed in vain at his wound, fingers useless in stemming that endless tide. He tried to cry out, but his yells only sounded as a gurgling until he fell forward on the thick carpet underfoot.

"I know you're still in there," Guy said, leaning down and using Jean's fine tunic to wipe the blood from his dagger. He kicked the body, but it was still. Guy landed another blow and another and another.

"Please," Julie whimpered.

"Shh, now," Bastien said.

He pulled a knife from his own boot, rubbed it gently along Julie's neck, then pulled away in one grand sweeping motion. Julie's cries faded as she choked on her own blood, the dark liquid spilling onto her dress of silk and lace. Bastien pushed her away. Eventually, she stilled and slumped over, as inert as her husband.

"What on Earth is going on?" Sophie asked, fists balled tight at her sides.

"We're executing the plan," Guy said.

"You mean the plan to obtain a document? How does murder factor into that? This is not what I agreed to. You lied to me. If I'd known—"

"What?" Guy asked. "You'd never have gone along with it? Forgive me if I misunderstood, but won't you be killing the lot of them when you destroy the source of their precious vitres?"

Sophie hesitated, her anger cooling and rationality taking its place.

"Relax. We're not asking you to get your hands dirty.

You just stand by and watch. That's your test. We don't do this without reason. This is a part of the lie." Guy threw his hand at Jean and Julie. "You'll understand why soon enough. Besides, it's not even murder. They're voyants. Given time, they'll rise again."

Sophie gazed at the two bodies with faces pressed into twin pools of blood. "You mean like the afflicted do? Or your poor unworthy?"

Guy shrugged. "But of course. They're the same. They all bear vitres. Now, ticktock. Bastien, wrap the wench in that rug. I'll use this one on him. Can't saunter past the guards with our clothes stained dark red in very suspicious splotches."

Bastien chuckled, and they both got to work moving chairs and tables off the carpeting. Sophie stood by, unsure what to do, her mind churning with countless thoughts. The voyants bore distortions, but unlike the afflicted, their sanity remained intact. The feeling their distortions gave off was eerily reminiscent of one Sophie had known well, one embedded in her own navel for so much of her life. How far did the similarities between her and the voyants go? While she'd borne her distortion, had she been timeless too? Immortal even?

Guy huffed, lifting the rug-rolled Jean up in both arms. Bastien followed with Julie. Sophie stepped aside to make way for them then trudged after the two men. Esme was waiting in the kitchen, the child nowhere in sight. Sophie's stomach sank at the thought of that poor thing, caught in the machinations of the Fleurs, oblivious to whatever the sins of its parents were.

"What happened to the child?" Sophie asked.

Before Esme could answer, a series of knocks sounded at the door that led to the courtyard. Esme rushed to it, unlatched the bolts, and cracked it open, the whole of her blocking the view. "Perfect timing," she said.

Helice slipped through the crack, hooded in dark robes. She glanced at her companions, noted the two forms wrapped in the rugs, and smiled. "Michel is waiting with the larger cart. Load those two on it."

Guy and Bastien heaved their burdens. Helice held the door ajar. In the backdrop, a man loitered, stooped and shrouded. Then, the door closed, and Helice advanced into the kitchen.

"He's in the nursery," Esme said.

"Good," Helice said then glanced at Sophie. "I'm sure you're confused. Follow us, and you'll learn some. Not all, mind you. Only Jean and Julie Bain have all the answers, and that will come later. First, we must fetch the child."

Sophie frowned but followed. There was no point in grumbling. She was utterly at the mercy of the Fleurs, complicit in whatever political games they were playing. Then again, that had been the point. Putting herself at risk was the only way for Sophie to prove her family's loyalty, to ensure they had access to Spirale's Link node.

Esme led them up the same set of stairs, but instead of veering right, as they had when heading to the study, they turned left. All the doors were shut, save the one at the hall's end. That's where Esme headed with Helice following and Sophie in the rear. A lonely oil lamp gave off its feeble rays, a pale-yellow glow exposing a small face peeking out of a tent constructed of blankets. He couldn't have been older than three years of age, his dark eyes locked on the women as they entered his sanctuary. But as Esme neared his textile fortress, he didn't retreat or whimper. He wasn't afraid of her. In fact, he crept out and extended his arms. So then, Esme was the trusted servant, a favorite of the boy's. Of course he would seek comfort in her, unaware of how she'd played a fundamental role in the kidnap and not-quite-murder of his parents.

"Come, Gael," Esme said, taking the child's hand and

guiding him to Helice. "I want you to meet my very good friend."

Helice crouched so her head was level with Gael's. She beckoned him over, and he advanced with that shyness of youth. The two of them shared tapered eyes and curled masses of black hair.

"This is Helice," Esme said. "Will you say hello to her?"

Helice smiled, even as her eyes threatened tears, the anguish so plainly written on her face. "Come, little sparrow."

Gael went to Helice and placed his hand in hers, the whole of it fitting neatly within her palm. The delicate and refined hands of a high-blood child contrasted against the ink-stained and chapped ones of a low-blood scribe. So different, yet so alike.

"May I see it, your secret?" Helice asked.

The boy's eyes shot to Esme, and his lower lip quivered.

Helice held up a finger between them. "It's all right."

Gael looked back and forth between the two women. Esme smiled and nodded. Gael relaxed then pulled his shirt free of his trousers and lifted it. That expansion and contraction, swirling, convection, the never-ending dance of a distortion as it defied the laws of physics even while it took up residence in the boy's navel. Just as one had with Sophie. She sucked in her breath, not because of the reality of the thing, but because Gael was so like her. The first she'd known to have existed as she had.

"I knew it," Helice said, rising to a stand, gazing down at Gael still holding up his shirt. "There's no taking on the first vitre well into adulthood to prove their worthiness. They're born with one." She turned to Esme. "You and Bastien will go with the child to Michel's. Your faces can't be seen in Spirale, not for some time. Take the smaller cart. We'll follow in several days."

Esme nodded and helped Gael tuck in his shirt before

leading him out of the room by the hand. He gave one last wistful look before moving out of sight.

"The child—" Sophie said.

"We're short on time. We need to make it back to the safe house before the Bains awaken. Come. Let's have the rest of those questions answered. Yours and mine both."

PERMISSION

ON THE PURPOSE OF THIS DOCUMENT

A most heartfelt congratulations to you and your family for Voyant Supreme Celeste Wilmot has bestowed upon you the immense honor of a Permission for one child.

ON THE NOT-MOTHER

Speak to your city's Voyant Superior for guidance on how to best secure the services of a not-mother. Refrain from seeking out a sightless on your own. The utmost secrecy surrounding this Permission must be maintained, and only the appropriate Sect officials know how best to achieve this.

ON THE IMPLANTATION

The not-mother must be implanted with the male seed. This can be done in whatever fashion you choose. Once the not-mother carries the seed, her and the mother must enter Courbe's birthing retreat to ensure complete isolation. Under no circumstances may the mother or not-mother been seen in public prior to the child's birth.

ON THE EMBEDDING

The embedding procedure for the vitre must be undertaken within the final two months of implantation. Only a qualified Sect official can perform the procedure at the birthing retreat. Thereafter, the not-mother must remain under constant watch.

ON THE BIRTH

Only qualified Sect officials may be present for the child's birth. Neither parent is permitted to observe the process. The child will be delivered to you once it is deemed safe to do so.

ON ACHIEVING VOYANT STATUS

After the child's birth has been approved by a Sect official, their status must remain hidden. To this end, only the parents may bathe and dress the child. Once the child is one year from adulthood, contact your local Sect for further information on the steps involved in claiming voyant status.

ON THE STORING OF THIS DOCUMENT

The contents of this document are highly sensitive. As such, this Permission must be treated with the utmost care. Ensure none but the voyants addressed view it. Once your child has been bestowed the title of voyant, destroy this Permission without delay.

ON CONCLUDING THIS DOCUMENT

Failure to follow these guidelines in any way will result in the child being labeled a poor unworthy. If you agree to the conditions set herein, sign and date this Permission and present it to your Voyant Superior when you wish to move forward with the process. Congratulations yet again. Your allegiance to the Sect is appreciated and rewarded accordingly.

This Permission is only valid if stamped with the Seal of the Voyant Supreme

THE NOT-MOTHER

The door to the safe house burst open, and Fenrir jumped from his seat. Lenore was up almost as quickly. They both knew exactly what would enter in short order. They had watched the entirety of the Sophie's mission through her eyes. Fenrir tried to project calm, but the truth was, he was agitated beyond belief.

Guy struggled through the doorway, carrying a burden wrapped in patterned textiles. Fenrir rushed in, intent on giving the man a piece of his mind, but the timing was ill-suited. Somewhere in the darkness beyond, Sophie stood in the street. Exposed. Tied now to these people and their crimes. Him starting a shouting match with Guy would be the height of folly. Better to do so in the privacy of the safe house.

"The head is on your end," Guy said, stepping forward, forcing Fenrir to take hold of the burden and assist.

Fenrir simply glared at Guy as he grabbed hold then backpedaled toward the cellar stairs.

"Down we go," Guy said. "The pretty one can help her Maman and Helice."

Lenore stood to the side, waiting for Sophie and Helice

to enter. Fenrir took the steps in reverse, one at a time with an excess of care, the wood groaning under the combined weight. The safe house was an old structure, ill-kept, but it did happen to have a cellar, an invaluable trait for clandestine meetings and for housing two highly-sought fugitives. Once Fenrir and Guy reached the ground, they deposited their load.

"You've an abundance of strength hidden behind unassuming trappings," Guy said. "A bit like me."

"You and I are nothing alike," Fenrir said.

Guy pointed to the rug. "Watch him in case he starts to wake." Then, he was jogging back up the steps.

Fenrir sighed and migrated to the bundle. Feet stuck out, velvet slippers with elegant embroidery framing the sole. But before he could inspect further, huffs and grunts sounded from above. It was Guy again, but now with Sophie and Helice helping to carry a similar burden of textile. As the others descended, Lenore appeared at the head of the steps, closing the door behind.

"Two chairs," Guy said, helping to guide the two women down the final steps.

Fenrir fetched the articles and set them next to the roll of rug that was now shifting and groaning. Sophie and Helice deposited their load which was motionless still, while Guy retrieved a rope sitting on the table nearby, slung it over his shoulder, then strode to the awakening captive. He kicked the bundle, and it gave off a moan. Then, he unrolled the rug with a push from his foot. The interior was soaked in a deep red. A tinge of iron floated in the air. A red gash sat on the man's neck, blood staining it and his shirt but no longer flowing freely.

"Hold the chair while I secure him to it," Guy said.

Fenrir placed his hands on his hips. "We need to talk about how you lied to us and made my wife an accomplice to murder."

"Not murder," Helice said. "Kidnapping perhaps, but as you can clearly see, the man isn't dead. The woman either." She moved in to do what Fenrir would not, gripping the wooden chair tightly.

Guy slapped his hands against the captive man's chest, took fistfuls of his billowy shirt, and heaved him up. Together, Guy and Helice managed to secure their prisoner to his chair.

"Now, her," Helice said, tossing a hand at the other rug.

She and Guy got to work on the other captive, and within minutes, both were tied to their chairs, rolling their heads and groaning.

Guy waved to a pile of rags on crates set against the wall. "Grab a handful of those," he said to Lenore.

But before his daughter could retrieve the articles, Fenrir grabbed her wrist and shook his head. "We don't raise a hand to help them further until we have answers."

Lenore nodded, and he released her. The three Roshems stood abreast, staring at the Fleurs, eyes hard. Guy sighed and grabbed the rags himself, balling them into tight wads, forcing them into the mouths of the prisoners, and tying them in place. The voyants were a pitiful sight in their blood-soaked clothing with twin gashes on their pale throats. Somewhere, underneath their fine garb, distortions roiled, and yet, Fenrir didn't sense a thing. Ignoring the pull from afar that originated at that massive shard of a tower or the lesser ones that were peppered throughout the city, unwarded, exerting their foul influence with impunity, Fenrir could feel nothing from the ones that had to be embedded in the man and woman sitting before him.

"We demand answers," Fenrir said.

"And you shall have then," Helice said. She tossed a hand at the captives. "These are the voyants Jean and Julie Bain."

"You claimed voyants bear distortions," Fenrir said, "only, I don't feel them."

"Feel them?" Guy said.

"I'm usually able to," Fenrir replied. "A sixth sense, if you like."

Sophie slipped her hand into Fenrir's. He looked at her, trying to read her thoughts without the aid of the Third Eye, but her expression was an enigma. Sadness. Eagerness. Determination. For what?

"Gaze at the voyants through your Third Eye," she said. "Nytho's update."

Fenrir turned his eyes back on the captives. All he had to do was think of what he wanted from the Third Eye. In this case, it was to have his vision supplemented, and in an instant, a kind of filter overtook his view. Shadows weren't so impenetrable. Details were sharper. But most significantly, ghostly spheres appeared embedded in the voyants underneath their clothing. One near their navels. A couple of others scattered elsewhere. Distortions, without a doubt.

"But I don't feel them," he said.

"Do you remember when we first came to know one another, to really know one another, in your home?" Sophie whispered. "When we shared secrets?"

Fenrir nodded.

"Did you feel anything then?"

He breathed in rapidly then exhaled long and slow. He hadn't. Sophie's distortion had been different for him. Visible but otherwise undetectable. These then were like that one.

Guy stepped to the table and retrieved the oil lamp sitting on it. He moved to Julie's side and grabbed a handful of her pale locks, exposing her face. He glanced at Helice and held the light closer. "You're sure this is her?"

Helice stepped forward, her back and head tall, only her eyes angled down to gaze at Julie. "Without a trace of a doubt. That's her, the woman who used my sister as cattle to birth her little voyant."

Guy released Julie's head and spat on the ground. Helice turned to face Fenrir, his wife, and his daughter.

"You lied," Fenrir said. "A document's theft, that's what Sophie agreed to. You didn't say anything about kidnapping these voyants."

"It was a part of the test," Helice said. "To see if you weren't really working for the voyants."

"You've got us caught up in something we didn't agree to," Fenrir said.

"Our goals are what they always were. This," she said, waving at the voyants, "is simply justice."

Helice walked to the table and waved Guy over. He pulled a folded parchment from his pocket and slapped it down. Helice leaned over, opened the document, and pressed on its creases, smoothing it out. Everyone stood arranged around the table in a circle.

Helice's eyes scanned the parchment's contents, then she stood back and crossed her arms. "Read it."

Fenrir, Sophie, and Lenore all migrated to the side of the table where the document could be read right-side up then ran through the text, their Third Eyes translating the written word almost instantly. The phrasing was vague, but even so, the meaning was blindingly clear. Voyants were granted a permission to have a child but were incapable of doing so themselves. If they were anything like Sophie had been, which seemed to be the case, their wombs would be stuck in a timelessness, the ebb and flow required for life to take hold and replicate an impossibility. Instead, they used sightless women as surrogates, what they called not-mothers, impregnating them with the male voyant's seed, forcing a distortion on the not-mother at a later stage in the pregnancy to ensure the child would be born with a different kind of distortion. But the fate of the not-mother was the same as that of any afflicted. It was Sophie's horrific past, one that had come about by unfortunate chance, done with purpose here in Spirale.

Fenrir glanced at his wife, her hand hovering over her open mouth.

"Now you see?" Helice asked. "You see what they do to us sightless? And the lie isn't just the women being used in such a way. The lie is they tell us the voyants are chosen by fate, that anyone can undergo the ritual of taking on a vitre, but only the voyants are able to do so without becoming a poor unworthy. Except that is a lie."

"They're born with a distortion and hide it," Lenore said.

"Their vitre enables them to take on other vitres without issue," Helice said. "It's not fate deciding this. It's the Sect."

"It's grotesque," Fenrir said, his eyes stuck on the final line of text: "This Permission is only valid if stamped with the Seal of the Voyant Supreme." Formal, bureaucratic, clinical. All to diminish the reality of the horrid act.

In the midst of digesting these revelations, movements sounded near Julie, hands struggling against bonds, a mumbling. Guy moved to her and pulled her head back. Julie squinted in the harsh light so near at hand, grimacing in pain at her hair pulled taut. She muttered behind her gag. Helice came to Guy's side and took the oil lamp from him. With his hands now free, Guy untied and removed the rags from Julie's mouth.

"Please," Julie said. "I don't know what this is about, but if it's coin you're wanting, we have plenty."

"Coin?" Guy asked. "What use do we have for such a petty thing? No, Madame Bain, you took something precious from us, something beyond all wealth and riches."

"Antonette Valin," Helice said. "You know the name?"

Julie's eyes flitted from side to side as she stammered. The Roshems arrayed themselves in an arc around the two Fleurs, staring at the captive caught in her lies.

"Maybe you see her in me?" Helice asked, lifting the light to illuminate her face.

Julie shook her head. "I don't know who you're talking about."

"Oh, I think you must. I have it on good authority she accompanied you to a birthing retreat near Courbe but only you and a child returned, a poor unworthy the only evidence of your crimes."

Julie looked at her captors, eyes pleading, then caught sight of her husband, bound to his own chair, slowly waking. "Where's Gael?"

"Just where he ought to be," Helice said, leaning in. "Far away from you monsters. Don't worry. We're not like you. We have hearts, battered and bleeding as they may be, but hearts still. Not the gaping voids you voyants have in their stead. Gael will come to no harm. He's my nephew, after all. But you? Well, I can't say the same."

"Release me at once," Julie said, straining against the rope, her wrists already raw. "You have to know this is futile, whatever it is you're trying to do. We're timeless."

Guy stepped forward and pulled a dagger from his boot. He balanced the tip on his gloved finger and spun it, the blade glinting with each revolution.

"That you are," Helice said, "which means we can inflict a kind of pain on you that's unknown to us sightless. Where we would perish, you persist. Under a knife. A rope. A scalding hot fire poker. You'll come to know these implements well, Madame Bain, you and your husband both."

"To what end?" Julie cried, her chair scraping with her frenzied movements. "What is it you want?"

"Just the truth," Guy said. "Admit to what you did."

Julie's face went slack, and her lips pursed until they turned white from the effort.

"Ah, well, one of you will change your tune," Guy said.

"Eventually. Though, I hope you'll be stubborn and resist as long as you can. I rather like the thought of introducing new kinds of pain to you. Just a shadow of what you did to us when you took Antonette away."

Julie spoke through clenched teeth. "You can't lay hand on voyants without consequences. You can't keep us hidden forever."

Guy laughed, moved in to Julie's side, then ran his dagger across her throat. She gasped and strained against her bonds, the blood pouring from a wound nearly indistinguishable from the gash that had already been there. Fenrir stepped forward, but Sophie grabbed his arm.

Helice sighed. "Let us try the man, and don't be so hasty this time, Guy. If you cut their throats, they hardly suffer."

Guy knelt and wiped the blood from his blade on the rug Julie had been wrapped in. "I lost control. I'll be more methodical with Jean."

"And once you've had your fill? What then?" Fenrir asked. "They'll come back again and again."

Helice and Guy glanced at one another.

"And we'll kill them again and again," Guy said. "Forever, if need be."

"If they're like afflicted," Lenore cut in, "we only have to sever them into innumerable pieces and keep those apart to ensure they don't rise again."

Fenrir and Sophie whipped their heads to their daughter, rage in Sophie's eyes, confusion in Fenrir's. Lenore was no fool. She knew what imparting such information would mean for the Bains. Guilty of horrid deeds or not, it was an awful fate, and one Fenrir wouldn't wish on even his worst enemy.

The Fleur-de-lis grinned at one another.

"Like your father did to the poor unworthy that chased me near the woods," Helice said, stepping to Lenore and holding out her hand. "We shake hands to truly mark our alliance."

"Oh?" Sophie said.

"You kept up your end of the bargain in assisting Guy," Helice said to Sophie. "A good sign you aren't in league with the voyants, but Lenore proved it really and truly. Never would their servants divulge such precious information."

"This is indeed the technique we used in Simetria when our city was prey to the afflicted," Sophie said, forcing a smile.

Lenore stuck out her hand and gripped Helice's. They held fast, executed one shake, and released.

"What comes next will be unpleasant," Helice said. "Please, go upstairs. We'll come to you when we're done."

Sophie and Lenore turned, and it forced Fenrir out of the stasis he'd been mired in. This was Sophie's mission, true, but he wasn't a simple lackey. He'd come here to help, which also meant to provide guidance. This is what they were to one another. Two people with their own fair share of flaws, but those diminished when taken in aggregate. Her weaknesses, his strengths. His weaknesses, her strengths. They looked to another to combat their own demons. What kind of husband would Fenrir be if he simply stood idle without voicing his concerns?

"To be clear," he said, "you're saying you'll come fetch us when you're done with your torture?"

Helice's eyes shot to Fenrir. Her grin faded.

"Look," he said, "I understand the situation, the voyants' crimes both to your people as a whole and to you two more personally, but I can't just sit here and accept this. We're willing to help you cleanse your Link node, but this cruelty isn't something I'm at all comfortable with." He glanced at Sophie.

She stayed silent and didn't even dare to bat an eye. It was so unlike her not to take a stand, not to voice her opinion. Something had her rattled, something beyond the pseudo-deaths of these voyants.

"Your compassion is touching," Guy said. "You have a kind heart, but these creatures don't deserve your pity. They aren't like us. They aren't even human."

"Papa, it's not our concern," Lenore said. "Besides, we can hardly judge, given all the questionable things we've done, you and Mama in particular."

Lenore stared at him with a pursed mouth and furrowed brow. What had she learned about them on her journey? What awful secrets had Sophie shared and why?

"We'll be waiting above," Sophie said, already heading to the stairs.

Lenore followed, but Fenrir stood firm. He couldn't understand it, the response of his daughter or wife. Were they really so callous?

"Come, my love," Sophie said in words and then through their minds added, *they have their minds set and no amount of arguing will change things. Imagine yourself in their position. If those voyants had used Lenore as they used this Antonette. Besides, there are other considerations. Let's talk above.*

Fenrir sighed but then trudged after Sophie and Lenore, the creaking of the steps masking the groans coming from Jean. Just as Fenrir closed the door, there was the telltale smack of flesh colliding with flesh. He shuddered then dropped into a seat at the kitchen table beside his wife and daughter. The room was only faintly lit, a single candle flickering, but Fenrir preferred the dark. Somehow, it made reality feel far away. Manageable. A kind of veil buffering him from turbulent emotions.

"I find it hard to understand why you told them about the mercy killings," Fenrir said to Lenore. "You either don't comprehend the hell that existence is or your journey has changed you."

"The voyants brought this on themselves," Lenore said. "They tortured Helice's sister, who's still out there somewhere, existing in the hell that's affliction. I'd say, a mercy killing is a balancing of the scales."

Fenrir put his head in his hands and stared down at the stained and scratched wood of the table. *We should send her back to Simetria,* he said to Sophie. *This place is no good for her. It's feeding something dark. It's killing me hearing her say these things.*

You can't make me go back, Lenore cut in.

Fenrir lifted his head and looked at his daughter with wide eyes. She'd overheard an exchange she shouldn't have been privy to. How?

You both forced me to come here, and now that I'm here helping, you want to send me away because you're afraid of exposing me to how the world works? You can't shield me forever, Papa. I'm not a child anymore.

"She's right, Fenrir," Sophie said. "It's her choice to make. If she wants to stay, she stays."

"What's the matter?" Fenrir asked. "You aren't being yourself."

"Because she's taking my side for once?" Lenore asked.

"Lenore, enough. I'm talking to your mother."

Sophie smiled, but her eyes screamed of pain and fear. When she spoke, it was in a whisper. "Did you happen to notice any similarities between the voyants and one Lady Roshem back in the time of the Rot of the Link?" She raised her eyebrows and looked knowingly at Fenrir. "How they're born. How they survive their distortion."

Fenrir glanced at Lenore who didn't seem confused by her mother's hints.

"She knows," Sophie said. "I told her."

"It seems you told her a great deal. 'All the questionable things we've done, you and Mama in particular.' What was that in reference to?"

"What do you think?" Lenore asked. "Vergil Holdsworth and how he happened to meet his end."

Fenrir glared at Sophie.

"Don't give me that look," she said. "Your letter set it all off. She wanted to know more, and us relaying the truth, the whole truth, was long overdue."

Fenrir shook his head.

Now, back to what I was saying," Sophie said. "The voyants, you see the similarities? They're timeless. Brushes with subsequent distortions don't cause them to become afflicted. The ones they bear are harmless if touched. If they are what Lady Roshem was, does that mean—?"

"Best not to dwell on questions that have no answers," Fenrir said, intertwining his fingers and squeezing them. "And this should be the last time we discuss such things so long as we're in Spirale. These people are not ours. If they learned about Lady Roshem, there's no knowing how they might react. We've already witnessed the lengths they're willing to go to for their cause."

The three Roshems let their eyes fall to the table, their hands, anywhere but each other.

"You're right, as usual," Sophie said. "Allies we may be, but it's best not to test already uncertain waters."

But were those waters only uncertain or, in fact, perilous? Had they made the right choice in allying themselves with the Fleur-de-lis? Then again, it hadn't even been a choice. If Sophie and Lenore hadn't thrown their hats in with the revolutionaries, they would still be locked away in the Sect's Sanctum.

Fenrir lifted his eyes and gazed through the darkness. Sophie was watching him, waiting. Their Third Eyes synced. He'd already seen what Sophie had in the Bain's Manor, but now he felt what she had, her pain, a wound long closed, seemingly healed, but now ripped wide open. To have caused her mother so much anguish, her shame at her horrid secret, her terror at her distortion being discovered. The walls and walls she'd constructed around herself, hiding who she was, what she was. Now here, in this city, to learn that everything she'd despised about herself would have been the very definition of normalcy or, even more, something to strive for or desire. It was too much. The juxtaposition. The irony. To come so far to a foreign land and find a likeness she'd never expected.

But it's not you/me. Not anymore. You/I have no distortion. You/I escaped the chains shackling you/me. You/I am free. You/I am nothing like these voyants who use their own people as chattel. You/I may not approve of their methods, but this is what must be done. You/I must destroy the Rot of the Link. What do you/I care about what comes after? This is not your/my city. It's not for you/me to meddle.

When they came out of the sync, they gazed at one another, twin sets of lips spread into smiles. They were content. They were of one mind. They were already set on the only path forward, and all that was left was to see it to its end.

"We may disagree with the methods of these Fleur-de-lis," Sophie said to Lenore, "but your Papa and I think it best to continue working with them. I take it you agree?"

Lenore's chin rested on her hands planted on the table. "That should be obvious. I have no qualms with the methods of the Fleur-de-lis. They're revolutionaries as I was before the Disaffected betrayed me. Their cause, at least, is real and true."

"The violence they employ doesn't upset you?" Fenrir asked.

Lenore lifted her head and cocked it at him, a wrinkle in her brow and wry smile on her lips. "What revolution ever succeeded without bloodshed? I would think the two of you would know that better than most."

"Our revolution was forced on us," Sophie said, "and we brought about change with minimal use of violence."

"Then you were lucky," Lenore said. "Usually, violence is

the language the oppressors understand best. In the case of the voyants, it might be all they even hear."

Fenrir's heart sank at hearing such words issue from his daughter's mouth. The world was hardening her, molding her into something callous and cold. Circumstance, that's all it was. This wasn't Lenore in her heart of hearts. How could it be? Her mother had no such darkness lurking. And neither did he. No, it was nurture, not nature. Spirale was doing this. Not his Lenore. The sooner they finished their mission, the sooner she could return home, forget this twisted city, and go back to being the Lenore he'd always known.

ALTER EGOS

Lenore waited by the barn door, her hand on the latch, her ears trained on the outside. It was silent. Autumn was fading into winter. No frogs or crickets any longer, the cold killing them off or driving them into hibernation. A gust of wind passed, and the barn groaned and whistled. Lenore wrapped her cloak tighter and readjusted the mask that covered the lower half of her face, playing at a bandit in order to take on the role of voyant in short order. The gala was only one day away. The delegation from the Sect city of Courbe was bearing down on them.

"I don't like it," Esme said. Her voice traveled with ease from the far end of the barn, despite her efforts to speak in a hushed tone. Some strange auditory effect of the space. She and her brother and fellow Fleur-de-lis, Bastien, were huddled against a bale of hay, wrapped in their cloaks, masks on their faces too.

"Well, it's not for you to decide such things," Bastien replied. "With the three foreigners added, that makes too many for us all to play as Courbeans now."

"I don't like you going into that danger without me."

"You'll be there."

Esme scoffed and tossed her hands. "As a servant. Nowhere near the gala itself. Probably locked away in your quarters, watched like hawks, useless."

"Until you aren't. Once we set things in motion—"

"*If*, Bastien, *if* you set things in motion."

Now, it was her brother's turn to toss his hands in frustration. "Ye of little faith. Don't let Helice overhear."

Helice leaned against the door just beside Lenore, motionless and grim. Bastien and Esme glanced in their direction. Lenore trained her eyes back on the crack between the two large doors and tried not to brood. This whole endeavor seemed riddled with holes, pinpricks that, on reflection, grew into gaping gaps in the cloth of their impossible plot. Their numbers were much too small for Lenore's liking. In the barn alone, there were only the four of them—Lenore, Helice, Esme, and Bastien. Out there in the dismal fields, prey to the increasingly caustic elements, there weren't many more of their party. Just Guy, her parents, and Michel. A handful of other Fleur-de-lis holed up in the farmer's hut nearby, no doubt. Someone had to be watching that voyant child they'd kidnapped. Or was it rescued? Helice, at least, would frame it as the latter.

"What if their clothes don't fit us?" Lenore asked, pulling back from the barn doors and glancing at Helice.

"There are three men and three women, so among the six of us, we should find attire that works. If not, we'll adapt."

"Improvised alteration?"

"Esme knows how to do such things. A useful skill for a maid, you know."

Lenore returned to her watch on the doors' crack. She kept having sudden flashes of panic like this. She wanted to believe the Fleur-de-lis had thought every aspect of their plan through, that there were no loose ends, no room for error after the months they'd been working on it, but she couldn't stop her mind from catastrophizing, not after the disaster that was the Disaffected's ill-fated strike on the Source. Her parents had known the whole time. If she had been so blind, couldn't the Fleur-de-lis be as well? The Bains' capture had gone smoothly, true, but stealing into one voyant manor was child's play compared to the complexity of infiltrating the gala, playing the part of voyants from Courbe.

Despite days of research—reading and learning about that city and its people from Helice and her books—Lenore only knew the broad brushstrokes. Courbe was the next-largest Sect city after Spirale, nestled in the heart of the landmass they found themselves on, built on the charred remains of a great city of the Old World. The people were proud and aloof. Of all nine of the Sect cities, Courbe was the most insular. Courbeans didn't like to mingle with voyants from other cities. Many of the voyants from there were only known by name. As an added benefit for the purposes of their mission, the Courbeans were infamous for their extreme modesty in dress. Covered from neck to toe, faces shrouded in lace veils, paints obscuring any exposed flesh. This was why Helice had settled on the Courbeans. But like so much in human nature, this reserve was a farce. Courbeans were more perverse than the other Sect cities. Orgies galore. Fantasies run wild. They were known far and wide for their strange and obscure fetishes.

The sun was sinking now, dusk not far off. They were a few hours out from Spirale.

"What if something went wrong?" Lenore asked.

"There's no use in thinking such things, not until we know them to be true. If Guy, Michel, and your parents fail somehow, we'll do damage control but only then."

"I always assume the worst," Lenore said.

"Staying in the present is useful, although it has the unfortunate effect of giving one tunnel vision. I've been so focused on the coup, I haven't had as much time as I'd like to plan what will come next, assuming we succeed."

"What would a Spirale freed from the Sect look like?"

"I know how I see such things. Rule by and for the people. No elite making the decisions on behalf of the many. Everyone having a say. It existed in the past, the Old Times, in the nation our cities were built on."

Lenore pulled her hand off the latch and forced it into a pocket. She hadn't even felt the cold of the metal until that moment, the burning of the frigid. She leaned her back against the door, facing Helice full on. "You would trust the people in all things then?"

"I would because I think, deep down, we have great potential. All the negative qualities come about from circumstance. People can be selfless. I've seen it time and time again. But when you pit them against one another or create a system that rewards bad behavior, of course it will flourish. The trick is to show people we don't have to live like this. That there is another way."

Wasn't this what Lenore had wanted for Simetria too? Wasn't it why she'd joined the Disaffected in the first place? They'd had no concrete plans for the future beyond the destruction of the Link and the fall of Order, but wasn't Helice's vision exactly what Lenore had longed for without knowing? Something whole and pure. A place that valued *us* over *me*. True connection, wholeness, unity.

"But this is just me," Helice said. "You'll get a different answer depending on who you ask. Even within the Fleur-de-lis, there are disagreements, and when you take the other factions into account, the picture becomes a mess."

"Is that why they aren't a part of this?" Lenore said, tossing her hand at the barn, Esme and Bastien, Helice.

"The only things we have in common with the Blindfold and the Porte is a disdain for the voyants. Beyond that, our beliefs and methods couldn't be more different. The Porte are intellectual pacifists; they'd never agree to a coup, let alone one as violent as ours. The Blindfold are too moderate. They want incremental change which would just form a new hierarchy with merchants at the top instead of voyants. And as for the handful of other factions, those are too small and inconsequential to bother with. No, better to use our own so we get the final say in the world that's birthed from all of this."

Lenore glanced at the siblings, still bickering, crossing their arms, tapping their feet, snapping at one another in whispers.

"But you're so few," she said. "I just worry we won't have the numbers to succeed. Voyants or not, their followers won't roll over at a moment's notice."

Smile lines formed at the edges of Helice's eyes, no doubt grinning broadly under her mask. "We seem few here, but there are scores more lying in wait. Trust me. Guy and I have spent years growing our ranks. The ones here are the inner circle. We'll have the numbers, and besides, the chaos of the voyants dropping like flies will work wonders on frightening the guards into submission. Their whole world crumbling before their eyes? It'll put them into a comatose state."

A temporary ugliness and brutality that would give way to a halcyon sanctuary. This was the revolution Lenore had imagined the Disaffected granting Simetria. How long since she'd thought of Deston? It felt like ages. So strange that, once, he'd consumed her thoughts, whereas now, the pain of his remembrance was like a dull throb. No doubt, it helped to occupy one's mind with other tasks, especially those of the life-and-death nature.

"Tell me about your city," Helice said. "How does it work in terms of governance?"

"I'm not the best person to ask. My mother or father

would be better suited to frame Simetria in a positive light; all I see are the cracks."

We're coming, Sophie said through Lenore's Third Eye. *Be ready.*

Lenore snapped her head forward, flexed her fingers, and breathed long and slow. "They're coming," she said.

Helice moved to the side, out of the door's path. Then there was a shuffling of many feet, grunts, whispers, one muffled attempt at crying out.

"Try that again and you'll regret it very much, fine lady." Guy's voice.

The sounds were close now. A set of five knocks, two slow, three fast, and Lenore tore open the door. A crowd rushed in. Four of theirs handling twelve Courbeans, half in well-tailored clothing, the others sporting simpler attire. Lenore slammed the door shut and put the latch in place. Guy herded their captives into the center of the barn. Bastien and Esme migrated over.

"Sit," Guy said.

The Courbeans' hands were tied and their mouths gagged with cloth. Six men and six women, the whole of the delegation. Bastien and Esme dived in and split the group in two—the voyants in one cluster, their servants in another. Esme barked at the latter group and had them sit off to the side near the hay bales where she and Bastien had been chatting. She kept a close eye on them with Michel joining her in her watch. The others arranged themselves in a circle around the six voyants. One of the women was sobbing, her eye paint smeared down her cheeks in little purple rivulets. Two of the men and the other women glared at their captors. The third man was pale, his eyes closed, muttering a kind of prayer even through his gag. These were the ones they would become. Lenore wondered which was hers.

"Ass cheeks on the dirt," Guy said, pointing at the ground. "Don't make me say it again."

All but one of the Courbeans complied, their fine travel gear getting a light dusting from the barn's bare floor. This place was far removed from any other dwelling, and the barn's owner was a relative of Michel's and a confederate of the Fleur-de-lis. Guy didn't hesitate to strike the one defiant Courbean with the back of his hand. The man crumpled. The sobbing woman shrieked.

"I won't resort to violence unless you force me to," Guy said, "but I do very much hope you'll force me to. Understand?"

All but the crumpled Courbean bobbed their heads in acknowledgment. Sophie and Fenrir were still both in body and mind. It was strange. Lenore was connected to them for communication, but she hadn't yet synced with either, and despite that, she had a kind of window into them. Less thoughts. More feelings. Ever since the Bains' mercy killings, the two of them had accepted the Fleur-de-lis's methods for what they were. Neither were upset by what Guy did.

"All yours," Guy said to Helice, stepping away.

She moved in and knelt until she was eye level with one of the quiet, defiant women. Her hair was raven black, her nose long and thin, eyes alert. Like all voyants, she looked somewhere in her late-twenties to late-thirties.

"We have questions," Helice said. "You have answers. You give us what we seek, and you make it out of this with your lives intact. Refuse, and we let our associate do what he likes with you."

Helice angled her head at Guy, leaning against the barn wall, legs crossed at the ankle.

"Now," Helice said, "I'm going to remove that cloth so you can speak, but that's not an invitation for you to howl or scream. No one will hear you anyway, so it would be pointless. Nod if you understand."

The woman nodded. Helice reached around her head

and untied the knot. The woman spit out the cloth. It hung around her neck and clashed with the finery of her velvet and fur.

"Good," Helice said, standing and putting her hands on her hips.

The woman watched her.

"Your name?" Helice asked.

The woman blinked several times. "Eve."

"Eve, you're going to tell me about Courbe. Everything."

"What?"

"Pretend I know nothing about you people. The faster you convey this information, the faster this is over."

Eve went to glance at the other voyants, but Helice leaned in and grabbed her chin, forcing her eyes forward.

"We don't have unlimited time, and my friends here are an impatient bunch. They get cranky when they don't get their way."

Guy whistled a tune then pulled a knife from his boot and tossed it, caught it, tossed it.

"What do you want with us?" Eve asked.

Helice held up her finger and wagged it. "You're answering my questions, not asking your own."

Eve grimaced but otherwise stayed obedient. Helice guided her, question by question, as the Fleur-de-lis and Roshems listened, committing as much as they could to memory.

What is the layout of Courbe like? The neighborhoods? The buildings?

How are the people, sightless and voyant? What are their lives like? How do they dress? Talk? Make merry? Grieve?

What is forbidden? Taboo? What is celebrated? Encouraged?

Who do the sightless love? Hate?

What of the voyants? How many are there? Who is powerful? Who powerless?

On and on it went. An hour of it, at least. Eve answered. Pointed, direct. It wasn't ideal, trying to learn about a society in this interrogatory style, forcing someone to distill their culture down into frantic words. But it helped. Delicate threads plugged the holes in their knowledge, just enough to get by. They hoped.

"The day has turned to night," Guy said, still at his post against the wall.

Eve was drained. The other Courbeans whimpered, voyants and servants alike. But to really and truly play their roles, the Fleurs and Roshems needed to know their alter egos, interact with them, learn what they could.

"Find the one who matches you best," Helice said, pointing to the voyants.

Fenrir, Guy, and Bastien inspected the men, made them stand, compared heights, weights, girth, skin tone. Helice, Sophie, and Lenore did the same with the women. It wasn't a perfect match. The Courbeans had two women with darker skin, and one of the men was short and wide, where Fenrir, Guy, and Bastien were all rather tall and lean. Still, the robes did wonders in masking these discrepancies. Once the Fleurs and Roshems had their Courbean counterparts, they all paired off, moving to different parts of the barn, ungagging the captives, speaking to them at length. This exercise wasn't quite as crucial as the other. Courbe's insular nature meant these voyants hadn't interacted overmuch with voyants in other cities. Nevertheless, they had to ascertain who had met who. Only Bastien's Courbean, Richard Roche, had ever been to Spirale previously, as came out when they reconvened to compare findings.

"He went several years back for a diplomatic mission," Bastien said.

"Who did he interact with?" Helice asked.

Bastien shook his head and shrugged. "He claims they were all low-level voyants. He can't recall the names."

"It's risky," Helice said. "Most of the Spiralean voyants will be there."

"Maybe Richard Roche falls ill and isn't able to attend the gala?" Guy said. "He arrives with us but is bound to his room."

Helice glanced at the voyants, gagged again, exhausted, afraid but hanging on to every word of their captors, desperate to know how things might end for them. "Let's move this conversation outside. Esme, Michel, can you watch them?"

The Fleurs nodded and combined the two groups of prisoners into one mass then stationed themselves on the sides. Legs wide. Daggers drawn. Helice beckoned the others to follow her out of the barn.

"Good call, Starling," Guy said. "Captives or not, best to avoid them overhearing."

"Let's keep our voices low," she said.

The fields in the distance were bathed in darkness. The sun had set, and a chill encroached. The moon was out and increasingly making itself known, a paltry substitute in the presence of the might of the sun, but in the nightscape, a lord amongst lesser beacons, those pale stars that shimmered in the haze. A fog was lifting, rising from the dewy soil, forming a discrete layer that hovered a few feet from the ground. Lenore marveled at the sharpness of the boundary, how the vapors all seemed to come to a collective agreement to sit just so. The moon bathed the environs, its soft illumination absorbed and reemitted by the fog so the vapors themselves appeared to glow. It was equal parts beautiful and eerie. Like this land and its people.

"If my Courbean can't attend the gala," Bastien said, "would I go as another? Switch Courbeans with him?" He pointed to Fenrir.

Fenrir started. "What? Why? If you're playing Roche, and Roche is sick, then you wouldn't attend the gala."

"I would play Renard instead," Bastien said.

"And why in the world would we do that?"

"Better to have more Fleur-de-lis in the gala for the coup. And, well…"

"Well, what?" Fenrir asked, hands on his hips, eyes locked on Bastien.

It was one of those odd power plays Lenore constantly witnessed amongst men. A duel of some kind, pitting their stubborn wills against one another, all while they could just use their words to clarify things and avoid the theatrics altogether. She couldn't imagine how her mother dealt with the tender egos of the less-fair sex.

"Out with it already," Lenore said.

Fenrir and Bastien both looked at her with widened eyes then back to each other.

"You are old," Bastien said.

Fenrir blinked.

"The voyants all look quite young," Bastien added. "Younger than you do. It just seems best if I were to go in your place."

"Nonsense," Guy said, "he looks fine."

"And the veil would cover my face," Fenrir said.

Sophie stepped in, pulling down her mask and smiling, laying a hand on each man's shoulder. With her mother and father standing side-by-side, the juxtaposition was clear. Fenrir was a handsome man, but he did look his age, slightly over fifty, whereas Sophie's youth held on tenuously. Now, Lenore knew the likely culprit—her mother's bygone distortion and the temporary though lingering timelessness it must have imprinted on her.

"Let's talk this through, hm?" Sophie said. "You make a valid point, Bastien, but I really must insist Fenrir accompany us to the gala proper. Before any coup can take off, we, meaning me, my husband, and my daughter, must cleanse your Link node. We're all required for this. Without it, your voyants keep their vitres, and, quite honestly, your coup is doomed to failure."

"She's right," Helice said. "If Sophie says Fenrir must come, he must come. Aged or not. Besides the veil, we'll use paint and makeup."

Bastien's face sagged. He was defeated and didn't fight the consensus.

"Make sure you're coughing at the inn tonight," Helice said to Bastien, "and also as we ride through Spirale and make our way to our rooms in the Fortress."

Bastien gave the briefest of nods.

"If that's settled," Fenrir said, "we ought to be going."

"I wish we had more time with the voyants," Sophie said. "I still feel like we aren't prepared."

"We're out of time," Fenrir said. "We'll have to do our best."

"I'll fetch the others from the house," Helice said.

Besides Esme and Michel, four other Fleur-de-lis would play the roles of the servants. All of them would take the Courbean's carriages to the inn these voyants had booked, the name and location of which they'd pulled during their questioning. Other Fleurs would stay behind to watch over the prisoners until they returned. If they returned. If they weren't found out at the gala, all their efforts in vain, everything undone. Lenore stilled the rush of dark musings, and in that sudden silence, something tugged at her, some weak link. But what was it they were overlooking?

As Guy and Bastien returned to the barn, Lenore caught a glimpse of the row of captives sitting on their knees, some heads hanging, others erect, fear on some faces, anger on others. She used her Third Eye to look at them, hoping it might provide some guidance on what it was she was failing to see. And it did in the form of complex, roiling, ghostly movements embedded in their navels and elsewhere on their shrouded forms. Their distortions.

The door shut. Still outside, Lenore migrated to her parents and spoke in low tones.

"Papa, you said you can't sense the voyants' distortions, but what about the voyants? Do we know they can't sense the distortions on each other?" She looked knowingly at Sophie.

Her mother pursed her lips. "I suspect they can. I can feel theirs, after all."

It would be a catastrophic error to go to the gala sans distortions. If they did, they might as well hang signs on their necks marking them as imposters. If they really and truly aimed to play voyants, they needed vitres of their own. And what luck that there were six warm bodies currently huddling in the barn with plenty of distortions to spare, ones that wouldn't cause affliction, that were safe to touch and handle and stow on their persons for the duration of the gala.

Lenore turned and marched to the barn. She could do the hard things, the things others would falter from. The Fleurs glanced at her as she entered. She approached Esme, plucked the knife from her hand, and pushed the voyant woman, Eve, onto her back with one thrust of her foot. She shouted through her gag. Lenore straddled her. To do this, to summon the courage for such violence, she needed to stoke the fires of outrage. She needed her blood to boil for bloodlust to grip her.

"Do you have children, Eve?" Lenore asked. "Children by way of not-mothers?"

She didn't need an answer. She already knew it to be true based on all their studies of the Courbeans. Eve Tirel had two children.

"How many of them are voyants? How many sightless women did you murder to get them?"

"What are you doing, pretty one?" Guy asked, now standing off to Lenore's side, surprised but not upset, simply curious to see what she was up to.

"Ensuring our mission is successful," she said.

Lenore looked the voyant over with her Third Eye, and there was a distortion, pulsing and twirling on her right forearm. Lenore used the dagger to rip Eve's dress at the shoulder then rent it all down the arm. Eve shouted and struggled until Lenore brought the blade to her neck.

"You ought to be still, or you risk getting a nice gash," Lenore said.

"You shouldn't ruin the dress," Esme said. "You'll need it."

"Oh, if these voyants are anything like our high bloods, she'll have scores more in her luggage. Probably three times as many as she needs. Isn't that right, Eve?"

Guy laughed. He seemed to like this side of Lenore. But the same couldn't be said of Sophie and Fenrir, just entering.

"Lenore, what in the world?" Sophie said.

She was too far away to intervene before Lenore jabbed the knife in, the distortion rippling and undulating around it, Eve howling.

"Keep them back," Lenore said to Guy.

He stood and barred her parents.

"Out of the way," Fenrir said.

"The pretty one is a grown woman capable of her own choices," Guy said.

"Lenore, stop this at once," Sophie said. "This brutality is pointless."

"Not pointless," Lenore said between Eve's screams.

She forced the knife farther into the flesh and traced a curve all around the circumference of the distortion. It was hard work with Eve's struggles and the complex movement of the distortion itself, but within a few seconds, Lenore had freed the foul mote. She held it up for her parents to see. Sophie and Fenrir went still. She stood and strode over to them.

"For you, Mama," she said, holding the distortion out, blood-covered, somehow smooth, harmless. "If you're playing Eve, you'll need one of her distortions. We'll all need one, or our mission will be in vain."

Sophie held her palm out, and Lenore dropped the distortion in. Her mother peered down and cradled it.

"Now, for the next one," Lenore said, eyeing the voyants who looked at her in sheer terror.

It was the strangest feeling and nothing like she imagined it would be. Nausea or disgust, those were the emotions she thought would accompany this act, but they were nowhere to be found. Instead, there was a kind of rush from knowing she wielded power and others cowered in her presence. It felt good, but it worried her that it did.

"Lenore, enough," Fenrir said.

"It's not pretty, I know," Lenore said, "but it must be done."

"This isn't the way—" Fenrir said.

Sophie put a hand on his arm, and he stopped, looking at her searchingly.

"Each voyant's distortions have their own flavors," Sophie said. "Retrieve one from each, Lenore."

Lenore walked to the other prisoners, knife in hand, hands bloody and slick, a metallic tinge in the air.

"I'll do it," Fenrir said, moving to Lenore's side and holding out his hand for the knife.

"I can do it," Lenore said.

"I'm sure you can, but I don't want you to. Now, get cleaned up at one of the buckets in the stables."

Lenore placed the knife in her father's palm and stepped back. She headed to the stables, found a bucket, then took to splashing water on her hands. A voyant let out a muffled cry, his gag blocking the bulk of the sound. Lenore got to work using her nails to scrub the blood, but the sticky substance only got lodged underneath. Despite feeling fine, or more than fine, her hands wouldn't stop shaking. Maybe it was less the action that was getting to her and more her reaction to it. She didn't want to like what she'd done.

A hand touched her shoulder, and she jumped. It had only felt like minutes had passed, but the barn was mostly silent now, besides the muffled groans from the voyants. Somehow, Fenrir had already retrieved the other five distortions. Sophie was looking down on Lenore whose hands were raw but washed clean of the blood.

"Come, little corvid," Sophie said. "Time to go and play our parts."

CHAT

———5 Apr at 01:23———

Marcos: You there?

Henri: I'm awake, yes.

Marcos: Still the night owl.

Henri: It's hard to get sleep these days. The world ending and so on.

Marcos: The worst is over.

Henri: That is what you said before those distorted pockets started to appear.

Marcos: Talking to Reya again?

Henri: Should I not be?

Marcos: She's trouble. She's chosen her side. Working against me, which means she's also working against you.

Henri: She said the Linkrot is causing the distorted pockets.

Marcos: There's no hard evidence for that. She's talking out of her ass.

———5 Apr at 02:05———

Marcos: Are you pissed or something?

Henri: No, I just happen to have other things on my mind. We will talk later.

————7 Apr at 11:47————

Marcos: How are you doing?

Henri: As well as can be. More riots last night. Margot is very worried. She says we should go into the countryside. Her family has a farm.

Marcos: You can't leave. You have to finish what you started.

Henri: I deployed your Linkrot just like you asked. That's the extent of what our past relationship gets you.

Marcos: So, you are pissed at me.

Henri: You lied.

Marcos: No, I told you what you needed to hear. If I had told you the truth, you would've still done what I wanted, but your conscience would have suffered. I did you a favor. This is all on me now.

Henri: How kind of you.

Marcos: Whether you believe it or not, I care about you. You and Margot. When all this has settled down, we need to meet up. Spend the day wandering Birmingham. Like old times.

Henri: The old times were with Reya too. Will you invite her?

Marcos: Reya doesn't want to have anything to do with me. Or I with her.

————18 May at 17:11————

Marcos: Are you there?

Henri: I'm here, yes.

Marcos: It's been a while since I heard from you. I was starting to worry the worst had happened.

Henri: It's bad here. You know that. I'm trying to keep Margot safe.

Marcos: I think it's time you seriously consider making use of the ideology we've got. This Church is hitting a chord with people, but that won't last forever. You've got a small window to make it work.

Henri: I have no interest in creating a false religion.

Marcos: It's not false. It's real. We've done tests. The diagrams and schematics have an effect on the distortions. We're going to turn this into something rigorous then apply it.

Henri: Distortions? That's what you call them now?

Marcos: Church doctrine 101—name your enemy.

Henri: I thought "the Others" were that.

Marcos: Yeah, and these are caused by them. As punishment for us kicking them out.

Henri: Dear God, you're really going all-in with this nonsense.

Marcos: As should you. Paris is burning, Henri. Calais could be next.

Henri: Paris is Paris. Calais is Calais.

Marcos: Ugh, spare me the intercity rivalry. People are going to get hurt if you don't step up. Someone in France needs to take the reins. I'd like it to be you.

Henri: I have nothing against "taking the reins," but I do take issue with your methods.

Marcos: It's not a religion, not in the sense you think of it as.

Henri: I don't mean that. I mean using fear to control people. I happen to believe in giving people something to strive for.

Marcos: What, so the threat of hell is no good, but the promise of heaven is fine, even if it's all a lie?

Henri: Yes.

Marcos: Come on, work with me here. We could do so much if we pooled our resources.

Henri: There's no point in that, and you know this. I already see it, so I know you do too. The world is getting smaller. People are retreating and entrenching themselves. How long until the last plane flies? When will the last ship sail between your land and mine?

Marcos: You're being dramatic and fatalistic.

Henri: You're not being honest with me. Reya told me about your Cleansing of the Synthetic. First, it will be the

Digisphere. Then, everything else. We won't even be able to communicate with one another.

Marcos: It's just a precaution until we can ensure the alfom really are shut out.

Henri: Excuses. I'm done with them. And you. Reya told me she tried to reason with you, but she was worried you couldn't be reached. It seems she was right.

Marcos: Reya isn't on our side. When are you going to realize that? If she continues to interfere, I won't hesitate to remove the threat she represents.

Henri: They say power corrupts, and I know it to be true, but ah, I thought maybe you weren't so cliché as all of that.

Marcos: This is bigger than me and Reya. Or me and you.

Henri: You've made that clear. You do things your way, Marcos. I do them mine.

Marcos: Understood.

THE GALA

Sophie lifted the black lace veil attached to a small cap clipped into her hair. She gazed into the oval mirror set above the vanity and into the reality reflected therein, one of the six bedrooms that composed their quarters in the Fortress. Opulence was the theme, all the wealth accrued by the Sect over the years seemingly funneled into this structure. Finery saturated the place, from the hemming of the carpets to the metalwork of the braziers to the carvings on the bed's wooden posts. Yet, despite the lavishness, an unease permeated it. The geometries were all wrong. The proportions off-kilter. A propensity for the asymmetric, for odd numbers, for irrational number sets that weren't related to *pi* or *e* or any other fundamental mathematical unit.

Sophie focused back on her own reflection, craving something familiar in this sea of the sacrilegious, only the sight that met her wasn't any more comforting. A stranger stared back at her, decorated in dark paints and wearing trappings even more bizarre than the traveling attire they'd liberated from the voyants and arrived in. This gala dress was loose, consistent with the Courbean way. Sophie being lost in fabric was the height of fashion for those strange people.

It had the added advantage of providing ample room for the combat gear they all wore underneath in anticipation of the bloodshed ahead.

Esme hurried by, a blur in the room's doorway, tending to the false Courbeans' disguises, using the deep purples and blacks of paint to hide the Roshems' Third Eyes and general visages just in case their veils were pushed aside in the chaos of the gala. The women's costumes were especially important. After all, Hubert Pomeau knew Sophie and Lenore's faces, not to mention the scribe he'd employed, however briefly, and, as the Voyant Superior of the city, he was sure to be in attendance.

Sophie lowered her veil, rose from her chair, and wandered into their suite's common room. It was crowded with boxes and chests. The five false Courbean servants were busy organizing luggage filled not with stores of clothing but rather the armor and weapons required for the coup. Sophie stood to the side, leaning against her room's doorframe, hands slipping into pockets hidden in the folds of her voluminous dress. The left grazed a velvet pouch masked by her trappings and hanging from her neck all the way down to her navel. It held the distortion retrieved from Eve Tirel, the voyant she was playing. Sophie's right hand slid against the smooth synthetic casing that protected the precious diskette stowed in that pocket. In short order, they would restore the Link node here then return home. They'd been gone from Simetria for too long already.

Sophie advanced into the common room then caught sight of Fenrir lingering in the room next to hers. She entered and inspected him, dressed in all black, a lace veil of his own though pushed aside for the moment. The only feature that distinguished the Courbean male dress from the female's was a sash that sat lower on the hips. A blank gaze met her, the one that told her Fenrir's eyes were attuned to another place entirely. This was his daily call with Nicolus, their Third Eyes connecting them. She waited until his pupils became less dilated, and his eyes again skimmed the contents of his surroundings.

Sophie migrated to his side. "How is Master Yevin and, more importantly, Simetria?"

"He's well, as is the city. Or well enough. Things haven't worsened."

Sophie laid a gloved hand on Fenrir's arm. "And you explained the situation to him?"

"I've kept him informed, yes, seeing how you refuse to speak to him."

Sophie laughed, if only to hide the scoff that involuntarily came out. "What nonsense. I don't refuse to speak to him. It's just better if you do. It was your idea to give him the Third Eye and leave him in charge of Simetria."

Fenrir looked at her blankly, and yet she knew without a doubt he was angry. Maybe it was the stiffened shoulders or how his breath came more rapidly than usual. This was no good. They couldn't afford to be out of sync in such a pivotal moment.

She ran her hand along his arm. "I'm only jesting."

Her words did little to appease Fenrir's brooding. He'd been cross all day and even back into the previous night. She knew the reason.

"She'll be fine," Sophie said. "She's ready for this. She's tougher than you give her credit for."

"Tougher? Is that what you call what she did in the barn? Hands drenched in blood, carving into a woman's arm, oblivious to her screams?"

Sophie didn't want to see the implications of Lenore's actions. Yes, it had been necessary, liberating the distortions from the voyants, but what troubled her was more the way in which Lenore had gone about it. Charging forward without discussion, almost as if she'd been eager to take part in the mutilation for its own sake.

To ease her own misgivings, Sophie forced herself to speak what she longed to believe. "Lenore made a difficult decision. She saw a weakness in our plans and engineered a solution."

"She shouldn't have had to make that decision in the first place. She shouldn't even be here. At the gala. In Spirale. Any of it. It's doing something to her."

Sophie saw it, that hint at the awful truth she fled from. Sophie would never have done what Lenore did. And neither would Fenrir. But there was one person who wouldn't have given it a second thought.

"There's nothing to be done now," Sophie said. "We're too far along, and we need her in this."

She went to walk away, but Fenrir grabbed her wrist. She turned and stared at him, the stitching of her veil's lace undulating with her breath, spirals retreating and advancing endlessly.

"I love you," he said, his voice thick, "both of you."

"I know you do, and we adore you in turn."

She moved in, brushed her veil aside, and kissed him long and hard.

"This charming clothing has that effect, no?" Guy said.

Sophie pulled away from Fenrir. Guy was leaning against the room's doorframe, attired the same as Fenrir with his veil pushed up and out of the way, caught on his braids.

"I hope you'll find me just as irresistible," he added, grinning widely at Sophie before his eyes flicked to Fenrir.

"Maybe you'll get lucky," Sophie said, "and I'll mistake you for him."

"I can only hope," Guy said, "but I come to say that Esme asks for the good Monsieur Renard. His makeup and paints are particularly important."

"Because I'm old, as Bastien so eloquently put it."

"Bastien is just jealous," Guy said.

"I'm sorry to have taken his spot," Fenrir said.

"Oh no, I meant he's jealous of the fact that even at what, forty, you look worlds better than him."

"Forty?" Fenrir said. "Are you flattering me now?"

Guy shrugged. "If it's deserved?"

Fenrir chuckled lightly as he slipped past Sophie and Guy and out of the room.

"You Spiralean men are such strange creatures," she said. "Flattering your rival? Is that some kind of strategy?"

"Who says he's my rival?"

A knock sounded on the suite's main door.

"Honored voyants," a voice said. "The gala is now underway. I'm available to escort you whenever you would like."

"Very good," Helice called. "We'll be out soon."

The false voyants trickled into the common room, one by one, as the finishing touches were put on their disguises. Fenrir was last, and after he entered, the five of them looked one another over one last time to ensure nothing was amiss. Helice nodded to the other Fleurs, their false servants, and the supposedly ill Roche played by Bastien.

"Renard," Helice said, waving her hand at the door.

Fenrir nodded and took the lead as expected of the ranking voyant in their party. And fortunately, in addition to translating their speech, their Third Eyes also managed to give the Roshems Courbean accents that were more convincing than the ones the Spiraleans attempted. Fenrir had done an admirable job in his role thus far, having steered them through all the interactions required from the Sanctum's gate to their suites in the Fortress.

Fenrir gripped the suite's door handle, all black and composed of irregular curves, then he pulled. The Courbean delegation filed out.

"Right this way, honored voyants," the waiting servant said.

The Courbeans nodded but didn't utter a word in response. Haughty, illusive, reserved. It was easy to be such things when their nerves were so on edge. Sophie clasped her hands to keep them from shaking, not so much from fear as from adrenaline. The servant led, and they followed in a line. Fenrir in front then Helice, Lenore, Sophie, and Guy bringing up the rear.

Here, in the heart of the Fortress, the opulence was overpowering in its potency. So too was the unease. Unlike the Bains' Manor, where practicality won out over dogma, the cradle of the Sect demanded the physical perversions their tenets held so dear were built into the very fabric of the structure. Sinuous corridors, undulating surfaces, illusions and tricks of the eye. But Sophie weathered the sensory onslaught. She'd already had practice in their journey from the Sanctum to their quarters, but even so, the vertigo taunted her and not only her. Fenrir's gait was unsteady. Lenore kept veering to her right. Only Helice and Guy appeared unaffected, accustomed as they were to the twisted ways of the Sect.

A thick, crimson carpet ran the length of the hall. The space was well-lit courtesy of a hoard of candles set in massive brass fixtures. Tables lined the way, overflowing with arrangements of flowers in a purple so deep it looked black. Spirale had put great effort into preparations for the gala and, as the carriage ride through the city had revealed, the festivities for Ascension Day as a whole.

They weren't long in reaching the gala, a line of voyants trailing back from what had to be the ballroom. They took their places, and their servant moved off to the side. Sophie eyed the other guests clustered into their delegations, wearing unique dress, styling their hair in distinct ways. Her and her companions wouldn't stand out in this crowd of heterogeneity. Their foreignness was appropriate.

A door loomed, a couplet of sentinels at the ready. The other delegates chattered excitedly, the newcomers obvious in their nervous energy, the veterans smug and smiling. Only the false Courbeans were stern, though none could tell past their veils. They moved forward one step at a time, each march preceded by a voice shouting out the names of the delegates. Fenrir reached the herald first and offered their invitation with their false names scribbled on it.

The herald inspected the contents. "I only count five here."

"Monsieur Richard Roche was taken ill," Fenrir said. "He's resting in our quarters. He sends his apologies."

The herald frowned, took a graphite stick from a pocket, then struck through Roche's name. "How unfortunate," he said, then projected his voice to the room at large. "The delegation from Courbe—Monsieurs Renard and Quint. Madames Martin, Savary, and Tirel." The herald waved them in.

The gala's ballroom was an extension of what the corridors and their suite had hinted at. All blacks and deep blues and vivid reds. That twisted penchant for the non-Euclidean reared its head here, concentrated and purposeful, spirals saturating nearly every surface and interspersed with eyes, eyes everywhere, watching Sophie as she moved. Her own eyes got lost in the irregular patterns of the curtains, the complex geometries of the painted screens. Her feet tripped on tiles that looked as though they led to gaping holes. It was a hall of mirrors and false leads.

In an attempt at grounding herself, she shifted her focus to the guests, but that view held no succor. In fact, it induced an even more potent vertigo. Attire fashioned in strange cuts that exposed parts one would never see openly in Simetria. A navel here. A bare breast there. A buttocks. But the lack of decorum wasn't what disturbed her. It was the thing that necessitated the chaotic glimpses at forbidden parts. Distortions. Paints highlighting them, accessories framing them, on hands and arms and chests.

This place was all wrong. These people, deranged. Laughing and chatting, acting as though their very society wasn't built on the foulest of all foundations. And yet, they weren't all that different from what she'd been before she'd destroyed the Rot of the Link. She'd done it not out of a seething hatred for the non-Euclidean but to free herself from Vergil's thrall. And if she was being honest without herself, she did wake some nights drenched in sweat, confused, groping for her distortion long gone.

Windows. That's what vitres meant, and losing her distortion had been like a closing of a portal. Some kind of feeling, a brush with the primordial, gone. She'd never admitted it to anyone. She barely wanted to acknowledge it herself. But standing in the gala, amongst so many others who bore a distortion and were free of affliction, she couldn't help but wonder if there wasn't a bit of truth behind what the Sect preached.

"Refreshments?" Fenrir asked, presenting his arm to his wife.

She hooked hers around his. "A fine idea. I'm parched." She turned to Lenore, Helice, and Guy. "We're off."

"Just make sure to stay in contact," Helice said to Sophie then angled her head at Lenore.

Without Third Eyes of their own, the Fleur-de-lis needed Lenore to act as an intermediary. Sophie would keep her apprised of their progress, and Lenore, in turn, would inform the Fleurs. Communication was key at this stage. If something untoward happened to Sophie and Fenrir, the Fleurs needed to know as soon as possible in order to adapt. As for the coup itself, the Fleur-de-lis wouldn't act until the Link node had been cleansed. That moment would be obvious to anyone within eyeshot of a voyant, as their distortions vanished and many of them perished in the process.

"Shall we?" Sophie asked Fenrir.

They migrated along the edge of the room. Slow, advancing at a leisurely pace. They found a servant with drinks and relieved him of two of his burden. While they drank, Sophie watched Lenore and the others attempting to blend in. To be both present but not draw attention to themselves. The equivalent of wallpaper. It was a tricky business, but it wasn't hers. She was meant to find the Link node. She could feel it even then, tugging at her, somewhere high above their heads, maybe off to her right, she would know once she and Fenrir managed to make it out of the main room and into the halls.

"Let's escape this nightmare," she said, draining the rest of her drink.

Fenrir offered her his arm again and handed their glasses to a passing servant. They headed to a door on the periphery of the room, manned by a servant.

"How do you want to play this?" Fenrir asked Sophie. "You're tired from our travels?"

"That's what we'll say with our words, but let's have him see with his eyes we're feeling a bit frisky."

"Very in character for Courbeans."

"Naturally."

They were close now, within earshot. Sophie laughed and stumbled against Fenrir.

He caught her. "Careful now."

The servant stepped forward, barring the door, young, his eyes a mix of terror and desire. To be amongst these gods, to want nothing more than to be one of their number. Poor fool.

"Apologies, honored voyants, but I've been instructed to

keep the guests in the main hall until the Voyant Supreme has given her toast."

"And how long until then?" Sophie asked.

"When both hands stand upright," the servant said, pointing to the clock.

Sophie's stomach sank. It was hours yet until midnight, which meant an eternity of this charade, one she wasn't keen to partake in.

"But of course," Fenrir said, bowing. He pulled Sophie aside. "We can't draw attention to ourselves. We'll just have to wait it out."

We can't leave, Sophie told Lenore. *They're keeping everyone in the main hall until midnight.*

Lenore, Helice, and Guy stood on the far side of the room, three of a small ring. They'd seemingly been trapped into conversing, their aloofness failing to free them this time.

Come to us, Lenore said. *Better to have numbers on our side in navigating these tricky conversations.*

Sophie nudged Fenrir and tossed her head toward Lenore and the others. They made their way leisurely and, within a handful of minutes, joined the larger group. The others widened their ring to accommodate the newcomers. Sophie nodded at her neighbors, almost forgetting no one could see her false smile beyond her veil.

"Our fellow Courbeans," Guy said, waving a hand at Sophie and Fenrir. "Madame Tirel and Monsieur Renard."

Sophie and Fenrir inclined their heads the barest of degrees. This reserve and lack of enthusiasm was perfectly in line with the ways of the Courbeans. The others ran through their names. Some sounded familiar from their studies and readings of Spirale's annals, which meant these were mostly Spiraleans they conversed with. Yet, they weren't destined to do much in the way of conversing after all because, just after

Sophie and Fenrir's introduction, one of the voyants pointed to a cluster on the far end of the room.

"She's here," he said.

Within seconds, the Courbeans stood alone, having been abandoned.

"I think we ought to follow the crowd if we don't want to stand out," Fenrir said. "We've still got a few more hours to blend in."

As they began to move toward the mass, the wall of voyants parted. A U-shaped arc of bodies decked out in various shades, men, women, all shapes and sizes, but of a limited range in age. The other commonality? That rhythmic pulsing, dissolution, blossoming they all bore. But the figure at their center, the one they clustered about, was unique. It was nothing tangible, no overt physical distinction but rather something nebulous that forced the eye to her.

Sophie recognized the inspiration for the statue she'd seen on her arrival in Spirale and the distant glimpse she'd had of Celeste during her speech. Long raven hair reaching down to her knees. That same black dress, simple, form-fitting, the plunging neckline only covering the outer halves of her small breasts and exposing her torso down to the navel. The skin there was covered in a deep blue ink tracing patterns reflective of Spirale at large. Organic, winding, asymmetric.

The Sect's leader. Daughter of its founder. A woman who'd lived centuries, made timeless through her distortions. As she approached, a haze followed her, and Sophie knew its source. She felt all Celeste's distortions as a complex jumbled mass, interwoven over the years, entwined into the very fabric of her. An embodiment of the non-Euclidean, totem to the Rot of the Link.

Celeste marched, not walked, to the Courbean delegation who was looking very much out of place. They stepped to the side of the room, but she followed. They were the object of her gaze, hidden behind a black lace veil of her own, attached to the brim of a smart velvet hat. Her lips, though, were visible and those spread into a wide grin the closer she got. Deep red, like fresh blood.

Fenrir stepped forward and gave a low bow. Guy did the same. Helice, Sophie, and Lenore followed suit. It was the Courbean style, the kind Helice had taught them, minimal flourishes, subdued, stern. They kept their heads down, hopeful Celeste would continue on, but she lingered. Sophie was the first to stand, back straight, chin down. She waited for Celeste to say something, but all she got was that wide smile. Then, the Voyant Supreme moved on with an arc of underlings following like a wave eager to break but denied satisfaction.

With the voyant leader's arrival, the gala truly came alive. The music started. The ballroom writhed and wriggled with bodies. The floors thick with them. Arms thrown wide then pulled in, trains of dancers tracing curvilinear paths, constantly moving in a chaos Fenrir couldn't make sense of. It was a microcosm of the gala as a whole and of Spirale. Incomprehensible. Foreign. Fenrir stood on the sidelines, along with the other false Courbeans.

"Is it odd we're not dancing?" Sophie asked.

"It would be odd *for* us to be dancing," Helice replied.

"That famous Courbean reserve," Lenore said. "Besides, could you even hope to join in that?" She nodded her head at the fray.

Sophie laughed. "I'd be swallowed whole, I suppose."

She was grateful for the dance distracting the voyants. Most were taking part in the chaos. When they weren't actively moving their bodies, they were catching their breath, dabbing sweat. It went on for ages, one song bleeding into another, the musicians switching out only when fingers were bloody or strings broken or lungs hoarse and aching. The dancers, though, seemed to grow more energized with each passing moment. They were tapping into a primal urge, letting this ritual infuse them with an otherworldly stamina. Their distortions meant they bore a kind of madness, after all. This was just letting that insanity leak out in a controlled way.

About an hour into the frantic, rhythmic chaos, a discomfort jabbed at Sophie. She glanced in its direction, and soon, sounds she knew all too well followed. Yelps and screams and hollow gasps. An amalgamation of pain and suffering distilled into the auditory. Within seconds, a lumbering form passed through the entrance of the ballroom. Servants used spears to steer the creature, their own eyes wide with terror both from the afflicted they guided and the voyants they did this in service of.

The Courbeans retreated to the wall. Nothing would give them away faster than their lack of immunity to affliction. They couldn't risk even brushing against the creature. But their aversion to it was the exception. As soon as the bulk of the voyants noticed the afflicted being directed into the center of the room, they descended on it, crowding it, reaching into its corrupted flesh, hands grabbing and groping for something. As soon as the first of the voyants pulled away from the mass, it was clear what they sought. Distortions pulsed in hands held aloft, and the voyants gloated to each other about their finds, asking where their fellows would put theirs. These distortions were different from the ones the false Courbeans held in their small wooden boxes. These came not from a voyant but from an afflicted.

Sophie watched in horror and disgust as the voyants pressed the foul motes into chosen spots on their bodies, muscles straining, chests heaving, sweat pouring as the distortions embedded themselves into the flesh. Not as eagerly as she would have expected. Nothing like the behavior she had seen time and time again as a surveyor. The voyants' relationship to the distortions was clearly quite different. Where a normal human would become afflicted, the non-Euclidean taking root and exerting its twisted geometries on its host, a voyant appeared to neutralize the influence of the distortions. After an initial discomfort of their bodies acclimatizing to the new addition, the distortions became as benign as the others they bore. Sophie gaped in wonder, seeing what should be an impossibility firsthand. A literal nightmarish scenario to an ordinary normal person. A petty game of vanity to the voyants.

Once the voyants had what they sought, the servants again corralled the afflicted beast out of the ballroom and away, down to some deep, dark corner of the Fortress until the unease associated with it was lost to distance for Sophie. She came out of her daze and looked at her companions.

"What in the world was that?" she asked.

"Voyants being voyants," Guy replied then pointed to them, back at their dance, now with a renewed mania. "Hours yet to go. I would guess this is just the beginning of their perversions."

"We're seeing things no sightless ever see," Helice added. "Or at least none but their most trusted servants."

The voyants now fell into their dance utterly and completely. Ribbons lost, hair dislodged, clothing discarded. First, it was one woman who was entirely nude, just dark paints covering a spattering of her body. The men started to fall toward her, like she left eddies in her wake, sucking them in. They pawed at her. She cackled and swatted them away until one struck her fancy. She locked eyes with him. The other men retreated and formed a circle around them. A solid wall of flesh blocked the view, but between the breaks in limbs, the empty spaces between legs, there were glimpses of the fornication unfolding there in the middle of the hall.

The carnal sights stirred the blood and other bodily fluids

of the voyants. Decency had been breached, and nothing held their appetites in check now. Men and women joined the tangling of limbs so two became four became eight became sixteen and on and on. There was no wall of legs shielding the view now. Exposed for all to see. An orgy of epic proportions. Pairs splintered, traded partners, women with women, men with men. This was nothing like Simetria.

"Hypocrites, even in this," Guy said, waving a hand at the mass of bodies. "They charge us sightless with perversion for doing the same."

"The men with men and women with women," Helice added.

"It's outlawed here?" Sophie asked.

"To them, we sightless are only reproductive vessels. A source of the labor they so rely on. Doing their bidding in all things."

"They're corrupt beyond measure," Lenore said.

"They're voyants," Helice added. "They play by different rules. Timeless and bored with life, they have to resort to extremes to feel anything. Celeste is the worst of them all."

Their eyes strayed to the Voyant Supreme, standing on the sidelines with an entourage, swirling a glass of wine, watching the orgy impassively.

As the carnal acts wound down, the voyants satiated in the realm of the amorous, the gala moved on to satisfying the next of the earthly desires—bloodlust. Servants shuffled in with trays of daggers, offering them to guests like hors d'oeuvres. Some eagerly plucked the weapons up. Others gazed on in confusion until the veterans amongst them flew into action, stabbing one another with gusto. Those not keen to join the fray retreated to the sidelines, but a sizable portion of the attendees took part.

As the carnage unfolded, the attackers became more creative. Bonds and gags were called for. Servants rushed to comply. A few who were too slow fell prey to the bloodlust. Sophie gritted her teeth but remained immobile. Drawing any kind of attention just now would be the height of folly. They'd come here to restore the Link node. Nothing else could stand in the way of that.

Voyants bound one another and used pain to heighten pleasure, a mix now of lust and mutilation. But such acts could only go on for so long until all the participants had fallen to their wounds. Servants ran to and fro, relocating the inert bodies, wiping away the blood. The voyants would rise again, given time. Even so, Sophie recoiled at the sheer madness of it. Of the willingness to be mortally wounded simply as a means of entertainment. If she'd had any doubt before about the mental soundness of the voyants, this gala had made it blindingly clear how lost the ruling class of Spirale truly was.

And it wasn't even the scenes they had witnessed that night. It was what they hinted at. The tip of the iceberg, darker deeds still lurking below the surface. If the voyants committed such heinous acts in each other's presence, what twisted activities did they get up to behind closed doors? Nothing was taboo. There were no limits. To gorge themselves by the mouth and genitals on whatsoever they pleased. The living, both young and old. The dead.

A DEFILEMENT

With the bloodlust past, the voyants swayed on the periphery while the ballroom was cleared of the recent carnage. The music again took center stage, altering by degrees, hinting at a progression. Eventually, its purpose made itself known. Just minutes shy of midnight, the cacophony reached a fever pitch. The music swelled, careening toward an awful crescendo. Then, silence. And darkness, the lights suddenly blown out. A hand grabbed Fenrir's. Even through the gloves they both wore, he'd know those fingers, that palm, anywhere. Sophie's.

"We are gifted the eyes within," a voice boomed, a woman's, deep and full. Powerful. Certain.

"Gifted the eyes within," the voyants repeated in near tandem.

"We are open to another sight," the voice said.

"Open to another sight," the voyants repeated.

"My voyants."

The lights flared, the room awash in a yellow glow. Celeste stood on a dais set against the wall that bore the enormous clock. Its wrought-iron hands reached upward. Celeste lifted her own in mimicry.

"On this day, we celebrate my father's life and not-death.

Five hundred and forty years ago, Henri Wilmot ascended to another plane. He's there now. Maybe watching over us. Maybe so changed he's incapable of seeing us anymore. But it matters not, for we have only one goal to guide us—to do as he did and ascend."

She brought her hands down. A servant shuffled to the dais and lifted a glass. She took it without deigning to gaze at the stooped boy trembling in her presence. Fenrir couldn't blame him. Even he, on the opposite side of the room, was terrified of Celeste. His fear stemmed from something innate, something in her aura. It didn't diminish spatially but rather seemed to bypass any normal Cartesian coordinates entirely.

She had eyes within. Her vitres. Distortions. But unlike the afflicted, hers were controlled. More so than Sophie's had been or even the other voyants because Celeste could bend hers to her whim. Fenrir hadn't been able to feel Sophie's distortion, and those of the other voyants too were muted somehow to his sixth sense. But Celeste's were different, more akin to the distortions borne by afflicted. Wild and unhinged motes of foulness. He felt hers. She felt him. A thousand eyes stared through him, tossing his veil aside, ripping his robes off, parading him nude through the halls of her mind.

Sophie's hand squeezed his, and the touch brought Fenrir back. He gasped, hungry for the air his lungs had been denied while he'd been under Celeste's spell.

Are you all right? Sophie asked.

How had she not felt it too, linked as they were?

That woman is powerful, Fenrir said. *She was toying with my mind.*

Celeste lifted her glass. The voyants hurried to grab vessels of their own, snapping at servants, kicking the slower ones as they retreated. A cowering boy offered glasses to the Courbeans. They each took one and lifted it.

"May we live endless lives until our time to ascend comes," Celeste said.

"To ascend," the voyants shouted.

Then, they all drank the deep amber liquid and smashed their glasses into the ground. Shouts and laughter rumbled as servants frantically swept the shards away. The lights returned to their usual sheen and intensity. The music was softer now, aimless, droning. The party was coming to a close.

Fenrir scanned the room. It was like a battle had passed through. Abandoned clothing, broken glass, splotches of blood, a few voyants still recovering. Their fellows laughed at them. The servants tried to rally them. Fenrir shook his head.

"You don't approve?"

He turned, and there was Celeste standing just next to him and Sophie. His heart jumped, and he dropped hold of his wife's hand. Celeste smiled at him, lips a brilliant red, full, soft. She pushed the lace of her veil up, revealing the whole of her face; it was exquisite. Heart-shaped with a small, straight nose slightly upturned. The eyes pulled him in. Large and round with thick, dark lashes, and the iris of the left an impossibly bright green. But it was the other eye that demanded his attention, forced him to take it in, to linger on it, get lost in its complex movements, because it wasn't just any eye but rather one with a distortion in place of a pupil.

"Voyant Supreme," Fenrir said, giving a stiff bow.

"Renard, is it?"

Fenrir offered another bow, this time lower and longer. He took the opportunity to peek out the corner of his eye at his companions. They stood by, radiating tension. This was no good. They couldn't raise suspicion here at the end. They were so close to their endgame. They just needed to make it through this interaction. Fenrir slowed his heart. He'd prepared for this, spent hours poring over Spirale's texts, interrogated a voyant, specifically for a moment like this.

He was a Courbean. His name was Louis Renard. He had a wife and son in Courbe. They lived in the 9th district, had a garden terrace, were well-regarded. To be at this gala was an honor. To speak with the Voyant Supreme, a dream. He was Louis Renard. He was in awe of this woman, dazzled by her, eager to exchange words with her, getting drunk on her attention. By the time Fenrir rose from his bow, he wasn't Fenrir anymore.

"It pleases me to hear my name on your tongue," he said.

Celeste blinked, pursed her lips, and softened her eyes. She moved closer to Fenrir until her dress brushed his robes. Her fingers reached out and stroked the silk of his garb. Fenrir could only glimpse Sophie from his peripheral, and worse, he couldn't feel what she felt. But that didn't matter. He wasn't Fenrir just now. What did Monsieur Renard care of Madame Tirel?

"Courbeans are such fine craftsmen," Celeste said. "It's a pity you keep yourselves so shrouded. Tell me, Monsieur Renard, what did you think of the dance?"

What would Renard have thought of it? Courbeans were prudish compared to other Sect cities, but how would that compare to a typical Simetrian? He would hazard honesty.

"I have complex feelings toward it," Fenrir said.

"Oh? Would you care to elaborate on them?"

"There was a freedom in that dance but also a barbarism. I applaud the one but flinch from the other."

Celeste smiled wider and wrapped her arm around Fenrir's, patting his hand.

"Your eyes within must be clouded to view it as anything but pure."

Fenrir's heart raced. How to reply to that? Was this it then? He could only hope Sophie might flee and rush to the Link node before his blunder undid them all.

"Maybe," Celeste added, leaning in and whispering, "it wasn't the acts themselves that disturbed you, but rather you not being a participant? See, I've known Courbeans before, and you may present yourselves as one thing but be, in fact, a very different thing, , especially in regards to amorous affairs."

Fenrir feared where this was going, but he had to play along. To the end.

"You know my people well," he said. "Maybe I'm similar to them, or maybe not."

Celeste laughed and dug her nails into Fenrir's gloved hand. Her eyes were alert, alive, hungry.

"I propose we test this," she said. "You and I. A private audience."

Fenrir glanced at the others, still standing nearby, tense, horrified, no doubt. He reached for Sophie's mind. It was hard to make the connection, but he managed.

I can't turn her down. If I do, we're as good as done. No voyant in his right mind would reject her.

Fenrir, forgetting the grotesqueness of it, of my personal feelings, you'll be undone if you go along with it, the moment she sees you don't, in fact, bear any vitres.

There will be much that comes before that point. I'll buy us time. He couldn't feel her, and it pained him beyond measure. *Do what you must to get to the Link node and fast.*

"I'd like nothing more than to spend time alone with your honored self, Voyant Supreme." Fenrir brought Celeste's hand to his lips. A distortion swirled there, set in its center, churning patiently. He steeled himself then kissed it.

"Good evening to you," Fenrir said to his companions, thankful he couldn't see Sophie's face past her veil and that she couldn't spy his.

He turned and walked with Celeste out of the grand room, away from the wild guests, past the humble servants, through winding halls until they reached an arch with spiral steps beyond reaching up and plunging down. The doorway was manned by a guard.

Something pulsed and pulled. It was that old familiar

feeling. A prickling like a thousand needles running up his spine, putting his cranium in a vise, forcing his stomach to churn. Fenrir gripped himself and controlled his breath. He made himself into an observer and was able to view the distortions again without being cowed by their strength. When he did that, he could cut through the chaos, the noise, to the heart of them. Spirale's Link node. It was there, high above.

Celeste tugged on Fenrir's arm, and they passed through the archway and trudged down the stairs. Round and round. As they traced the spiral of the staircase, the air grew chiller and damper. The lighting became irregular and infrequent. It was odd because even though they ought to be moving away from the Link node, that familiar unease of distortions only seemed to grow with each step.

"Your quarters are here?" Fenrir asked.

"We'll have privacy."

They reached a landing with a thick wooden door and an iron padlock. Celeste drew a key from the folds of her dress and granted them entry. She led Fenrir into a darkened hall then pulled him along, not needing light to see. They had to be deep in the bowels of the Fortress now.

Celeste stopped and moved to the wall. She fumbled with a door latch, inserting a key, then pulled Fenrir into a room. It was even darker than the hall but slightly less chill. It smelled of wine and something sour. Celeste struck a match and set it to a lone candle atop a table. The flickering flames cast horrid shadows, but through them, Fenrir could inspect his environs. The room was sparsely furnished, just a bare wooden table, two chairs, a few crates piled in the corner, a barrel near the door, another door opposite but made of metal with a thick bar crossing its center. The unease originated from beyond it. Blocked and buffered but noticeable. Celeste settled into one of the chairs and tossed her hand at the other.

"Sit," she said.

No bed. No place for amorous forays. A trap, and one he'd blundered into blindly. Fenrir glanced at the door they'd come from. Something sounded on the other side—the clank of metal armor, keys fitting in the lock, the heavy thud of boots, the huff of a man. He was hemmed in.

"I take it we won't be trying our hand at that test you mentioned," he said.

"Sit."

Fenrir moved into the chair, ready to spring up at a moment's notice, curious why Celeste was locked in this room with her prisoner, the guard out there, powerless to assist her.

"Who are you?" she asked.

Fenrir's mind went to his companions. If he'd already been found out, what was happening to them? He tried to reach for Sophie and Lenore, but a flash of eyes was all he got in return, one a bright green, the other bearing a distortion. He cried out in pain, doubled over in his chair, his head throbbing.

"Don't do that," Celeste said. "Answer my question, or else I'll increase the unease tenfold."

Fenrir jumped from his chair, and as he did so, there was a kind of rush bearing down on him, like a massive wave building and building. Despite that, he resisted. Fenrir had known the darkest despair more than once in his life. The loss of his son, Amilia, his name. A hint of light cut short when Sophie was wrenched away from him by Vergil. A lifetime of bliss with her and Lenore before they'd both been captured by these foul voyants. All his pain and anguish hadn't been felt in vain. He'd learned from it, taught himself to weather the maelstroms of the mind, and this was what Celeste used, or tried to use, against him. His own mind. But his mind was his still.

She glared at him defiant before her. Then a smile fluttered at her lips, and the wave transformed, no longer broad but honed to a point. She jabbed, puncturing holes in the fabric of him, in search of something. He didn't know what until she neared it, a forbidden truth from decades past. Sophie at his shack's door, her belly swollen with child, him answering, letting her in, their embrace, tears, kisses. This memory was a beautiful thing, one of his happiest, the moment he'd opened himself up again and let himself really and truly feel. When he'd chosen to be a father a second time. But there was a shadow hovering around it, and it was that shade Celeste tugged at.

Fenrir winced. He didn't know what it was, this memory he'd hidden, but every fiber of his being told him to reject it, to not glimpse it for fear of losing himself. But his thoughts weren't his alone anymore. Celeste felt his resistance, and she pushed hard to force him to see what he wouldn't. What he couldn't. A sync, there in his shack. Sophie wanting him to know everything, their minds becoming one, her thoughts his, no walls, no secrets.

And there it was. That awful possibility he'd glimpsed before locking it away tight, him and Sophie both pretending it didn't exist, silently agreeing to forget it altogether. Lenore, his darling daughter, the apple of his eye, everything that was good in him, except that reflection he saw might only have been an illusion of his own making. Sophie had joined with him in that fungal grotto their last night in the Old World. That had been when Lenore was conceived. Only, that wasn't the whole truth. He hadn't been the only one to give Sophie his seed. There had been another, days after, Sophie locked away in Nicolus's cellar, Vergil visiting her night after night. The question of Lenore's parentage. The very real possibility she wasn't Fenrir's after all.

Celeste's next blow was potent and sudden. In an instant, Fenrir's sight turned white, his ears rang, and his whole body went numb. By degrees, his senses returned. He was curled into a ball on the cold stone floor, rocking himself. Celeste stood by his side, the train of her dress brushing up against him. She knelt, took his chin in her hand, and gazed at him.

"What an unhappy truth to learn, or rather, relearn," she said. "But if you had listened to me and given me what I wanted, you would've been spared such unpleasant remembrances."

Fenrir shut his eyes and gripped himself, trying to prepare for the next blow, but nothing came. Just a soft touch on his arm, lifting him to a crouch then a stand, easing him back into his chair. A hand brushed his veil aside then pulled the cap it was attached to off.

"Make me happy, stranger," Celeste said, "and I can take that awful memory away. Make it like it never even happened. Restore you to the bliss of ignorance. All I need in return is for you to tell me about your enigmatic self."

Fenrir peeled his eyes open. Celeste stood before him, his chair angled away from the table now. She leaned in, the view down her plunging neckline unobstructed.

"So tantalizing in your mystery. Besting my people's wits. Fooling the lot of the voyants. I'm rarely moved by anything these days, but you, stranger with the golden hair and emerald eyes, you surprised me."

Celeste reached out and grasped Fenrir's throat. He grabbed at her hands, but she squeezed hard, harder than her thin frame seemed capable of. He gasped for breath and clawed to get out, but she was immune to his assault. She laughed then released him. He bent over and swallowed mouthfuls of air. She pushed him against his chair's back, moved in, straddled the seat, sat on his lap, pressed her body into his.

"The women we captured and who escaped," she said, "they're your allies?"

He shook his head, too exhausted to speak. Celeste brought her face to his, just inches away.

"Where do you come from? And why come to Spirale? What are you after?"

"To learn."

She rubbed her lips across his cheek then whispered into his ear. "Don't feed us the same tired lies they did. It's too far gone for that. Don't you see, this is the end?"

She bit his ear then grabbed his jaw and pressed her lips to his, hard. She rubbed her hands in his hair, ripped at his robes, exposing the armor he wore underneath and the pouch with Renard's distortion.

"More surprises," she said.

He moved to push her away and stand, to at least attempt to flee, but that searing pain locked his limbs. That horrid memory was a puncture wound ripe for exploitation. With it, Fenrir was frozen, powerless. Celeste set about tearing his trappings away, exposing his chest, reaching around, feeling the skin, every surface, in search of something. She pulled back and looked him over.

"No vitres," she said, "except the one you carry outside your skin." She ripped the pouch from his neck and dropped it to the ground.

Her hands rummaged in his robes, from his chest down, finding his sash, tossing it aside, article by article, undressing him then groping, wandering, touching, lingering. She fixated now on him, this stranger, this new and novel being. So, he was serving his purpose after all. Maybe buying time for Sophie and the others? He wouldn't know. He couldn't. Celeste had his mind in her cage.

And his body too. She toyed with him. Used him as she saw fit. In the chair. On the cold, slick stones of the floor. She rocked and moaned, him ashamed he wasn't able to make himself deny her, his own body betraying him, giving her what she wanted. He longed to fight back, but he was too weak. And if he tried to retreat to somewhere quiet and safe inside his mind, she utilized that wound, dragging him back out, lashing him in retribution with white hot slashes from a cerebral whip.

He raged. She reveled in it. And after an eternity of being trapped in her thrall, of being her plaything, she released him, satiated. Fenrir was limp, barely able to keep his eyes open, but she dragged him to a stand, draping his ruined robes around him.

"Still defiant," she said. "After all of that? You're a worthy opponent, stranger. I'd like to keep you as my toy, but I'm afraid I've already done too much damage. Broken you, or brought you near enough to ruin. Alas, this is what I do. So, let's bring this to its finale, shall we? Tell me who you are and why you're here."

Fenrir dragged his eyes to meet Celeste's, then he did the unexpected. He laughed. She frowned for the first time, off put by his resistance, grown bored with the game. She lifted him by his ear and pulled him toward the other door, the one of metal. She unlatched the bar and swung the door wide then pushed Fenrir in, the unease all around him now, potent. She followed behind, forcing him forward with kicks.

"Onward," she said. "You've been most disappointing, and my patience is spent. You'll give me my answers."

The hall was pitch black, and that sourness from the other room was overpowering in here. Something lurked. The echoes reached further than the walls, and as Fenrir's eyes adjusted, thanks to his Third Eye, glimpses of iron bars came into view. He walked down a row of cells. A prison. And each enclosure radiated the unease of distortions. Afflicted, scores of them, mumbling and moaning and sucking and slapping. Screaming. Howling. Weeping. This was where they kept their poor unworthy, the ones they got tired of seeing skulking about their twisted city streets.

This was to be his fate then? Here at the end? To be turned into an afflicted at long last, just as Sophie was set to destroy the Link node. But was she? Through all his pain and anguish, he hadn't been able to think or put the pieces of the puzzle together. If he was caught, the others would be too. And they must be because it had been so long already, hadn't it? So that was it then. Failure. Their doomed mission over.

Fenrir stumbled on the uneven stones and collapsed into a pile. He wept, not for what had happened but what was to come. To live in unending torment. To feel what his son must have for years. It was a cruel jest of fate but one long overdue. He should have seen it coming. He'd been too happy, his life too good, and now, his mistakes were catching up to him.

"There, there, stranger," Celeste said, kneeling to the ground, rubbing his back, stroking his hair. "All you have to do is answer my questions, and you escape this fate. But here, come, let me share a secret with you. Then perhaps you'll be more obliged to do the same with me?"

Celeste lifted Fenrir with her inhuman strength, supporting him under the arm, and carried him to the end of the hall, past the scores of afflicted. Fenrir nearly toppled over before they even reached it, the foulness and wrongness of whatever lay beyond the bars almost overcoming him. He was too weak to bear it, but Celeste forced his head upward, pulling him by the hair.

"Look on him, stranger. Look on the wise and lauded Henri Wilmot. Gaze on the beauty of his ascension."

Fenrir cracked his eyes open and stared, stared at a complex movement, of countless limbs, and many heads, of ears in mouths, of teeth on hands, and eyes everywhere, on the outside and the in, seeing everything, being everything, the beauty and horror of it, of reality, of existence.

"Our little secret," she said. "Not on another plane. Just locked away in the Fortress. He was a poor unworthy after all. Oh, the complexities of familial relations. Take heart in knowing you aren't so badly off. Maybe it's a mercy the girl might not be yours. That darkness you sensed in her, that wouldn't have anything to do with you. Just her nature finally revealing itself."

Celeste released Fenrir's hair, and his head sank, shoulders bowed.

"Now, tell me who you are, and why you're here."

If he could just find the strength, but to do what? These were afflicted—Henri and Celeste—and afflicted never die. He'd failed both his families now, hadn't he? Amilia and Trevon. Sophie and Lenore. All his talk of protecting them, of keeping them out of harm's way, but that was what he was doing, even still. He hadn't come down here to complete their mission. That was on Sophie now. His role was different, and it didn't require him to do anything at all except persist. To direct all of Celeste's focus on him and him alone.

Fenrir gave a savage grin. "I'm Fenrir Roshem, and I'm here to destroy your world."

HENRI'S OBSERVATIONS

10 August

- I'm going to start taking notes on my studies of the distortions. I'm building off what Reya sent me. I know Marcos was lying. The Linkrot virus definitely played a role in creating these. The question is, how? And what exactly are they? Everybody is very quick to curse them. Maybe it's just me being me, but I find them beautiful in a strange way. I've managed to track down the location of one such distortion in Calais. At the Link node's old server site. A coincidence? Unlikely. I'll start measurements on it tomorrow.

11 August

- Day 1 of measurements. Distortion 1. Link node server site. Floor 2.
- Size: a small thing, barely detectable even with Reya's device, difficult to measure without being able to touch it. I'll have to figure out a technique for that. I'm sure astronomical texts will have something I can use.
- Shape: spherical, irregular, pulses
- Other attributes: slight temperature and pressure fluctuations?

- But what is it? No idea. I do know it's dangerous. Deadly if you touch it, based on what Reya's people found. It's like the thing defies the laws of physics. I wish I'd taken more of those classes. Comp sci isn't doing me much good here. I'll have to do what I can. Reya's notes help. I wish she were here instead of rotting in whatever cell Marcos must have thrown her in. Bastard.

14 August

- No progress on finding a technique for measuring the size. I need to make more regular measurements to say if the distortion is changing at all. It's hard to make it out here though. The streets aren't safe. Margot doesn't want me to risk it. Maybe we relocate to this place, and that way, I can study it better. She won't be happy about that, but this is important.

21 August

- I've been very bad about my studies, but it will be better now. We've relocated to the site, after many arguments, shouting, tears. Margot understands.
- I was able to find a way to measure the distortion. It turns out astronomy wasn't as useful as I'd hoped. Stars emit light. Distortions don't. I'll write out my method in more detail in a separate document, but in short, interferometry is key.
- Size: 4.2 cm
- All other attributes appear unchanged or similar enough. I need better equipment.

22 August

- Attributes unchanged
- Leading theory on what the distortions are: singularities/mini-black holes? I don't know enough about this stuff to say.

23 August

- Attributes slightly changed, in particular the size increased by 0.1 cm

- I toyed around with some of Marcos's rituals (wards, he calls them) that he's supposedly using to "contain" these distortions. Let's see if they do anything to stop the growth.

29 August

- I let some time pass to see if the wards work. The size increase continues but is slow. I'm not being methodical enough about this. I should have done measurements for several days before making use of the wards. A control, in scientific method terms. Ah well. Too late to go back.

5 September

- The wards definitely did something because since I removed them, three days ago, the distortion has grown noticeably. I guess Marcos isn't completely full of shit. Too bad his Church is more interested in controlling the growth of the distortions than in understanding them.

- There's not much more I can do here with my limited knowledge. With the Digisphere gone, I can only learn from what I find in the libraries that haven't been burned and gutted. I should've been working on this from the beginning. I let too much time pass. Marcos was right in that way. There was a limited window to act, and I wasted it worrying about a girlfriend who hates me.

10 September

- I reintroduced the wards. They still have an effect, but it's not as strong. The trick seems to be catching the distortions when they're small. Need to find another one. I'll hunt through the building today. If the Linkrot creates them, they should be clustered around the node. This still begs the question, how did a computer virus create a warping of space-time?

- Note: Margot doesn't hate me. She's been so snappy lately partly because she's pregnant. Three months along, it looks like. What a time to bring a child into the world. Poor thing.

12 September

- I tried visiting the Link node today, but no luck. Everything is locked down past the fifth floor.

16 September

- I dug into Reya's notes and read them all. So much was jargon, but I think I understand now. The Link wasn't just a means to communicate with the alfom, it was an anchor to their reality, some other universe? I have no idea, but it's why the Linkrot is causing the distortions. Somehow, the virus is corrupting this portal, fracturing it, and sending those little shards all over the place, centered on the Link nodes. The distortions aren't nefarious anomalies. They're windows, windows into that other reality. We just haven't learned how to look through them yet.

6 October

- I see it now, where this all needs to go. I've been staring at the distortions or where they should be; there are ten of them now. They hold an answer. But just looking at them like I am is not enough. You can't view them from the outside. They're opaque to us that way. They're meant to look in.

22 October

- Vitres. That's their true name. Distortions sounds ugly and implies they're unnatural, but they're the furthest thing from that. They're a gift. We just don't know how to receive them yet.

6 November

- I forced a mouse to touch a vitre. It was horrible to see. The creature squeaked until it went hoarse, but it didn't die. That was five days ago, and it still lives. It's changed though, the vitre giving it another kind of sight. How to harness that without going insane? Those are the reports I hear of people who come in contact with the vitres; they go mad. I can't ask the mouse this. As it is, I can only vaguely study the effects.

28 November

- Another mouse, another vitre. I've done this a dozen times now and have learned little, but yesterday, I stumbled on a discovery. One of the mice must have been pregnant; you can't tell with mice. She birthed her pups—Margot tells me that's the name for baby mice—and would you believe they're whole? One exception. They bear a vitre, but unlike their mother, they're not affected by it. Even stranger, I can see theirs with the naked eye.

10 December

- The pups grow and flourish even while their mother suffers. They rub against her vitres and are unharmed. Their own are clearly different.

21 December

- I took a huge gamble today, but I felt I had to. There was no getting around it. I need answers. I touched one of the pups, nearly full-grown mice now, and its vitre didn't harm me. This confirms my suspicions. The vitres of these mice are different because their mother bore one. Somehow, they've developed an immunity. They can see through those windows. They have eyes within. Too bad they're mindless creatures. If only there were a way to test this on something more intelligent.

15 March

- So much has happened. Maybe it's for the best I didn't bother to record it. I'll live with the scars the rest of my life. Why set them to paper? Why set this? I guess I want Celeste to know in case I'm not able to tell her when she's older. In case I don't make it.

- She was born two days ago, a small vitre embedded in her navel. Perfection coming from a monster. Margot was so far gone by then. How strange that the vitres are things of beauty, but the poor ones who are unworthy of their gift turn into such horrible beings. I didn't know what to do with her. Once Celeste was given to me, Margot was just a liability. One stray touch, and she would drag me into her misery. I coaxed her out of the tower today then hurried back in and shut it up tight. Her mind is gone. She didn't even try to follow me, just wandered away through the weed-choked streets. Calais is so changed.

20 April

- There was no reason to delay the inevitable. I needed to know if Celeste was the perfection I imagined her to be. The longer I waited, the more attached I would get. I didn't put her mother through all of that just to shrink from difficult choices in the end. Today, I subjected Celeste to a vitre. She took it up, unchanged. The pupil of her right eye is now a window into another world.

June

- I've shared my findings with those I trust, the ones I could find. I've spent too much time holed up in the tower. Marcos is an idiot in most ways, but he was right in one. He said I needed to lead my people. I have something to guide us now, and I'm eager to share it with them. It's just a matter of building our movement. I hope it's not too late for that.

...

I've accomplished so much. The Sect of Sight is secure. We lead Calais, and soon, we'll send representatives to other cities. And yet, the holy grail eludes me. I gave Celeste the gift I crave, but I can't, for the life of me, find a way to have the eyes within. I should be content to lead the Sect, but how can I when I can't be what they need? I'm sightless. They need a voyant. There's nothing for it. Tomorrow, I take on a vitre. If I fail, I fail. I leave the Sect for Celeste to lead. She'll know what to do. She has that other sight I crave. She can see through to impossibility. I created perfection. For that, at least, I'm grateful.

VOYANT SUPREME

"I'm surprised you let him go with her," Guy said.

"Fenrir knows what he's doing."

Sophie only wished she felt as confident as her words sounded. In truth, the thought of Fenrir facing Celeste on his own made her heart scream and her ears roar. He was buying them time, and Sophie had to ensure his sacrifice wasn't made in vain.

"Come with me," Sophie said to Guy.

"Me?" he asked. "That's not the plan."

"I need someone to help, and if Lenore goes, you Fleurs will have no means of communication. She has to stay, which means you must come."

"Better yet, we should all go," Lenore said. "Papa is buying us time, but we don't know how much. The faster we restore the Link node, the better."

"But the coup?" Sophie said.

"Will still happen," Helice replied, "but Lenore is right. Fenrir's ability to distract Celeste is all that stands between us and exposure now. I'm afraid he underestimates her. She's so much more than she seems."

"If you're all dead set on coming with me, then come."

The others nodded, and Sophie marched to the exit. As they entered the halls, they tried masking their agitation as excitement, at least for as long as the servants, voyants, and guards were in sight. Sophie followed the feel of the distortions to where a veritable hoard of them were concentrated high above, what had to be the Link node. This led them to a set of stairs with only one lonely, hulking guard barring their path. Sophie herded the others out of sight around a bend in the corridor. She bit her lip and wracked her brain.

"Should we pounce?" Guy suggested.

Sophie shook her hand then placed it on her forehead. She needed to think, but that was no simple task, not given the innumerable trains of thoughts vying for her attention. She kept having flashes of Fenrir and that horrid woman. Her fawning over him then the two of them walking out of the ballroom. Buying them time could only mean one thing in the context of that conversation. All manner of carnal images sprang to Sophie's mind.

She halted the onslaught of useless musings. Her inaction was only harming Fenrir. The best she could do by him was to find the Link node and cleanse it as quickly as possible. But how to bypass the guard? The four of them would surely be enough to subdue him, but what of the sounds of combat? Those would, no doubt, travel through the halls with ease, piquing the interest of other guards. They couldn't afford a confrontation. Not at this stage.

In the midst of her debates, a group of five voyants traveled down the hall and approached the stairs. Hubert led them. They stopped on reaching the guard. Sophie couldn't catch what words they shared, but whatever was said worked in their favor because the guard turned and headed down the stairs. The voyants moved into the stairwell and began their ascent.

"Does that make things easier or harder, do you think?" Lenore asked.

"They must be going to the Link node," Sophie said. "So, harder. Now, we have five people between us and it."

Sophie and the others crept around the corner. The voyant's echoes rang out, bouncing violently off the thick, slick stone of the stairwell. The exact contents of their words got lost in the chaotic geometry of the space, but the rapidness had a mania to it. Sophie peeked her head through the entryway, looking down then up, the central well of the spiral open, permitting a dizzying view both below and above, ten stories in each direction, at least.

"What are they doing?" she asked.

"Trying to ascend like Henri before them," Helice said.

How much time did they have? Sophie feared what she might experience if she reached for Fenrir, but she had to know how things were faring for him. Could they take the climb slow and steady, weasel their way past the voyants with clever excuses, or did they need to barrel through, consequences be damned? Sophie concentrated in an effort at locating him, but in place of that telltale tug, there was only a blankness.

She gasped. "I can't feel him."

"Me neither, Mama, but that's how it's been from the moment Celeste approached us. Some kind of interference with our Third Eyes."

However it was, it wasn't good. They wouldn't know what was happening to him. Again, those flashes of scenes, her mind running wild. Sophie clenched her jaw and forced a smile, savage and grim. She couldn't afford to feel anything. So, she didn't. Instead, she acted. Rushing into the stairwell, climbing, two steps at a time, arms pumping, breath fast and deep. The others hurried after her, whispering for her to slow down, to come back. All at once, a few stories up, she stopped and turned to face them. They looked at her expectantly.

"We're going to the Link node," she said. "Voyants or not, be prepared to do whatsoever is required to get through."

The next floor brought distortions, a mote here and there. Their progress slowed. They moved into a linear train with Sophie at the helm, guiding them. Only she and Lenore could see the distortions, courtesy of their Third Eyes. Helice and Guy might be able to spot the largest ones by their effects, but the small ones would be invisible. The voyants ahead of them had been a stroke of luck. Their passage through had already carved a kind of path.

By the time Sophie and the others caught up, the journey's toll on the voyants was apparent. Two of the five bore a peppering of distortions, new ones that they were trying to acclimatize to. As they'd seen firsthand in the gala, taking on a distortion was an ordeal, even for voyants, and to take on so many in so short a span of time? They were groaning, slumped on the steps, with sweat streaming down brows and teeth barred.

Hubert glanced over his shoulder and caught sight of the new arrivals, his amusement showing in an arching of his brow and flaring of his nose. "More hopefuls?" he asked then, noticing their attire, added, "and all Courbeans. Well, come along."

He gripped the handrail and plodded up, slow and steady, weaving through the maze of distortions. The voyants who could move followed. Sophie and the others trailed behind. They were close to the Link node now. She could feel it. Just a couple more floors, and they would be there. But the party stalled.

"This is where I leave you," Hubert said, waving a hand upward. "Those who wish to ascend must do so on their own."

Sophie bobbed her head to see past Hubert. The distortions were thick. There was no way through without coming into contact with them.

One of the voyants nearest to Hubert straightened her back and held her head high. "I'll go first."

Hubert stood to the side. She marched on, three distortions embedding themselves in her before she was even out of sight, then she was lost in the spiral of the stairs. A few seconds passed, and all they heard was the huffing of her labored breath then gasps and groans. There was a crashing, her body rolling down. Hubert jumped aside while the other voyant got knocked down and cursed at the woman.

Hubert laughed. "Is that all? You must not be as eager to ascend as you thought."

Sophie leaned toward Helice. "How exactly does this ascension work?"

"From what I've heard and read, the voyants can ascend by coming in contact with the Hole. They give up their body and move to a higher plane of consciousness."

"But more likely," Guy said, "they just become overwhelmed by their vitres, becoming more akin to a poor unworthy than a voyant anymore."

The voyant who had fallen rose, hung her head, and retreated down the steps. She was wheezing and crawling with distortions.

The man she'd knocked down looked at Hubert. "Not this year," he said before slinking away.

"Anyone else?" Hubert asked.

Sophie and the others shook their heads.

Hubert frowned and shrugged. "Typical."

He brushed past them on his way down, glancing at Helice, then stopping mid-step. Her veil was gone; all of theirs were to better spot and avoid the distortions.

Hubert's eyes narrowed. "Don't I know you?"

Guy lifted a leg and thrust it into Hubert's abdomen with all his might. Hubert yelped then crashed down the stairs. They followed for the first few steps, but his fall went on and on. They listened and waited. After several more seconds, there was just a lonely groan then silence.

"He won't be getting up anytime soon," Helice said.

"That's all fine and good," Sophie said, "but it doesn't help us with the matter of getting past these foul motes to the Link node." Before she could follow up, a deep-seated terror and wave of pain ripped through her. She doubled over, grabbing at her chest.

"What's wrong?" Helice asked.

Sophie cracked her eyes open and found Lenore at her side, mimicking her posture.

"Papa," Lenore said.

"My god," Sophie said, "what's she doing to him?"

There was no concrete thought, no rational decision made, just Sophie standing, pulling the diskette from her robes, and handing it to Lenore. Her daughter gazed at her with a furrowed brow and parted lips.

"He's been found out," Sophie said. "I'll be damned if I don't do something, but we still have to finish what we started."

Lenore grabbed the diskette, and Sophie let it slip from her fingers.

"Do you remember the console I showed you at the Source in the Old World?" she asked.

Lenore nodded and licked her dry lips. She looked so aged, haggard even, skin gray, eyes milky. Had she been even more affected by Fenrir's pain than Sophie, despite the fact she'd never synced with him? It didn't make sense, but there was no time for making sense of anything. Action, that's what was needed.

"Put the diskette in it," Sophie said. "It will likely look similar. Some kind of box of synthetics with a slot in it. Maybe a button and lights near the slot."

"And after that?" Lenore asked.

"It should do the rest," Sophie said. "All you have to do is put it in place."

Lenore cradled the diskette. "How do we get through the distortions?"

"That, I don't have answers for." Sophie pulled Lenore to her and squeezed her tightly. "You can do this. I know you can. Now, I'm going to go save your Papa. You save the world."

Then Sophie was tearing down the stairs, round and round and round, moving past dizziness and nausea, taking on the discomfort like it was a mantle, something to protect her against the elements roiling within, screaming at her not to go, not to leave this impossible task for her daughter. But that was it—Lenore was her daughter; she could do this.

Sophie jumped over Hubert's inert body. She went down and down, passing the landing on the ground floor, plunging farther still. The tugging of the Link node lessened, but a new cluster of distortions grew. There was something else down here, some other threat. She moved faster, feet sliding on the stone, skidding down the steps. She reached for Fenrir, and this time, she felt him. In agony, anguish, his mind splitting asunder. Sophie clenched her teeth and flew, hitting a landing with a door, knowing it was where she needed to go. She burst through.

In the hall beyond, a guard came barreling toward her, the pointed steel of his sword glistening in the wavering torchlight. Sophie dodged the blow, but she had nothing to fight with except her hands. She scampered farther down the hall, planting her left leg and lifting her right one high, using the ball of her foot to dislodge the sole torch. She stamped on the embers, ignoring the sharp pangs from the flames licking at her feet.

The hall went dark. She used the moment to free herself of her voyant robes, her movements easier now in her light leather armor. She filtered her sight through the Third Eye and could see again with ease, the color lost but the details there. The guard groped in the dark.

"Fight me like a man," he said.

"Well, I'm afraid that's not possible, seeing how I'm not, in fact, a man."

The guard used Sophie's voice to guide him. He wasn't as dim as he looked. She pressed her back to the wall on the opposite side of the hall and inched along it. She needed to get in close to disarm him. Once he was only a few paces away, she slipped in, grabbing hold of his hand, pulling it with her as she twisted around to his back. He howled as she broke the delicate bones there. Sophie released him and dove for the sword. The guard was too busy with his pain to notice the arc of steel. He was still dumbly looking at his wrist when she brought the blade down and lodged it in the gap between his helmet and breastplate.

For the third time now, Sophie had killed a person, a non-afflicted, but to save Fenrir, she would murder all the world. She didn't let herself feel a thing. Instead, she simply pulled the sword free and rushed to the door the guard had been manning. It was locked. She hurried back to him and rummaged through his armor. The metal was warm and slick with his blood. Her hands were coated with it by the time she found a ring of keys in a pouch. She tried one after another, dropping them a few times, cursing at herself. Fenrir's horror was still there, which meant he was alive at least, but she didn't know for how much longer.

Finally, Sophie found a match. The key shoved the lock out of place, and she slammed the door open. A small square of a room greeted her. A lonely table with one flickering candle. A bundle of clothing on the floor, his leather armor. Her eyes fell on a door at the far side of the room. She strode there and opened it.

The stench, the throbbing, the horridness of this place. A horde of afflicted behind thick iron bars. At the end of the corridor, two figures. A woman in a fitted black dress stooped over, pulling at hair the color of straw. The body attached to it weak but not yet limp, barely covered in tattered black robes, flesh exposed, bruised, battered. In an instant, Sophie knew what Fenrir had suffered. Defilement. In mind and body.

She tore down the hall. She must have shouted or given off a battle cry, because something alerted Celeste to this new threat but too late. She was just turning, releasing Fenrir's hair, letting him slump to the ground, when Sophie came in and executed one fine arc of the sword. A limb severed. A fountain of blood. Celeste stumbled then screamed, clawing at the stump that had been her left arm.

Sophie grinned savagely, but before she could repeat her success, lopping off the head this time, a lumbering form emerged. There was a blackened gap, barred iron on each side, a cell with its door opened. The afflicted was on them in seconds, moving past Celeste, ignoring Fenrir, bearing down on Sophie. A thousand arms came at her, fingers ending in talons, she ducked and weaved and did the dance of the surveyor. She dodged its blows with twists and twirls, a beautiful feat. But she was a surveyor without her polearm. There was no way to take the offensive.

She kept her distance, maintained her advantage, but at some point, she would make a mistake, and in this most deadly of games, that would mean the end. For her. For Fenrir. He was strong. Sophie knew this, but she sometimes forgot just how strong. All that he'd been through and come out of. His mind was reeling but not yet broken, his body aching but whole. He reached for Sophie, Celeste's hold over his mind shattered by the pain of her severed arm.

Sync with me, he said.

Sophie did without hesitation, even knowing what it would

mean. Her mind being his and vice versa. His sufferings hers too. And they were great. A slaying of pride. A degradation of the worst kind. An unraveling of the self. A horrid secret unearthed, one she herself flinched from. But they were two minds now, bearing the weight one had before. Sophie lifted him up, cleared his eyes, helped him put aside the suffering for the moment, and focus on their task.

They danced. Toying with the afflicted, leading it to where they wanted it to go. False starts. Feigned failings. They kept it occupied, its attention fixated on them. But so too was theirs on it, only realizing too late Celeste was gone. Gone where? To tend to her wounds? No, what did she care for such things? She was timeless, unfazed by the corporeal, an inconvenience to be rectified. But first, there was protecting her domain.

The Link node. Lenore.

THE NODE

Lenore trained her eyes forward, straining to see the distortions. She didn't have her parents' gift. She couldn't sense the non-Euclidean, not without aid. But her Third Eye served her well in this regard, revealing the cancer infecting reality. The distortions showed themselves as inversions, their cores a sickly black, their extremities a ghostly white, tendrils reaching out, turning all that was right wrong. They were everywhere. This was the last hurdle, the final obstacle between her and the Link node, and it felt insurmountable. How was she meant to get through?

"Any ideas?" she asked.

Guy paced the steps. Helice furrowed her brow. Lenore looked at them then at the distortions then back. Think. Think. But the harder she tried, the more hopeless it all was.

"What about using a body as a kind of shield?" Guy said.

"What kind of body? One of us?" Lenore asked.

"No, one of them. A voyant." He tossed his hand down the stairs.

"Not a bad idea," Helice said, "but also impractical."

"Nonsense," Guy said. "I lift the body and carry. The two of you follow behind and steer me."

Lenore didn't understand the dynamics of the distortions. Were they like matter, picked up by whatever came into contact with them? Or were they more ephemeral?

"What body though?" Lenore asked.

They all leaned over the railing and gazed down. Hubert was there somewhere. It would be a long trek, first down however many stories he'd tumbled then back up and onward. They set off. After a few turns around the spiral, they found him, splayed out, bleeding. Guy squatted then grabbed at the voyant's arms and pulled him onto his back. Hubert groaned. Helice helped steady Guy. Lenore took the lead, using her new sight to steer them and avoid the distortions. Helice assisted Guy as she could, catching him when he staggered, pushing Hubert from behind. The ascent was painfully slow. Guy was drenched in sweat within minutes. But they advanced, however glacially.

Lenore tried to focus. On her steps. On the distortions. But her mind kept leaping to her parents, fretting about them, imagining all the worst fates they might suffer. And when she did that, she felt them, their pain and fear and despair. They were battling something horrid, and it was winning. But that was all she could get. Nothing concrete or substantial, no actual answers, just vague emotions, and she didn't dare reach out with words. She couldn't distract them just to appease her own anxieties.

Round and round the spiral she went with Guy and Helice behind. Then they were back to where they'd started from, the voyant still in tow. Guy put Hubert down and gasped for air. He was spent. He needed a rest. The three of them sat on the steps, gazing at Hubert's bruised face, that once straight nose now crooked and swollen. His lips murmured something, but he didn't open his eyes. They were about to put him through a great deal of suffering. It was the barn all over again. Lenore felt fine, but her hands were shaking. From fear or excitement?

She's coming. Can't do anything. Trapped fending off beast.

The words came from two minds, spoken in unison, her parents synced. They were struggling, using all their concentration to tell Lenore what she needed to hear in the midst of a fierce battle. The "she" they referred to could only be one person. Lenore hurried to the railing and looked down the depths. She trained her ears. Closed her eyes. Let her Third Eye work its magic. Feet in thin shoes padded on the stone. A breath came hard and fast. She was closing in on them.

"We have to move," Lenore said. "Celeste is coming."

Guy jumped up and hoisted Hubert on his back. He ascended the steps in reverse, so that Hubert was foremost. The voyant had already taken on a distortion or two, but they hadn't yet hit the mass of them. They hurried upward and took a few more turns before they hit a blockade. It was a wall of distortions, tall and wide and thick. Using Hubert wasn't even an option. These were all encompassing. They would swallow them whole.

"Put him down," Lenore said.

Guy draped Hubert on the steps. The voyant was groaning more often, his eyes flickering open now and then.

"What do we do?" Helice asked.

Lenore pulled the diskette from her robes and stared at it. Her mother had given her this task, this most important of all tasks. She had to do whatever she could to ensure they succeeded. She wasn't going to let them down. Lenore leaned over the railing. This time, she caught sight of Celeste, a stream of black fabric twirling around and around. She was close now. She'd be on them in minutes. Lenore thought and thought, but she could only ever see one path forward. She steeled herself. She turned.

But the diskette was plucked from her fingers. Helice's hand. Her body running up the steps, away, into the wall of distortions. Lenore cried out and reached for her, but Helice was already gone, engulfed by the non-Euclidean. Lenore went to follow, but two arms grasped her, one about the shoulders, the other about the waist. She fought them and cursed, but they were too strong. Guy pulled her down and away.

"No," Lenore shouted. "She can't."

"Shhh, pretty one," Guy said. "She can. She will."

Seconds and Celeste was there, just below them, mere steps away, her bright red lips smeared into an awful grin, eyes strained and wide. She reached for Lenore and Guy. Lenore braced herself, shut her eyes, tried to block it all out—Celeste's shrieking laughter, Guy's haggard breathing, and Helice's screams of agony.

Lenore was ready to die. She'd been ready to the moment she'd pulled the diskette out, but Helice had stolen that from her, shaken her to her core, left her with nothing but this awful death, Celeste's remaining hand ready to rip her to shreds. But it never grazed Lenore.

There was a bubbling, a rippling of reality. Celeste froze, face slack and stretched, and emitted a groan of immensity from between those lips, now cracked and pale. She collapsed and convulsed. Lenore and Guy pulled away. The wall of distortions so near at hand jittered in fits. The foul motes fell inward then outward then inward again until they got sucked into nothingness, faded, and vanished entirely. A roar. A cerebral shockwave. Then there was a ringing of the ears and an unreality draped over everything.

Despite that impossible stretch, Helice must have made it through, inserted the diskette, thwarted Celeste and the voyants, gotten her revenge on them, for her people, for Antonette. Guy rose first and staggered up the steps. Lenore followed in a daze through a door, into a room of synthetics, shining and clean, timeless. Light gray floors, white walls and ceiling, stacks of black boxes releasing heat and whirring away. Wires snaked and fed into a singular console in the center of the room, providing it with that electric energy it so craved. It was a near duplicate of the one in the Old World, even that haze hovering, a physical manifestation of the Link. The Link node was cleansed. There were no distortions here, those black and white sores of reality purged by one selfless act.

And the executor of that? There she was lying on the floor near the console, staring up at the ceiling, eyes seeing through to somewhere else. Helice's body was left in a ruin from the innumerable distortions she'd borne there at the end. Guy knelt by her side. Her chest struggled to rise and fall. Her eyes moved to his, tears streaming down her dark cheeks. He took her head and rested it in his lap then held and kissed her hands.

"Goodbye, Falcon."

"Goodbye, Starling."

THE FALLOUT

The afflicted who had once been Henri was relentless. All his pent-up anger, over five hundred years of sitting in this cell, locked in the dark, forgotten, tuned into that song of beauty and horror. What would that do to the mind? Fenrir couldn't fathom it. His own mind was unraveling from mere moments of a horrid act.

He faltered at the recollection. Henri lashed out a fleshy appendage. Sophie swooped in, severing the mass with the sword she wielded. Fenrir had nothing. Just his hands. His body. His defiled flesh. Another quake rattled him. But he wasn't alone in his mind. Sophie was there. They were synced, but this time was different. They weren't wholly in tune. There was a dissonance that only became more pronounced with time.

Suddenly, the afflicted Henri wailed. In that call was loss, fear, wrath. He raged. Fenrir and Sophie retreated. They knew what this moment was. They'd seen it before in the Old World in Simetria, years past. The Rot of the Link was dying, the diskette eating away its foul code, cleansing the system, restoring the Link node. She'd done it then; Lenore had saved them.

In their minds, Sophie reached for Fenrir, an embrace of victory, but he retreated from her. Touch. Touch was an awful thing. Of mind. Of body. He severed the sync then staggered and caught himself on the wall. Henri was in his death throes now, his thrashing slowing. The afflicted in their cells went still too. Silence. It was done then. Fenrir slipped to the ground, lay down, pressed his cheek against the cold stones. Sophie rushed to his side, but he shrank from her, cradling himself in his arms, forming a tight ball. She stayed her hands.

"Fenrir," she said.

She'd risked her life to save him when he was supposed to be the one to protect her. And what of the other one he was meant to protect? Had he failed with that too?

Lenore? Fenrir said. *Are you there? Are you safe?*

I'm here, she said. *Guy and I both. But Helice...*

Lenore's grief slapped Fenrir. He groaned and held his head in his hands.

"Shhh," Sophie said, "that's enough. We'll make our way to her. Don't reach out again. Your mind is raw. You're both in too much pain."

Fenrir hurried to an unsteady stand. "I want to leave this foul place."

Sophie offered an arm, but Fenrir rejected it and moved on his own. They exited the hall of cells and entered the small square room adjacent. Fenrir kept his eyes trained down.

"Fenrir," Sophie said, "your clothing."

He glanced at himself, covered only in tattered robes. Exposed. It brought the moment back, the one that had unfolded right here. His eyes caught the chair, the floor. His defilement. He was reeling. He staggered through the room and into the corridor beyond, dark and still. Sophie came after him and nudged his arm with a bundle of cloth.

"Your armor," she said. "It's mostly intact. Try to put it on."

Fenrir ripped at his robes with a sudden spurt of energy, desperate to be free of them and the scents that lingered on them. His. Celeste's. The clothing clung to him. He grew frantic trying to get it off, one sleeve wound tightly around his arm. His tore at it then clawed, but it hung on, eager and tenacious. Like that horrid woman. He collapsed against the wall, spent by his efforts, tears streaming. The shame. To be reduced to this husk in front of Sophie. He couldn't bear it. He slumped to the ground and buried his face in his hands.

This wasn't how it was meant to be. But wasn't it? He didn't understand his reaction. He'd come down here knowing what it meant, ready to use his body to buy the others time. And that's what he'd done. So why did it shame him so? Why did he feel like he'd never get clean again?

"It's over," Sophie said, kneeling at his side.

But it wasn't. Those scenes wouldn't disappear, refused to fade into memory. They played out over and over again. Why had his body betrayed him? He hadn't wanted it. That's where it all went wrong. When he'd been the one to make the decision, thinking Celeste didn't know who he was, playing a role, it had been in his control. But that loss of control, that lack of a choice, that was undoing him.

Sophie reached for the knotted remnants of his robes on his wrist. He gritted his teeth as she worked the fabric loose. As soon as he was free of it, he stood and hurried away. Exposed again, even in darkness, cradling himself and the parts that had so betrayed him.

"Where's the armor?" he said.

He was suddenly impatient and angry. Sophie moved too slow, offered him the coverings too gently. He snatched at them and scowled. She moved in to help, but he held a hand up and glared. She stood by and waited as he shrouded himself. Piece by piece. Trousers, frock, boots. Once he was covered, he breathed a little easier.

"It's a long climb," Sophie said. "Let's rest here a moment."

Fenrir leaned against the wall then slid to the ground. Sophie sat beside him.

I can hear you again, Nytho said. *And I see you've succeeded in restoring the Link node.*

Those sweet, sweet words. Confirmation sorely needed. And more than that, Nytho was something to divert Sophie's too-ardent attention to, away from Fenrir.

Lenore did it, Sophie said.

Congratulations, and I don't say that lightly. The Link node is safe for now, but we need to ensure it stays that way. There's more to be done.

We're well aware, Sophie said. *But we need rest. This has been an awful ordeal.*

Fenrir didn't hear the rest of the conversation. A roaring came and crowded his thoughts. Images kept flashing into view, staining his eyes, embedding themselves like distortions. He couldn't keep his focus. His mind wandered.

After a few more minutes, Sophie rose and offered a hand. He ignored it, using the wall as a crutch instead and grunting to a stand. He followed Sophie down the hall and up the stairs, step by step, then waited while she went farther to find Lenore and Guy. The three of them came down not long after looking haggard and worn. Guy and Lenore's cheeks were tearstained. There was no Helice.

Lenore was suffering. This Fenrir knew. And yet, he couldn't feel anything in response to that. All the violent emotions that had accosted him in the bowels of the Fortress had drifted away, leaving only a hollowness in their wake. A spectral residue.

Sophie led the way through the Fortress. It lived up to its name, like a battle had passed through. Voyants staggered about, some dying a slow and painful death, their anatomy disrupted by the distortions' sudden disappearance. Others were already dead, eyes staring into nothingness, in disbelief at how their timelessness could come to an end. Servants scurried about trying to lend aid where they could. Guards trotted by, lost and aimless without their Voyant Supreme to give orders.

"The Fleur-de-lis," Lenore said. "The coup."

Guy was in a stupor from losing Helice, but Lenore's words seemed to rouse him. "I have to go to them. Deliver word if they haven't already sprung into action. Aid them if they have."

"Lead the way," Sophie said.

Guy shook his head and pointed down the hall in the direction that led to the tunnel connecting the Fortress to the Sanctum. "You've done your part. Leave while you can."

"Nonsense," Sophie said. "You need all the help you can get."

Guy smiled sadly and sighed. "You're in no state to help. More trouble than anything."

Fenrir grimaced. There was only one of their party who was useless at present, and everyone took great pains to avoid glancing in his direction.

"Please," Guy said. "Go. Back to the safe house. You know the way?"

"We'll manage," Sophie said.

Lenore stepped in and laid a hand on Guy's shoulder. "You'll come to us, when you've finished here?"

"If I live, yes." Guy grinned widely, crushing his grief under a show of fatalism.

"You'll live," Lenore said sternly. "You must. Spirale needs you."

Guy took Lenore's hand and pressed his lips to her palm then he sprinted away.

"Well, shall we?" Sophie said.

The chaos worked to their advantage. No one took note of the erstwhile Courbean delegation. Not as they stole through the Fortress, sounds of battle echoing through the halls. There was no way of knowing if it was the Fleur-de-lis enacting the plan or not. They retraced their steps to the tunnel that connected to the Sanctum, navigated that labyrinth, and exited its ironclad gates. Courbeans turned strangers. They let Spirale swallow them, its streets bright with celebration. A kind of heroes' welcome even if no one was aware of the sacrifices made on their behalf.

The sightless were still reveling in Ascension Day. For now, they were oblivious to how much their lives would alter, but when dawn stole in, when sunlight flooded the curvilinear streets, following the irregular bends and twists of the thoroughfares, their new reality would make itself known. Sightless no longer. Poor unworthy all dead. Streets and buildings free of distortions. How would they react to this? Would they sing praises for the three Simetrians and Fleur-de-lis who had liberated them? Or would fall prey to the age-old fear of change?

Fenrir and the others slipped through the city. Red and white fireworks exploded. Horns blared. Flutes called. Bells rang. Spiraleans ran by laughing and smiling in crude and simple approximations of the elaborate costumes of the voyants. Spirals. Eyes. But other motifs too because these people weren't timeless. They weren't stuck in a past, static and unchanging, but rather lived moment to moment, dynamic and loud. They bore flowers, leaves, birds. So many colors too, not limited to the blacks, whites, purples, and reds of the voyants but a kaleidoscope of hues.

It should have been beautiful. It ought to have filled Fenrir's heart with joy or brought him some kind of peace, but his eyes were only attuned to ugliness now. The shabbiness of the people's dress. The peeling of their paints. The strangeness of the words on their lips.

This was not his city. These were not his people. He had

no business being here, should never have come. Fenrir was tired. Not just his body and mind but his soul. After all he'd done, after everything he'd given, he was spent. His familial bliss was shattered. Glancing at Lenore, her eyes flitting over all the activity, he couldn't fail to see the resemblance to a man he'd helped his wife murder. Spirale had taken Lenore from him, and for that, he despised the city with all his being, what tattered remains were left.

NEXT STEPS

The safe house wasn't the haven Lenore had hoped it would be. There were too many memories tied up in it, too much to remind her of Helice and what would be her eternal absence. The cellar was the worst. Helice's tomes were still spread on the table down there, her careful script showing on parchment.

That pang returned, Lenore's newest companion, visiting her all the previous night and into the following day. She hadn't slept well. None of them had, nestled together on the floor of the main room. Fenrir in particular tossed and turned, even crying out several times. Sophie tried to comfort him, but he lashed out then crept down into the cellar. When Lenore rose for the day and searched for Fenrir, she found him curled on a mat. He was shivering, still wearing his damaged leather armor. Something awful had happened to him in the Fortress, but she dared not probe his thoughts. Her own mind was too wounded to stand for any added pain.

She missed Helice. Her sphinx smile, her surety, the energy she emanated. She fretted about Guy and the other Fleur-de-lis. Her whole family was on edge. Even after their success, after achieving their goal, so much uncertainty lay ahead. What would happen to Spirale? To them? Fenrir brooded. Sophie flitted about. All that morning, her mother was too attentive to Fenrir. He didn't take the coddling well. After Sophie had asked if he needed anything for the fifth time within an hour, Fenrir slammed his hands on the table and rose from his chair.

"I'm going for a walk," he said.

"I don't know if that's a good idea," Sophie said.

She moved to go after him, but Lenore grabbed her arm and shook her head. Fenrir stomped out. If it wasn't for the door's tendency to get stuck on its lower left corner, it would have slammed shut. Instead, it sent a strong gush of air in.

Sophie sighed and huffed and paced. "I don't know what to do with him. He's being so difficult."

"I imagine that's because he went through something difficult," Lenore said.

Sophie stopped then stood with her hands on her hips. "You think I don't know that? Me? I synced with him, little corvid, just after his ordeal. I felt everything he did, as if it had happened to me. I know too well what he suffers, but that's what I just don't understand. We were synced. I was there for him, willing to take on some of the burden, and he wouldn't let me. Even still, he refuses my help."

"He just needs time," Lenore said. "We all do."

Sophie softened and flopped into a chair. She rubbed her hands over her face then patted her hair. It was freshly braided. She alone looked put together. "Spirale won't wait for us. Nor Simetria. I understand that we need time, but we don't have that luxury. Besides, sometimes action is the best antidote. Let's talk next steps."

"Should we wait for Papa?" Lenore asked.

"No," Sophie said. "He can be involved if and when he's able. First and foremost, we have to secure the Link node. Last night, I reached out to Nicolus and requested he send word to the wardens just across the water. Journeyman Frye and the others are a good first start for reinforcements."

"Do you think it's a good idea to bring in foreigners en masse?" Lenore asked.

"Just a few extra hands," Sophie said. "Some of the guards in the Fortress might still be blindly doing their duty."

"What if the coup didn't go as planned?" Lenore asked. "What if the Fleur-de-lis don't control the Fortress or Sanctum?"

"The voyants will be mostly gone, so it would only be a matter of time until they lose their grip on power completely, especially once the truth gets out. Permissions, not-mothers, the whole system rigged to keep the sightless out."

Lenore folded her hands one on the other and rested her chin on them. "There's the matter of actually getting the word out. For Spirale, I'm sure the Fleur-de-lis will have it all in hand, but what about the other Sect cities?"

"They have a long path ahead of them," Sophie said. "I speak from personal experience. To craft a new government, to win the people to their side, these things won't happen overnight."

"They'll need help," Lenore said. "From us. If we want the Link node to be truly secure, we need to ensure things stabilize. We can't afford to just leave. Not now."

Sophie sighed, hung her arm over the back of her chair, and gazed at the milky glass of the sole window in the room. "Don't I know it. The trouble is, there's much for us to do elsewhere. There are other Link nodes in other cities, corrupted by the Rot of the Link, which must be cleansed, eventually. More pressing is Simetria and the unrest. We've been gone too long already. I'm afraid at least some of us will need to return soon."

"But not all of us," Lenore added. "Let me stay. Let me represent Simetria."

Sophie side-eyed Lenore. "Spirale needs the wardens, and the wardens need one of their own to lead them."

Lenore glanced at the clouded window bearing faded plaid curtains. Someone had hung those with care. Maybe even someone with ink-stained fingers and an enigmatic smile, someone who saw the potential in everyone and had envisioned a better future for them all.

Lenore had sworn she would never be a warden, but she'd mistaken her disdain, thinking the wardens were synonymous with the guild system. Here in Spirale, she'd learned what they really were.

"I want to stay," she said.

***

It was midday when Fenrir returned, freshly washed, at some public bathhouse no doubt, and sporting new but simple clothing. Neither Lenore nor Sophie commented on the change. Fenrir took a seat at the table then glanced around the room.

"Any word from Guy?" he asked.

"Not yet," Sophie said.

Fenrir nodded then went silent. The three of them sat like that, each lost in their own thoughts. A half hour later, Guy arrived carrying bread and news. Sophie cut the loaf while he explained the state of Spirale.

"We couldn't take the Fortress. Or the Sanctum. The guards were too many. As soon as battle erupted, they came out of their daze. We'd hoped being leaderless would weaken them, but it wasn't enough. I called my people off. We must regroup and strategize."

"The important point is, the voyants are out of the picture," Lenore said. "It might take time for their house of cards to fall, but fall it will."

"No doubt, but the fall won't be as quick or painless as we'd hoped. It seems some of the voyants survived and are holed up in the Fortress, frantically trying to maintain their grip on power. The sightless are confused. Rumors abound. A plague hit the gala. Someone poisoned the wine. Assassins broke in. You can see, we have much work cut out for us."

"Did you release the story about the Permissions?" Sophie asked.

"To those who would believe it and agree with our cause, yes. Now, we just wait for word to spread."

Sophie offered slices of bread then fetched a slab of butter and jars of jams. She set a kettle on the stove before taking a seat at the table. The last food any of them had eaten had been before the gala. Lenore was suddenly famished and attacked the bread, slathering it with spreads. Guy grinned at her, and she blushed. What would other high bloods think of her if they could see her now? What would Deston? It had been ages since she'd thought of him. So much had happened. So much had changed. To the world. To her.

"What next then?" Fenrir asked. He picked at a chunk of bread but didn't eat.

Sophie took delicate bites of her own. "I've already sent for the wardens in the village. Once they arrive, I'm heading back to Simetria."

"So soon?" Fenrir said.

"I've been away too long, but we obviously can't leave Spirale in this tenuous state. The Fleur-de-lis need all the help they can get."

Fenrir frowned. "You want me to stay?"

Sophie shook her head. "I suspect you'd like nothing more than to be far away from this place, my love. Besides, you're in no state to do the hard work of securing Spirale. Lenore offered, and I think it's a fine idea."

Fenrir frowned deeper. Lenore's father had always been a handsome man, in her mind and many others', but how strange that one event could affect him so much. He looked aged, but what was even more heartbreaking was seeing him so snappy and guarded.

"You're going to leave her alone in this festering wound of a city? Haven't we given it enough?"

"Papa," Lenore said, "I can do this. It was my idea. Besides, I'm not alone. I'll have the wardens and Guy and the Fleur-de-lis, not to mention all the people of Spirale the Sect wronged."

Fenrir turned his emerald eyes on Lenore. So sad. Aching. Pleading.

"I've done well, haven't I?" she asked. "I'm capable. Can't you see that?"

His mouth quivered, and he rose from his chair, retreating to the window, pushing the curtain back a sliver and pretending to inspect the clouded view.

Sophie turned in her chair, angled toward Fenrir. "She can do this. She's strong."

Fenrir stayed fixed to the window. "She'll need more than strength to deal with this fallout. A kind of ruthlessness is required." His eyes snapped to Sophie's.

Her mother looked down at her hands. "She can do it."

Lenore rose from her seat and migrated to Fenrir's side. She laid a hand on his shoulder, but he tensed at the contact.

"I can make the hard choices, the decisions others are reluctant to make."

Fenrir continued to look out the window, refusing to meet her eye. "Oh, I'm aware, Lenore. The question is, do you want to become that kind of person?"

She frowned and hardened. "I want to help. I'll do what's needed."

Fenrir sighed and finally looked at her. His eyes always so soft and full of love, now empty and vacant. "I suppose I always thought you were more like me, but I understand now that's not the case. Maybe I forced myself to see something that wasn't there and to ignore what was actually lurking."

Lenore shrank from the comment, but before she could mull her father's words, Guy came to her side and rested a hand on her shoulder.

"I pledge to stand by her," Guy said.

"It's settled then," Sophie said. "Lenore stays. Fenrir and I return to Simetria." She lifted a finger and wagged it at Guy. "But no funny business, Monsieur Zanon. Hands stay off, yes?"

Guy and Sophie smirked. Lenore blushed. But Fenrir stayed fixed to that window, a distance between him and them, physically, mentally, lost in his thoughts, a thousand miles away. That wall that had existed between Lenore and her mother had crumbled at long last only to reappear, erected anew, now sundering her from her father.

***

Fenrir and Sophie walked through the circuitous streets of Spirale. Their forest green wardens' frocks fluttered in the late autumn wind. Their wardens' chains on their black sashes sent blazes to Lenore's eyes, reflecting sunlight bursting through the fitful cloud cover. They were getting lost in the crowd of people, only their tricorns visible bobbing in the distance. When even those were gone, Lenore's stomach wrenched.

But she couldn't afford a show of emotions. She'd learned that from her mother. Wardens valued stoicism, and she had five of them alert at her side. She turned, head lifted, back tall, arms clasped in the small of her back. She gazed at them, one after the other. These were the ones she'd traveled with from Simetria to the fishing village across the water through the forest. She knew them, but they didn't know her, not the Lenore Roshem she'd become.

She wore the warden's uniform, a mirror image of her parents' and these others at her side, even down to the chain link sitting in her black sash. That last adornment was new; she hadn't borne it before. When she'd left Simetria, petulant and aloof, she'd refused to take the oath. Despite that, she'd done the duty of a warden after all. She'd protected the Link and would continue to do so. She'd found purpose in this calling, not because it had been expected of her, but because she'd finally seen the truth in what the wardens pledged loyalty to.

She was one of them now, the oath having issued from her lips minutes before her parents' departure. And yet, the pledge didn't feel like the chain she feared it would, weighing her down, limiting her aspirations. Instead, she felt free but also apprehensive because she wasn't just a warden. She was Simetria's envoy to Spirale, which made her the senior-most warden in the city.

It was a strange feeling, having power. Not unpleasant but laced with unease. Lenore was afraid of it, fearful it would manage to corrupt her as it had done to so many others throughout history. More than that though, she was afraid of herself. This journey to Spirale had shown her another Lenore, as alien and incomprehensible as the sights beyond the vitres. One who got a rush from carving a knife into captives. One with a link to something more. Her Third Eye had hinted at it again and again, tapping into others' feelings without a sync, a kind of bond with synthetics? She didn't understand it.

There was at least one who would—the alfom called Nytho. All she had to do was call out to him through her Third Eye, ask him her question, and find the answer. But she didn't. Maybe it was because she didn't want the answer or maybe because she wanted him to reach out to her first. They'd never spoken, and for some reason, this grated on her. After everything she'd done for him, he didn't deign to give her any notice. So be it. She wasn't chasing after approval anymore, her mother's or anyone else's. If Nytho wanted her to take her parents' place one day, to be his champion, he would have to woo her.

SECOND SEDUCTION

He talked of you often. He thought of you even more. Yes, this is who you think it is. I know they warned you about me. I'm aware you're hearing my words through a very biased lens, but I'm also hoping Vergil's opinion of you was well-founded. He said you were sharp. He said you were loyal. Are you, Nicolus Yevin? Formerly Priest Yevin of the Most-Holy Church of Impermanence, stalwart champion of the Lady? Because that's who speaks to you. But you don't sing my praises anymore, Master Yevin of the Wardens Guild of the Order of the New Day. Now, you curse the Lady and all I did for you. But what of the artist in you? The Paper Airplane Poet? Surely, he sees more than the other faces?

Tell me, Nicolus, do you understand why I did it? Did Vergil share those secrets with you? No, of course he didn't. I asked him not to. I told him to use the utmost care and avoid any mention of me to anyone. All of our caution was wasted though. The alfom caught on to our clandestine meetings and enacted their revenge on him. Except this was done differently than you were told. Not through synthetics. Not by frying his brain via his Third Eye. Lies. No, Vergil's death came by another hand, one that used his trust and love against him—Sophie Roshem.

I know you see it, the connections taking place. Maybe you always knew but couldn't admit it to yourself. Let me spell it out clearly, the truth—Sophie Roshem killed Vergil with help from Fenrir Mey. They cornered him in his workshop, used synthetics to overpower him, and framed his murder as an accident. Sophie swooped in and claimed Vergil's throne where she sits to this day, Fenrir at her side, both of them puppets to Nytho and his dark schemes.

I only ever aimed to help you, all of you. I know it doesn't seem that way, but it's the truth. Nytho and the other alfom are no friends of yours. They only care about the Link. Nothing else matters to them. Not Vergil. Not you. They discard useless tools at a moment's notice. A time is coming when they'll use your world in their machinations. It's my hope to avoid that altogether, but the only way is by keeping them out of your world. Sever the Link. The Linkrot is the only means, but it doesn't have to be the flawed program it was. I've improved it. It won't grow to consume your world. It will barely leave a mark.

You doubt me, I know, but if you dig, you'll find evidence to support my words. So, what would you say, Nicolus, to an alliance? Help me finish what Vergil and I started. He trusted me, and you trusted him. Give him one last gift. Bring his vision to life. Make his murderers pay for his death. I know he loved you. Tell me, did you love him?

FROM THE AUTHOR

Thank you for reading *Blessed is the Link*. Your feedback is important to me and will help other readers. Please consider leaving a review on your chosen platform. Please note that *Blessed is the Link* is the second book in the Bit trilogy. Stay tuned for book 3. If you enjoyed *Blessed is the Link*, you may also be interested in "Disaffected", a short story inspired by the novel. Lastly, everything I write falls in a shared universe. For a more immersive reading experience, check out my other novels and short stories. Visit my website at sherisingerling. com for more details.

ACKNOWLEDGMENTS

The family: Mom, Dad, Alan, Shaun, Shannon, and Shea. My beta readers: Ben, Isaiah, Sarah, Seren, Tessy, and T.R. Mainstone. The French translations: David Fleur.

ABOUT THE AUTHOR

SHERI SINGERLING is a US native living in Germany where she works as a laboratory manager, lecturer, and research scientist. Sheri spends her days staring at rocks and dust from space and her nights crafting worlds via the written word. Outside of her work and writing, she enjoys coaxing plants to grow, walking up and down steep inclines in nature, and listening to repetitive electronic beats.

Her publications all fall in the Alfom shared universe and include the novels *Nytho, Neuen, Blessed is the Rot,* and *Blessed is the Link,* and several short stories. Her short fiction has appeared in *Clarkesworld Magazine.* For updates on Sheri Singerling's work, subscribe to her newsletter at sherisingerling.com/subscribe and/or follow her on Instagram (@shersingerling), Facebook (Sheri Singerling - Author), and Bluesky (@ sherisingerling.bsky.social).

9 781968 638009